Indian
Ocean

Mombasa

nbara Mts

Lushoto

Mombo

Tanga

Pemba
Island

Zanzibar

Dar-es-Salaam

# THE
# VOLUNTEER

Kwa Josh Feldstein,

Karibu nyumbani kwangu,

Kama utarudi Tanzania!

Salaama,

*[signature]* Feb. 99

# THE
# VOLUNTEER

·················································

## CARTER COLEMAN

**WARNER BOOKS**

A Time Warner Company

*Upendo na shukrani kwa:*

Dee Dee & Kevin Reilly for two years on a mountaintop.
Julian Ozanne & Aidan Hartley, my Niarobi brothers, for nursing
me back to mental and physical health.
M.L.H. for Africa and my pen.
*Amu* Jim McGehee
Susan Minot, *Mhariri Bora*
The Dream Team: Lynn Nesbit, Larry Kirshbaum & Jamie Raab
Allen, John & Dudley of Penniman, Noland & Coates
My Long-Suffering Family

Copyright © 1998 by Carter Coleman
All rights reserved.

Warner Books, Inc., 1271 Avenue of the Americas, New York, NY 10020
Visit our Web site at http://warnerbooks.com

 A Time Warner Company

Printed in the United States of America
First Printing: March 1998
10 9 8 7 6 5 4 3 2 1

**Library of Congress Cataloging-in-Publication Data**

Coleman, Carter.
    The volunteer / Carter Coleman.
        p.  cm.
    ISBN 0-446-52203-1
    I. Title.
PS3553.O47376V6    1998
813'.54—dc21                                                97-46659
                                                            CIP

*Book design by Giorgetta Bell McRee*

For Julie
*Nitakupenda Milele*

&

For Bret Easton Ellis
*Mwalimu Katili*

It is the blankness that follows gaiety, and Everyman must depart
Out there into stranded night, for his destiny
Is to return unfruitful out of the lightness
That passing time evokes. . . .

—John Ashbery

# Aprili 1

The sun was a moon. Rutledge Jordan followed the sounds of Modest Mbungu's footsteps up through the mud. The faint globe of light glowed every few minutes through a hole high in the canopy. The trail rose up a mountain slope through a long tunnel of dinosaur ferns. Noon now, it was dark as night. Cold wet leaves curtained the path. Jordan dreaded passing through the giant ferns, where once he had nearly stepped on an Usambara bush viper.

"It's not too late to turn back," Mbungu said in English.

"Go on back," Jordan said in Swahili. He bumped into him. "Sorry." He could make out Mbungu's light shirt, the whites of his eyes. He groped for Mbungu's hand and held it loosely while he spoke, deliberately using the Bantu custom. "Turn around now if you feel compromised."

Mbungu grunted and dropped his hand. Disappearing, Mbungu answered in Swahili, "You might hurt yourself."

Jordan jogged blindly on. Branches slapped his face. He wondered if Mbungu was trying to strand him in the darkness. Jordan found himself at the bottom of a steep slope. He moved the straps of his pack wider on his shoulders and listened to the silence. Panic floated in the back of his head with the thought that he had strayed off the trail. He leaned forward on his knees, dug his hands into mud and started climbing up slope. Muttering, he cursed Mbungu for insisting on taking a new shortcut. Mbungu was deliberately getting him lost. *"Mm-boon-goo!"* Jordan yelled. The darkness was still.

The trail opened into dim light falling through a grove of tall camphor trees ten centuries old. Out of a tremulous ceiling suspended a hundred and fifty feet overhead by burnt-orange trunks, shafts of cathedral light slanted down to a floor of dry peat. Jordan saw Mbungu leaning against a tree at the edge of the camphor grove and walked over without speaking. Mbungu peered into the canopy, wearing a faded ranger's shirt and gray chinos, a black wool sweater given him by a Norwegian botanist tied around his waist and a pair of L. L. Bean duck boots that Jordan had ordered for him last year at the end of the long rains. The boots looked new, but then, Jordan thought, Mbungu probably cleaned and oiled them every night.

Mbungu turned to Jordan. "Coming up that ravine saved us fifteen minutes."

Jordan glanced at his watch and nodded, breathing heavily.

*"Kuluzu,"* Mbungu whispered, pointing to a tree fifty yards away on the other side of the colony of ancient camphor trees.

Jordan focused in on the colobus monkeys with a pair of Nikons, reducing the hundred yards to twenty. Black-furred three-foot midgets with white beards and white capes hanging from their shoulders grazed and groomed each other, combing fingers through their beards and tails. The *kuluzu* were born and died on narrow branches high off the ground, never once touching the earth. One shrieked at the two men on the forest floor. The whole troop ran along the branches to the far side of the tree. Jordan sprinted across the slope beneath them. The monkeys chattered louder and began to leap in place on the branches until the limbs sprang up and down like diving boards. One by one the caped figures flew fifty feet through green light and shadows and caught limbs in another camphor farther down the mountain.

"The alpha male." Mbungu pointed.

One monkey remained in the tree where the clan had been resting.

*"Bwana Mbolo Kubwa,"* Jordan said.

Bwana Big Dick jumped four, five times until the limb was a blur and he launched into the shadows.

A loud *whooshing*, the sound of air compressed through a bellows, broke the stillness of the forest.

"Here she comes," Mbungu said in English. *"Chui ya anga."*

The leopard of the sky appeared from the gloom, laboring its eight-foot wingspan open and closed. The crowned eagle slung its talons into the monkey's back and whisked him upward, bursting through the leaves high overhead. The troop raised a unified scream against the execution, a primal keen that drew Jordan's hands to his ears. The colobus clan gathered into a huddle around the great trunk of the camphor.

"Was that one of the parents?" Mbungu walked across the clearing.

"I doubt it." Jordan watched the colobus. "Romeo and Juliet's hunting ground is on the other side of the ridge."

A quarter mile down the trail, the men could still hear the monkeys howling.

"Today is April Fools' Day." Mbungu shook his head. "You're a fool."

Jordan took Mbungu's hand, looked him in the face. "There are only two dozen sky leopards left in the mountains."

"Nestlings are so fragile," Mbungu said quietly. "The shock of leaving the nest could kill it. You might give it a disease." His steady gaze induced a moment's anxiety. He was a forest conservator, and his humility and deep knowledge of the forest made Jordan feel like a sham, a fast-talking American of no particular expertise or moral depth.

"*You* know that one of those eaglets is doomed. The runt never survives. Cain will kill Abel," Jordan said quickly. "This time maybe Abel will be lucky."

"'The eagles are dying. The habitat is shrinking. This way there may be one more'—you've told me." Mbungu frowned. "Are those your true reasons?"

"Why else?" Jordan let go of his hand.

"It's too late now," Mbungu said in Swahili. "We won't make it back before nightfall. You can try again tomorrow."

"*Kesho.* Tomorrow." Jordan tied fishing line to an arrow. "What an African."

"It's true what they say." Mbungu's face was serious. "White men are crazy."

"Long rain fever." Jordan drew back an arrow against the gut string of a Maasai bow.

"You were crazy in the dry season," Mbungu said.

Jordan aimed high overhead and fired: the arrow rushed up a hundred feet and bounced off the lowest limb.

"Shit." Jordan straightened out the monofilament line and picked up the arrow. He shot again but the arrow fell short of the limb. Jordan followed the line into a tall bush, scratching his arms and face. He tried a third time, a fourth, and a fifth.

"Give it to me." Mbungu extended one hand impatiently as Jordan crawled out of a bush.

"You're abetting a criminal."

"Is there not honor among thieves?" Mbungu shot the arrow cleanly over the limb.

"Have a beer, comrade," Jordan said in Swahili, tossing a green Heineken can. He tied together two lengths of smooth red climbing rope, then tied one end to the fishing line. They pulled the rope up over the limb and back down, where they secured it to the tree trunk. Jordan stepped into a waist harness and clipped two Jumar ascenders to the rope. He tested the device: the alloy brake slid up the rope but not down. With long slings for his feet attached to the ascenders, Jordan could toil straight up, stepping into one sling while sliding the other one higher.

He lashed a bag of nylon netting on the back of the harness then started. Grunting, huffing, he clambered slowly. Sixty feet up, his left knee began to convulse involuntarily, bouncing like a sewing machine needle. "Relax," he whispered. He knew he was perfectly secure, but the sensation of dangling in space and twisting in a slight forest wind affected some nerve center and sent disturbed signals to his knee.

Drenched with sweat, Jordan reached the lowest limb. After un-clipping the harness, he stood and gazed up into the tangled branches. The nest was another fifty feet higher. Climbing quickly, he lost the fear of falling as the limbs grew closer together and paused once to look at an orange orchid flower clinging to the trunk. "My beloved Mother and Father," he composed aloud, drawing a short Maasai sword from a scabbard on his belt. "After all this time my heart is still restless. Today I climbed a big tree to try to save an eagle." His voice trembled. He hacked off a branch the size of a walking cane and trimmed off the twigs, fashioning a light pole for self-defense. He wiped the sweat off his hands and pulled on a pair of motorcycle goggles. "It's not part of my job. I did it pro bono."

At the top of the tree's crown, the nest was a sphere of sticks larger than a queen-size bed. From below, Jordan could hear no movement, only a light wind stirring the leaves. Hugging the limb, he crawled slowly up a wide branch that supported one side of the nest. If one of the sky leopards comes screaming in, shout. Wave your arms and shout it off like shouting down a charging rhino, Jordan coached him-self, afraid of panicking. Swat him in the gut if he keeps coming. Get your bearings, somersault across the nest, grab the chick, and keep rolling until you reach the wide branch on the other side.

❖

A female sky leopard, a mother in her thirties, was perched in the bright light above the canopy in a tree thirty yards from her nest. Slowly she scanned the blue dome. Her eyes could discern a rabbit at six miles. Her gaze rose and fell while her head twisted slowly, a strong anxiety rushing through her with every hungry chirp from the two nestlings. In the morning while her mate stood watch over the nest, she had flown in widening circles through the rain forest, search-ing for monkeys and bush buck; but without her partner to execute diversions, she was soon spotted by monkey clans that quickly with-drew behind thickets of branches. She was hungry but large enough to go days without filling her crop. The crying reminded her that nestlings must eat at dawn and dusk. Two instincts competed within her: to hunt for the chicks or to guard them from goshawks and augur buzzards and vengeful monkeys. Suddenly, in the periphery of her wide field of vision, a primate emerged slowly through the leaves at the edge of the nest. She spun her turret head, saw it was human, then swooped off the perch and circled around the treetop.

His eyes were an inch above the leaves. Jordan slowly turned his head from side to side. He climbed higher on the limb and searched the sky over the nest and the undulating surface of the surrounding canopy. Fifty yards away, poking out of the green crown of an abutting tree, brown leaves of dead branches betrayed the wall of the hide that he had started building three months after arriving in Africa, over a year ago now, in the bleakest period of his exile. Through the short rains of November and the dry season after, the days and nights he stole away from his work and spent in the hide were the only moments of escape from his melancholy.

He stuck his hands into pockets of thatch, pulled himself onto the pile of sticks, and stretched to peer into the nest. The heads of the nestlings lay back on furry S-shaped necks with their beaks wide open, crying with hunger. Cain was nearly twice the size of Abel, though they were born a day apart. Cain stole the runt's food. Abel's head was wounded from his brother's gouges. Jordan readied himself to roll over the rim.

Flat on his back, midway through a barrel roll, Jordan saw the sky leopard diving out of the sun: talons the size of human hands thrust forward from a broad breast spotted orange and black, eight-foot wings with undersides checkered black and white. Jordan's hoarse shout stuck in his throat. He was rising up on his knees when the eagle hit the back of his head, knocking him face first into the nest floor. He pushed himself up and spat out a mouthful of decayed colobus fur.

Suddenly he felt as if eight syringes were piercing deep into his shoulder.

A vise began to crush his clavicle and a big beak pecked against his goggles like an ice pick. Jordan screamed.

One goggle lens cracked. Jordan's focus blurred then returned to a close-up of liquid yellow eyes set in a large black head crowned by dark feathers edged in white.

*Go ape shit.* Jordan remembered from childhood the advice of a kid down the block about the only course of action when you find yourself outmatched with nowhere to run. He rolled onto his back, pulling the sky leopard off balance. He slapped her in the head; she sliced his palm with her beak. The talons clinched tighter on his shoulder. Jordan balled his fist and punched her spotted breast. She screeched and came back with a fierce peck on his cheek. Jordan grabbed her by the neck and tackled her to the nest floor, trying to wrench her claws from his shoulder. He squeezed her throat. Finally she released her grasp, then struck wildly with both claws and ripped a deep hole in his forearm.

Jordan lunged across the nest and scooped up Abel. Its eyes were closed, but it cried out. Cradling the nestling between his cupped fist and forearm, he rolled up over the rim and straddled the big branch. The sky leopard leapt after him.

Talons raked across his head as she sculled out over the canopy.

Jordan ducked out of the sun's glare into the quiet gloom of the giant albizzia. He panted and shivered, full of adrenaline. Abel looked up at him without fear or malice, the gaze of a puppy. He placed the chick in the nylon bag hanging from his harness and scrambled down. On the lowest branch he sat and fumbled with a small length of climbing rope, trying to push it through an alloy figure eight. "Exterior . . . narrow focus . . . concentration." He repeated some Outward Bound jargon learned on high school trips to the Smoky Mountains. Finally he threaded the rope, clipped it to his harness and swung clear of the branch. Descending in measured lengths like a spider, he slid down, spinning as he dropped.

The sucking sound of a projectile cut the air, and Jordan turned to see the sky leopard, its wings tucked to its sides, angling out of the shadows.

He kicked off the tree and swung around the trunk. The eagle altered her course, homing in on him. He covered his face. The sky leopard swept past, knocking him on the side of the head with balled talons. The pain eclipsed his vision for a moment and he fell backward. He found himself dangling from the rope.

Mbungu appeared upside-down, shouting, throwing stones at his head.

The yellow eyes and huge black beak hovered a few feet away. Jordan shielded his face with his arms. The eagle clawed his elbow.

*"Taremka! Taremka!"* Mbungu shouted. Come down!

Jordan pulled himself upright and freed the rope jammed in the figure eight. As he dropped to the floor, the eagle dove in and dragged her talons across his back, then swooped high and dove again. Jordan screamed and played out the rope. Mbungu jabbed at the eagle with a long spear and sent her flying off into the trees.

*"Pumbavu!"* Mbungu called Jordan an idiot. He drove the spear into the ground. "Are you okay?"

Jordan bent over, taking long, deep breaths.

*"Poleh,"* Mbungu said sympathetically, turning Jordan's forearm gently to look at the wound. Sorry. *"Poleh sana."* Very sorry.

"Please don't say *poleh*." Jordan stood up straight. "I hate that word."

Mbungu unclipped the nylon sack from Jordan's harness and looked inside. "Where are you going to keep the little leopard?"

"I was thinking of your house for a while until it's bigger." Jordan unbuckled the harness.

*"Hapana,"* Mbungu refused, then in English: "Not without a permit from the wildlife division."

"You fuckin' bureaucrat." Jordan clutched his forearm to his side and hunched his hurt shoulder. "It's a doomed runt."

"It's *your* damned runt." Mbungu dangled the sack inches from Jordan's face.

Jordan pulled the rope down from the tree, stuffed the climbing gear in his pack and hoisted it on his back. "Let's go," he said, taking the eaglet from Mbungu.

"Give me the pack." Mbungu laughed. "Calm down. The mother won't be back."

"Maybe not." Jordan broke into a run down the mountainside. "But I'm too scared to be rational."

They stepped out of the forest at the top of a mist-shrouded field of emerald tea. Rows of round bushes ran several hundred yards down to the Forest Research Station, a white colonial chalet with a red roof that had been the home of a Swiss planter. Beyond the mountains the horizon stretched twenty miles east to a dark line where the coastal plain met the gray haze of the Indian Ocean. Tufts of cumulus raced across a sky of the radiant blue that preceded the brief tropical twilight.

"Told you we'd make it back before dark," Jordan said in Swahili.

"Because you were so scared," Mbungu said, bending to drink from a stream. "You bolted like a bush buck."

Jordan eyed the stream. "That water gives me the trots."

"It's pure," Mbungu said between gulps from his cupped hand. "Can't hurt you."

"You sure there's no way you can keep the bird until it's big enough to travel across the mountains?" Jordan asked.

Mbungu stood up and wiped the water from his face with his sleeve. He looked at Jordan with crossed eyes like the ragged madman who begged at the entrance gate to the forest reserve.

Jordan led the way down through the tea rows and across a lawn to the veranda of the chalet, where a houseboy waited by a table set with a thermos and teacups. Mbungu told the boy to bring hot water and raw chicken innards, then followed him inside. Jordan swaddled the nestling in a sweatshirt and watched its head rock from side to side. Transparent purple lids sheathed its bulbous eyes.

"Take off your shirt." Mbungu set a bowl and bandages on the table by the nest.

Jordan winced while Mbungu scrubbed dirt and dried blood from the puncture wounds on his shoulder and bathed them with iodine.

Laughing, Mbungu said, "*Mzungu* are such babies."

"Since you're aware of the white man's low threshold," Jordan said through clenched teeth, "you could try to be gentle."

"*Stephanoaetus coronatus*," Mbungu enunciated the Latin syllables slowly, trying to distract him. "What are you going to name it?"

"I don't know." Jordan stared out at the rain forest. A line of dark peaks formed a green island rising out of the rolling sea of maize fields that ringed the forest. A wide flat-bottomed cumulus sucked vapor from the rain forest up through invisible tentacles, listing overhead like a gargantuan Portuguese man-of-war, dwarfing the other clouds in the sky.

"This one needs a doctor," Mbungu said, wrapping Jordan's forearm with gauze.

"I'll go tomorrow."

"Don't mention how you hurt yourself." Mbungu clipped off a piece of surgical tape with his teeth.

"Of course not." Jordan wiped sweat from his forehead.

The houseboy returned with a tray. He offered Jordan a bowl of little livers, hearts, and kidneys.

*"Sio chakulu cha mzungu."* Jordan told the boy that raw chicken was not a white man's delicacy.

Mbungu laughed, chopped a heart in half and dropped it in the mouth of the nestling lying on the table. Its black eyes blinked. Jordan and Mbungu took turns feeding it. Color drained rapidly from the sky. The big cumulus settled over the forest, wrapping fingers of fog around the peaks. Jordan shivered and looked for a sweater in his rucksack and found a week-old *Daily News* he bought in the morning for Mbungu.

"Sorry it's crumpled." Jordan handed him the paper.

"I thought you had forgotten," Mbungu said, and walked inside.

Jordan put on a sweater, picked up the eagle and followed Mbungu into a paneled room with a fireplace. Mbungu lit a fire and then settled into an armchair with the paper. Jordan set the eagle on the sweatshirt on the floor by the hearth.

" 'The Return of Democracy,' " Mbungu read a headline aloud and laughed forlornly.

Jordan watched the eaglet close its eyes.

"Does it work in your country?"

"Good question." Jordan pulled a couple of tepid Heinekens from his pack.

"You'll be gone by the end of the year." Mbungu popped the tab of a beer can. Behind him, at the edge of the firelight, the houseboy set a table.

"That's right." Jordan stretched out on an old brocade sofa. "So?"

"I was just thinking. . . ." Mbungu's voice trailed off. He took a sip of beer. "How *mzungu* come and go."

"I'll be here long enough for the bird to grow up," Jordan said.

Mbungu nodded. He reached for a piece of eucalyptus on the floor and lobbed it into the fire. "It'll make a good story to tell your friends. More exciting than teaching peasants to raise fish."

Jordan stared at him through the shadows. "Bwana, I've worked hard on my appointed rounds."

"True." Mbungu glanced at the dinner table and stood. "But isn't that what you want? An African adventure to take home?"

"Look, Modest, I want to do something of value before I leave." Jordan pushed himself up from the sofa. "*Sawa*, so I'm doing it for excitement. But it's worthwhile. When I saw Abel hatch I knew I had to save him."

"Have you thought it through carefully?" Mbungu moved to the table. "You won't have time to take on any new farmers who want to raise fish. No time for quick trips to Nairobi or Dar to chase white women. No visits to the hide. No—"

"I know," Jordan said. "I'm going to put the bird before everything else."

The rain on the roof was like waves of gravel. Jordan woke from a dream in darkness, unsure for a moment of his location in space and time. He thought he was in his own house on the other side of the mountains, then saw Mbungu's boots in the glow from the embers of the fire and remembered his grandfather's tin-roofed hunting cabin on the other side of the world. Imagining the rain would puncture holes in the tin, he stared into the grayness above the lamp until corrugated sheets materialized over the rafters. The roof billowed in and out like some great lung.

"'Rain, midnight rain, nothing but the wild rain,'" Jordan recited to himself, a habit of the solitude of the last sixteen months. As he rose from the sofa, his shoulder ached. He pumped up a pressure lamp and the room filled with white light and a loud roar beneath the pounding rain. The sky leopard was sleeping. He opened the wide front door and passed from the light and lantern noise into wailing wind and black night. Misted rain blew in under the veranda roof. He sat on a bench against the wall and wondered what Anna was doing on April Fools' Day. He pressed the light on his watch and saw: 11:51. It was nearly four in the afternoon in Memphis.

You want out of this hillbilly town?" Fred Goldberg whispered to Rutledge Jordan as Charles Coates left them at the bar and headed for the back of the restaurant. "Come work for me in Dallas."

Jordan glanced at Mr. Coates picking his way through the tables.

"Charlie can't hear too well anymore and he's too vain to wear his earpiece," Goldberg said louder.

"That's a very kind offer, Fred." Jordan raised his glass, thinking there was nothing he would loathe more than working for an auto parts magnate in Dallas. "But I like Memphis. My family's been here since the War of 1812."

"The Rutledges or the Jordans?" Goldberg asked in a Texas accent that was twangier than the delta's. He was short, round, and bald and wore a tan poplin suit and matching lizard-skin cowboy boots.

"Both," Jordan said. "I must sound like a pretentious peckerhead."

"I take it your family's fortunes have declined since the golden age of King Cotton." Goldberg somehow managed to talk rapidly despite the drawl.

"Beg your pardon?" Jordan said.

"Otherwise you wouldn't be busting your balls fourteen hours a day for Penniman, Noland and Coates, waiting another five years for them to make you a junior partner so you can cut it to twelve. All that grunt work while they play golf." Goldberg laughed and clapped him on the back. "I envy you, son. I don't know anything about my grand-daddy except he was killed by Nazis in the Second World War."

Jordan looked up helplessly, unsure how to respond.

"Don't take it so hard." Goldberg stepped up on the railing at the bottom of the bar, gaining four inches so the bartender could better see him, and ordered another round.

"Listen, son, I'm glad you're wearing that pair of buff elk."

Goldberg nodded at the pale leather cowboy boots showing under Jordan's seersucker trousers. "I gave them to you so you'll fit right in. General counsel for CarZone. I'm sure I can double whatever Charlie is paying you. You'll love Dallas."

"Fred, I've become well acquainted with national auto parts retail over the last three months—"

"You picked up the scent quicker than a redbone coon hound," Goldberg shot in as the bartender set down three tumblers of bourbon and ice on the steel bar.

"Thank you, Fred." Jordan grinned. "But I'm not sure it's the field I want to pursue."

"But there's piles of money to be made!" Goldberg squealed. "You could come back one day and buy the Rutledge plantation back. Make your parents proud, restore 'em to the gentility of the past."

Jordan laughed. "My parents?"

"I heard your daddy took a hit on the futures market and that his building business isn't exactly booming."

"To whom have you been talking?" Jordan tried to keep his voice civil.

"I've been doing business in Memphis for years." Goldberg looked over his shoulder and called, "Welcome back, Charlie."

"Have you been filling young Jordan in on the golden rule?" Charles Coates was tall and thin. He wore a dark suit that set off his silver hair, a white shirt against his deep tan and a blue tie with mallard ducks. His face was set in sour severity from a lifelong struggle with dyspepsia.

"He who has the gold makes the rules." Goldberg chuckled. "No, Rut and I were just discussing his illustrious family history."

"The Rutledge Raiders." Mr. Coates nodded solemnly. "Elijah Rutledge died defending Vicksburg."

"One account has it he was hung for stealing horses," Jordan said.

"Yankee propaganda." Mr. Coates looked at Jordan.

"Well, there is some debate in the family, Mr. Coates."

The senior partner gave Jordan a frown he used in meetings to silence his juniors.

"Do you know where the name 'Jordan' comes from?" Goldberg asked.

"The Jordan River," Mr. Coates replied.

"And the root of the river's name?"

"I don't think it's Latin," Jordan offered.

"Of course not. It's Hebrew. It means 'the descender.' It comes from the word to go down. You're the one who goes down." Goldberg laughed and waved one hand in front of his mouth, making a V with his forefingers.

Jordan tried to smile.

Mr. Coates didn't seem to get the pun. He looked down at the floor then at Jordan. "Why are you wearing boots?"

"Well, sir, Mr. Goldberg gave them to me." Jordan tried not to smile. "I thought it appropriate on the day we closed—"

"Don't make a habit of it."

"Of course, I—"

"Fred, our car is waiting outside," Mr. Coates said, moving him toward the door.

"We'll be talking." Goldberg winked at Jordan and shook his hand with a fierce grip.

"Look forward to it," Jordan said.

Jordan sat on a stool and looked at the Peabody Hotel across the street in the evening. The blocks of limestone, yellowed by the streetlights, reminded him of a painting, though he couldn't remember which one. Wavering on the front window was his own reflection: a thin twenty-eight-year-old in a double-breasted seersucker jacket with dark pouches under his pale blue eyes and short sandy brown hair. He could see himself as a gray-haired old man, his mouth set tight. In the afternoon the managing partner had called Jordan to his office and told him that he was getting a "substantial bonus" for closing the CarZone deal. Ten thousand dollars. About ten dollars an hour.

An attractive brunette came into the restaurant. Black jeans, black sleeveless shirt, push-up bra. Black cowboy boots. She crossed the terrazzo floor and sat a few stools down.

"Howdy," Jordan said. "Are you a cowgirl?"

"No." The woman's face was not friendly. "I'm a lesbian."

"What's a lesbian?" he asked.

"I like to kiss girls." The woman turned away. She signaled the bartender then looked down at Jordan's buff elk boots. "Are you a cowboy?"

"No," Jordan said. "I guess I'm a lesbian, too."

The woman ordered a drink. Jordan checked his watch and looked out the front windows. The reflection of the steel bar trembled as Anna came through the glass door. Her dark hair was down, and she wore a simple navy dress that hung loosely from her shoulders, skimming her curves.

Jordan waved. "Hello, beautiful."

"Hello, lover." Anna's voice was deep, throaty. She stepped in close. Her head just reached his neck.

He bent down and kissed her. Brown eyes, a whiff of perfume.

"You look like a zombie." Anna slid onto a stool.

"I can't wait to get up to the mountains."

"Dewar's on the rocks," Anna ordered then leaned sideways and whispered, "That pretty woman over there is a dyke. New teacher at the art college."

"I know."

"How'd you know?" Anna furrowed her eyebrows.

"She told me." Jordan swirled the ice in his glass. "Not that she was an artist—that she was a lesbian."

"Were you trying to pick her up?" Anna laughed, but she was serious.

"Oh, sweetpea," Jordan said, putting his arm around Anna's shoulders. "I got a nice bonus today. Got enough now for a down payment on the house."

"That's terrific, baby," Anna said brightly. Her parents had long ago offered them the down payment. There was something wrong in her eyes.

Jordan squeezed her shoulder and waited for the accusation he had been expecting for the last three months. "What was your day like?"

"Packing and paperwork." Anna looked into his face. "Boxing up the exhibit."

Jordan wanted to confess to her, to ask for forgiveness and swear that he would be faithful forever, but he was scared that she would never trust him again and not sure he could honor the pledge. "Where does the show go next?"

"Atlanta." Anna sipped her Scotch. "You want to go to the opening?"

"You bet." Whatever was wary in her eyes had passed. "I like Atlanta."

"You can misbehave with your frat brothers," Anna said. "Pretend you're still at Vanderbilt."

Jordan ordered a third bourbon and water. "It's funny. I was watching my reflection in the glass there, and there I was forty years from now in the same suit."

"Did you see me in your reflection?"

"There you are. . . ." Jordan took her hand and looked at the window. "A beautiful grandmother."

"You'll never trade me in for a newer model?"

"Never," Jordan said to her reflection.

# Aprili 2

In the morning a cloud lay over the rain forest, shearing off the peak with a flat gray roof just a few hundred feet up slope from the Swiss house.

"Better see a doctor about stitching your forearm," Mbungu said.

"*Sawa,*" Jordan said. Okay. He put a double handful of straw in a small box strapped to the rear rack of a little Peace Corps–issue Honda motorcycle, then picked up a sheet of cotton wool and lined the sides of the box.

The nestling wallowed on the ground by the rear knobby tire.

"Don't drive like a demon," Mbungu said.

Jordan bent to pick up the eaglet.

"Or you'll kill the bird," Mbungu emphasized in English.

"Don't worry about the bird, bwana." Jordan ground the back of his hand gently in the cotton and straw and hollowed a cavity for the nestling. He placed a wire screen over the top of the box and lashed it to the rack with strips of cut inner tube. "I need someone to love."

The ride across the Usambara Mountains back to the western escarpment usually took two hours. After two hours in steady rain, with streams of mud coursing through deep ruts in the road and his vision reduced to thirty feet, Jordan was only halfway home. To distract himself from the wet and cold, he sang loudly and kept glancing back at the canvas top tied on the box. The nestling was no worse off than sitting out a storm in the top of a tree. Jordan worried about how long he could hold the brake lever on the steep slopes with his left hand aching from the rip between his thumb and forefinger. The rain showered on for two more hours while the throbbing in his hand became a piercing pain. He yelled each time he hit the brakes. After a while he stopped singing and rode on grimly, wondering if he should have taken this nestling after all.

Jordan passed through a curtain of rain into a clear sky. A hot savanna wind rushing up the escarpment held the storm away from the cliff edge. He could see the reaches of the Maasai steppe, a desert blue as a sea in the soft light of a low sun. Row after row of distant ridges, invisible all day in the glare, delineated into purple teeth that ran jagged across the far horizon. He coasted past a derelict Lutheran church of gray clapboard with broken windows and an open roof long stripped of tin sheets, its yard overgrown with tall bougainvillea bushes. In the lane children in ragged shorts and torn dresses pushed each other on a handmade bike with wooden wheels.

Jordan waved and turned into a gap in a row of tall bushes that enclosed the lawn in front of his home, the old rectory of the ruined chapel—a stone cottage with a roofed front porch and back porch that faced a three-thousand-foot cliff. He always arrived behind the hedge walls with a sense of relief from the thousands of eyes that watched him wherever he went and the hordes of children who appeared from nowhere to surround him. The watchman, Omali, sat on the front porch, cutting a face in a pumpkin. Omali was the one luxury that the Peace Corps allowed volunteers.

"The other pumpkin was rotten." Omali pointed his knife across the yard to a pile of compost. The jack-o'-lantern was a custom imported into Tanzania via seeds smuggled from America that had become a permanent talisman meant to scare off Sambaa thieves.

"Thanks, bwana," Jordan said, coming to a stop by the porch. He untied the rear rack and carried the box to the front door, pausing to wave his hand over the pumpkin. Omali watched gravely while Jordan mumbled an English incantation from an illustrated medieval prayer that had hung on the wall of his room as a child: "From ghoulies and ghosties and long leggity beasties and things that go bump in the night, good Lord deliver us."

Jordan walked into the rectory, a central room with a bedroom on each side and a kitchen along the back. There were light fixtures put up decades before by a German priest in hope of electric lines that were never erected. In the sinks were rusty faucets and pipes that ran to a rotten wooden tank on stilts overgrown by bushes in the side yard. Jordan collected water from the tin roof of the cottage and carried it during the dry season from a stream a quarter of a mile away on the back of his motorcycle. He set the box on a round table in the main room. Gently he dried the sleeping eaglet, then fashioned a nest with the towel. He slowly pulled off his soaked clothing and fell naked onto the couch. Dreamily he studied the wound in his right hand. He unwrapped the gauze on his forearm and gingerly folded back the deep V-shaped gash. There was a gray line of pus. He dropped the skin quickly, scared to look further, and started to think through the procedure: Scrub wound with Betadine solution . . . apply—

*Quee-quee-quee!*

Jordan started at the unfamiliar sound.

*Quee-quee-quee!*

Jordan remembered there was no meat in the house. Painfully he pushed himself off the couch and walked out to the porch and Omali.

"Get the goat," Jordan said.

Omali looked horrified.

"What's the ma—" Jordan realized he was naked. He rushed inside and frantically searched his bedroom.

*Quee-quee-quee!*

He found some dirty clothes in a basket, pulled them on and ran back outside.

Omali was walking around the corner of the house.

"Where's the goat?" Jordan looked across the yard at the rotting church.

Omali turned slowly around to face him.

Jordan repeated: *"Mbuzi iko wapi?"*

"It ate through the rope and . . . and . . . fell over the cliff." Omali's speech was slurred. He stood listing in a long quilted lime coat that Jordan didn't recognize, a castoff that must have turned up recently at the market in Lushoto in a shipment from America. He'd probably sold the goat and bought the new coat.

"*Mwongo*," Jordan said. Liar.

"*Mimi sio mwongo,*" Omali denied it, glancing at Jordan, then staring at his own feet.

"It wasn't your goat," Jordan said slowly. "You never help anybody. No one would ever give you a goat."

"It wasn't my fault." Looking up, Omali wiped his mouth with the back of his hand. "It was an act of God."

"I'm deducting it from your salary," Jordan said, turning.

"But that's two weeks' pay." Omali followed him across the porch.

"I'll take it out over six months." Jordan could hear Omali staggering behind him.

"Please, bwana, it was an act of God."

"You worthless drunk," Jordan said in English. "You sleep through the night and rob me in the day." He wanted to fire him, but Omali came with the church; his cousin worked for the diocesan office in town. It was impolitic to break a single strand of the web of an extended African family. If Jordan fired Omali, the cousin might try to throw Jordan out of the house, and being on this edge three thousand feet above the plain was Jordan's single most reliable source of pleasure in the Usambara Mountains.

"You know I don't speak English." Omali looked ridiculous in the woman's ankle-length coat. "Please, bwana. I am a poor man. I've got eight children to feed."

What a life, Jordan thought. "Okay, bwana."

"*Ahsante, bwana,*" Omali thanked him.

"If anything else vanishes, you're sacked." Jordan tried to glare at him.

"*Ahsante, bwana.*" Omali smiled. "*Ahsante.*"

Jordan rode down the lane, sucking the wound on his hand. He came upon a group of barefoot boys in shorts, kicking a ball made of crushed plastic bags held round by twine.

*"Jambo, Bwana Samaki,"* the children called out. Hello, Master Fish. He was known by his trade to thousands of Sambaa in the mountains, a celebrity because of his white skin.

"Anyone around here have chickens for sale?"

"My mother does," one boy said, dribbling the ball in the air with his knees.

"Quick. Run ask her."

The boy kicked the ball and ran off through a gap in a hedge.

"Let me ride the bike," one boy said, smiling with his arms wide as if holding invisible handlebars.

Jordan regarded him silently.

Another boy mimicked Jordan sucking his hand.

The first boy ran back through the hedge. "Sorry, Master Fish. She sold her last chicken yesterday."

Jordan rode on until he came to a cluster of huts where a group of women sat on mats, braiding each other's hair. Before they could initiate an annoyingly long traditional greeting, an interminable series of questions on the condition of the weather and crops and work and family, Jordan asked quickly, "Any chickens for sale?"

The women's faces hardened at his bluntness.

"Excuse me. I'm in a hurry. Does anyone have any chickens?"

"All the chickens here got sick and died," one woman said.

"That's horrible. I'm sorry." Jordan twisted the throttle.

He rode farther down the road, asking everyone he saw. It seemed that some sort of plague had killed every chicken in the vicinity. Jordan stopped alongside a line of girls wearing bright wraps and balancing five-gallon plastic buckets of water on their heads. He asked one, "Do you know where I can buy some chickens?"

She passed without answering, keeping her eyes on the road.

Jordan repeated the question to the second girl.

She walked by silently.

Jordan asked the third girl.

She didn't seem to hear him.

He asked the last girl.

She hurried to catch up with the others.

Muttering, he rode down a rocky slope. Near the bottom a man staggered drunkenly uphill. Jordan hit the brake and slid through the mud. The man jerked upright, his eyes wide, yelled and fell into elephant grass off the roadside.

"Sorry," Jordan said, looking down at the man. "I just wanted to ask if you know where I can buy some chickens."

"Ngolo," the man said.

"Ngolo village?" Jordan stayed on the bike as he pulled the man back on his feet.

"Yes." The man brushed mud off his patched trousers. "Mama Zanifa has plenty."

"Thanks." Jordan released the foot brake so the bike rolled down the slope before the man could ask for a handout. "Mama Zanifa," he repeated to remember. The mother of Zanifa.

*"Mzungu! Mzungu!"* A dozen children ran toward the Honda as Jordan coasted into the Ngolo village ten minutes later. White man! White man! *"Mzungu! Mzungu!"*

"I am the king of the witches, the night spirits and the vampires," Jordan said in Swahili, and then, his voice lowered, "Don't touch the motorbike."

"Give me money." A boy with a fluoride smile practiced his English.

Dizzy, Jordan ignored him and looked around at the village on the sloping mountainside. He asked for the home of Mama Zanifa.

"The last house. The big one." The boy pointed to a roof in a grove of banana trees.

Jordan walked along a path. Cattle peered out from the doorways of the adobe homes. Old women with creased faces sat on dwarf stools and canvas chairs under the shade of tall tropical hedges that divided the little yards. On the ground, flanked by formations of motley chicks, hens veered through the village. Darting about like nervous schools of fish, they seemed to head up the slope toward a two-story house. Except for colonial plantations Jordan had never seen a house like this in the mountains. Smooth pink wash covered the adobe, and the windows, large like *mzungu* windows, were trimmed in a bright red wash.

light, took on sinister shapes. His helmet heated up like some sort of facial sauna. The eye shield fogged over completely, forcing him to flip it up. Sweat streamed down his chest and back, soaking his shirt. Jordan knew he had a fever, but the sudden heat wave in his body deadened his wounds and he was grateful. A praying mantis flew into his right eye, and he coasted off the road into bushes and fell over on his side. He picked up the bike and kicked the starter, again and again. Seething, he pulled off the steamy helmet and shoved his foot down on the crank. Finally the Honda engine ignited. He rode on through the night, squinting against flying creatures swarming in the headlights until he saw the evil eyes of the pumpkin on his front porch.

In a sweaty daze Jordan hacked the hen apart and diced up the heart and liver for a cropful of the richest cuts. He glanced through *Hawks and Hawking* at the photographs of falconers feeding nestlings with tweezers. The book referred to a hatchling taken from the nest as an "eyas." Even when the eagle was grown it would be an eyas, one taken at the most impressionable age from the natural world into the world of humans.

The eyas looked to be a deformed creature crying out for protein from the bottom of a woven basket, where she lolled on a mat of sticks. As she gulped the chunks of chicken organs, her crop swelled into a goiter the size of a golf ball. Full, the eyas let her beak rest on the bulging crop. The impossibly long neck drooped over her toadlike body. Her wings were stubby flippers. Jordan thought of her as a female after reading that raptors were referred to in the feminine out of deference to the largest sex.

In the kitchen Jordan found the choloroquine malaria pills in the bulky Peace Corps first-aid box and tried to remember when he had last come down with the parasite—January, perhaps. He set the lantern on the counter and lit several candles, placing them in an arc around the operating area. He opened a big bottle of Eusol, the Edinburgh University antiseptic solution invented years ago for cheap and easy manufacture in the colonies. With a sterile prod, Jordan drew back the flaps of torn skin on his forearm and looked hard at the vivid colors underneath. It looked as foreign as the slaughtered chicken. The fat cells were grapes of fluorescent yellow, the muscle a rich dark purple. A green vein wormed through the opening uncut. The wound was filthy.

Jordan crossed the room and gagged down two shots of local gin. He twisted open a bottle of hydrogen peroxide with his teeth and poured it into the wound until the white foam ran over onto the counter. He squirted red Betadine onto a sterile gauze pad and scrubbed the wound. His natural squeamishness made the process almost unbearable. He tried to drown the pain by singing.

Jordan squirted more Betadine on another piece of gauze, took a breath and scrubbed the naked flesh. He washed the burning foam from the wound with cool Eusol and saw more dirt. One more time. Jordan thought of the Maasai warriors who neither flinched nor screamed while an elder pared away their foreskin with a crude blade. Their mothers, standing on the periphery of the ceremony, wailed and convulsed for them. He thought of his mother on the other side of the planet. Scrubbing, he squeezed his eyes shut and saw Mama Zanifa tearing open sterile packets and emptying rabbit fur into the deep wound. He wiped his hand across his forehead. It was covered with sweat.

Jordan staggered into the bedroom, lurched under the mosquito netting and pulled the crawl space taut, tucking the netting down between the frame and mattress. He felt safer here than anywhere else in Africa. No rats or insects or snakes could reach him. The webbed-off space was soothing and secluded, an enchanted gazebo in a dangerous garden. This is malaria, Jordan thought. Malaria always recurs when you are exhausted and psychotic.

# Aprili 3

Jordan woke to the screams of the eyas. Pale gray light gathered in the stillness as the turning planet swung the mountains toward the sun. His feet pushed through the net to the cold floor. In the kitchen, rats had chewed holes in the carcass of the chicken left on the wooden counter. Jordan sawed off several ounces of meat and fed them to the eyas, wondering about a name. He stared down at the furry eaglet, alone and out of place. The name came to him. Pasipo. Where there is not.

"Pah-SEE-poe," he said sharply. "Naughty, Pasipo."

The fever returned in a sudden sweat shower. He lay under the mosquito net, too weak to move, knowing that the malaria was not responding to the chloroquine, that this strain was almost certainly resistant to the synthesized quinine. That left Lariam, a new drug that was known to induce hallucinations that lingered long after the malaria. He remembered the girl fresh out of a Bible college in the Midwest, a Peace Corps math teacher in a desert village two hundred miles west who spent every hour of every school day for several months reading the Bible aloud to her students before the head office in Dar es Salaam identified her as a nervous breakdown. She had been taking Lariam once a week as a malaria prophylaxis.

The rain hammered on the tin roof of the rectory. Unsteadily Jordan navigated the slippery painted floor to the kitchen. The medicine box lay open amid spent candles and bones and bits of meat and dried chicken juices. He found the Lariam, tore open the aluminum wrapper, and chased it with filtered water from a small cylindrical tank on the counter. After feeding Pasipo, Jordan collapsed on the sofa with one arm over his eyes blocking out a painful light.

*Hodi . . . Hodi . . . Hodi.* Someone's call woke Jordan from malaria dreams to a room of shadows. Slowly he gathered himself up from the sofa. He could see figures outside the screen door on the porch. He staggered toward them but they seemed to vibrate and merge together. The world began to spin around him and he stumbled to the wooden floor. He closed his eyes against the turning room but his mind was filled with rushing images. "Mama," he mumbled. Someone lifted him onto the sofa. He opened his eyes. The room swung by horizontally, flashing repeatedly across his field of vision.

He closed his eyes. A cool wet cloth was put on his forehead. Silky fingertips stroked his arm. Someone unbuttoned his shirt and toweled his chest dry, then lifted his *kikoi* wrap and wiped his legs and feet. He heard words without meaning. An eternity passed. He screamed.

Someone's hand gripped his tightly. A blurry figure circled him. Shards of static spun off a comet's tail.

"Please stop," he begged. "Please stop. Please stop."

*"Poleh. Poleh,"* said a soft voice. Quiet. Quiet. *"Poleh. Poleh."* The word cut through the mad orbit of images soothing as a mantra. Don't panic, Jordan told himself. Control your breathing. Slow your breathing and your vision will follow. He felt the muscles between his ribs stretch as his lungs filled with air and listened to his ribs creak as he exhaled. *"Poleh."* The voice spoke so slowly, each word seemed filled with the rhythm of his lungs. *"Poleh."* The comet tail of yellow static dissipated into a cloud of red and white. Jordan opened his eyes.

Black eyes stared down into his. The young girl Zanifa knelt beside him. "You have returned. Your fever was too high. Have you taken medicine?"

Jordan could not speak. He gazed at the warm hues of her face, her soft dark curls coppered by the light. Out the back windows over the escarpment a red sun hung low over the plain. He squinted at the girl, sweat stinging his eyes, mumbled in English: "You're beautiful. So sweet . . . perfect."

"I don't understand," she said softly.

Jordan stared at her. He couldn't think in Swahili.

Zanifa turned her face from his stare.

"Zanifa, we gotta go—it's time to get the water," said a girl behind her.

"The men should . . . get their own . . . water," Jordan struggled with the Swahili.

The two girls looked at each other and laughed.

"They would never carry water," Zanifa said. "The men? Never!"

The other girl moved toward the door.

Zanifa reached down and picked up his forearm. "The wound is really bad. I should clean it."

"I'm running home to carry the water before my father hits me," her friend said.

"Tell my mother I'll be home soon," Zanifa said.

The screen door slammed behind the girl.

Zanifa looked at Jordan. "We must wash your wounds with boiled water and pack them with boiled salt."

"I thought you were going to suggest rabbit fur." Jordan was beginning to feel lucid.

"I learned from my great-grandmother." Zanifa stood up, straightening her skirt. "She was a doctor famous among the Sambaa who knew the herbs of the forest and the medicines of the white man. She was married to a German."

Pasipo cried from the table. Jordan tried to sit up but the room began to shift. He lay back and asked her if she would chop up some meat and feed the baby hawk.

"The hawks eat better than the people of the mountains," Zanifa said.

Jordan smiled at her, motioned toward the eyas.

Leaning over the basket with the tweezers, Zanifa said, "She is ugly now, but she will grow up to be a beautiful eagle. Everyone hates them because they steal the chickens."

"Pasipo will grow big enough to take a baboon."

"I say!" Glancing at Jordan, Zanifa used the English exclamation often heard in Swahili conversations. "The bird has had enough. Now we must clean your wounds."

"Okay, get the big box of medicines on the counter," Jordan said. The thought of scrubbing the wound again left him nauseated. "We don't need to use water and salt until we run out of my medicine."

Zanifa set the box on the floor by the sofa.

Jordan rolled on his side and leaned over the edge. He found the Lariam, ripped the foil wrapper off one capsule, and swallowed it dry. He shut his eyes as Zanifa peeled off the bandages.

"First pour in the peroxide," he said through clenched teeth. "Wait for the bubbles to settle and then pour in the Eusol." He tried to hum as she cleaned and dressed the wounds. Soon his brain was too far gone on the Lariam and fever to feel the pain. He concentrated on the sensations of her hands on his skin.

"You need a woman to take care of you," Zanifa said finally, simply.

"My problem is that women always took care of me."

Anna sat in the stern, calling directions. The canoe dropped over a blind shelf on a bend in the river. Directly in their path a huge boulder rose, with a fountain splashing off the black rock. Jordan's whole body jerked back. Anna shouted, "Hard right!"

Jordan hesitated.

"Hard right!"

Jordan dug the paddle in the water, and the bow of the canoe swung away from the rock. He looked back.

Staring past him at the river ahead, Anna held her paddle vertically in the water behind her, using it as a rudder. She laughed and said, "Ole Turn-n-Run." She pointed downstream to a formation of rocks in a stretch of white water. "There's a whirlpool at the end of the rapid. Stay to the high side of the hole and paddle like hell or it'll suck us in."

The white water heaved the aluminum canoe from side to side. Jordan rode with his hands clutching the gunnels. The canoe sailed over a ledge and plunged into the stream. "High side," Anna yelled. Jordan leaned out over the bow and drew back his paddle through the green water with both arms. The bow rose and the stern of the canoe swung into a swirling hole six feet in diameter. Jordan was certain they were sliding backward. *"Paddle!"* Anna shouted, spiking the side of the whirlpool in a blur of strokes. Jordan paddled furiously, driven by the adrenaline of pure fear, aware nevertheless they were not in much danger. After a few seconds the canoe broke back into the main current and slipped downstream.

The river slowed, widening into a deep pool in the bottom of a sheer sandstone gorge. They drifted out of the sunshine into the shade of trees along the edge of the river and grounded the canoe on the little beach of the Gentleman's Swimming Hole. Jordan dragged the canoe out of the water and stumbled toward a gray boulder, breathing deeply, thinking he should buy a StairMaster. Anna tackled him from behind, landing on top of him. She pushed his face into the sand.

"What a chicken." Her voice came from above, gravelly and slightly winded.

Jordan spat out sand and rolled over. Her legs pinned his waist. He looked up into her face and thought of waking in the cottage naked beside her and of the way their bodies clung together as they slept and how they started to make love still half-asleep, long before dawn, and he wondered how he could have ever betrayed her.

# Aprili 4–7

For three days, driven by strong winds from the south, the rain came each night, waking Jordan with the sound of waves crashing upon the tin. He lay in bed listening to the storms, afraid to go back to sleep. The line between waking and sleeping was blurred by Lariam hallucinations. One night three figures in black robes and hoods stared at him through the mosquito net. Jordan sat up and cried out, "Who are you?" The figures pulled down their hoods with white hands. Their heads were missing. Vines and white lilies grew out of their severed necks. One of them reached toward him with a bloody amputated arm. The veins and tendons and flesh of the stump twisted into a vagina that opened and closed like a mouth.

In the bleak dawns he would wake to Pasipo's cries. The eaglet looked up from Zanifa's green mattress of new leaves in the dining room with the innocent eyes of an infant. Brain dead, Jordan dropped bits of raw chicken into the eyas's little mouth. When the plastic container was empty, he would mindlessly slit a chicken's neck and gut the carcass and heave the bones, head and feet over the cliff. At times his vision would skip and spin. He would sink to his feet and lie still with his eyes shut, watching colors flash against the black of his eyelids until his sight returned.

Mama Zanifa came the first morning and found him half-awake in fever, tangled in bedsheets. It took Jordan a minute to recognize her through the mosquito net. She tried to persuade him to go to the hospital, but Jordan said he would wait it out, that he couldn't bear the idea of sleeping in a ward of AIDS patients. A few hours later he was not sure if Mama Zanifa had actually visited.

Zanifa came with her friend Subira every afternoon, bringing fruit and vegetables and chickens. Zanifa would change Jordan's dressings and force him to eat papaya. If Pasipo cried out while she was there, she would feed her, talking to the eaglet in Swahili, congratulating her on her appetite, telling her of the coming days when she would fly high in the sky.

On the fourth day, in the gray light before dawn, Jordan woke with a clear head, feeling at home again in his body. He kicked away the mosquito net and stood naked in the room. He stretched his arms upward, touched his toes. He tied a *kikoi* around his waist and ran through the house to the porch. The clouds a thousand feet below formed a flat plain of snow stretching to the horizon.

*Quee-quee-quee*, Pasipo called. Already she seemed a few ounces bigger. Jordan placed the bits of meat in front of her to see if she could eat on her own. She bent over and pecked one.

Jordan brought a bowl of *uji*, cream of cornmeal, the local porridge, out to the back porch. Bright sunshine bleached the snowfield and fell through vaporous crevasses to spotlight patches of yellow grass another half mile below on the floor of the steppe. For a time the panorama seemed to fill him with dumb happiness. He was alive. He stared into the distance, listening to the wind. He remembered a mountain sunrise in New Mexico with Anna and the old sadness came rushing in. It was best to keep occupied. He finished his tea and thumbed through his Sierra Club appointment book, noting three dates he had missed with farmers in the last few days. There was one entry today: Ayubu Waziri, Harvest, *Saa 3*—the third hour of the Swahili day, which began, logically, at sunrise.

Hurriedly Jordan cleaned and dressed his wounds. A V-shaped scab was hardening on his forearm. It was too late to stitch it now. Three of the eight punctures on his shoulder were still infected. He would have to be careful not to get them wet.

Outside, Omali was sleeping on a cotton mattress on the porch by the door. Jordan looked across the yard to the old Lutheran chapel. The weathered clapboards were black from the rain. Vines climbed the sides, curled under the roof beams. Omali was breathing heavily, wrapped in the big quilted lime coat. Jordan picked up a green bottle from the futon and sniffed the rancid odor of raw cane liquor. He poked the dirty down coat with his boot. *"Omali!"*

The watchman groaned and stirred.

"Greet the sunshine before it rains, bwana," Jordan shouted in Swahili, stepping back.

Omali shielded his eyes with his forearm. Slowly he managed to stand.

"What would happen if thieves came while you were drunk and asleep?" Jordan unscrewed the cap on the fuel tank of the little Honda, dipped his finger, then squinted inside. "What kind of watchman are you? Get out of here."

A large pale gray raptor floated slowly upward from the one-armed cross atop the chapel's steeple as if climbing an invisible ladder with sluggish strokes of overwide wings—a gemnogene, a nest robber. Jordan watched it ascend vertically and then dive toward the escarpment. When he looked down, Omali was gone. He locked the front door and pushed the bike off the porch and rode out through the gate in the picket fence. The dark rotting wood of the church steamed in the sunshine.

On the far side of the church, Jordan saw Omali shouting at his wife. A muddy yard sat in front of an adobe house with a rusty tin roof and one hole for a window. Several children ran toward the motorcycle. Invariably Jordan felt guilty living in the large rectory alone while Omali and his family shared one room. They were like the other quarter million Sambaa living in crowded huts as they had for centuries in the mountains. "Omali," Jordan yelled, coasting. "Don't forget to buy some candles for the pumpkin."

*"Ndiyo, bwana."* Omali waved and turned back toward his wife.

Jordan gunned the throttle, losing himself in the rare sunshine and the rush of the speed through cornfields, past lone homesteads and clusters of mud huts.

Ayubu Waziri was waiting with a gaggle of his children a quarter mile below the village of Sala, a dozen adobe huts in a copse of spindly wattle and eucalyptus trees rising against a barren mountainside of red clay. On the steep slope in soil depleted by decades of cornfields, Jordan and Waziri had dug two pairs of ponds in a stepwork fashion and linked them with small channels. From the village looking down, Jordan could see two were dry. The other two looked like dark green cat eyes in a fur of golden maize stalks. Jordan took long leaping strides down the hill. Ayubu Waziri was one of his few students he believed would persevere.

"You're late!" Ayubu Waziri shouted up, smiling, waving extravagantly with both arms. A wiry little man, he was barefoot and wore trousers rolled up to the knees and a Harvard T-shirt. Waziri was forty but looked sixty-five.

As Jordan neared, Waziri yelled again, "You've been lost."

"I've been ill."

"*Poleh.*"

"Thanks."

Waziri's children gathered close. Jordan told them hello, and they responded in unison: "I kiss your feet." Waziri embarked on a long, old-fashioned greeting. What's the news of the morning? Of your family? Of your work? Jordan responded with one-word Swahili rejoinders. Peace. Good. Cool. He thought of a polite way to end the exchange: "What's the news of your fish?"

"We'll find out today."

"For real," Jordan said. "Shall we drain the pond or drag the net?"

"We'll drain this one but drag the other," Waziri said.

Jordan and Waziri spread the net by one pond then lowered the weighted end down in the water. The old man told one of his boys to pull the gate below the pond. The reflection of a cloud on the surface of the pool wrinkled, then broke apart as a small whirlpool appeared in the deep end. White water coursed down the narrow cut in the earth and splashed into an empty pond below. The water inched down the sides of the upper pond. After several minutes only a puddle remained and silver tolapia jumped and gasped in the net.

The smallest children scrambled to fill glass jars with minnows, wiggling them out of the holes in the net and rushing the minnows to the low pond. Three older girls gathered fish in five-gallon buckets. Everyone was laughing, marveling over the number of fish. The tall girls raised the plastic buckets to their heads. They dropped their hands to their sides and paced easily up the trail to the village.

"*Tumeshenda, bwana,*" Waziri said. We have conquered.

"*Tunakwenda, tunashenda,*" Jordan replied, intoning the refrain of an old East African army song. We are going. We are conquering.

Waziri laughed and slapped his knees.

Chanting the refrain, Jordan marched toward the full pond. He thought of the partners at Penniman, Noland and Coates, parceling the year-end bonuses. He decided that if he was not shadowed by regret, this moment might be more satisfying than a big check. He wondered how long would it take to outlive the shadow.

"*Tunakwenda, tunashenda.*" Waziri's twelve-year-old son, Hamisi, pranced behind Jordan, following him around the pond. Smiling, the other children took up the song. We are going. We are conquering.

Jordan stopped at the deep end. "Who's dragging the net with me?"

"That pond is too cold for an old man," Waziri said. "Let the boys."

"What about the girls?" Jordan said.

"Their job is to carry the fish and dry them."

"Let the boys put a five-gallon bucket of fish on their heads for a change."

Waziri laughed.

"Okay, you and I'll drag the pond. Set a good example." Jordan dug in his pocket for a sheet of plastic and a roll of waterproof tape.

"You and I are *wazee,*" Waziri exclaimed. "It's unbecoming of elders to slop around like frogs."

Jordan taped the plastic around the bandage on his forearm then took off his boots and long trousers. Underneath he wore a pair of cut-off khakis. The cool water soothed his hot feet. He remembered the tepid ponds in South Carolina where he and his fellow volunteers, most of them five or six years younger, right out of college, spent two months. Every day he had thought about quitting. All his friends had thought he was mad to give up his career for the Peace Corps. At the end of the training, his mother had nearly fainted when she learned he was going to Africa. His father told him, "Don't leave any café au lait babies behind and pray every day."

A year and a half later he had taught thirty odd Sambaa who showed any real promise of sticking with the fish ponds after he was gone, a decent record by Peace Corps standards, if statistically futile. As he dragged the net against the water, his shoulder ached, but he felt strong, fit from his short life in the mountains. He called across to the tall boy, who looked to be about eighteen. "Pull hard. Pretend we're in the waves of the Indian Ocean."

The boy caught up. "I've never been in the ocean. I saw it once from the top of the mountains."

They dragged the net to the far side of the pond and up onto the bank. About a dozen three-pound tolapia flopped in the net.

"*Tunakwenda,*" a five-year-old girl said, bending to pick a fish. "*Tunashenda.*" While the children laughed and collected the fish, Jordan walked across Waziri's maize fields into a stand of wattle and watered the dry, feathery ground at the base of a tree. The soil was poisoned by wattle toxins that killed off other plants. The spindly trees, brought by the British colonists to produce tannin for curing leather, were still invading the country inch by inch.

Jordan returned to the pond just as two of Waziri's boys started to drag the net again. He caught sight of Waziri's three daughters coming down the trail, their empty buckets swinging by their sides.

Jordan asked the old man, "Do you know a half-caste woman, Mama Zanifa, who lives in Ngolo on the other side of the second mountain there?" He pointed to the blue ridges to the north. "She has a daughter about the age of your oldest."

"*Haaah!*" Ayubu drew his breath in quickly. "That child is an abomination."

"What?" Jordan asked. "What do you mean?"

"The Sambaa forbid incest," Waziri explained righteously. "In the days before the Europeans, children of incest were killed at birth. That child is a sacrilege against the ancestors. She should never have been allowed to live. Disaster will follow her."

"Who's her father?" Jordan asked.

"Her mother's brother." Waziri stared at him.

"No wonder her skin is as light as her mother's," Jordan said. "Where is he now?"

"He went mad. You could always find him drinking cane liquor, telling the others that the curse would kill him." Ayubu appeared to enjoy the fatalism of the story. "One day he threw himself off the mountain."

"The girl is beautiful," Jordan said.

"What?" Waziri's face looked shocked. "You whites are strange. She has no *butt.*" He pointed to one of his daughters, whose Bantu bottom protruded far enough to carry a melon—the kind of rump Tanzanian men in a bar would cheer, *Whoa-whoa.*

"*She* is a Sambaa beauty," Waziri said. "That girl Zanifa would have been killed had her mother not fled to Dar es Salaam. Mama Zanifa came back when the girl was five years old. After that no one would marry the woman."

"But Sultani Kimweri is going to marry Zanifa." Jordan waited for a reaction.

"I have not heard that," Ayubu said, and then, sighing, "I'm surprised. His father would never have taken an abomination for a bride."

Riding back to the rectory, Jordan passed Omali sitting with a group of vacant-faced men at an open bar. On the lawn of the rectory Omali's daughters were playing something like hopscotch.

"Did you bring me a fish today?" the oldest asked, smiling.

"One for everyone." Jordan dug into his rucksack.

Inside, he fed Pasipo a chicken liver, heart and intestines, then lay down in a canvas lounge chair on the back porch. The blanket of clouds had vanished beneath a faultless sky. The cliffs beneath him dropped a vertical thousand feet, then sloped steeply another three thousand down to the long orderly green grids of sisal plantations making a pointillistic carpet along the mountain wall. To the south, the green carpet was broken for a half mile by the town of Mombo, a collection of shiny tin roofs hugging the base of the escarpment. To the east the flat, empty savanna of the Maasai steppe stretched for thousands of square miles. On the horizon the Nguru Mountains appeared to be black shark fins.

Jordan looked at his easel, set in the shade of the porch, and considered starting another watercolor of the vista. Painting was therapy, absorbed his loneliness and self-pity, but he was anxious to check his mailbox in town for the first time in a week.

Jordan rode on a dirt track a mile to the outskirts of Lushoto, the district seat, and turned onto the only asphalt road in the mountain range. The road linked Lushoto and Mombo, twisting from the cool highlands twenty miles down a river gorge to the sweltering savanna. Jordan rode past lines of Sambaa whose reposed faces seemed innately hostile. Their faces always unsettled him, though he knew if he stopped and said hello, they would break into wide smiles. Women trudged beneath baskets. Men walked hand in hand, a custom that no longer struck him as odd. Jordan rode by the low white buildings of a primary school, a gloomy Victorian house occupied by Irish Rasminian Brothers, a lumber mill, a small tannin factory billowing smoke with a sign that read *Giraffe Extract*, then passed the tennis courts and gardens of the Lawns Hotel, a soccer stadium, a Lutheran bookshop, a BP station with old-fashioned pumps out of a Hopper painting, a row of noisy bars by the bus stand opposite the Catholic cathedral and the colonnaded National Bank of Commerce. He pulled into the driveway of a gingerbread British-era post office.

His box was one of three hundred set in a wall along the back of a veranda. Always there was the question: Had she written back? He opened the box with an antique key and found a single envelope that contained clippings of weddings and debutantes from the *Memphis Commercial Appeal* and a card from his mother telling him of the birth of his sister's second daughter. Jordan read the note and the clips twice, slowly, then walked across the veranda to a counter and wrote on the back of a postcard of zebras on the Serengeti:

*Dear Sophie,*

*I'm so happy to hear that you've brought a healthy new baby into this strange world. I can't imagine. Mom must be in heaven. Longer letter later.*

*Love, Rut*

Placing a pink flamingo stamp on the card, he heard another motor-cycle pull up at the post office.

"Do you think you can get AIDS from eating out a girl?" asked a tall man in black leather sitting on a big 1,000-cc BMW enduro-bike. His yellow hair was short, almost crew cut, his face tan, and his mouth hung open in a smile. African drums and pygmy voices could be heard pulsing softly from waterproof earplugs around his neck.

"Hey, Ernst." Jordan put the card in an old cast-iron mailbox.

"I met this beautiful girl last night in a hotel in Tanga after eight hours on the road from Nairobi." Ernst shrugged, suggesting the fu-tility of self-restraint.

"Hit and run," Jordan said in Swahili slang. He knew Ernst had been replaying the episode to himself on the ride back to the moun-tains from the coast until now he was aching to tell it aloud. "You know, bwana, you're just like Kurtz in *The Heart of Darkness*. You've gone utterly native, but you still have to share your experience with one of your own."

"Kurtz was a great man."

"Uh-huh," Jordan said absently, remembering Ernst's advice on these steps the day his mother's clipping of Anna's wedding arrived over a year ago. A teenage sleeping dictionary, Ernst had said, would keep his mind off the American bird and improve his Swahili in the bargain.

"She was . . . wild." Ernst was saying from his motorcycle. "Half Zulu. Half Zanzibari."

Jordan said nothing, stepping from the porch to the driveway.

"What happened to you?" Ernst clicked off the Walkman and looked at the scab on Jordan's face. "Crash the bike again?"

"Remember Romeo and Juliet?" Jordan said, touching the wound. "Yeah?"

"I fought Juliet for one of her chicks," Jordan said.

Ernst whistled and smiled.

"Keep it to yourself," Jordan said. "I don't want the game officer on my back."

"Maybe the eagle will improve your mood," Ernst said, climbing off the BMW.

Jordan watched Ernst walk to the porch of the post office, envying his attitude. Eighteen months ago Jordan had been put off by Ernst's promiscuity, but he had come to admire his endurance. Ernst was a veteran content to propagate his own highly educated hybrid tribe with a string of African wives from the villages where he had worked in Uganda, Kenya and Tanzania. His dozen children were sent by the Dutch development agency to the best international schools in their respective countries and to college in Holland. The energy required to travel by motorcycle among the families scattered across East Africa was immense, and Ernst was nearly fifty, though he appeared much younger. "You went to Nairobi to see your kids?"

"Yeah, bwana, they grow up so fast." Ernst turned on the veranda to smile.

"So that's why you keep having more." Jordan swung one leg over the seat of the Honda.

"I like children around." Ernst dug for his keys in his pocket.

"Just like the Africans." Jordan gazed up at the blue sky and smiled. "I was starting to have fantasies of jumping off my back porch."

"There was an American in Uganda who killed himself in the long rains." Ernst looked solemn. "We called him the Peace Corpse."

"Bullshit."

"It's true." Ernst's face was serious. "Keep yourself occupied."

"It's shitty weather for building fish ponds." Jordan twisted the throttle mindlessly. "And it's so fucking pointless."

"But you never give up." Ernst edged his laugh with madness. "You're one of *us*."

Jordan ignored him. "And it's too fucking wet to paint outside, anywhere interesting."

"Ah, that reminds me—I've been meaning to ask if you would paint a mural on the side of my office." Ernst nodded across the road at a new alpine-style split-level.

"What? Like a portrait of your extended family? Not exactly an appropriate family planning message."

"Very funny. No, a mural of the mountains with properly terraced fields and aqueducts and villages of families with two children—"

"I get the picture. Sure. After the rains," Jordan said without enthusiasm.

"I'll pay you," Ernst said over his shoulder, pulling mail from a box. He unrolled a newspaper and whistled. "Five more parties have been registered."

"Get ready for democracy." Jordan put on his helmet.

Ernst thumbed through a handful of envelopes. "Prepare for chaos."

# Mei 7

Jordan gunned the Honda through the rain on the tarmac road, descending from Lushoto toward Mombo, late for an appointment with a fish farmer. His shoulders were hunched up against the rain. He forced himself to relax, felt the rain splattering his neck. Rivulets ran down the helmet across the eye screen. The road, empty of travelers who usually lined the sides, was a black smear cut through a mountainside of red clay that in the rain looked dark brown like dried blood. Jordan followed a black Leyland bus with a motto painted on the back: "Never Get Back." All the buses in Tanzania carried amusing slogans. Jordan hit the throttle, passing the black bus on a short straightaway between blind curves. His side mirror caught the bus name: Satellite.

Halfway down the mountain gorge to Mombo, Jordan turned off the tarmac onto a road that climbed to Vooga, the old royal capital where the sultans ruled the mountains for three hundred years. On the slick clay, the rear tire of the bike fishtailed through the corners and the front tire sprayed his pants legs with red mud. Jordan was tempted to turn back, but the farmer had walked twelve hours round-trip the day before to beg him to visit his ponds to see why his fish were dying.

The road ran through eroded fields stripped of all trees save candelabras, fat cacti thirty feet tall with thin limbs that arced upward. On a ridge above was a grove of eucalyptus with a red roof and white steeple poking through the treetops, a nineteenth-century Lutheran

mission, the first foothold of the white man in the Usambara
Mountains. Jordan passed the turnoff to the mission and leaned into
a blind curve, trying to hold the rear wheel steady. Rounding the
bend, he saw a boy in a school uniform in the middle of the narrow
road.

Jordan hit both brakes and the horn. The rear wheel swung forward
until the bike was skidding on its side across the mud.

The boy turned around.

The metal plate beneath the engine thumped into the boy's bare
legs, tossing him over the bike in a slow somersault.

Up the road at the edge of a village, barely visible through the rain,
a woman screamed. Jordan lay on his side in the mud, one leg caught
under the Honda. There was a burning in his knee. He groaned and
twisted from the waist to look back at the boy, who lay facedown in
the road, his blue shorts and white shirt muddied red. Raindrops
splashed on his black skin. Midway down one of the boy's thighs, the
leg jutted backward abruptly at an unnatural angle.

Women's voices joined the screaming. Men began to shout.

At the sight of the fractured white femur poking through black
skin, Jordan choked back the impulse to vomit. He pulled off his helmet, pushed the frame of the Honda up a few inches and jerked his
leg from under the bike.

The screeching and shouting grew louder as the villagers ran down
the road. The sound became an inhuman buzz.

Jordan crawled through the mud toward the boy. Gently he lifted
the boy's head and wiped the mud from his face. He bent and put his
ear to the boy's mouth, but the buzzing behind him was too loud to
hear anything. He cupped his hand over the boy's mouth and nose,
felt weak breath against his palm.

A stick whacked Jordan in the side of the face, scattering bursts of
color across his field of vision.

Jordan yelled and fell over into the mud. He was surrounded by villagers shouting in Sambaa, accusing him in a language he couldn't
understand. Men waved machetes. The stick crashed down on his
shoulder. He covered his face with his arms.

"You killed the boy!" someone shouted in Swahili.

"He's alive!" Jordan screamed through his arms.

"You killed my brother!" A young man held the stick over his head. The crowd wailed and screamed. The man brought the stick down toward Jordan's head, but he rolled away. Someone kicked him in the stomach. The buzzing sound was amplified as the throng gathered. An old man with a machete pushed through to the front and pointed the blade at Jordan, screaming in Sambaa.

"He's alive," Jordan shouted in Swahili. He couldn't see the boy behind the legs of the villagers. "He's alive!" No one heard him.

Jordan tried to stand, but someone shoved him down from behind. He curled into a fetal position. The rain kicked up red spouts in the mud by his face. The stick pounded his arms. Jordan screamed, realizing the mob was bent on blood justice, beyond caring whether the boy was dead or alive. The stick hit Jordan's kidneys. The buzzing roared, cheering the beating.

A car horn honked up the road behind the crowd. The horn honked again and again, then blared in a long blast. The stick stopped pounding his arms and head. The buzzing sound was deafening. Jordan raised himself up on one elbow, felt what was too warm to be rain dripping down his chin.

Behind the crowd, a tall man in a long white *kanzu* and red fez, standing on the hood of a Land Rover in the rain, shouted and waved a staff. The noise of the mob dropped a few decibels. The man was shouting in Sambaa. Two men in black pants and white polo shirts broke through the crowd, pulled Jordan to his feet, and dragged him through the villagers to the car. Their faces were hard and empty as they shoved him into the car and shut the door.

Inside, the mob was muffled by the low rumble of the engine and sixties psychedelic jazz on the stereo. Jordan watched the man in the robe gesticulating from the hood. The two men in polo shirts came through the crowd with the boy in their arms. One said something to the man in the robe as they drew alongside the car. They passed Jordan and opened the rear door of the Land Rover and placed the boy on the floor behind the backseat. The boy moaned and cried out.

The crowd streamed by the car. One man stopped at Jordan's window and raised a stick. Jordan flinched and shielded his head.

Through the gap between his forearms he saw one of the men in polo shirts shove the man along the road. The man in the robe opened the door on the opposite side of the car. The crowd outside had gone almost silent. They peered in through the windows, the mania no longer in their eyes.

The man in the robe climbed into the backseat beside Jordan. "You are one lucky *mzungu*," he said in an elegant British accent.

Jordan was confused, still trembling. He stammered, "Thanks, you . . . you."

"If I hadn't been on my way to Lushoto to pick up mail, they would have ripped you apart." The man laughed. "Don't you love Africa?"

One of the men in polo shirts slid onto the front seat, put the Land Rover in gear and started slowly down the road, pushing through the silent crowd. The other man in a polo shirt sat on the little Honda, waiting for the car to pass.

"Julian Kimweri." The man in the robe extended his hand. His skin was lighter than most Sambaa, his features sharp, hermetic.

"Rutledge Jordan." He shook the man's hand.

Kimweri clutched his hand firmly, signaling that he intended to hold it for some time.

"The sultan of the Usambaras?"

"Yes." Kimweri smiled. "Are you all right?"

"My head aches, but I'm okay." Jordan looked over his shoulder at the boy, who was staring at the roof of the station wagon. "I'm worried about him."

"He appears to have slipped into a state of shock," Kimweri said. "We're driving straight to the hospital in Lushoto."

"With that leg, they're going to send him to Dar es Salaam." Jordan ran his fingers through his hair and found a big bump rising over his ear. "The Peace Corps will pay."

"He'll be fine. Put him out of your mind." Kimweri squeezed his hand. "Jesus, I'm soaking. Beg your pardon." The sultan let go of Jordan's hand and took off his fez. He leaned over the front seat, then sat back with a folded towel that he set on the seat between them. Kimweri bent forward and pulled the white robe up his dark legs, rose a few inches off the seat to slide the bunched cloth over his naked ass, sat down, and jerked the *kanzu* over his head. His muscles were rippled like an athlete's. "So you are a volunteer?" Kimweri reached for the towel.

"What?" Jordan said, looking away.

"Are you a teacher?"

"Oh." Jordan stared at his muddy hands. "Yeah, fish ponds."

"Isn't it really too cold to farm fish in the mountains?" The sultan unfolded the towel; it was another *kanzu.*

"Yeah," Jordan said as the sultan pulled on the robe. "But a few guys do pretty well."

The boy cried out. His gaze, no longer fixed, darted around the car. He babbled rapidly in Sambaa. Kimweri leaned his long frame over the seat back. He squeezed the boy's shoulder and whispered until the boy quieted down.

They reached the tarmac and turned uphill. The driver used the hazard flashers and sped through the curves, honking before each blind corner. A cloud filled the gorge at the edge of the road.

"Have you been in the country long?" Kimweri took Jordan's hand again.

"Sixteen months." Jordan started to ease his hand away but it was clasped more firmly as if to make him deliberately uncomfortable.

"How do you find Tanzania?"

"Beautiful. Friendliest people I've ever met," Jordan answered automatically, then laughed uneasily at the irony. "It's like they were . . ." His voice trailed off as he sought words to explain what had happened. "They were transmogrified by some atavistic instinct. They suddenly turned into . . ."

"Savages?" Kimweri smiled. "*We are* friendly. But beneath the surface is a violence that can remain subconscious for years, a lifetime even, before the right event triggers it." He clasped Jordan's hand tighter. "But you are lucky."

It took effort to concentrate. Under the slicker Jordan's clothes were wet with cold sweat. He wished the sultan would let go of his hand and looked over the seat at the boy lying silently with his eyes closed and face clenched, both hands gripping the thigh of his good leg, his fingernails sunk in the bare skin. Jordan couldn't bring himself to look at the naked femur. He was awed again by the African ability to endure pain. "I'd be screaming bloody murder if I were him."

"They make them tough around here."

The rain drummed harder on the roof.

"You know, my ancestors came from Abyssinia, but the Sambaa made them kings because we had the power to call the rains."

Jordan could feel the sultan's eyes on his face as he focused on the repetitive sweep of the windshield wipers, figuring the sultan was trying to distract him with small talk. He said, deadpan, "Can you stop the rain?"

"Don't you believe in magic, Mr. Jordan?" Kimweri's grip tightened slightly.

"Only in my pumpkin." Jordan laughed weakly. "The jack-o'-lantern scares off thieves."

The sultan did not laugh. "The British jailed my father for two years early in his reign. There was utter drought. The people began to starve. Finally they stormed the jail. When the British freed him to the crowds, the sky opened up with rain. It's a fact. Look it up in the June 1942 *Tanganyika Notes and Records.*"

Jordan sucked in his breath like a surprised Tanzanian. "So now you've come back from England to start a political party? Sort of taking up where your daddy left off? That's what they say around town."

At last Kimweri released his hand. He offered Jordan a cigarette from a pack of Sportsman. Jordan shook his head, and the sultan lit one and exhaled a stream of smoke. "The country needs leaders who are more concerned with the welfare of the people than lining their own pockets."

"Good luck, bwana. That's a tough row to hoe." Jordan glanced back at the boy, who was staring again at the pebbled vinyl roof. Jordan sighed. "God, I feel tired."

"It's only natural," Kimweri said. "We'll be at the hospital soon."

Jordan laid his head against the seat and closed his eyes, trying to put the throbbing in his leg to sleep. The disk changed on the car stereo, and Miles Davis's "Kind of Blue" came through the speakers. Beneath the jazz was the sizzling of the wheels speeding over the wet tarmac. The boy moaned.

Jordan jerked up and opened his eyes. He crossed his arms over his chest, sandwiching his hands in his armpits before he turned toward Kimweri. "I've met your fiancée."

The sultan tapped the ash of a cigarette into a tray in the back of the driver's seat, then looked at Jordan.

"She delivers chickens for a crowned eagle that I'm raising."

"Of course. I should have put it together. *You're* the mad American." Kimweri's laugh was vaguely feminine.

The car bounced over a speed bump, and the boy cried out.

Kimweri drew on his cigarette.

Jordan wanted to ask how he could marry a schoolgirl. "Congratulations. Zanifa is a wonderful little girl."

Kimweri paused, letting "little girl" hang in the air. He spoke through a curtain of smoke. "The wedding is set for the start of the short rains. I hope you'll attend."

"That's nice . . . to invite me," Jordan said. "Thank you very much."

On the outskirts of Lushoto they pulled off the road onto a circular drive in front of the old colonial hospital, long low buildings with wide verandas connected by covered walks. The driver rushed inside, and a moment later two orderlies appeared with a gurney.

"I've got to run." The sultan offered his hand. "My man will be along shortly with your bike."

"I can never repay you," Jordan said, opening the door.

"Do you play tennis?"

"I played the country club circuit growing up." Jordan laughed at the pretentiousness of his reply and with an acute sensation of being so far from home. He stepped down from the car and felt dizzy.

"You can repay me on the court. Tennis is the only thing I miss from the outside."

"*Sawa*," Jordan said, smiling wanly. Okay. "But give me time to recover. I pick up messages at the Lawns."

"Cheers." Kimweri leaned forward and pulled the door shut. The Land Rover pulled away.

Jordan walked slowly up the hospital steps, wondering if his body would have been sent home in a bag or on ice, if Anna would have come to his funeral.

Rut is such a chicken," Anna said. "You should have seen him in the canoe. He looked like Barney Fife in Mayberry."

Everyone laughed, and Jordan's face went red. He stared at the azalea bushes and magnolia trees at the end of the yard.

"Rut never was much of a jock." Vernon Taylor stood sockless in loafers, madras shorts and a polo shirt, holding a beer can.

"Vernon, that's not fair," Anna said. "He won the state championship in the cross-country."

"That's because he was too scared to play football and not coordinated enough to play basketball," Vernon said.

"You want to square off on the tennis court?" Jordan yawned, thinking the three days in the mountains hadn't helped his chronic fatigue. "Or in a court of law?"

"Vernon Taylor, the only exercise you get anymore is on the golf course," Sandy Taylor said. Eight months pregnant, she had cut her bleached-blond hair short and wore a loose, sleeveless dress. She sat in a wrought-iron yard chair, fanning herself with a copy of *Southern Living.* "Or driving down to the casinos in Tunica. I often wonder what happened to my dream quarterback."

"Gone to seed in ten short years with the rest of them," Anna said, moving across the patio with a pitcher. She was in a white tennis dress and barefoot. Jordan admired her tan, lean legs and long, elegant toes. "May I refill your tea?"

"Please, darlin'." Sandy smiled.

"You never stop smiling now," Jordan said to Sandy. "Your eyes are so, uh . . . serene."

"Wait till Anna's pregnant," Sandy said. "You won't believe how good it makes you feel."

Jordan looked at Vernon, who was staring up at a cloud in the sky.

Anna handed Sandy her glass. "Jordan's not ready. He wants to travel before he settles down."

"You want to, too," Jordan said quickly. "You want to as much as I do."

"It's true," Anna said. "I want to go to Tuscany on our honeymoon."

The phone rang in the house. Jordan got up and walked toward a sliding glass door.

"I'll get it." Anna set the pitcher on a round metal table. "I think it's my mother."

"Mrs. Demange calls every evening at seven on the dot," Jordan said to Vernon, watching Anna go into the house, a white Spanish bungalow shaded by tall oaks and elms. "She says she doesn't care where we sleep, but we have to keep separate residences until we marry—'two rents until the ring.'"

"When are y'all going to get married?" Sandy said.

"I don't know. We've been together so long that it doesn't seem very important," Jordan said, reaching for a beer in a cooler by the table.

"That's a cop-out," Sandy said.

"Last month you were goin' to tie the knot as soon as you could buy that big house in Harbor Town," Vernon said. "You're movin' the goal line."

Jordan looked at Vernon and remembered his bachelor party. Vernon had passed out while a hooker was giving him a blow job. What would Sandy do if she heard that? As far as Jordan knew, Vernon had been faithful in the two years since the wedding.

"Will you start the grill?" Anna said from the doorway.

"Sure, sweetpea," Jordan said.

"Sweetpea?" Sandy laughed. "That's so nice."

"Rut's always been a sweetie-pie," Vernon said. "When I met him in ninth grade I thought he was a yag."

"Yag?" Sandy asked.

"Gay." Jordan poured charcoal in the grill. "That's what his golfing buddies call gays—yags instead of fags. Their idea of clever wordplay is spelling backward."

"Jordan fancied himself a poet in college," Vernon said. "Another yag trait."

"One of Rut's poems broke my heart," Anna said.

After you had broken mine, Jordan thought. "Did you know Fred Goldberg offered me a job?"

"No kidding," Vernon said. "What did you say?"

"No, of course. I mean, *CarZone.*" Jordan squirted fluid on the charcoal. "But lately I've been thinking that maybe I should get out of town. Atlanta, maybe."

"See what I mean about moving the end zone," Vernon said.

"There was no call to say that." Sandy looked at Anna sideways. "They'll get married before they move."

"I'll follow him anywhere," Anna said with a mock dreamy expression.

"Watch out, y'all." Jordan knew he should let the fluid soak longer, but he went on and flicked a match. Flames burst three feet over the grill.

Swatting at an insect, Vernon spilled beer on his shirt, and he walked inside through the glass door. Anna and Sandy started talking about the Diane Arbus exhibition Anna was curating for the Memphis American Museum of Art.

Jordan wondered if Anna had ever been unfaithful to him. They had dated through their freshman year in college, and then she had left him, though they had remained close friends. They had gotten back together senior year and crewed on a sailboat across the Atlantic after graduation, then she'd worked for Sotheby's in London while he was in law school and they'd traded letters about their affairs. When she'd moved back to Memphis, he had started coming home from Nashville on weekends to see her. That was nearly three years ago now. He felt certain that she hadn't slept with anyone else since she'd gotten back. She saw their love as a fort against the world, sheltering them with walls of honor. What did that say about his love?

# Mei 9

Jordan sipped his tea and looked over his watercolors. Thirty-two studies of the eaglet's first thirty-nine days as an eyas were pinned chronologically across the wall. There were empty spots where Zanifa had asked for the pictures. The differences between the daily sketches were so minute as to be undetectable except for slight shadings in color, but if you skipped from the first sketch to the twenty-first, the toads seemed to be two entirely different creatures. The nestling's raincoat of down changed from gray to white, and her legs and talons turned from a fleshy pink to an enameled yellow. The long thin line of her gape also had turned from pink to yellow. She had grown several inches taller, and a great hooked beak had become the central eye-catching feature, too big for her long triangular head. From the third week to the fifth, the eyas did not change color so much as grow, but in the last few days black-tipped quills were poking through her white down.

There was no sound from the living room. Jordan figured Pasipo was sleeping, so he undressed outside on a small square of stones he had built by the back porch. He put his clothes in a bucket for Omali's wife, Sisilia. A few months before, she had approached him about cleaning the house. He knew that at least *her* pay would go to their children, rather than Omali's drink. Sisilia worked a few hours five days a week and was paid the equivalent of twenty dollars a month, more than a local teacher's salary, from the shillings Jordan made selling the quarterly harvest from his own fish pond. The pond just covered the cost of Sisilia and the boy who was paid in fish for feeding the pond leaves. Jordan thought of the pond and his employees as his small contribution to Tanzania's gross national product, his effort to "Rebuild the Economy," a battle cry of the republic heralded every day in the newspapers. He stood under a stream of solar-heated water from a black hose that curled along the tin roof. After he showered he wrapped a faded purple *kikoi* around his waist. Leaning against the wall of the house, he gazed out at the great plains and a line of clouds defining the far horizon, letting the sun dry his skin.

"*Hodi,*" Zanifa called from the front porch.

"*Karibu,*" Jordan yelled and hurried to the back door.

*Quee-quee-quee.* Pasipo screamed from her nest.

Jordan came into the living room from the kitchen and saw Zanifa in her uniform, standing in the front doorway. "*Karibu.*"

Zanifa opened the screen door.

"*Jambo,* Zanifa."

"Hallo, Mr. Joldan." Zanifa pronounced the English "r" like an "l."

Jordan moved toward Pasipo's nest on the table. Zanifa followed from the other side of the room. Jordan looked at the nest. There was something odd about the eyas, something askew. She was too tall.

"Pasipo!" Zanifa shouted. "You can stand!"

*Kew-kew-kew.*

"That's a new word Pasipo started saying yesterday." Jordan laughed.

*Kew-kew-kew.*

"Pasipo. You're learning to talk and to stand. You're clever just like your daddy." Zanifa took a long slice of liver from the container and held it out to Pasipo, who leaned forward and pulled it from her fingers, swallowing it whole, appearing to choke on the slick red slab until somehow compressing it all into her crop. Front heavy from her bulging crop, Pasipo staggered around the nest, looking up at them and chirping. She waddled and fell. Jordan watched, entranced, a proud father.

"Pasipo can walk already! Pasipo, you're too smart!" Zanifa reached over the rim of woven banana leaves.

*"No,"* Jordan said, grabbing Zanifa from behind by her arms and pulling her back from the table. "Don't ever touch them. Eagles never touch each other."

He was suddenly aware of the warmth of her shoulders through her blouse against his bare chest. Her arms were absolutely smooth. The tension he felt was so strong that he wondered if she felt it. He let her go and stepped toward the nest, forcing a smile. "Soon she will start to grow feathers."

"It takes a long time for her to grow up and fly," Zanifa said, feeding the eyas. "I'll be married before Pasipo is learning to hunt."

Jordan did not detect any expectancy or sadness in her voice. He almost asked if she was happy about the coming marriage to Kimweri but said quietly, "I'll do a portrait when Pasipo is fully feathered and can stand on your fist."

"I'm doing a project on crowned eagles." Zanifa looked up from the bird at Jordan. "Can Pasipo come to the fair in November?"

"Why not?" Jordan glanced around the room for a shirt. "By then you ought to be able to fly her across the gym to your fist in front of the judges. Who's judging the fair?"

"Father William and the sisters." Zanifa took another piece of liver from the plastic box.

"That monk is a good man," Jordan said. Father William, a Franciscan from Connecticut, was the only American in the Usambara Mountains that Jordan really liked. The others were evangelical missionaries from Nebraska who spent their time holding revivals on a continent that already had more Christians than anywhere in the world. But Father William had built St. Mary's girls' school in Lushoto from nothing, raised enough money to renovate an old mansion, arranged scholarships for the African sisters to get teaching degrees in the States and designed the school to be self-sufficient. St. Mary's was solar powered, and the girls grew their own vegetables and kept livestock while studying an American high school curriculum.

"What do you like best about school?" Jordan asked, pulling on a T-shirt.

"Science." Zanifa wiped her hands with a towel. "I want to be a doctor."

"The Sambaa people could use a few more," Jordan said. "Will your husband let you go on to medical school?"

"I don't know. I haven't asked him." Zanifa picked up her sisal bag. "I must run home."

"See you next week," Jordan said flatly.

"Get a good weekend," Zanifa said shyly, trying a new phrase.

# Juni 14

Pasipo waddled across the tongue-and-groove floor.

The nestling was no longer a downy toad but now a cross between a toad and a hawk. Splotched with black half feathers and patches of down, Pasipo teetered across the back porch toward the railing, which Jordan had eaglet proofed with a lattice of wattle poles. She stuck her black beak through one grid and stared out into the gulf of air over the Maasai steppe. The young crowned eagle resembled an old country preacher, stooped with long black shoulders and a white neck. Her breast was not yet the orange and black spots of her parents but a rich white. When the resident ravens circled in close, cawing with their grotesque beaks agape, Pasipo staggered back, spread her wings and hissed. Then the black tiara with its flame tips was revealed.

Jordan slid across the porch in front of Pasipo and snapped a photo of the threat display. He turned back to his tray of paints, mixing the eye color of the day. When the brown gray seemed right, he knelt and belly crawled across the peeling planks. "Pasipo, kew, kew, kew."

The malign gaze that Pasipo cast upon the ravens softened, the eyelids closing slightly, the pupils widening, when she regarded Jordan's face. It was not his imagination—Zanifa had witnessed it, too. It was the raptor's expression revealed only to kin. Jordan slowly raised the brush up to Pasipo's head, whispering, "Kew, kew, kew." He compared the color on the brush and the eyes of the raptor.

On the other side of the house, the front door opened. Jordan scuttled ass backward several feet, then sprang up, spun around and saw Zanifa skipping toward him with a basket under one arm.

"Hallo, Mr. Joldon."

Jordan sang out a bit of a Swahili radio tune: "I love you, angel, but I have no money to marry you, *what can I do?*"

Zanifa laughed. "But you have money. You are a *mzungu*."

"Not all white faces are rich."

*"Poleh,"* Zanifa said, bending over Pasipo.

Jordan couldn't help looking down her school blouse at her full breasts and the black bra, then felt a flash of shame.

"Pasipo, you're getting bigger every day." Zanifa stood up.

"Hey, let's take Pasipo for a walk. She's never been outside," Jordan said, pulling on a leather welding glove. He got a fish from the plastic container on the table with the gloved hand and laid his arm on the porch floor, holding the fish out to Pasipo. "Kew. Kew. Kew." He wiggled the bait. Pasipo waddled a few inches closer, hopped onto his glove and proceeded to rip apart the fish.

Jordan slowly raised Pasipo, whose talons cinched down tight. She remained fixated on the shredded fish, well perched on the glove. He braced his left bicep against his body with his forearm at a right angle and carried Pasipo through the house, shutting and locking the windows and doors with his free hand.

Jordan and Zanifa followed an overgrown trail along the escarpment, weaving slowly around bushes and boulders and trees. Wide gray-bottom clouds shaped like saucers floated a thousand feet over the mountains. Between the patches of cloud shadow, Jordan was drowsy in the heat and humidity. Pasipo ignored the fish now, gradually twisting her head back and forth, taking in the wide world. She stared up into the blankness of the sky.

"Wonder what she sees," Jordan said in Swahili.

"An eagle," Zanifa replied in English. "She sees like a witch doctor."

Jordan laughed.

They paused in a small grove of tall albizzia. Long beards of a pale gray green moss hung from the white branches, a beautiful parasite slowly killing the trees.

Zanifa pointed to a clump of white and black at the base of a tree down the path. The clump moved jerkily around the trunk. Jordan jogged over.

*Koi-koi-koi*, Pasipo screamed, a new but familiar sound. She spread her stubby wings and raised her crown. *Koi-koi-koi.*

Jordan recognized the female territorial call. Pasipo was truly a girl.

The clump was a wounded augur buzzard, a hawk with an orange tail.

*Kow-kow-kow!* The auguar buzzard's call was harsh.

*Koi-koi-koi!* Pasipo screamed back.

"Someone stoned that hawk. That kind is a clever chicken thief." Zanifa was speaking Swahili now.

*Kow-kow-kow!*

*Koi-koi-koi!*

"A *fungo* will eat her," Zanifa said.

*Fungo.* Jordan drew a blank and then a vague image in the moonlight of a spotted cat he had mistaken momentarily for a leopard. A civet cat. The *fungo* he once saw was as big as a German shepherd.

*Kow-kow-kow!*

*Koi-koi-koi!*

"Watch after Pasipo. I'll try to pick it up," Jordan said.

He placed the eaglet twenty paces down the trail and then crawled slowly toward the wounded buzzard.

*Kow-kow-kow!* The buzzard screamed and hissed, backed up against the tree. *Kow-kow-kow!*

Pasipo answered from behind: *Koi-koi-koi!*

Jordan pushed his gloved fist toward the buzzard. It seemed small, perhaps a male. Jordan wiggled the headless fish at the buzzard, whose eyes were darting back and forth between Jordan's face and his fist. Jordan inched his fist closer.

*Kow-kow-kow!* The buzzard attacked with a blur of talon strikes that would have lacerated bare fingers to the bone but only glanced off the glove.

*Koi-koi-koi!* Pasipo screamed.

Jordan glanced back. Pasipo waddled down the trail, her gray brown eyes enraged, her inchoate crown raised. Zanifa crouched along behind Pasipo, laughing.

*Koi-koi-koi!*

*Kow-kow-kow!* The buzzard let loose another series of talon slashes.

*Koi-koi-koi!*

Jordan could hardly think in the noise between the two raptors. He tried to grab the buzzard's legs with his bare hands, but one talon caught his palm. He jerked his hand away, but it held in one of the buzzard's claws. He wrenched it free, but the buzzard gouged his forearm with its beak before he pulled his hand out of the wounded raptor's range. He backed away, and both birds quieted down. Zanifa was sitting on the ground beside Pasipo, blocking the eyas's advance with one hand, her head bent back, laughing hysterically.

Jordan stood grinning with embarrassment. He spoke in English: "You want to try?"

"Okay." Zanifa stood and walked toward him. "Give me the glove."

*Kow-kow-kow!* The augur buzzard screamed again as Zanifa crawled in close. Jordan couldn't make out what she was murmuring, Sambaa or Swahili. She slid her fist forward and left it a foot from the buzzard with the fish swaying slowly back and forth. She held perfectly still for a long time. Fifteen minutes after Jordan first checked his watch, the buzzard stopped screaming. Zanifa murmured softly. The buzzard folded her wings to her sides.

After a half hour the buzzard stepped forward and snapped at the swaying fish. The raptor leapt back, then hopped forward and hooked the fish and tugged. Zanifa raised her fist a few inches off the ground so that the buzzard was stretching to maintain her beak hold. Zanifa inched her fist higher, and the buzzard leapt off the ground and landed on the glove.

Zanifa whispered to Jordan, "Go ahead of me—I'll see you back at your house."

Jordan was dumbstruck. She had brought the bird to her fist with extraordinary patience—the cardinal virtue of a falconer. It was true that Africans possessed a profound patience, but how did she *know* to wait until the hungry raptor broke down and trusted her? Jordan took off his boots and put both socks on one hand and coaxed Pasipo up onto his fist with a dry slice of chicken breast he had pulled from his leather falconer's bag.

Jordan shut Pasipo on the back porch. In the empty bedroom he wrapped a long strip of cloth around the top of the chair back for a cushioned perch. He knew raptors didn't drink water, but he put a round plastic tub, half filled with water and weighted with a stone, near the perch for bathing. He pulled a peeping chick from the back porch, twisted its neck and left it as a gift on the seat of the chair.

On the front porch, Jordan waited for Zanifa. Two birds now. This is the family you've made for yourself. He saw Zanifa come through the gate and asked himself, Could you ever love her? Is that a crazy thought?

"Where do I put her?" she asked at thirty yards.

"In the empty bedroom. It's ready."

*Kow-kow-kow!* the augur buzzard cried and then fell silent.

"Okay," Zanifa whispered in Swahili. "Clear out."

Jordan wedged open the screen door and withdrew inside the house.

*Kow-kow-kow!* Nearing the door, the buzzard raised her wings, but she stayed on the glove. Inside, the buzzard saw Jordan and screamed.

*Koi-koi-koi!* Pasipo answered from the back porch.

The buzzard launched from Zanifa's fist. Flapping one wing, it veered into a wall. Zanifa sat down and sidled slowly toward the buzzard, who was looking to escape, pivoting around the injured wing. Zanifa herded the hawk into the guest room and stopped at the door. The buzzard saw the dead chick on the seat of the chair and leapt up.

Zanifa closed the door to the bedroom and walked out to the front porch. Jordan handed her a glass of orange juice and sat on a windowsill. "You have an amazing touch with animals."

Zanifa walked to the railing. She told him that her *bibi-mzee*, her great-grandmother, used to remark to others about her great-grandchild's ability to talk to animals, to calm down goats and cattle, even chickens. "She said that in the old days, in my thirteenth year I would have been taken out with other girls my age to a bush school."

Bush school—Jordan had never heard that expression before. Zanifa spoke rapidly in Swahili, and Jordan had difficulty following her. He interrupted: "Bush school?"

"The old women taught the girls what they needed to know before they got married. The old women looked for girls who had the special gifts of the shaman." Zanifa looked directly at Jordan. "*Bibi-mzee* told me that I would have been a great shaman."

Jordan smiled, touched by her pride, asked, "Why didn't she teach you herself?"

"She was as old as the mountains. She began to teach me the uses of the forest plants, but she died when I was ten," Zanifa said, looking away.

An afternoon wind picked up from the south, whistling across the porch.

"You must have learned a lot from her," Jordan said.

"I remember one custom she told me that's been forgotten." Zanifa leaned against one of the posts that supported the roof of the porch. "In the old times, after a woman had a child she returned to her mother's house until the child was old enough to fetch a glass of water for the father. Only then would she go back to her husband's house and make another child."

"Traditional family planning," Jordan said in English. That would space the kids with three years between them. Now the village women are dropping kids every ten months. If that old custom could be revived, it would slow down Africa's runaway population.

Jordan looked Zanifa in the eye and wondered if she could see his longing. Softly in Swahili he said, "Bringing the wild hawk to your fist was incredible."

"When Chahingo, the first sultan of the Usambaras, tamed his first wild dog to train for hunting, he cornered it in a cave and stared into its eyes for three days and three nights without stopping. *Bibi-mzee* told me how he offered a piece of bushbuck until the starving dog gave up and ate out of his hand." Zanifa hoisted herself up and sat on the porch railing. "From that day the dog and Chahingo were brothers. The dog called together all his family and friends until Chahingo had a huge pack. He brought the pack from the dry savanna

to Usambara Mountains, a land of many streams, good soil, tall bananas, cool weather and few mosquitoes."

"And beautiful women," Jordan said, leaning against the wall.

Zanifa giggled and looked at the floor.

"Go on. Finish the story." The people here are still storytellers, he
thought. The tradition lingers south of the Sahara. Television has yet
to sweep it away.

"The crops of the Sambaa people were always stolen by the fierce
wild pigs with beards and sharp tusks. They had always plagued the
Sambaa, killing the hunters who tried to drive them away." Zanifa
looked at the wall beside Jordan while she talked, occasionally glancing over at his face for a split second, speaking slowly in Swahili for
his sake. "Chahingo, a stranger from the lowlands, told the Sambaa,
'Every year these wild pigs eat your crops and kill your young men. I
will kill every pig in the forest if you make me king.'" Zanifa crossed
her ankles and started to swing her legs as she talked. "The Sambaa
said okay, and he took his pack of dogs and hunted for three months.
It was a great slaughter. It was before the Arabs had come with the
news of Mohammed, and so all through the mountains there was
feasting." Zanifa smiled at the myth's happy ending.

"For the first time they were able to harvest all of their crops. The
people were very happy, and so they made Chahingo their king." Zanifa
sipped from the glass. "The Sambaa agreed to Chahingo's terms, and
the king could choose any girl from any village as a wife to live at Vooga
without having to pay bridewealth. All of the villagers would give a por-
tion of each harvest to Vooga. In return, he would bring rain to the
mountains each year to ensure a good harvest. In times of famine, the
sultan gave out grain from the stores collected each year from the trib-
ute." Zanifa looked at Jordan as she said: "Even after many years the
people were not sorry that they had made a stranger their king."

"Why was Chahingo a stranger?" Jordan wanted her to keep talking, to linger.

"He looked different. He was a Kilindi." Zanifa set the glass on the
rail and didn't know what to do with her hands. She placed one in her
lap and started picking her nose. "The Kilindi came south from the

deserts of North Africa. He was taller than the Sambaa, more slender, with a nose like a sharp hoe."

"Like yours." Jordan considered telling her that *mzungu* girls didn't do that in public.

Zanifa dropped her hand. "Of course. Didn't you know I am Kilindi!"

"Well, your mother told me her father was a German," Jordan said. "So you're related to the sultan?"

"A cousin," she said.

"That could mean anything," Jordan said. "Everyone's cousins. The Kilindi is a big clan."

Shyly Zanifa said, "Will you come to my wedding?"

Jordan answered quickly. "I'm up for a holiday at the start of the short rains. I was thinking of taking a trip to Nairobi to see some *mzungu* and watch some American movies." He ventured a question that had been on his mind for weeks: "Who was your father, Zanifa?"

"My mother told me that he was a German doctor working in the Lushoto hospital when she was young." Zanifa looked down at her legs and pushed herself off the railing. "In her shame she ran to a cousin in Dar es Salaam to have me."

"And you've never heard from your father?" Jordan couldn't help pushing.

"No." Zanifa frowned, breathed deeply and clasped her hands at her waist. "I'll come back tomorrow afternoon to feed my passard." She said this in English. She had been reading *Hawks and Hawking* and knew that the wounded augur buzzard was referred to not as an eyas, but rather as a "passard," a wild bird. "Just keep the door closed and throw her meat on the chair."

Jordan watched her walk around the outside of the old church. She was sixteen. She believed in magic. She had never seen a great painting. She had never used a telephone. She knew only these dying mountains, her first five years in a sweltering suburb of Dar es Salaam, a few school vacations with friends to the coffee town at the base of Kilimanjaro. She didn't know or didn't admit the identity of her father, though she had heard the taunts of villagers that she was an abomination of incest. She was a virgin.

From his office on the ninth floor of the Cotton Exchange, Jordan looked out at the brown waters of the Mississippi curling around the peninsula of Harbor Town, where he could just make out the Cape Cod–style house that Anna and he were thinking of buying. As clouds moved across the sky, the steel sides of the Pyramid glinted like a signal mirror. A steamboat chugged upriver. Jordan looked down at the stacks of papers on his desk, scribbled, "White is a difficult thing to capture," on a yellow legal pad, then stared across the room at the white oak paneling and a framed watercolor he had painted of a sunrise over marshland. He had liked it when he finished it, but it seemed to grow worse every day that it hung on the wall.

"Yo, Rut." Vernon Taylor stood in the door. "What's the difference between in-laws and outlaws?"

"What?"

"Outlaws are wanted." He waited, and Jordan was quiet. "You're in a good mood."

"I wasted four hours on a conference call. Some jackass in New York scheduled in lieu of actually reading the documents." Jordan balled up the top sheet of the pad. "How can we do this for the rest of our lives?"

"It's the price you pay for the good life." Vernon swung an imaginary golf club. "Don't you love the long summer twilights? You can play until nine."

"I feel like I'm working on a fucking chain gang."

"*Huh,*" Vernon chortled, lining up for another swing. "It'll get easier when you get children. Then you can tell yourself you're doing it for them."

"I ain't sure I'm ready, boss." Jordan tossed the paper into a can decorated with a painting of the surrender of Robert E. Lee that had been in his grandfather's office.

"Kids. You think they're going to be a pain in the ass, but then you love 'em," Vernon said, visoring his forehead with one hand to follow his long drive out the window.

"Packin' up for the day now, boss." Jordan jammed some papers into his satchel.

"You should start playing tennis again. Something to take your mind off everything."

"Anna wants us to study yoga."

"Perfect for you. New age. Effete. The Zen attorney." Vernon laughed, looking at the picture of the sunset. "I wouldn't advise you to quit law to paint."

"Bright and early, boss." Jordan shuffled across the carpet as if dragging shackles. He followed Vernon down a hallway past empty offices. To fill up the silence in the elevator, Jordan asked, "How are Sandy and Elizabeth?"

"Happy as clams. A child makes a woman's life complete. They are born to nest. Get Anna pregnant and you'll see."

"There's a conspiracy to turn everyone into parents. Everybody our age is having kids and talking about it. My mom keeps telling me how happy *she'll* be," Jordan said as they came out into a parking lot. "The species perpetuates itself through social pressure. I can't handle it anymore. I think I'm one of those guys meant to have children late in life."

"Maybe you aren't meant to have them at all." Vernon bent over to put his briefcase in his Volvo. "Maybe you're gay."

"Maybe, baby." Jordan pinched Vernon's ass.

"Do that again and I'll kick your ass."

Jordan climbed into a new Wagoneer and drove to a booth by the gate. He handed a card to an elderly black attendant. "Howdy, Homer."

"Hel-lo, Rut. You's the last one ta leave agin."

Jordan looked up at the fleets of matching cumulus clouds. "The sky's clear every mornin', yet every evenin' it's full of those clouds. Where you reckon they come from, Homer?"

"Oh, I don't know, Rut." Homer smiled wide. "South 'merica, I guess."

"I thought that dinner would never end." Jordan set his jacket on a hanger. "All people talk about is buying houses and joining the country club —"

"They talk about more than that. You just don't listen." Anna washed makeup off her face. "You didn't make much of an effort to raise the level of conversation."

"Lately the days stretch before me in endless tedium." He hurried to add: "Not you. Everything else."

Anna stood in the door, wearing only her panties and bra. "Baby, I spent an hour this afternoon at St. Jude's with a little girl dying of cancer. Wake up."

"I need Prozac or something."

"No, you don't." Smiling with her lips closed, she laughed through her nose.

Jordan lay on the bed and picked up a copy of *Outside* from a nightstand. Anna walked naked across the room and crawled over him. "God, I've got to get up in six hours to make the plane."

Jordan kissed her ear and traced his hand around her breast. "I wish you weren't going to Chicago. You won't be here to cheer me up."

"You're a sweet boy." Anna put her tongue in his mouth then dropped her head back on the pillow. "Baby, I'm sorry. I'm tired and it's late." She spread her legs and laughed. "You can have sex."

# Juni 15

A d in. Match point," the sultan said formally, bouncing the ball on the baseline. The late sun cast shadows of jacaranda trees over the southern half of the court. Kimweri served with heavy topspin, coming up over the ball just at the top of a high toss, a classic graceful motion reminiscent of the British great Fred Perry, whose brand whites the sultan sported. *Phwok!* The yellow ball angled fast across the court, rising then falling, the topspin springing it high as it nipped the line in the backhand corner.

Sideways, on his toes in worn-out Tretorns, cut-off khakis and a Vanderbilt T-shirt, Jordan swung down on the ball with both fists on the leather grip of the Head racket. *Phwak!* The ball shot back spinlessly at a hard angle. Jordan considered following the strong return, but, unnerved by Kimweri's last fast ball, which had evaded his rusty reactions and punched him in the gut, nearly knocking out his breath, he retreated to the baseline, watching the ball throw up a puff of red dust deep in the sultan's territory.

Kimweri grunted, executing a long, graceful topspin backhand with a single fist, the Slazinger graphite racket meeting the ball low and lifting it high. *Phwock!* Rising, the ball came straight down the line. Jordan scrambled behind the baseline. The ball landed in the forehand corner, scattering lime. *Phwick!* Jordan countered with a delicate chop, spinning the ball back on itself, pitching it softly toward the lip of the net. Kimweri sprinted forward. The ball tripped over the lip and dropped to the court. Kimweri lunged, scraping one knee on the clay as he stretched low to spoon up the ball before the second bounce.

The yellow ball rose in a weak, low lob. Jordan moved in for the kill, choosing a backhand smash over a forehand, dropping the Head low and whipping it up over the yellow ball. *Phwak!* The ball rocketed behind Kimweri, who turned and dropped his racket uselessly. A wisp of red dust burst at the baseline.

"Out!" Kimweri shouted breathlessly. "Close, though. A mere centimeter back. Why did you even bother to slam it?" His Oxbridge accent seemed stronger in victory.

"The singular satisfaction of the smash," Jordan said, panting. "I always choke." Hooker, Jordan thought, the old teenage word for a tennis cheat. "Good game."

"Excellent match," Kimweri said. They shook hands over the net, then walked toward the fence. "Seven–five. Six–three. Seven–five. It's marvelous having this sort of competition right here in Lushoto. We must establish this as a routine."

"Absolutely." Jordan preferred his opponent's steely prematch silence to the chumminess of the victor. A waiter in a white coat and black pants came down the steep green lawn from the hotel. Jordan followed Kimweri to a table beneath an umbrella of palm fronds. Jordan shifted his chair into the sunshine and stared up at the green peaks. "This could easily be the Smoky Mountains."

"The Germans called the Usambaras Little Switzerland," Kimweri said. "To each *mzungu* his own."

Signing for the brown half-liter bottles of Safari lager, Jordan noticed that the waiter was barefoot.

"Your backhand is a bazooka," Kimweri said affably, tipping back a Safari.

"You never double faulted," Jordan replied.

"I've been practicing by myself." Kimweri laughed. "In the palace courtyard."

Jordan laughed and closed his eyes, felt the sun on his face, the sweat evaporating, a rare sense of camaraderie. "You lived half your life in England. What do you miss most?"

"You mean what or whom do I miss most?" Kimweri sighed. "I

told you—tennis for the former query and the Honorable Victoria Watson for the latter."

"Honorable?" Jordan opened his eyes.

"A lord's daughter. The Brits stamp the word on their passports." Kimweri spoke without irony, pursing his lips at this affirmation of royalty. "I used to stay at her father's coffee plantation on Kilimanjaro. He underwrote my education. We were lovers for years, but . . ." He looked at Jordan, whose gaze had drifted to a jacaranda tree. "It seems I've been afflicted with that insidious disease that infects *mzungu* who've been too long in Africa. They tend to divulge their secrets to the first white face who pitches up."

Kimweri took his hand, and Jordan wondered if he was a lover of Lord Watson's rather than his daughter's. His hand was dry. He leaned over the table and looked intently at Jordan with dark brown eyes. "How is Zanifa's project progressing?"

"Great, I guess. She's got her own bird now. A wounded augur." Jordan edged his hand away, but Kimweri tightened his grip. Jordan babbled on, "I'm continually blown away by Father William. The winner of the science competition at St. Mary's gets a trip to a big fair in Cape Town. Where did he get the money for that?"

Kimweri stared at Jordan for a long time. Not reading his expression, Jordan realized he didn't know this man at all.

"Did you know that Father Damian has two half-caste daughters who teach at St. Mary's?" Kimweri relaxed his grip but did not remove his hand.

"I heard," Jordan said. He suddenly felt guilty by intent, fearful that his eyes would betray a crime that he had not committed. He waited.

Behind the sultan a purple bloom fell from a jacaranda tree.

"Zanifa's ranked at the top of her class, maybe she'll win the trip to South Africa," Jordan said to fill the uneasy silence. "Can you imagine what she will make of a real city?"

"Well, she couldn't go. She'll be married." Kimweri dropped Jordan's hand and fished a warm-up jacket from his Slazinger bag.

"You could go with her." Jordan was startled by the nervousness in his own voice.

"Perhaps." Pulling on his jacket, Kimweri regarded Jordan. "How is the boy?"

"He just had his second operation in Dar es Salaam. He'll be walking soon." Jordan drained the brown bottle of Safari. "I was thinking of taking his family some fish."

"Probably not a good idea. You might stay away from that village." Kimweri picked up the bag. "Same time next week?"

"*Sawa, bwana. Tutaonana saa hii weeki ijayo,*" Jordan said.

"The only word you pronounce impeccably is *weeki,*" Kimweri teased. "Until next *weeki,* then." The sultan walked down the alley of jacarandas to his Land Rover.

Jordan pulled on a sweatshirt and jogged up the hill to the Lawns, a U-formation of German colonial white plaster buildings with green tin roofs and long verandas. In the gallery between the dining room and the bar hung an oil portrait of Julian Kimweri's father, a strikingly handsome young man in a flowing white *kanzu,* embroidered vest and headdress fashioned from the white cape and black fur of a colobus monkey. Jordan studied the painting then passed through an archway into a long narrow room with pale blue walls, bay windows, a beamed ceiling, and a semicircular mahogany bar.

"*Shikamoo, Mzee,*" Jordan said. I kiss your feet, Elder.

"*Marahaba,*" Nikos Ionides barked from the far end of the room. The pear-shaped old Greek sprawled with a large book on a leather chair by a fireplace that curved out from the wall. He wore a baggy safari suit of olive cotton, his legs stretched out and safari boots propped up on a Maasai stool. "Who won?"

"The sultan," Jordan said. "I let him. . . . *Don't* tell him I said that."

"Never. I am a gentleman." The bushy black eyebrows on Ionides's tan face arched toward a clean line of oiled white hair. His voice was loud and gravelly.

"Just remember who imported the *Encyclopedia Americana* for you. At great expense, I might add." Jordan turned to the barman, a stooped Sambaa in a red fez and white uniform. "*Shikamoo, Mzee* Steven."

"*Marahaba.*" The barman smiled. Perfect teeth in a creased dark black face. Delighted.

"Gin and Sin." Jordan ordered the house special. On the wall behind the bar, between the shelves of liquor bottles, hung the requisite large photograph of the president of the United Republic, an affable-looking Zanzibari in a safari suit and white Muslim skullcap.

"Why did you let Kimweri beat you?" Ionides shouted, widening his sparrow-hawk eyes.

"I'm supposed to be an ambassador of goodwill," Jordan said. "There's always next week."

"Let him keep winning," Ionides said. "That's a wise policy. He's not the same man as his father. I remember the time we picked up the sultan at the airport in Mombo upon his return from the coronation of Queen Elizabeth—"

"Haven't I heard that story twenty times, *mzee?*" Jordan crossed the room with his drink and sat on a sofa. "I'm starting to dislike Julian Kimweri. It sounds like he's buying a cow, not getting married."

"The African, dear Rutledge, is the most chauvinistic man on the planet. . . . Next, perhaps, to the Arab." Ionides rasped this last phrase as an afterthought, rubbing his knees. "My gout always returns with the long rains."

"She's a schoolgirl."

"Don't worry yourself over some bitch," Ionides said dismissively, then, in a lower voice: "Paul sent a message. He's desperate for a courier."

"Why?" Jordan heard footsteps and glanced back at the door of the bar.

A *mzungu* man, probably a Dane or Norwegian development expert, looked at them without expression.

Jordan smiled slightly and nodded. The *mzungu* averted his eyes and stepped to the bar.

Ionides shouted for the barman to turn on the radio. A speaker squawked static until Steven found an English station from Nairobi: "Drink Deworm once a month and say good-bye to intestinal distress!"

Jordan turned back to the old man. "Why? Did another runner get caught?"

"In Zambia. But with your passport you'd never get caught. You said yourself you slipped through last time like a diplomat."

"Not interested." Jordan swirled the sugary mixture of Cinzano and Tanqueray around his mouth. "Last time I needed the money to build the hide in the forest. I don't need anything now. And I'm raising Pasipo. It's like taking care of a baby."

"Five thousand dollars," Ionides sang, closing the encyclopedia.

"Tell your brother that, uh, tell him I was traumatized by the last run and I don't want to push my luck." Jordan got up. "Traumatized, bwana. Do you understand?"

Agnes, an enormous woman a foot taller than Jordan, trundled into the bar, her Bantu butt like the stern of a dinghy. Ionides's choice of a concubine was evidence that he had been here long enough to become African in sensibility—*mafrik*. Agnes put Jordan in mind of the legendary concubines of the king of Buganda who were force-fed honey and goat butter until they were too big to walk.

"I'll tell him you're thinking about it," Ionides said, eyeing Agnes. "You're thinking about it."

"I'm thinking that your hearing is starting to go." Jordan squeezed Ionides's shoulder as he walked past. He gave Steven an African wave, raising both arms like a referee declaring a touchdown.

# Juni 25

Two black dots tumbled high in the azure sky.

"*Haaah,*" Zanifa gasped, looking through Jordan's binoculars.

Jordan rose up on one elbow from the deck where he lay beside Zanifa, saw no thunderheads on the 360-degree horizon and lowered himself back on a boat cushion. The deck listed in the wind, creaking audibly. It's suicide to come up here before the end of the long rains, Jordan thought. He tried to ignore the swaying of the groaning deck. The wind gusted higher. The leaves on the branches that surrounded the deck sounded like crinkling cellophane.

Jordan squinted at the tumbling dots. They were still too high to distinguish clearly. He shut his eyes and remembered building the hide. The day that the clipping of Anna's wedding arrived in his box, four months into the two-year contract—fifteen months ago now—Jordan rode the Honda as fast as it would go, redlining the engine beyond the limit, from Lushoto to the rain forest. The Honda was never the same, and afterward in the villages along the road, Jordan, who had previously been known exclusively as *Bwana Samaki*—Master Fish—was now called *Pikipiki Zimu*—Biker Possessed. A handful of Muslim elders had witnessed Jordan fly off the bike while sliding through a corner, pick himself up, leap back on and race down the road as if fleeing a ghost. Later that day Jordan conceived the idea of building the hide while smoking *bhangi* with Mbungu, the forest conservator. A hide would be the best way to paint the sky leopards, which could be glimpsed only from the forest floor. A hide would be a grand distraction.

The hide had been paid for by running tanzanite and emeralds from Dar es Salaam to Mombasa. In both ports the customs officers saw the Peace Corps sticker on his blue American passport and waved him through. Crossing had been easy, but Jordan had been terrified and nauseated. He rationalized the crime with an embassy estimate that a full third of the country's gross domestic product left illegally each year in the form of gold and precious stones. What was three thousand dollars out of tens of millions? Besides, the money ended up perpetuating the survival of an endangered species. Had Jordan not built the hide, he never would have seen the eagles mating and never would have saved Pasipo. The hide took three months and thirty Sambaa to build. They had nailed a ladder up the trunk and hauled beams and planks a hundred feet up with ropes and pulleys and bolted the beams to the tree with elaborate wooden harnesses without damaging the fifteen-hundred-year-old branches. Now the hide was a destination listed in a guide for backpack travelers. While Jordan was waiting for Cain and Abel's eggs to hatch, he had been annoyed to find a party of long-haired Germans in the hide, drunk and shouting at the eagles. He had decided then that he would remove the ladder before he left the country.

*Koi-koi-koi!*

*Kewee-kewee-kewee!*

Jordan heard the crowned eagles and opened his eyes. The wings and bodies were distinct now. If you traced their flight pattern, the intertwining paths would resemble two threads of a twisting strand of DNA, repeated over and over in a sort of ladder, each rung lower in the sky.

*Koi-koi-koi!*

*Kewee-kewee-kewee!*

"It's the first time I see them from the bottom," Zanifa said. The binoculars were big in her small hands. Jordan noticed the rise of her breasts beneath her sweater and the curve of her hips in blue jeans. He wondered what he would remember of Zanifa and what she would remember of him. He looked up at the eagles. The spots of black and henna orange were visible on their breasts. The thick legs had small spots of black and white. The shoulders were henna. The undersides of the huge wings were striped black and white.

"Those are Pasipo's parents," Zanifa said in an awed tone.

Sometimes locking talons, all the while twisting slowly around each other and screaming, the sky leopards tucked their wings and dove a hundred yards at seventy miles an hour. Opening their wings, they let their own velocity carry them into an upward swoop and slowly lost momentum. Then they slid tail first toward earth in a long arc until they were upside-down and diving again.

*Koi-koi-koi!*

*Kewee-kewee-kewee!*

"The dance is a supremacy duet. Sometimes they start three thousand feet over their nest, sometimes three hundred," Jordan told her. "Always at sunset."

"Why?" Zanifa said, still peering through the binoculars.

"To let all the other sky leopards know that this territory is taken. I hate to think what happens to the eaglets. They spend two years with their parents, much longer than any other eagle, learning how to hunt in the forest. Then their parents push them out of their territory. And they have nowhere to go. Ninety percent of the forest is gone. Cut."

"So where *do* the babies go?" Zanifa murmured.

"I guess most die of starvation a week after they get thrown out on their own. I've found one. Some find a little patch of forest and adapt to preying on goats and chickens instead of monkeys and bushbuck." Jordan had the urge to reach out and stroke her cheek.

"The villagers hunt them down," Zanifa said, scratching her elbow with one hand while the other propped up the binoculars. "When I was little a crowned eagle took a baby. The villagers have never forgotten."

"They sure haven't." Jordan sighed. "There's probably only five or six pairs left in the Usambara Mountains."

"What will you do with Pasipo?" Zanifa sat up to follow the eagles lower in the sky.

"Let her loose at Mafi Mountain." On his knees, Jordan peered through the dead branches of the wall at the nest tree thirty yards off. The eagles circled and landed. "They've probably used that tree for hundreds of years. It was sort of passed down by their parents."

Zanifa knelt beside him, poking the Nikons through the branches. Cain, black shouldered with a white breast, hobbled around the nest. He was no bigger than Pasipo now, perhaps because Pasipo had a steadier diet. The parents stood on the rim, watching Cain with their heads cocked.

The azure was draining from the sky. The wind rustled the leaves. Zanifa shivered. Jordan put his arm around her shoulder. *"Twende."* Let's go.

He stood and pulled her up. They crossed the deck and peered over the rail. From their perspective on the crown of a camphor tree situated near the mountain summit, looking down the steep slope across the folds of the mountains, the green canopy top of the rain forest undulated like dark waves on a stormy sea. Dizzy, Jordan backed away. He stared out over treetops and ridges to the haze of the Indian Ocean twenty miles east then turned northwest.

"Look." Jordan pointed over two ridges to a cluster of tiny buildings on a mountainside forty miles in the distance. "Lushoto. It doesn't look like it takes two hours to get there, does it?"

"A sky leopard could fly there in no time." Zanifa pointed just west of the town. "Do you see the old church by your house?"

On the other side of a peak that threw a long shadow over Lushoto, at the sharp edge of the escarpment, Jordan could see the black steeple of the ruin. The flat savanna beyond was blue gray in the late light.

"Past your house you can see Mafi Mountain." Zanifa pointed to a lone cone rising from the savanna, the bottom light green grass, the top half the dark green of a rain forest. "When Pasipo lives there she can fly here to visit her family."

"They wouldn't recognize her. They would drive her away."

"Thanks for bringing me here," Zanifa said, looking at Jordan. "Now I know what the mountains look like from above. I feel like an eagle."

Jordan smiled sadly. Time was running out. In six months he'd be back in Tennessee or he could look for work with one of the development agencies. He could end up like Ernst.

"I'll never forget seeing the sky leopards in their super—What do you call it?"

"Supremacy duet." Jordan placed one hand around the back of her smooth neck. "It's in the book I gave you. I'll give you a photograph of it."

"That would be great for my project." Zanifa put the binoculars in their case. She swung her legs over the edge and started down the ladder. Jordan watched her disappear and looked back across the savanna at the rows of peaks receding into the west. Red flames rimmed the farthest ridgeline and the sky beyond was a sheet of liquid gold.

It was dark when they came out of the forest by the Swiss house.

"*Karibuni, bwana na kijana,*" Mbungu said, waiting on the porch. Welcome, master and youth.

"*Shikamoo,*" Zanifa said shyly. I kiss your feet.

Mbungu ignored the formality and patted her on the back, saying warmly, "*Karibuni chai.*" Welcome to tea.

They followed the young conservator into a large room where a fire roared in a semicircular hearth with a copper flue. Umber light glowed from lace shades hanging on cords halfway down from the high ceiling, illuminating the room just well enough to steer between the antique furniture.

"You need to get that water generator fixed," Jordan said, taking a wingback chair by the fire. "You can't see well enough to think, much less read."

"The generator was manufactured in 1958. It's difficult to obtain parts." Mbungu poured tea from a porcelain pot into three dainty cups. He started to repeat the explanation in Swahili to Zanifa, but Jordan cut him off.

"Stick to English. Zanifa speaks very well." Jordan reached for the tea.

"You saw the eagles dancing?" Mbungu asked Zanifa, handing her a cup first.

"My English is not good enough to tell you," Zanifa said, sitting in a chair near Jordan. "It was very great."

"Beautiful," Mbungu said. "Without *Pikipiki Zimu* we could not see the eagles." Mbungu laughed and slapped Jordan's hand African style. "A patio in the sky. These Americans have big imaginations." Turning to Zanifa, Mbungu asked, "Is he taking care of the nestling?"

"Like a mother," Zanifa answered quickly in Swahili. "He takes her for walks. Every day he paints her picture. His name should be *Mama Mzimu.*"

Mbungu burst out laughing. "You catch that, Jordan? She says you should be called 'Mama Possessed.'"

Jordan asked himself why he could not enjoy these moments. "She's clever."

"I'm very happy to know you are taking care of the eagle. If you can put her back in the wild, it will be a great accomplishment." There was a rare expression of approval in Mbungu's eyes. "Where do you plan to leave her when you go?"

"Mafi Mountain."

"A good choice." Mbungu sipped his tea. "I've known a number of Peace Corps volunteers in my life. My chemistry teacher was a boy from Illinois not much older than I was then." He smiled and nodded his head toward Jordan. "That one acts crazy, but he's the most serious."

A black storm front from the Indian Ocean appeared like ink across the sky, blotting out the Milky Way. Riding down the rutted slope, Zanifa clung to Jordan, bending her head under his arm to watch the oncoming road in the weak beam of the Honda's headlight.

"I should have made you wear the helmet," Jordan said.

"It's too big," Zanifa said. "It falls off."

"If it rains, we're going to crash, and Bwana Kimweri will kill me."

"It's not going to rain." Zanifa laughed.

"What do you call that storm eating up the sky?"

"It doesn't feel like rain." Again Zanifa laughed. "Believe me."

Jordan labored the handlebars through a steep switchback, struggling to keep the front wheel out of a deep rut that ran to the edge of a long drop. Safely through the hairpin corner, he relaxed his shoulders and felt Zanifa's breasts pressed against his back, her head resting on his shoulder. Jordan whispered to himself as heat gathered in his crotch, but he could remember only bits of the prayer. An erection pushed against his khakis. He tried to distract himself with multiplication problems.

The Honda lit up the narrow road that led to the village of Ngolo. They passed in and out of pockets of fog. The dirt road ended at a clearing bordered by a tall hedge. Outside of the headlight, the village was too dark to distinguish from the trees and mountainside. Jordan cut the engine, surrounding them in blackness. A dog barked. It was about eleven P.M., *saa tano*, the fifth hour of the night. The whole village had gone to bed.

"Tell your mother I'm sorry we got back so late," Jordan said in English.

"*Nini?*" Zanifa asked in surprise. "You're not coming to greet her?"

"Okay." Jordan climbed off the bike. "You can't see a thing."

Zanifa giggled and took his hand. "I'll show you."

Jordan followed her on a path between the small huts. Most were completely dark. Candlelight glimmered in the slits between the small wooden shutters of a few. Laughter came from one. He stumbled where a shallow watercourse crossed the path. The only outdoor light in the village was a hurricane lamp hanging on a post by the gate of Zanifa's house. Jordan let go of Zanifa's hand as they turned into the yard.

Zanifa scampered to the doorway. "*Mama, tumefika!*"

Fog rolled through the yard.

The door opened. Mama Zanifa stood holding a lantern. Her skin looked white in the yellow light.

"*Zanifa, tumechelewa sana.*" Mama Zanifa scolded her for being late, then called out to the yard. "*Karibu, Bwana Joldon.*"

"*Ahsante,*" Jordan replied, and crossed the yard. Someone brushed by him. He thought it was Zanifa. The figure unhooked the lantern from the gate. It was another girl. He stepped into the light at the door. "I'm very sorry that we got back later than we had expected."

"Bwana, you are so late. Why are you so late?" Mama Zanifa led him into a hallway that ran through the center of the house. The light moved along in front of her. "Where have you had my daughter?"

"It took a long time coming from the forest." The desire he'd felt on the way back made Jordan feel guilty. "We saw the sky leopards dancing and talked to the conservator."

"I don't get it—all the trouble she is going to over a bird."

On each side of a hallway were smooth adobe walls. Jordan had wondered what the second floor looked like, as it was so rare in a house in the mountains. The wall on the right of the hallway rose to the ceiling, closing one big room that was reached by a ladder. On the left, the upper floor was a loft piled with corn ears. A cat peered down at him from the edge of the loft.

"*Karibu*," Mama Zanifa said, turning into an opening in the wall by the ladder. Welcome. "*Karibu kiti*." Welcome to a chair.

On the sills of two windows burned small oil candles, lighting only the surface of the closed shutters. Shadows filled the room, encircling a glowing orange mound of embers in a small charcoal brazier a few inches off the dirt floor.

"*Karibu hapa*." Mama Zanifa sat him down on a wooden sofa with kapok-stuffed cushions and set her lantern on a coffee table at his feet. She plumped down beside him. Jordan saw she was wearing a nylon windbreaker with the Greek letters kappa sigma, a secondhand fraternity jacket, over a *kanga* skirt.

"It's cold this time of year," Mama Zanifa said. Her voice resembled her daughter's.

"*Masika*." Jordan said the Sambaa name for the cold season.

"You speak Sambaa?"

"No. Only a few words."

The girl appeared with a tray and put a thermos and plastic teacups on the table, then vanished in the shadows.

Jordan heard footsteps upstairs and imagined Zanifa studying by candlelight like Abe Lincoln.

"*Chakula?*" Mama Zanifa asked.

"No, thank you. I'm not hungry."

"I just returned from Dar es Salaam." She bent over the table, positioning her bottom two feet from Jordan's face, and poured tea into the cups.

Jordan was pretty sure that she was coming on to him. If he was an African man, he would just reach out and grab her ass. That would be the signal. He said to her rear, "Zanifa told me you had gone to sell chickens."

Mama Zanifa shifted her hips to one side, turning around from the waist. "Eat ees good beesniss." She spoke for the first time in English, sounding nothing like Zanifa.

Jordan took the cup from her hand.

She turned to the table, swinging her butt back in his face. He thought he remembered reading that female gorillas in heat wag their asses like this at the alpha male. He admired the curve of her hips, felt the stirring again and shifted his hands in his lap, counting the months. Nine. He glimpsed Daniela naked, staring up at him from the bed in her apartment in the UN compound in Dar. His hand hung in the air.

Mama Zanifa's leg grazed his fingertips as she moved to the sofa. She settled next to him so that their legs were touching and said in Swahili, "It's not proper for a girl to be gone late into the night with a man."

"Forgive me, Mama Zanifa—"

"Cull me Mayree."

"Okay, Mary. I'm sorry that Zanifa was out so late. It was for her schoolwork. I think she really liked seeing the eagles."

"Are you chasing my daughter?"

"No! Of course not. I was just helping her."

"Zanifa says that you don't have a girlfriend. That's not right for a young man. Are you sick?"

"Mama Zanifa!" Jordan laughed.

"Mayree."

"Mary. No, I'm not sick. I'm just, uh, I have a girlfriend in America."

"Zanifa says that you are very sad because your girlfriend married another man."

The servant girl appeared with two brown bottles of Safari lager.

"No, thank you." Jordan shook his head as the girl placed one bottle in front of him.

"Please," Mama Zanifa said. "It's not often that I get a chance to talk with *mzungu*. I had many *mzungu* friends in Tanga."

Upstairs Zanifa tuned a short-wave radio to the BBC. Jordan could just hear the news in English.

*"Sawa,"* Jordan said. Okay.

"I had a boyfriend from Russia. He worked on a big farming project. I learned to speak Russian."

Jordan imagined them meeting in a disco. With her light skin and *mzungu* features, young Mary would have been a magnet for randy expats. "Did you want to marry him?"

"He had a wife in Russia," Mama Zanifa said cheerfully. "Sometimes he spoke of taking me outside." She sipped her beer. "Just words. I've told Zanifa that she should never believe a *mzungu* who talks of love. They talk and talk, but they always go back to the outside alone."

"Some *mzungu* take African wives."

"Very few." She placed her hand in his lap. "I am too old to be someone's wife now. I am happy here with my chickens and cows." She rubbed her hand on the inside of his thigh. "I could have stayed in town. I came back because I like the mountains. This is home."

Jordan looked at Mama Zanifa. She was not more than ten years older than him. He imagined that under her clothes her body was lean and hard from a life in the mountains. He remembered her plump breasts from the first day he'd met her. Her hand moved deeper between his legs.

"I think you like me." Mama Zanifa gripped him through his khakis. Jordan looked down at her brown hand; her fingers looked callused and chapped.

"He likes you very much," Jordan said. "But this is not a good idea."

"It is not good for a man to go too long without using this. That can turn you into a *msinge*."

Jordan laughed at the idea of prolonged celibacy making you gay.

Mama Zanifa rubbed the bulge beneath his pants roughly with the palm of her hand. "I think you need a woman," she whispered, then in English: "Isn't it?"

"You are a very beautiful woman, but this is not good," Jordan said.

"Are you a *msinge?*" Mama Zanifa unzipped his pants.

"No. This feels good. I would like to, but I don't think it is right."

"*Kwa afya,*" Mama Zanifa said. For your health.

The ceiling creaked overhead as Zanifa moved about in the room.

"It's late." Jordan sat forward and zipped up his pants. "I have to ride back in the dark and I am dead tired already."

Mama Zanifa looked surprised then laughed.

"I'm sorry to hurry off like this." Jordan stood up.

"I will not tell Sultan Kimweri that you took Zanifa to the forest today," Mama Zanifa said gravely. "He would not like to hear that someone had the chance to spoil her so close to the wedding. But many people must have seen her on the road. Maybe because she wore a helmet, no one knew her."

"We just went to look at the eagles."

"Yes. I would know if you had changed her. But the sultan is a man. If I had been here, I would not have let her go. Don't take her on your motorbike again. You could make trouble. You understand?"

"*Bila shaka,*" Jordan said, surprised at the fear in her tone of voice. Without a doubt.

Mama Zanifa told the servant girl to lead him back to his bike with a flashlight.

# Juni 27

Jordan coasted off the pavement onto the dirt road to Vooga. As he rode through steep, barren fields in broad daylight, his fear felt distant, controllable, but passing the turnoff to the old mission station, he became uneasy, and, a few minutes later, coming around the blind corner where he'd hit the child, his heart raced. A group of young men stood in front of a shanty bar, watching the bike approach the village, a half dozen houses and a couple of closet-size stores. Jordan waved as he came alongside. They stared coldly. He accelerated out of the village. In the rearview mirror he saw the men walk out on the road, looking at him.

Flat and narrow, the road curved around the mountainside, bringing him parallel with the village, now a mile across a valley of maize growing on slopes so steep that the topsoil ran down to the plains with every rain, draining the fertility into rivers that emptied into the sea. Looking over the vale, Jordan stopped, wondering which house was the boy's, and saw a group of men gathering on the road. One of them pointed at him.

The road climbed steeply through dense banana gardens, then emerged in a painful light on the summit of a flat ridge with a panorama of the high peaks of the Usambara range, a point where a king could survey the entirety of his mountain realm. The thousand mud huts of Vooga spread out on both sides of the road, which ended at a wide double gate set in a wall of thorn hedge. Women balanced baskets on their heads, children chased each other and kicked homemade balls, men sat in groups under the eaves, walked hand in hand. Everyone stopped and stared silently at the *mzungu* riding slowly through the center of town.

At the gate Jordan told the keeper, an old man in faded green fatigues and cap, that he had come to see the sultan. The old man swung open the wrought-iron gate, and Jordan rode in. On one side was a tall A-frame with a rotten thatch roof and charred weatherboard and broken windows. A peeling sign read "Usambara Council." Eighty feet away, the sultan's Land Rover was parked in front of a covered walkway that closed a semicircular formation of round adobe rooms with conical thatched roofs. A few giant trees shaded the whole compound. Jordan stopped by the Land Rover and noticed that the palace encircled a patio with flame and jacaranda trees growing up through the flagstone.

"*Karibu,*" said a woman in red kangas under the walkway. "*Karibu ndhani.*"

Jordan followed her down the walkway through an ornate arabesque door studded with brass spikes, a decoration originally meant to deter elephants, into a gloomy parlor with dark, heavy Zanzibari furniture and Oriental rugs on an orange clay floor. Jordan heard the slow tempo of delta blues coming from an adjoining room.

*Oh sad, bad days*
*Since my sugar, she ran away.*

Jordan crossed the room and studied framed black-and-white photographs on the wall. In one, under the inscription "Five Tanganyika Chiefs at the Coronation of Her Majesty the Queen," were four men in baggy, ill-fitting suits, but in the middle, regal in a long white *kanzu,* embroidered vest, and fez, was Julian Kimweri's father, the last sultan.

"He was something, wasn't he?" Kimweri's voice came from behind.

"Stunning." Jordan turned.

Julian Kimweri was dressed in chinos and a blue sweater and leather deck shoes.

"Muddy Waters." Jordan tilted his head toward the next room.

"That nigger can sing the blues." Kimweri smiled.

"He used to live on my friend's father's plantation in Mississippi," Jordan said without thinking.

"You're proud of that?" Kimweri sat on an orange camphor throne with an inverted V-shaped back fluted like organ pipes and an imperial British insignia of a standing lion carved just over his head. He motioned Jordan toward a chair.

"Just making conversation." Jordan sat on a Zanzibari chair with arms and legs carved into black intertwined snakes.

Kimweri nodded silently, appraising Jordan. "You were one of those rich white boys who hung out at blues bars?"

"I was never rich," Jordan said quickly.

"Rich is relative," Kimweri said, half smiling. "Compared to the coons in the blues bar."

"Compared to the Sambaa you're rich."

"There's nothing wrong with rich." Kimweri laughed. "So what's up?"

"My tennis elbow has come back." Jordan shrugged. "I think riding the bike irritates it."

The woman in red kangas returned, carrying a tray, and offered Jordan a cup of tea.

"Bored? Lonely?" Kimweri lit a Sportsman. "Singing them expat blues?"

"Yeah." Jordan wanted to say how he couldn't stop missing Anna, how hurting her had driven him here, how the whole idea of absolution was a silly fantasy.

"You'll be home before you know it." Kimweri blew a perfect smoke ring.

"I'm not sure I want to go back." Jordan sipped the tea, tasted the spicy tang of cardamom.

Kimweri drew on the cigarette. "Fed up with the getting and spending?"

"That and . . . I don't know." Jordan set the teacup on a table. "Progress. So many places I loved are gone now."

"It's unfortunate." Kimweri stubbed out the cigarette in an ashtray on the arm of the throne. "But what can one do? It's too late to change the course of civilization."

"Too late," Jordan murmured.

"Still, you're fighting the good fight." Kimweri smiled. "The great test of first-rate intelligence is the ability to hold two contradictory ideas in your mind at the same time. You know that everything is doomed, yet you remain determined to make it otherwise."

"That's it."

"So it was your idealism which brought you to the turd world to teach fish farming?"

Jordan laughed.

"Come on." Kimweri rose from the throne. "I want to show you something."

Jordan followed him into the yard. A warm wind gusted across the compound, carrying the sounds from the village.

"That was my daddy's supreme court." Kimweri pointed to the ruined A-frame. A white-necked raven surfaced from a hole in the roof and flew off. "A nesting place for crows."

"You leave it wrecked as some sort of memorial?" Jordan looked up at the sultan's profile, the long nose and sharp chin.

"A challenge," Kimweri said, walking toward the gate. "The day the Teacher nullified the old chiefs' authority, the party officials in Lushoto sent a mob to ransack the building. I was only three. It's one of my earliest memories."

"I'm surprised they didn't get carried away and attack your house," Jordan said, remembering the frenzy on the road.

"The village stopped them." Kimweri looked at Jordan gravely. "They would die for us."

As the old man in fatigues opened the gate, a bodyguard in a white polo shirt and black trousers appeared from out of nowhere. The sultan dismissed him in Sambaa, and he and Jordan walked out into the town. The people waved with both arms high, bowing and saluting the sultan, who waved back and returned their smiles, walking along the thorn hedge. Soon the houses stopped and the fields began.

Jordan whistled at the enormous work in progress. "Amazing. I've never seen anything like it. I'd heard about your scheme, but it's incredible." A stepwork of soil terraces traversed the ridge beneath Vooga and the ridges on the far side of the mountain valley. In the distance, from the top to the bottom of the mountainside, tiny figures stooped over the terraces.

"When I'm an old man," Kimweri said, sweeping his arm from one end of the range to the other, "I want to be able to fly over the mountains and see the erosion scars healed, the denuded ridges covered again with trees."

"How many square kilometers have you completed?" Jordan followed Kimweri down a path between the terraces.

"We're averaging fifty square klicks a year." Kimweri pointed to rows of saplings planted along the backs of terraces. "We're using only indigenous trees."

"Smart," Jordan said. "How'd you do it? How'd you convince the people to terrace? It's so much work. The Brits never could."

"Simple." Kimweri bent and pushed his hand into the soil. He pulled out a potato and, standing up, pitched it to Jordan.

"It's five times as big as the potatoes in the market." Jordan turned the potato in his hand.

"Water." Kimweri raised his eyebrows. "A potato is nothing but a sack of water."

"Eureka." Jordan brushed the dirt off the brown skin.

"I showed the people how you can sextuple the size of your produce if you irrigate your fields and trap the water and topsoil with terraces." Kimweri gestured to a line of black pipe running along the top terrace. "Then I promised to supply the irrigation *if* they terraced their fields."

"Rain magic. Way to go, bwana." Jordan laughed. "Conjuring water in the dry season."

"Here"—Kimweri smiled—"there is hope."

"Hope, oh, that," Jordan murmured, staring out at the green landscape banded by degraded slopes of red clay.

"What?" Kimweri said, taking Jordan's hand.

"You've done a great job." Jordan looked away from his eyes, struck by the thought that Kimweri had heard that he had taken Zanifa to the forest.

Kimweri turned, pulling Jordan back up the hill. He squeezed Jordan's hand slightly. "How's Zanifa? I think you see her more than I do."

"She's a natural falconer." Jordan felt sweat collecting on his hand.

"Some of my Arab friends keep falcons." Kimweri looked ahead as they stepped up the terraces. "She can keep them for me here at the palace."

Jordan watched the sultan through the corner of his eye. "She'll be good at it."

"Can you teach her to hunt with her hawk?"

Jordan drew his hand away. "I can try. I've never done it, but I have a good book."

They reached the top and walked along the palace hedge.

"Will you do that for me?" Kimweri looked at him.

"Of course." Jordan tried to smile. "But I can't guarantee good results."

✦

On the bike Jordan dropped down through the dark banana gardens then out into the softening light of late afternoon against the red dying mountainside. The sultan's land reclamation scheme was the most promising development project he had seen in Tanzania, much better than any of the foreign programs, a real reason to be optimistic about Africa. But the idea of Zanifa living in Vooga left him melancholy, awakened the sadness that brought him here, and made him wonder what Anna was doing at this moment. He saw a waterfall far below near the plains and remembered the last trip he took with Anna, canoeing in the Cumberland Mountains three years ago on the Fourth of July. He was a fool, he thought, to have lost someone so smart and funny and beautiful.

He hit the flat stretch of road that wound around the valley of corn to the boy's home. Across the vale he saw a crowd gathering at the near end of the village, and he forgot everything.

"They won't attack you on the road. Not as a group. Not now. Not after you sent the boy to the hospital." Jordan repeated the assurances

Kimweri had given him before he had ridden off. "That sort of mass hysteria comes only when they see blood." Still, he was worried as he neared the men and women clogging the road.

Their faces were vacant. They showed no sign of parting to let him through. Jordan was reluctant to use the horn. He came to a stop a few feet short of the crowd. He tightened the strap on his helmet, then flipped up the visor and smiled. He waved. Talking together, the Sambaa closed in around him. Jordan recognized the man with a machete. Other men carried bush knives. An old woman held a hoe. They pushed in closer, shouting.

"*Jambo, mzungu.*"

"*Habari, bwana.*"

"*Salama, mzee.*"

"*Vipi, bwana.*"

They called out too rapidly and numerous for Jordan to reply. At the front of the bike the crowd opened just wide enough for a woman in a green *kanga* to approach. Everyone was quiet when she reached Jordan.

"*Karibu, Bwana Samaki,*" the woman said. Welcome, Master Fish.

She was middle-aged, wore her hair in rows, and held a bundle of corn ears out for him.

"Thank you." Jordan reached for the corn.

"My son is coming home soon," the woman said. "He's walking again."

"Oh, you're Mama Georgi." Jordan smiled. "I'm happy to meet you. I'm happy to learn that Georgi is getting better."

Mama Georgi smiled and looked at her feet.

"Thank you for the corn." Jordan turned around on the seat to strap the bundle to the rear rack with inner-tube strips. He handed the woman some shilling notes, telling her he must hurry home.

The woman spoke to the people standing beside her, and they moved back to let Jordan pass. He kept checking the rearview mirror until the village was out of sight.

THE WAY I FIGURE IT," JORDAN YELLED OVER THE MUSIC, "A WOMAN'S basic instincts drive her to home in on one mate to nurture her one egg while we are designed to scatter countless spermatozoa far and wide."

"You've put a lot of thought into this," Garret Stoval said, watching several girls pass through the half-dark into the bar. They were sitting on a torn couch in Ernestine and Hazel's, a maze of shabby rooms in an old riverfront building that used to be a brothel and was now a late night bar that Garret referred to as Last Chance. "That tall one was a head turner."

"I think every woman is beautiful." Jordan sipped bourbon from a plastic cup.

Garret loosened his tie. "How many times have you fooled around on Anna?"

"Five or six. The last time was four months ago."

"All one-nighters?"

"Yeah."

"Each time you weren't looking to get laid, right? They just sort of fell in your lap?"

"Pretty much."

"Then they didn't mean anything." Garret rolled his eyes dismissively. "You love her, right?"

"Totally," Jordan said. "She's it."

"You're not married yet. As long as you don't fall in love with someone else you haven't done anything wrong. It's like you said. It's only natural."

"That's license for adultery." Jordan thought it was pointless discussing infidelity with a hound dog like Garret.

"Then control your animal instincts. Stop tormenting yourself.

Stop tormenting me." Garret gulped down the last of his drink. "My libido rules."

"I'm not going to do it again."

"Uh-huh." Garret's eyes followed another girl. "Did you see the warheads on that one?"

"Why do they call out to me like sirens?" Jordan said. "Anna's breasts are beautiful. If I had a girlfriend with big boobs, then I would want smaller ones again. It's the part of the design to keep men on the move."

"You've got it all worked out, Rut." Garret sprang up from the couch. "Let's get another drink."

"I'm too tired to move, man," Jordan groaned. "Fetch one for me. You don't work the hours I do."

"Come on." Garret took his arm and pulled him up.

The blood rushed into Jordan's head and the room seemed to teeter, then settle. Robert Johnson was singing "Dead Shrimp Blues." Garret shouldered his way toward the bar, between a hippie couple wearing tie-dyed shirts and some cotton traders in business suits talking to women who could have come from a Junior League meeting. Jordan saw it was almost midnight and remembered Anna was supposed to call from Chicago an hour ago. Garret handed him a cup, and Jordan turned around just as a girl stepped into him. Her hand hit his, spilling the drink on his jacket.

"Oh, I'm sorry. I never watch where I'm going." She had short dark hair, large eyes and a ski-jump nose, and her breasts swelled against a tight ribbed T-shirt. She had probably just graduated with a marketing degree from Memphis State. She smiled. "I'll get you another."

"No, no. I've had enough anyway," Jordan said. "My horoscope warned me to beware of beautiful women in blue jeans. I should have been more careful."

The girl laughed and took the napkin from his hand. "What's your sign?"

"Sign?" He smiled. "I was born under a neon sign that said 'Cold Beer to Go.'"

"That's a new one." She laughed and dabbed his jacket. "If you're not careful, it's going to leave a mark. I live right close by on Front. I'm sure I've got some stain remover."

"Uh, well, I . . . ," Jordan mumbled, looking at her bright eyes. He felt wide awake. The floor vibrated to Iggy Pop singing "Lust for Life."

"Anna's in Chicago. You're bulletproof tonight," Garret whispered in his ear. "You can't pass up a ride on a filly like her. She's rarin' to go, God bless her."

"Man, I was trashed last night." Garret's voice sounded preternaturally cheerful even for a Saturday morning.

"Me, too." Jordan yawned and shifted the phone to his other ear. "I dragged myself out of bed at nine and went jogging, but I still feel hungover."

"So, what was her name?"

"Sarah something."

"Did you tell her yours?"

"Hell no. I said I was John Major."

"You're kidding." Garret chuckled. "She'd never heard of him?"

"Don't think so." Jordan reached for a carton of orange juice in the refrigerator. "I got to go to the office."

"Tell me the details."

"Shit, Garret. Use your imagination. When you're peeling off her clothes you think you're in heaven and as soon as you come the guilt hits you like a freight train."

"Hits you, bro. Not me. I just lie back and wait for round two while you're pulling on your pants and mumbling excuses." Garret laughed. "But I know what you mean. It's like that line from the Penn Warren poem we read in Southern Lit."

Jordan said, " 'The old pain of fulfillment-that-is-not-fulfillment.' "

"Yeah," Garret said. "I hit the jackpot after you left, this blond babe from Arkansas who—"

"Anna left about six messages last night. She sounds suspicious."

"You called her yet?"

"I left a message, said I was out late with you."

"When's she back?"

"Tomorrow."

"Then let's go whoop it up tonight." Garret howled like a dog at the moon.

"Lead me not into temptation." Jordan looked for his car keys. "If I stay sober, I'll stay out of trouble."

"Listen up, Rut. I know you. You're gonna want to get it off your chest. Don't do anything foolish."

"Maybe she heard something." Jordan didn't bother to hide the worry in his voice. "Not about last night, but about that wedding in New Orleans."

"I don't care if she saw you in bed, it did *not* happen. Deny it and keep denying it. Tell her she's imagining things. Eventually she'll believe you."

"That's not very original, Garret. The big lie."

"It works."

# Julai 6

When I came from Cyprus, the white men were the chiefs of Africa. You could mail a letter from Lushoto and in three days it would be in London. *Three days!*" Nicholas Ionides, in a wool three-piece, addressed a group of Dutch embassy personnel. "These days it takes three weeks if you're lucky!"

"I beg your pardon," whispered a middle-aged diplomat. "The Tanzanians will call you a colonialist."

"*I* am Tanzanian," the old Greek said in a stage whisper. He cocked his back, laughing, then shouted across the room: "Bwana Rajabu! How long did an airmail letter take to come from London in 1936?"

"Shut up, you senile old bastard," a retired member of Parliament, standing with a group of officials in short-sleeved safari suits, replied in Swahili.

"What?" the Dutch diplomat asked Ionides. "What was that?"

"You might trouble yourself to learn the local language," Ionides told the Dutchman, and raised his glass at the retired MP. "Cheers!"

Jordan sat behind Ernst's desk in a wrinkled seersucker suit, sipping a Safari lager. Ernst had built the office with thick walls and beamed ceilings, in a style sympathetic to the German-era government buildings next door. Tonight Ernst's staff had decorated the walls with Swahili banners. *"Irrigation Means More Food." "Save the Soil from Washing to the Sea." "Conserve the Mountains for our Children."* Father William, an American Franciscan in his sixties, was wearing a yellow cardigan and light green slacks and looked more like a golf pro than a monk. He was talking to the district commissioner, a bald, light-skinned Zanzibari in a Nehru suit.

Jordan looked around for the single white female. He spotted her in the next room: a blonde from the Dutch embassy in a blue dress. She was talking to Ernst by the reception counter that served as a bar. Jordan felt an involuntary sense of relief in his natural territorial aggression; Ernst would never go for a white woman.

As Jordan moved through the crowded room toward the woman, someone took his arm.

"Bwana Jordan, I want you to meet a friend," Julian Kimweri said in Swahili, sporting Savile Row pinstripes, an Oxford college tie and a red fez. "The Freedom Party candidate from Kilimanjaro, Samuel Nkosi." Tall and thin, in round wire-frame glasses and an elegant suit, Nkosi could have been an erudite jazz musician.

"Nkosi? You're the son of the chief of the Kilimanjaro tribe?" Jordan shook his hand.

"One refers to my father as the paramount chief of the Chagga." Nkosi had an American accent.

"Sorry. That's what I meant." Jordan's face reddened. "You studied in the States?"

"Stanford," Nkosi said.

"Stick to Swahili! Bwana Jordan's Swahili is excellent."

"The sultan is adept at flattery," Jordan said in Swahili.

"Do you have a sleeping dictionary?" Nkosi asked in English with a sly smile.

"Bwana Jordan doesn't like chocolate," Kimweri said, draping his arm around Jordan's shoulder. "Fundamentally Bwana Jordan is an old-time redneck racist. Sure, some of his closest friends are . . . But under it all he has a basic aversion to black . . . ah, what is your word, Nkosi?"

"Poontang." Nkosi laughed and slapped the sultan's hand.

"Nothing personal." The sultan clapped Jordan on the back.

Nkosi looked at Jordan and said, "I feel the same about white women."

"Maybe if I met some educated African women," Jordan said. "I simply prefer to be able to have a conversation with a lover."

"Why?" Nkosi asked.

Ernst waved at Jordan from the bar.

"Excuse me. Our host is calling." Jordan shook Nkosi's hand. "Nice to meet you. Good luck in the elections." He touched Kimweri's shoulder. "I'll see you on the court next week."

"Excellent." The sultan smiled warmly.


"This is Nicole." Ernst was wearing a thin red tie with his leather jacket.

"*Jambo.*" The blond woman smiled. Her eyes were green. Jordan was not sure if she was gorgeous or if she just appeared so because she was the first white woman he had seen in months.

"You must be glad to get out of the heat in Dar." Jordan smiled, hoping he wasn't leering.

"The weather here is lovely," Nicole said. "Dar es Salaam is a furnace."

"And have you seen the stars from the mountains?" Jordan nodded toward an open doorway that framed the night outside. "You can really see the Milky Way up here. Would you like to walk under the stars?"

Nicole's face went cold, not imperceptibly.

"Rutledge painted the mural outside." Ernst handed Jordan a beer. "He comes off as a loud American, but—"

"I apologize if I was forward," Jordan said. "Beautiful women always disorient me."

"The mural is very nice," Nicole said indifferently.

"Thanks," Jordan said. "Turner's my hero."

"Who?" Nicole asked. "Turner?"

Ernst was shaking his head behind her, signaling that Jordan was blowing it.

"An English Romantic painter," Jordan said, trying to think of a subject that might interest her.

"I'm familiar with J. M. W. Turner. I just couldn't believe you said that," Nicole said.

"Oh," Jordan said.

"Have you painted long?"

"Is the mural that awful?"

"No." She laughed. "I was just—"

"I started painting game birds—doves, quail, ducks—when I was seven. Every season we'd go out to my grandfather's hunting camp in Arkansas," Jordan said, hope rising. "The others shot birds. I painted them."

"I see." Nicole turned and spoke to Ernst in Dutch.

"I'll be here by eight in the morning," Ernst answered in English.

"It was good to meet you," Nicole told Jordan. She called to her driver and walked out into the dark.

"I hate to see a man miss his last chance of getting laid for a year." Ernst shook his head.

"It's only been nine months." Jordan looked at the door. "I counted the other night."

One of the men from the embassy started speaking to Ernst in Dutch.

Jordan set the nearly full beer on the counter, went out into the darkness and watched the taillights of Nicole's car disappear. He walked up the road toward the post office, gazing up at the stars and listening to the night sounds as the loneliness settled in. He turned around suddenly, wanting to find Father William. Home seemed so far away, and talking to an American made it exist for a few moments and briefly made Jordan feel his isolation more keenly, a sharp sorrow that filled the void inside him. In the parking lot outside Ernst's office, Jordan saw Father William talking to the sultan and Nkosi. He stopped in the shadows, trying to hear their conversation. The three men shook hands, then walked to their cars.

"Thank God that's over." Ernst propped his black boots up on the desk. "Brace yourself for a bitter dose of vitamin G."

"Gossip?" Jordan mumbled, tired and vaguely drunk, sitting in a chair facing the seat back. "What gossip around here could I possibly care about?"

"The sultan told Nkosi that he is having that schoolgirl go through *jando* before the wedding."

"*Jando?*"

"Initiation."

"Initiation?" Jordan couldn't concentrate. "What are you talking about?"

"You know, an old witch will remove her *kisimi.*"

"What?" Jordan kneaded his temples with his fingertips. "What the hell is a *kisimi?*"

"*Kisimi* means clitoris." Ernst yawned noisily. "In *jando* an old witch cuts off a girl's clit."

"Bwana, this is a sick joke." Jordan dropped his hands. "Are you serious?"

"*Kwa kweli,*" Ernst said. For real. Stretching his arms above his head, he yawned again. "The sultan is going to send your little friend through *jando.*"

"It can't be true. Julian is an educated guy."

"*Kwa kweli.*" Ernst closed his eyes. "Calm down. It's an old custom here."

The Honda's headlamp cast a pool of light across the parking lot of the Lawns Hotel, reflecting off the green diplomatic plates. Jordan coasted between a Range Rover and Nicole's Nissan Patrol, rested the Honda on its stand and walked to the bar, which was empty except for the barman Steven and Ionides, still in his suit, sitting by the fire.

Ionides looked up and waved at Jordan, who stood silently by the door.

"Cheer up!" Ionides cackled. "Only a hundred and seventy-two days till Christmas!"

Jordan slumped onto a barstool.

"Give him a Gin and Sin," Ionides yelled. "We're completely booked up! Every bed!"

"Happy to hear it." Jordan loosened his tie. "Did you enjoy the party?"

"It's always a pleasure to socialize with civilized people," Ionides said.

"You're such a racist it's amazing you're still alive." Jordan stepped to the bar.

"You look ill," Ionides said. "Have you got malaria?"

"Have you heard that Kimweri is going to send Zanifa through *jando* before the wedding?"

"I've told you not to worry yourself over some *bitch*," Ionides's voice was high and coarse. "The practice lingers in parts of Africa. Tragic, but there is nothing you can do. What can you do? *You* just arrived yesterday."

"Zanifa is a beautiful girl," was all Jordan could say.

"You know it is the women who perform the rite. It's a women's ritual," Ionides said wryly. "They believe the clitoris"—the Greek pronounced *kleye-tore-ees*—"is the equivalent of the penis, much as modern scientists view the organ. In *jando* they are removing the one male organ of their bodies."

Jordan shook his head. Excising the maleness so they could become completely female? He picked up the drink and looked at it.

"You fancy the lovely young lady, do you?" Ionides asked.

Jordan sipped the sweet martini. "She's a bright girl with a lot of promise. She deserves—"

"Oh, don't bullshit me. You want to fuck her."

Jordan just stared at Ionides. "Did I say that?"

"You are jealous. You must be mad. *Terrá più di una locomotiva. . . .*"

"That's Italian?"

"Yes," Ionides said in his crow's voice. "Mightier than a thousand-horsepower locomotive is one hair of a woman's cunt."

"She just comes by to deliver Pasipo's food," Jordan said quietly.

"It's not your country. You can't alter their behavior," Ionides said. "I threw up my hands a long time ago."

"This isn't like teaching villagers to farm fish," Jordan protested. "The bastard knows better. He has a degree from Oxford. I'd like to kick his ass."

"*Don't* cross Kimweri. He'll have you poisoned or run down by a truck. He'll spread the word around that you are a *mumiyani*, and one day when you're visiting a pond ten men will jump you and hack you to pieces, truly believing that they are killing a vampire." Ionides laughed cruelly. "You should go to Nairobi. Chase some white women for a change."

"I can't. I have a child to think of," Jordan said. "Pasipo."

"Put the girl out of your head. Buy your chickens somewhere else. Forget about her." Ionides shouted at Steven to bring the little bwana another drink.

Jordan sat on the sill of a bay window, watching Steven mixing the drink. The old man wore a red fez like the sultan's. Outside in the darkness a tree hyrax screamed like a terrified baby.

# Julai 7

Jordan opened his eyes. He was in a cloud, surrounded by a shifting white mist. He tried to lift his head. It was too heavy. He poked his hand beneath the netting and patted the top of the table by the bed until he found a matchbox, then removed a half-smoked hand-rolled cigarette from the box, a common hangover cure in the Peace Corps. Sweet smoke filled the gauzy enclosure, and Jordan softly sang "Rastaman Vibration" off-key.

Jordan turned over, pushed himself up with shaky arms and kicked through the netting. Wrapping a blue *kikoi* around his legs, he fumbled for a minute, trying to tie it tight at his waist. He proceeded carefully into the kitchen to the blue water filter on one end of the wooden counter. The plastic mug beneath the tiny faucet trembled in his hand. He drained the cup in one gulp. He filled the mug again and again. Gin and Sin—the idea made him shudder.

On the back porch he gazed out over the Maasai steppe. The noon sun glared off the bleached cloud tops level with the cliff edge, as if the vapor were a snowfield you could step out onto. *Kiu-kiu-kiu!* Pasipo chased a live chick around the floor of the porch, but the yard bird easily outmaneuvered the eyas. The scampering and the cries of the birds assaulted his ears.

Back in the kitchen he noticed a red fez on the floor. For a moment it was as if he were in a Russian novel, waking to recall a terrible crime. He might have gone to the sultan's palace at Vooga in a drunken rage. Then he remembered his midnight discussion with Steven about the waning popularity of the fez. Common in colonial days, the fez went out of fashion in the sixties, and now all the Muslim men wore white skullcaps. An old fez had gotten pulled out from under the bar and been given to Jordan.

"*Hodi!*" A call came from the front porch. He staggered toward the door. Zanifa stood smiling with a woven basket in her arms.

Jordan fell into a big kapok-stuffed chair. "*Karibu.*"

"I came early today. There's a big funeral in the afternoon. Mzee Sechonge of the Makuzi village died. He had thirty wives. I'm not going to school. Hundreds of our clan are spending the night at his home."

"Everybody in one house?" Jordan thought that he had misunderstood.

"No, bwana." Zanifa laughed and shook her head. "Everyone sleeps outside on the night of a burial. People stay up all night talking and singing. The men get drunk."

Jordan was dizzy. He focused on the girl. Her dark hair was longer than an African's usually was but still short, falling around her ears in soft curls tinged golden brown. She wore matching blue gray kangas of a Zairian fish pattern, wrapped around her as a skirt and a shirt. He imagined her held down by the shriveled hands of old women, her legs spread, one crone kneeling between them, bending closer with a paring knife.

Jordan struggled to sit up in the chair. "When do you enter *jando?*"

Zanifa's eyes widened. She gasped slightly. "Men are not to speak of it."

"Men are hyenas."

Lowering the basket, Zanifa looked at him quizzically. "I must hurry."

"Men began the custom." Jordan tried to get her to talk. "The men want to weaken the women. They want to have something that the women don't have."

"What?" Zanifa's face was uneasy.

"They are going to hurt you, Zanifa. They are going to cut . . ." Jordan couldn't finish the sentence. "God gave it to you for a reason. There's a reason women have those things."

Zanifa looked through the front door at the porch and the yard beyond.

"God gave it to you."

"Our mothers and their mothers have all gone through . . ." Zanifa couldn't bring herself to pronounce the word.

"There's a secret that some of the old men know, but they keep it from the women, just as the old women keep all the men away from the *jando* ceremony." Jordan pulled himself higher in the big chair. "A long time ago, before Chahingo came to the mountains, women were the chiefs because they are most important for the tribe. They make babies. Without the mamas the tribe would die away." He paused. "Do you follow me?"

She nodded. "The women were the chiefs."

"Yes—a woman could choose three husbands so that she could pick the men she thought would make the best babies to make the strongest tribe." Jordan noticed Pasipo watching them from the porch through the back screen door. "How would you like to choose your husband?"

"The world is not like that," Zanifa said simply.

"But if you could choose . . . Who would you pick?"

"You." Zanifa laughed and slapped his hand.

"Why?" Jordan stared ahead gravely.

"I want to go to America." Zanifa grinned.

"Has Kimweri said that he would take you to England?"

"Yes."

"I don't believe him. Why would he take a *jando* woman to the outside when none of the *mzungu* women have been through *jando?* You might learn the secret of the African men."

"He promised he would take me," she said, the smile no longer on her face.

"Has he taken his other wife?"

"No, but she doesn't count. That marriage was arranged when he was very young. He says none of his friends in England even know he is married because she does not count."

Jordan stood and steadied himself on a chair frame. "Listen, Zanifa—because the women were chiefs, the men were jealous and they decided to revolt and make the women into slaves." He made his way slowly back to the kitchen. "The men wanted the women to tend the fields. They wanted the women to carry water. They wanted to marry more than one woman. The men went to their villages and they collected all the young girls and took them into the forest. Then the men went back to the villages and killed all their wives so that there would be no woman left who could remember the days when the women ruled the mountains."

Zanifa looked shocked.

"After they had buried all the women, they brought all the little girls back and told them that the Maasai had come and taken all the women." Jordan mixed a mug of water with black current cordial and held it toward her.

She shook her head.

"One little girl was crying because her mother was gone. She asked the men, 'But why didn't the Maasai steal the cattle? The Maasai like cattle more than women.' One of the elders lied to the girl, 'We scared them away before there was time.' The elder thought, This is a clever girl. She might realize that the women are stronger than the men because they make the children in their bellies and fight through much pain to bring children into the world." Jordan drank the tepid juice slowly, thinking, The toothless barroom bards have rubbed off on you. Now you can lie with the best of them. Not that you weren't a liar before you came to Africa. *Where is this story leading you?* "You've seen that, Zanifa? A woman fighting to give birth?"

Zanifa stood still, her back perfectly straight, a shadow from the window curtain falling across half her face like a veil. "Many times in the village. I told you my grandmother was a midwife."

"The elder told the other men, 'One day the clever girl will discover that she can make her own pleasure by herself. That she does not need our *mboro.*'" He returned to the front room a little more steadily, Zanifa following a step behind.

"Way back then women went off to lie alone in the bush and give their bodies a special pleasure that was all their own, simply by touching their *kisimi*. Haven't you ever felt that pleasure?" Jordan said, sitting on the edge of the sofa.

Looking down at her feet, Zanifa shook her head.

"The elder felt very guilty over the terrible murder of the women and was scared of the clever girl learning the evil secret." Jordan settled into the cushions, his face pinched by the headache. "The elder told the other men, 'We must cut off her *kisimi* so she does not know that women have their own little *mboro*, so she does not learn that we are equal. We must teach the older girls to perform the ceremony for the younger girls so that they do not suspect that it is really the men who are enslaving them. We will use the older girls to trick them, to tell them that they need to cut it off so that they can have many children. Without her *kisimi*, a woman will need us to give her pleasure.'"

"Why don't the women know that their *kisimi* can give them pleasure?" Zanifa's tan face blushed.

"They were tricked a long time ago. They have forgotten," Jordan said. "Don't enter *jando*. Tell the sultan that you will not let the old women cut you."

"He told my mother that he will not marry me until after *jando*. She wants me to marry him." Zanifa looked at his face and then looked away. "He is family. He is a wealthy man. He is—"

"But you will be hurt badly. And when Kimweri gets tired of you, he's going to marry another woman." Jordan raised his voice: "And when he's sleeping with his other wives you won't even be able to give yourself pleasure because he had you cut."

Zanifa's mouth was half-open, but she couldn't find words.

"Zanifa, don't let—"

"If I don't go through *jando*, he won't marry me and the next husband will want me to be clean, too." Zanifa sounded lost. Her hands fidgeted with the hem of her *kanga*.

"*Safi?*" Jordan almost shouted. "*Clean?* There's nothing unclean about you the way you are now. If you get infected from when they cut you, *then* it will be dirty." He changed to Swahili, said quietly,

"You are clean. Don't let your mother or anyone tell you that anything about you is filthy. You are pure."

Zanifa stared at him steadily, her eyes red and watery. She wiped away a few tears with her palms.

"You know that these days most girls don't go through *jando*." Jordan leaned forward and took her hand. "You don't have to, either."

"It can't be a bad thing if all of the older women have gone through it," Zanifa whispered.

A wave of nausea made Jordan sink back into the sofa.

"Would you like some Ribena?" Zanifa asked. "You look sick."

"Please." Jordan smiled faintly.

She ran into the kitchen and returned with the mug. She laughed and said, "You drank too much *pombeh* last night."

Jordan nodded. "Listen, Zanifa, you don't *have* to marry Bwana Kimweri. If he won't change his mind about *jando*, don't marry him."

"But my mother . . ." Zanifa's voice trailed off as a look of distress returned to her face.

"You always wanted to be a boarder. We can find a good school in Kenya. I'm sure I can afford to send you there. You don't have to marry Kimweri and spend the rest of your life as his servant. His slave. He's going to have you cut like a dog. You don't have to do that."

Zanifa was quiet for a few moments. She wiped her face dry with her hands. Finally she said in Swahili, "Bwana Jordan, I'll think about this. But don't tell my mother. She won't understand. She wants me to quit school when I marry so that I can be a good wife."

"Okay." Jordan felt a sudden release and a brief pleasurable sensation he associated with taking a set off Kimweri on the tennis court. His headache seemed to fade away.

"Have you fed Ophelia?" Zanifa looked at the closed door to the second bedroom. She had named the injured buzzard the day after they'd found it. At Saint Mary's she'd read *Hamlet* in English and the Swahili translation by Julius Nyerere, the Teacher, the first president of Tanzania.

"Oh, God, I forgot. I'm so hungover," Jordan said.

"What?"

"No. Sorry. I slept late and she hasn't eaten."

"Father William says responsibility is hard practice," Zanifa scolded him playfully. She ran into the kitchen then came out carrying a plastic box and a falconry glove Jordan had made for her by a cobbler in Lushoto. She opened the door and went into the empty bedroom. The buzzard squawked.

Stretched out on the sofa in the front room, Jordan listened to her talking to Ophelia. He wondered how much it would cost to send her to school and on through college and where he would get the money. He whispered to her, "Run away."

JORDAN LAY ON A COUCH, WATCHING A TENNIS MATCH ON TV. Pretend it never happened. One day you'll forget and then it will be as if it never happened. He felt as though he were dragging a garbage barge of lies behind him wherever he went. He laughed ruefully and thought, No country will take it. He flicked the remote to change channels: stock cars raced around a track. The doorbell rang and he took a deep breath, composing his face.

"Hey, Rut," Anna called from outside.

Jordan opened the door. "Welcome back, baby."

"I missed you." Anna smiled and touched his cheek.

"Missed you, too." He kissed her, circling his arm around her back, then pulled her inside out of the heat. He saw nothing suspicious in her eyes. "You're a sight to behold."

"Sex," she said, pushing him backward.

"How was your flight?"

"Sex."

"Any turbulence?"

"Sex." She shoved him and he tumbled over the arm of the couch. She fell between his legs and popped the button on his shorts.

*"Mmm,"* Anna purred, curled against his side with her head on his chest. Sweat glistened on her forehead. Jordan stroked her hair, letting himself drift off. Anna ran her finger down his sternum. "I saw Mary Tisdale in Chicago."

"How's she?" Jordan mumbled with his eyes shut.

"Fine. She said she'd seen you at Emily's wedding."

"Oh, yeah?" Jordan pretended to yawn.

"Said you and Frank Davis were shit-faced."

"Everybody was wasted." He felt her sit up on his legs, straddling his waist with her thighs. He yawned again.

"Did you fuck Nan Grant?"

He didn't want to open his eyes. "Yeah . . . in college. You, um, knew that. What's this all about?"

"No. In April. At the fucking *wedding*, for Christ's sake."

"Baby . . ." Jordan saw a vague image of Mary Tisdale down the hotel corridor as they'd gone into Nan's room, Nan stepping out of a long white bridesmaid's dress. I just walked her to her room, he could say, then catch the lie as it came out of his mouth and toss it over his shoulder into the barge. He opened his eyes and knew fear showed in them. He fought a smile that formed involuntarily on his face, like a child who'd been caught.

Anna stared at him with her brow wrinkled.

Jordan felt the lie on his face, spoke to free his mouth of the stupid smile. "We saw each other a long time ago. It doesn't mean anything. We were drunk. It was a mistake. I'm sorry."

"You asshole." Anna stared at him. "You were out chasing tail on Friday night with Stoval. Did you get lucky?"

"No, baby," Jordan said lamely, wanting to cut loose the heavy weight, afraid that he had already confessed too much. He wondered if kindness and lies were sometimes worth more than truth. He looked away from her eyes at her hand resting on his belly. Her knuckles were like a small spine that he had broken.

"I hoped it wasn't true." Anna looked down at her hand. "But I knew it was."

"'This living hand . . . would, if it were cold And in the icy silence of the tomb, So haunt thy days,'" Jordan recited reflexively, an inane diversion, "'and chill thy dreaming nights—'"

Anna slapped him hard on the cheek. "Save Keats for your next victim."

He jerked his head to his shoulder, shaking off the impulse to strike back. Her eyes burned in a way he'd never seen and he thought, That's hate.

She slid her legs to the floor and knelt to pick up her clothes.

"Let's talk about this. Don't walk out angry. I love you." Jordan stood up as she pulled her dress over her head. "I fucked her, but I wasn't unfaithful to you in my heart."

She started to speak then shut her lips in a scornful smile and walked toward the door.

Jordan cut her off and tried to hug her. "I love no one but you."

She turned her head away, stiff-arming his chest with one hand, and hurried outside.

Jordan dashed back to the sofa, pulled on his shorts and ran after her, taking the steps from the landing down to the street two at a time. The humidity was so thick, it was painful to breathe. The asphalt scorched his feet. He reached her as she got into her car. "Please, baby, come back in. Let's talk about this."

Anna closed the door and hit the electric lock.

"I'm sorry. Forgive me," Jordan shouted at the glass. "Wait."

Anna started the car, then looked at him. Her eyes were sad now, red and swollen, but her face was dry. The car rolled forward slowly. She mouthed a word: Why?

# Julai 8

Zanifa sat at a table on the terrace of the Green Valley with three other girls in St. Mary's uniforms. They all wore maroon skirts and matching wool sweaters tied at their shoulders over white long-sleeved blouses. They sipped bottled sodas from straws and leaned together shyly, surrounded by tables of men in worn dark suits and colorful shirts, traders waiting for cross-country buses parked in the lot outside.

Ernst saw her first, coming out of the bright sunlight into the shade of the terrace, his head nearly grazing the bamboo ceiling. He looked down at Jordan and said, "There's your girlfriend."

"She's too old for you, huh?" Jordan took a seat at a table by the door. "Your mind's so single tracked. I guess that's very African."

"Africans are just less hung up about sex." Ernst put his leather jacket on the back of a chair. "I'm not as perverse as you imagine. I don't seduce virgins."

"Never?"

"Once. In Holland. I was fifteen and a virgin myself." Ernst ordered two chicken and chips and coffees from the waitress, a young woman in a long white lab coat. "What good is a virgin?"

"That's a question that has undoubtedly perplexed philosophers for centuries." Jordan looked over Ernst's shoulder at the girls' table.

"Why waste the time when there are so many who already know what they want?" Ernst smiled. "Has she seen you yet?"

"No."

"You want only what you can't have," Ernst said.

"What?"

"You're surrounded by women, but you only want the one you can't have."

"I don't *want* her."

"Don't kid yourself. You're drunk with lust. Six months from the end of a two-year drought. She's a sexy little mulatto. And there is nothing more beautiful than a *mzungu*-African cross," Ernst said as the waitress set a thermos and cups on the little table. "Sometimes they have big identity crisis, you know. A foot in two cultures. Never at home in one. Ah, bwana, my own kids, *Yesu Kristo.*"

"Your kids are okay." Jordan poured milky coffee into the cups. "Your daughters are college graduates with responsible jobs in the West. What else is there to aspire to?"

"Henry is a mess. He quit university in Holland." Ernst heaped sugar in his coffee like an African. "He's on the dole. Spends all his time in rock clubs."

"That sounds pretty normal." Jordan watched Zanifa. "Some of her genes are *mzungu*, but she grew up like an African with no white faces in sight." He looked back at Ernst. "One of them saw us."

Ernst smiled. His teeth were as perfect as an African's. "Do you think you're attractive to a Tanzanian woman—other than as a rich *mzungu?*"

"What?"

"Do Tanzanian women find you physically attractive?"

"What?" Jordan saw that all the St. Mary's girls except Zanifa were stealing quick glances at their table.

"In your American opinion, do Tanzanian women—"

"I don't know." Jordan looked at Ernst. "I feel like I'm in high school."

"I think they're intrigued because you're a rich *mzungu.* I know the Peace Corps are the poorest paid volunteers in Africa, but those girls don't have a clue. Physically, hmm . . ." Ernst lowered his gaze slowly from Jordan's wild, sun-streaked hair and lean face down his patched and faded canvas hunting jacket. "Think of it this way, in America women find you attractive, but here you're just a skinny, funny-looking white face with hair like a girl."

"Good. That's what I feel like."

"You look sort of like a hawk," Ernst said as the waitress set two plates on the table.

"What?" Jordan said, staring across the room.

"Your nose is aquiline. Your face has lost all its baby fat. You're not a boy anymore."

"I've always wanted to know what it meant to 'come of age.'" Jordan poured gelatinous, unnaturally red Kenyan ketchup on his chips. "What does it mean—to become a man?"

"If you got to ask, you'll never know," Ernst said. "You look exhausted."

"All these farmers have seen their neighbors harvesting fifty kilos of fish every three months and suddenly they all want in on the good thing." Jordan groaned. "I thought I was going to cruise through the rest of my contract. Just paint and raise Pasipo. I'm working harder now than when I was a lawyer."

"But you're doing something good."

"Yeah," Jordan said. "But after a while that becomes meaningless, you know? Like, so what?"

"You're in a cynical period." Ernst grinned. "You're all bottled up."

Jordan looked across the room. "They're coming this way."

The St. Mary's girls wove through the tables, turning the heads of the men as they passed.

"Look at all those bastards undressing them with their eyes."

"Schoolgirls are popular because they're less likely to carry the plague," Ernst said.

"Halo, Mr. Jol-dan," the first girl said slowly in English.

Two of the girls giggled. Zanifa was behind them, out of sight.

"Hello, Subira," Jordan said. He heard a slight quiver in his voice but wasn't sure if it was audible to anyone else. "How's school going?"

"Very wheel," Subira said.

"*Kwa moyo . . .*" Jordan quoted their school's motto in Swahili and English as Zanifa pushed through to the table. "From the heart."

The girls all laughed.

"This is Bwana Van Liere," Jordan said in English, standing up, the tremor in his voice fainter. "Bwana Irrigation."

Ernst spoke to the girls in Sambaa. They started laughing hysterically. Jordan didn't understand a word. He waved to Zanifa. She smiled and waved back. She wore a blue ribbon in her hair. Ernst switched suddenly to English, "Would any of you like a soda?"

None of the girls replied.

"Don't be shy," Ernst said in Swahili. "Sit down."

The girls looked at each other.

"*Sisi sio mumiyani,*" Ernst said. We aren't vampires.

The girls giggled.

Zanifa looked at Jordan and then said to Ernst in a small voice, "Thank you, Mr. Van Liere. I would like a Pepsi."

Still sitting, Ernst pulled a chair from the table with his long arm.

"Come on, everyone," Zanifa said in Swahili.

One of the girls whispered to Zanifa. They talked for a moment quietly, then two of the girls left. Subira and Zanifa and Jordan sat down. Ernst called for the waitress, then spoke in Sambaa to Zanifa. She laughed and covered her mouth with one hand. He seemed to say the same thing to Subira. Her eyes widened and she looked at her hands.

"What's so funny?" Jordan asked.

"Bwana Irrigation asked if you look like a girl," Zanifa said.

The waitress appeared. There was a large wet gravy stain on her long white coat. Zanifa and Subira ordered Pepsi.

"Don't you think he needs a haircut?" Ernst said.

"I would like to have hair like his," Zanifa said. Subira nodded.

"There's not a decent barber in Lushoto," Jordan said.

"Go to Dar," Ernst said.

"Two hundred miles for a haircut?"

"Shave it," Ernst said.

The waitress returned with the sodas.

Ernst handed her the empty thermos. "Zanifa, I hear you're rehabbing an injured hawk."

"An augur buzzard." Zanifa pronounced the name perfectly now. "I think soon she will fly again."

"*Safi sana*," Ernst said. Very cool.

"Subira, what are you doing for your science project?" Jordan asked.

"Maize," she said softly.

"Maize?" Ernst said. "What are you doing with maize?"

"Experimenting with fertilizer," Subira almost whispered in Swahili.

"Very good," Ernst said in Swahili. "There's a future in agriculture."

Subira sipped through her straw.

Jordan stared at Zanifa's innocent face and wondered if she had touched herself in the night. If she knew what she was going to lose, she might try to resist, but even then her mother might force her to marry Kimweri. Would going through *jando* be more horrific if she knew what they were taking from her?

Zanifa looked at him, a trace of a smile on her closed lips. She bent forward and drank down a quarter of the bottle through the straw.

"Zanifa, what do you want to do with your life?" Ernst said.

She looked Ernst in the face. "I want to become a doctor."

"I've never heard an African girl say that," Ernst said. "That would be a fine thing."

"She can do it, too. She's very smart," Jordan said.

Subira whispered to Zanifa.

"We have to walk home before dark. It takes an hour." Zanifa rose from her chair. "Thank you for the soda, bwana."

"You're very welcome," Ernst said. "Father William wants me to take some girls on a tour of the irrigation project."

"Those are the seniors," Zanifa said. "Next year I'll be a senior."

"*Sawa*, next year."

"Bwana Jordan, I'll come by to feed Ophelia tomorrow afternoon." Zanifa smiled. Subira whispered her thanks and ran off the terrace into the sunshine.

"See you tomorrow," Jordan said.

"Good-bye." Zanifa hurried to catch up with Subira.

"Zanifa's more confident than the others," Ernst said.

"She knows me. She's not nervous around me," Jordan said.

"It's more than that."

"She's a big shot in her class because she's friends with a *mzungu*."

"That too." Ernst smiled. His blue eyes seemed to blaze. "She's ready. It happens to African girls overnight. From the time they are six they believe what their mothers tell them about being stricken by the spirits if they fuck a man. Then around fifteen or sixteen something happens. Usually an older sister tells them that it was all bullshit, that they're missing out on something really fun. The next day they're ready to try."

"How do you know this if you don't seduce virgins?"

"What do you think?" Ernst tilted his chair back on two legs. "I've lived with a lot of African women."

"I'm not going to seduce her." Jordan spoke quietly in English, nervous suddenly that someone might hear. "I'm going to try to talk to Kimweri."

"Be very diplomatic," Ernst said. "Don't underestimate the gap between your worlds. He doesn't see things the way you do, even with his English education."

# Julai 9

Waiting for the sultan to arrive, Jordan practiced his serve. The sky was drab. A gray pall, thousands of square miles in size, hung over East Africa. The dreary days of July, the beginning of winter.

In white warm-ups, Kimweri jogged up through the alley of jacaranda trees. The branches were bare, and rotting blooms dark as wet crepe paper were swept in piles around the trunks. "Awfully sorry," the sultan said. "I don't usually operate on such an African sense of time."

"*Hamna tabu,*" Jordan said, not returning Kimweri's smile. No problem.

They faced off on the baseline. Jordan dropped a ball and whacked it high to Kimweri's backhand. *Phwock!* Kimweri's return was caught by the net. *Phwack!* Jordan hit another ball. They batted the ball back and forth twenty times before Kimweri came casually to the net behind a shot that was obviously going to land long. Jordan dropped his racket as if he were letting it pass, watched Kimweri bend for a ball in the net, then returned the shot at the last moment with a flat, two-fisted backhand. *Phwack!* The ball bulleted over Kimweri's back. He stood up, glaring at Jordan.

"*Samahani,*" Jordan apologized. *That* was rational. *That* was real smart. "I was daydreaming."

*Phwack!* Jordan served the ball hard and flat, with no spin, deep into the corner, and followed the serve to the net. Kimweri's return came straight at him. Jordan calmly blocked it back. A puff of red clay burst a foot inside the baseline fifteen feet from the sultan.

"My set," Jordan said, bent over on his knees, breathing heavily. Kimweri was better than he thought. For the first time he had tried to beat him, and he had taken only one set. "We're even."

"So steady." Kimweri walked to the bench on the side of the court. "You've lost your recklessness. Last time you didn't care. Now you're playing to win."

Jordan picked up a towel from the bench and wiped his face. "You play to win. You play to lose. You just play."

"You lost me there," Kimweri said.

Jordan shrugged and walked out onto the court.

In the final set, neither Kimweri nor Jordan could break the other's serve. They played almost wordlessly, calling out the score in flat tones, communicating with their eyes when they switched sides or found themselves a few feet apart across the net. At six all Kimweri suggested a seven-point tiebreaker, but Jordan shook his head and they drove the score up to ten games apiece.

Jordan leaned against the fence behind the baseline, his body coated with sweat. The light had not changed in the last three hours under the gray dome. Fifty yards above, on the veranda of the Lawns, several *mzungu* guests with drinks in their hands looked down at the court. Jordan wondered how long they had been there and thought, If Kimweri loses, especially in front of the *mzungus*, he's going to be in no mood to talk about Zanifa. He called across the court, "This could go on till nightfall. Let's play a tiebreaker."

"No," Kimweri said. "We've come too far now."

"I've got to meet a man at a pond in an hour."

"This is Africa. He can wait."

Jordan lost the next game, trying to set up Kimweri's winners rather than deliberately hitting the balls long or in the net. Switching sides, Jordan noticed that Kimweri's white togs had turned pink from the dust. In the final game, with three match points against him, Jordan saw Kimweri hanging back behind the baseline. He served without power. Kimweri rushed in and threw back a deep lob. Letting it bounce, Jordan ran around his forehand and took the ball on its second descent with a backhand smash. *Phwack!* The ball angled fast across the court and landed just outside the baseline.

Kimweri stared at Jordan.

"I choked," Jordan said breathlessly.

For effect, he tossed a ball high and smashed it again, sending it arcing over the fence, and then walked painfully toward the center of the court. Beneath the scar tissue of the wound on his forearm, a muscle throbbed. Above, the *mzungu* guests on the veranda clapped as Jordan and Kimweri shook hands at the net.

"They see us as an emblem for the meeting of first and third worlds, of black and white." Kimweri smiled and waved up the hill. Red dust plated his arm. A waiter in a white coat and black pants came down the stone steps with a tray. Jordan found a jug of water on the bench by the gate and poured it over his head.

"To a memorable match." The sultan smiled and raised a mug.

"You played well." Jordan tapped a brown Safari bottle against the mug. He slumped in the canvas chair and gazed at the mountains.

*"Unayo shida gani, bwana? Nini inakula wehweh?"* Kimweri leaned forward in his chair and took Jordan's hand. His eyes were friendly. His hand was dry. Jordan's felt clammy. What's the problem? What's eating you?

"Julian, I heard that you're going to put Zanifa through *jando* before your wedding."

*"Haah."* Kimweri smiled faintly. "For generations the women of the Kilindi lineage have been initiated. They are happier than most women in the world. They carry on the traditions themselves. It's not for you to question, is it?"

"This is . . . the modern world," Jordan stammered. He pulled his hand away. "You're an educated man."

"Remember the rain magic?" Kimweri sat back. "You may not respect those forces, but I do. Historically, we are living in a crucial period. It would be an offense to my Kilindi ancestors and many of the elders to marry a girl who is unclean. The elders would never forgive me."

"Unclean?" Jordan inhaled slowly, straining against his anger.

"Come off it. *Jando* is an act of enslavement. Primitive. Dangerous. You're the one who should condemn the practice as an example for your tribe."

"You see the world through a prism of Western prejudice." Kimweri's voice was low and collected. "You're an alien, from another continent, from another world, for God's sake. You *mzungu* believe you will show us the path."

Leaning forward, Jordan said without venom, "Mutilation is mutilation."

"Your opinion, *mzungu*." The sultan smiled as if to a subject.

Jordan grasped Kimweri's right hand. "Don't do this to her."

"You've crossed the line here, chappie." Kimweri brushed Jordan's hand off his own.

Jordan thought it futile and risky to argue, but he couldn't stop now. He said in a calm voice, trying to sound offhand, "Can it be protested at the *boma?* It must be illegal."

"There is nothing in the least illegal about it." Kimweri shrugged.

Jordan hesitated. "What if I went to the newspapers?"

"No one will take you seriously. No one cares." Kimweri emptied a Safari bottle into his mug. His eyes were indecipherable, his voice carried a trace of contempt. "In the papers, I am a hero, I'm the great black hope."

"A difference of opinion, I guess." Jordan sank back in his chair, thinking, Kimweri might order Zanifa not to see you anymore. He could have you thrown out of the mountains or the country. Surely he wouldn't hurt you. Ionides has got to be over the top about that. "I can't help playing the American, you know, compelled to voice the imperialistic view."

Kimweri appraised him silently. He smiled and offered his hand. "I'm going to Dar tomorrow for a week or two. When I return we'll have dinner here and discuss the role of traditional practices in African culture."

Jordan took his hand. He was certain Kimweri would never change his mind.

ANNA VANISHED FROM MEMPHIS. JORDAN GUESSED SHE WAS AT ONE of her parents' summer homes, in the Cumberland Mountains or on the Florida Panhandle. When he called, only machines answered. On a Friday afternoon, five days after she'd run out of his apartment, he drove six hours across the Cumberland Plateau to Rugby, but the clapboard Victorian cottage was empty. He walked in the dark through a cemetery, looked at tombstones with small ceramic photographs of the dead, stumbled through the woods down to the Gentleman's Swimming Hole, where he saw a water moccasin in the moonlight in the middle of the river. He slept in his Wagoneer and on Saturday drove sixteen hours south to a hotel in Pensacola.

On Sunday morning he met Anna's parents dressed for church beside a white Mercedes station wagon in the driveway of their beach cottage.

"Good morning," Jordan said, trying to sound cheerful.

"Good morning." Their replies were not warm.

"What brings you down here, Rut?" asked Mrs. Demange. Her voice was polite and her eyes were cold.

"Fishing." Jordan tried to laugh but made a strange noise.

Mr. Demange opened a car door for his wife. She stepped into the Mercedes without saying good-bye. Mr. Demange shut the door. "Don't want to be late for the service."

"Where's Anna?" Jordan didn't want to ask him but couldn't stop himself.

"I can't reveal that, Counselor," Mr. Demange said, walking around the car. He was a tax lawyer who had asked Jordan to join his firm a few years before, an offer Anna had made him refuse. "But you're in the wrong state." Mr. Demange shut the door, and the Mercedes drove down an alley of live oaks draped with Spanish moss.

# Julai 10

"I hate shoes." Zanifa sat on the edge of the porch, peeling her white sneakers and white socks off her dark legs. She folded them carefully, then looked at Jordan. "Do you think she'll fly?"

"No," Jordan said. "Not on her first day out of the house."

"I think she'll fly." Zanifa walked out into the fenced yard of the rectory under a gray sky, barefoot in her school uniform with one hand in a welder's glove grasping a squirming chick. Jordan watched her from the porch, wondering if she had touched herself yet. Fifteen feet from Zanifa, the passard augur buzzard perched on a post in the yard, looking around and occasionally emitting a quizzical whistling note: *Peee-ooo.*

"It would be more humane to break the chick's neck instead of frightening it," Jordan called out from the porch.

"Humane?" Zanifa pronounced the word slowly. "Like human?"

"It's same root, I guess. Humane means compassionate."

"Come what?"

"Compassion. Kindness. Concern for other's pain," Jordan said. "C-o-m-p-a-s-s-i-o-n."

Zanifa repeated the letters, then said, "Comb-pash-own-ate."

"Perfect," Jordan said.

"Ophelia hasn't flown in a month." Zanifa gestured to the buzzard with her bare hand. "She might not fly to a dead chick. She likes them live."

Jordan spotted Omali in his lime coat, loitering outside the picket fence despite instructions to stay clear of the hawk training. He waved him away.

Zanifa shifted from foot to foot and braced the gloved arm with her left hand. Twelve minutes passed slowly on Jordan's watch. The yard was quiet. Occasionally a voice carried from the lane on the other side of the hedge.

"You didn't feed her this morning to quiet her, did you?" Zanifa glanced at Jordan accusingly.

"Of course not. I wanted to. She started screeching at dawn. Pasipo went berserk. It turned into a screaming match." Jordan sighed. "I was gone all day. Omali wouldn't feed her. He thinks it's a crime to give good meat to an animal. He might eat a piece of meat and *say* that he fed it to the hawk."

"Berserk?" Zanifa shifted her weight onto one hip.

"Violently crazy. *Kichaa sana.*"

*Kow-kow-kow!* The buzzard cried out.

"She's gotten used to the outside and she's hungry again," Jordan said.

Across the yard Omali peered around the corner of the ruined church. Jordan shouted, "Go home and come back at dark!"

The hawk almost fell off the post at Jordan's shout. He focused the binoculars on the glove. Terrified, eyes frozen on the raptor, the chick squirmed and peeped.

*Kow-kow-kow!* The hawk walked around on the post, tilting its red tail and slate black wings. Her throat was white, her breast ermine. She stared at Zanifa with brown eyes set in a black face.

"Ophelia," Zanifa called.

She opened her wings, revealing the white undersides, the three-foot span. *Kow-kow-kow!* She demanded her food. *Kow-kow-kow!*

Finally Ophelia leaped, flapped her wings unsteadily, and glided to Zanifa's fist. Ophelia ripped the head off the chick, swallowed it with her beak tipped to the sky, then devoured the body in small, rapid bites.

"Now what are you going to do?" Jordan called in Swahili.

"I am going to start hacking her right now," Zanifa said in English.

Jordan smiled at "hacking," the ancient falconry term for returning a bird to the wild. He'd never heard it spoken aloud.

Zanifa reached into the leather falconry bag and pulled out a chick. She dangled it in front of Ophelia. The hawk swiped at it with one claw. *Kow-kow-kow!*

"*Chukua mwinyewe.*" Zanifa held her gloved fist high over her shoulder as she bent to set the chick in the grass. Get it yourself.

The chick began to flee across the yard. Ophelia left the glove, swooped down and plucked it up off the grass with one claw. Jordan winced and noticed that Zanifa didn't. She was used to the summary execution of animals. Ophelia rowed up to an Ethiopian flame tree and parachuted through the leaves.

"*Safi,*" Zanifa pulled off the glove. Cool. "Ophelia can fly." She walked toward the porch. "The book says we must put food out for her until she stops coming back. Then she's hunting on her own."

"The sooner the better." Jordan laughed. "The bird food is breaking me."

Zanifa pulled another live chick out of the bag. She pitched it overhand like a baseball at the tree. Ophelia dove from the limb, caught the chick on the wing, and flew back to the tree. Zanifa came onto the porch and sat beside Jordan on a bench along the wall.

"You are a natural falconer," he said. "You'll be able to train hawks for Kimweri."

"I want a falcon." Zanifa swung her legs in and out from the bench.

"What kind?"

"A lanner."

"Why?"

"They're bigger than peregrines." Zanifa looked at Jordan. "I think they would be easier to train."

Jordan thought that she met his eyes more often now. "Yeah, a peregrine would be harder."

"I want a lanner eyas."

"Exactly. A nestling would imprint on you." Jordan tried to think of the best way to ask her.

"Like you and Pasipo." Zanifa crossed her legs and began swinging them again.

"Yeah. Listen, Zanifa . . ." Jordan was about to tell her that he had spoken to Kimweri yesterday but thought that might undermine his case. "You want a Sprite?"

"Please." Zanifa stood up. "I'll get it. You want one?"

"No thanks." Jordan thought, What are you trying to do? Kimweri's going to make her his toy, and there's nothing you can do.

"Will you help me look for a falcon nest?" Zanifa said, coming out of the house.

"*Bila shaka*," Jordan said. Without a doubt.

Zanifa sat on the bench. She sipped her Sprite and gazed at Ophelia, a shadow in the branches of the flame tree.

"Have you thought about what we talked about here the morning of Mzee Sechonge's funeral?"

Zanifa kept staring at Ophelia.

Jordan waited for her to speak.

She looked at him and back out at the hawk.

He asked softly in Swahili, "Have you touched yourself?"

She looked down at her hands holding the bottle and whispered, "Yes."

Jordan paused for a full minute. "Did you feel anything?"

Zanifa stayed still, her head bent down.

This is probably how a child molester starts off, Jordan thought.

Zanifa looked up at him. She was blushing, and her eyes were not afraid. She spoke in Swahili almost too low to hear. "The last two nights. Before I went to sleep. I touched myself. I felt very . . . warm . . ."

Jordan leaned closer to hear. He felt ashamed of himself for getting hard at the image of Zanifa lying naked.

"It's only natural." Jordan gently took one of her hands from the bottle. "That's the way your body gives you pleasure."

"Afterward . . ." Her face was no longer flushed. Her eyes were vaguely uneasy. "I had trouble falling asleep. I lay in bed a long time, thinking that I had done something bad."

"No. Nothing bad. That was good. You're learning about yourself. About the body that God gave you. Keep going. One night you'll feel something more and you'll be tired and happy afterward. You'll fall right asleep." Jordan stroked her hand. "You know, Zanifa, nowhere does the Bible or the Koran say women should go through *jando*. It's something man made up a long time ago. God wants you to keep your body the way it is."

Zanifa gazed up at him silently.

He smiled and let go of her hand and stood up.

Her eyes looked uncertain.

"*Hodi*," a voice called from the far side of the yard.

Jordan saw a girl in a St. Mary's uniform standing outside the picket fence.

"It's Subira." Zanifa moved to the porch rail.

"*Karibu*," Jordan called.

"*Asante*," Subira thanked him, and opened the gate.

"Does your mother think Subira is here with you all the time?" Jordan asked Zanifa.

"Yes." Zanifa pleaded, "Don't tell her that sometimes I'm here alone."

"Of course." He watched Subira come closer and thought Zanifa didn't want to share her *mzungu* friend with anyone. He asked Zanifa, "Does your friend have a boyfriend?"

"Subira has a boyfriend who is older. He goes to the University of Dar es Salaam," Zanifa whispered.

"So, has she, you know?"

Zanifa blushed and looked away. "Yes."

"Want a Sprite?" Jordan offered in Swahili as Subira stepped onto the porch.

"Not today, thanks," Subira said. "Come on, Zanifa. We're going to be late again."

"Look at Ophelia up in the tree!" Zanifa pointed across the yard.

"Cool," Subira said. "Let's go. I'm not in the mood for my father to beat me."

Zanifa grabbed her book bag on the floor by the bench. "I'll come by tomorrow after school to feed Ophelia."

"If she's still here," Jordan said.

"What?" Zanifa looked stricken by the thought.

"I'm sure she'll hang around for a few days. I mean, who would pass up free food?"

"Okay." Zanifa looked relieved.

*"Twende,"* Subira said again. Let's go.

Jordan watched them leave. At the edge of the yard they were hard to tell apart. He wondered if Ernst was right. If Zanifa was ready for the passage.

# Julai 11

Jordan kicked open the gate and rode into the rectory yard. The gray dome high above was drizzling. Thousands of feet lower, an obelisk-shaped cloud rose up behind the stone cottage, its top curling slowly over the tin roof. Jordan searched the trees in the yard but didn't see Ophelia. He climbed off the bike and lumbered into the house. After nine hours repairing a broken dike with a fish farmer, he was covered with mud and wanted only to shower and sleep.

The house was half-dark. He heated water in the kitchen on two kerosene burners. It had been weeks since the sun had shone long enough to use the solar heater on the roof. He saw Pasipo staring in through the screen door from the back porch. Talking to the eyas, he pulled off his clothes and left them in a bucket for Omali's wife.

*Quee-quee-quee!* Pasipo screamed when Jordan started to eat a banana.

"All right already." Jordan walked naked across the kitchen to the plastic container full of raw meat.

*Quee-quee-quee!*

"I hear you." Jordan carried the box out to the porch. The flat plains of the steppe stretched bleakly into nowhere. Below the cliff edge, tiers of ragged clouds floated in a narrow band along the sheer escarpment, rising slowly on a cold wind.

*Quee-quee-quee!* Pasipo leapt up to a padded leather perch on a pole that was nailed to the floor. She was nearly full grown, three feet tall from the tip of her tail feathers to her crown, her body covered with feathers and patches of down.

Jordan shivered in the wind and tossed a chicken leg at the perch.

Pasipo snatched it out of the air with one claw. She stripped the meat off the bone and dropped it on the floor. *Quee-quee-quee!*

Jordan threw a breast to her and dashed inside out of the cold. He filled a bucket with warm water and carried it to the bathroom. Standing on a stool, he poured the water into another bucket that hung from the ceiling. The water drained out in a weak shower from holes punched in the bottom of the bucket. Jordan lathered his hair and body quickly and finished rinsing off just as the bucket was empty. He wrapped a *kikoi* around his waist, pulled on a sweatshirt, and walked back to the kitchen.

Through the screen door he saw Pasipo had finished the breast. Her crop was swollen. She was quiet. Her eyelids slid slowly down her gray corneas and hung three-quarters closed for a few seconds before shutting completely. Then she appeared to have solid white, irisless eyeballs.

Jordan grabbed a handful of finger bananas and lay down on the couch. Zanifa would arrive in an hour or so. He wondered if it was right to encourage her sexual self-discovery and how much of his motivation to help her was selfless. Maybe he was helping her because he wanted to fuck her. But he hadn't and wouldn't. So he was sublimating his sexual instinct into a higher motive. A Freudian paradigm. He yawned and rolled flat on his back, which ached from shoveling dirt. Perhaps he should drop the whole thing before someone got hurt. He closed his eyes and a few moments later drifted off, one hand resting on the floor by a bottle of water.

Jordan dreamed he was in a big, old-fashioned sea plane, gliding low over a blue bay. He was talking to Garret Stoval about Anna. They were on their way to meet her and her husband, Truman Tharpe, and their baby. The plane was coming in to land. Jordan dove through an oval hatch into the shimmering sea. He landed unhurt in a few inches of water and looked up. Stoval stood shaking his head in the open hatch of the plane. Someone whispered and touched his shoulder.

"Bwana Joldan." Zanifa was kneeling on the floor, leaning over the edge of the sofa. "I'm going to feed Ophelia."

"*Sawa,*" Jordan said groggily. He saw she had her glove and falconry bag. "I'll be out in a minute."

"*Baadaye,*" Zanifa said. Later.

Through the windows Jordan watched her walk barefoot out in the middle of the yard and raise a chick in her gloved hand to the sky. Ophelia emerged from the flame tree and dove down to the glove. Jordan got up from the couch. From the kitchen door he saw Pasipo was asleep on her perch. Her round white eyelids made her look like a blind prophet. He found some bread and cheese in a cupboard and went back to the living room couch. Outside, Ophelia swam from Zanifa back to the flame tree.

"She wasn't very hungry," Zanifa said, coming in the door.

"She must have killed on her own. You better start jessing her to a perch between feedings or get used to the idea that she will leave soon."

"Ophelia can go." Zanifa set her falconry gear on the large table where she had built Pasipo's nest three and a half months ago. "At the end of term, I'll start looking for a falcon."

"You're lucky." Jordan was too tired to speak Swahili. "In most parts of the world raptors breed once a year, but they breed all the time in tropics."

"I read that, too." Zanifa smiled.

"Could you light the lanterns for me?" Jordan said, rubbing his temples.

"It won't be night for two hours."

"Yeah, but it's so dark in here already." He yawned. "And I'm afraid I'll fall asleep and wake up when it's pitch black."

"You're working too hard," Zanifa said. She moved around the house, lighting hurricane lamps and opening windows to let out the kerosene fumes.

Jordan closed his eyes. He thought he could sleep right through to morning. Two more ponds. Measure. Dig. Stock. The fish pond rush was finally slowing down. Tomorrow he had to leave before dawn to reach Mlalo by noon and make it home by nightfall. Bwana Rajabu had better be there on time. And sober. Jordan wavered on the edge of consciousness, wanting to talk to Zanifa but wanting more to sleep for thirteen hours.

"Get up, bwana." Zanifa woke him, pulling him by the shoulders. "There're too many mosquitoes this time of year. You must sleep under your net."

"I'm okay." Jordan rolled away from her.

"No, bwana." Zanifa pulled his arm out from the sofa and tugged hard. "Come on."

"All right. I'm coming," Jordan said irritably. Very slowly he stood up from the sofa, then he let his legs carry him quickly through a door into a darker room. He dove on a bedspread sewn from matching *kangas.*

Zanifa loosened the mosquito net, which hung in a big knot over the center of the bed.

Jordan cleared his throat. "I was thinking of talking to your mother. I want to tell her that I will send you to school in Kenya and college in the States if you would rather become a doctor than marry Kimweri."

Zanifa tucked the net under the mattress at the foot of the bed. She moved around to one side and looked at him. "No, bwana, she won't listen. She wouldn't want me to go away. She wouldn't even let me room at St. Mary's when Father William said I could stay for free."

"Maybe if I talked to her." Jordan yawned. "If you went to good schools and became a doctor, you would be rich one day. You could take care of her. Buy her a house and a Land Rover."

Tucking the net along the side, Zanifa shook her head. "It is her dream for me to marry Sultani Kimweri. If you talk to her, she'll stop me from coming here. Your ideas will scare her."

"Don't you want to go to America? Don't you want to go to the places you've seen in magazines?" Jordan sighed. "If you marry Kimweri, you will never leave here. You're too smart for that. It would be a waste. You're the best student in your class—"

"Second best." Zanifa pulled the net behind the headboard. "There is a Chagga girl who always beats me. The Chagga are smarter than the Sambaa."

"Zanifa, listen to me. I'm offering you the chance for a first-class education. I'll bet the Chagga girl would go, don't you?"

Zanifa walked around the bed. "Yes. She wants to study in Europe."

"Do you love Kimweri?"

"I don't know. He's okay. He has only visited me a few times." She began closing the net along the open side. "I went once to his house. But he talks mostly to my mother."

"In the modern world, girls don't have to marry the men that their parents pick for them." Jordan thought she was much more collected than when they had met. "You don't have to marry someone if you want to do something better."

"Every night I lie in bed thinking about leaving," Zanifa said. "I don't know. My mother would be very angry."

Jordan realized Zanifa saw her own situation so clearly because she had grown up an outcast, never truly a part of clan and village, an outsider looking in. "Your mother will get over it. She'll always be your mother. If you take care of her, she would love you again. You can give her a better life than she would have as one of Kimweri's mothers-in-law."

"I hadn't thought of that." Zanifa stood in a narrow opening left between the net and the headboard.

"I need to get some water." Jordan crawled toward the gap in the net.

"*Pumzika tu*," Zanifa ordered, moving for the door. Rest only.

Jordan propped a pillow against the headboard and leaned against it. He heard her talking to Pasipo from the kitchen. Leave her alone. Let her walk out of here. He felt wide awake now.

Zanifa glided through the shadows to the bedside and set a tray on the nightstand. She poured him a glass of cordial from a pitcher. "You'll have to brush your teeth."

"Right." Jordan reached through the gap for the glass. "Thanks."

Zanifa filled a glass and took a sip.

"*Karibu ka.*" Jordan patted the bedspread with one hand. Welcome to sit.

Zanifa looked around the room, but there were no chairs. Turning to Jordan, she blushed and looked away.

Welcome inside, Jordan said, handing her his empty glass. *"Karibu ndhani."*

She put down his glass and slid onto the bed. The net shifted in a damp wind that came in through a window facing the cliff. Zanifa sat with her back to the net, her legs stretched out across the bed.

"Did you touch yourself again?" Jordan said.

Zanifa nodded. She drank from her glass.

"How did you feel?"

"It was like the night before," Zanifa whispered in Swahili, looking at Jordan with an earnest expression as if talking to a teacher. "Except then my *kisimi* hurt and I was worried that God was punishing me for doing that."

"No. God would never do that. He gave it to you for your own pleasure," Jordan said slowly, picking up the role. "Maybe you were touching yourself too hard. You have to be gentle. I should teach you."

Zanifa laughed. "How could you teach me?"

"I could touch you and show you how good you can feel."

Zanifa's face was suddenly uneasy. She looked through the net.

A wisp of cloud flowed in from the window facing the cliffs and passed through the half-light of the room and out the window into the front yard.

"That's so beautiful, isn't it?"

Zanifa nodded.

Jordan wondered if she had a sense of the beauty of the mountains. She would appreciate them if she ever left. He took the empty glass from her hand and leaned over her shoulder, setting it on the tray.

"I think I should teach you." Jordan placed his hand above her knee.

Zanifa jerked slightly and looked at him with uncertain eyes.

"You need to know what you are going to lose." He dragged the hem of the maroon skirt slowly up her legs.

Zanifa placed her hand on his. "What are you doing, bwana?"

"You know that I am your friend. I'll never do anything to hurt you. I'll always help you. I'll always be your friend."

On his knees Jordan backed toward the foot of the bed. He looked up at her as if praying. Her face was blank. Her eyes kept moving from his face to the window.

"There's nothing to worry about. I'm just going to touch you."

Zanifa sat perfectly still, looking at him fearfully.

Jordan smiled warmly. He slowly lifted her skirt. Zanifa's skin grew lighter, more luminous nearing her white cotton panties, in contrast with the deeper hues of her calves. Jordan could hear her breathing above. Slowly he reached up and pulled down the elastic band of her panties. Zanifa grabbed his hand.

"No, bwana."

"Don't be afraid," Jordan said softly. "I am not going to hurt you. I'm just teaching you."

"No, bwana." Zanifa gripped his hand tightly but didn't push it away.

"Don't be afraid." Jordan's face was tender, his brow furrowed with concern. He put his arm around her shoulders and pulled her gently down on the bedspread. Lying alongside her, Jordan stroked her hair. "This is something you should learn before you make up your mind."

Zanifa did not reply.

Jordan thought she was torn between staying and going. He inched the panties down her legs and pulled them free of her feet. Her toes and soles were thick and callused from years of going barefoot. The skin of her legs was smooth and hairless. He turned toward her.

Her eyes were frightened, her face flushed. She pushed her skirt back to her knees, clenching the hem in her fists.

"It's okay. You're okay." Jordan balled his hands over hers and lifted them until she held the hem at her waist. Where her legs came together there was no hair, only a smooth chevron lighter than the surrounding skin. Jordan remembered Ernst telling him that Sambaa women shaved this at the onset of puberty.

*"Bora kama lulu,"* Jordan quoted a Swahili expression. Beautiful as a pearl.

Zanifa looked ashamed at her nakedness.

Jordan let go of her hands.

She did not move. Her hands bunched the folds of her skirt at her waist.

"I'm not going to take your virginity," Jordan said. "You have nothing to—"

"Please, bwana, no." Her voice was diminished by fear. "Another day. You shall teach me another day."

"I'm not going to rape you," Jordan said so that he would believe it himself. He was hard beneath his *kikoi* and possessed by the desire to unbutton her shirt. He stroked her face. "It's okay."

"You shall teach me another day." She laughed nervously.

"No. If I can't make you change your mind, you will enter *jando* and then it will be too late. It must be today." Jordan tried to pry her legs apart. "Relax," he repeated in Swahili. *Stareyheh.* Silently he caressed her face. "I am your friend. I'll always be your friend. I'm just going to touch you the way you have been touching yourself."

Zanifa let her arms fall to her sides and stared at the round disk at the peak of the net.

She'd decided to go on, Jordan thought. She was crossing the threshold. He moved her legs slowly apart and stared at the naked vulva. He kissed the inside of her leg, planted his mouth and ran his tongue along two small petals of flesh. He pushed his tongue gradually inside then out again. His tongue returned to her clitoris, swollen now. He cupped his hand around her and slid one finger in tenderly, listening as the rhythm of her breathing deepened. He pushed his finger inside, deeper, but came up against the veil of tissue he had never felt before. Propped up on his elbows, he lay between her legs. He kept his mouth on her for a long time, until his neck was starting to hurt. Then her breathing quickened, rising higher in her throat. His breath paced itself with hers. Zanifa drew her knees up slightly. Her mouth was open, her eyes rolled toward her forehead.

His mouth still on her, Jordan reached down and began to fumble with the waist of his *kikoi*. Her rapid breaths turned into long sighs. He gave up trying to untie his wrap and focused on touching her lightly with his tongue. Zanifa cried out as if in pain. He stopped, but her face appeared swept away. He put his mouth on her. His chin was wet. She took long, halting breaths, then cried out and pushed his head away. He sat back and stroked her legs. She held one hand between her legs and looked at his face, seeming not to see him.

"You were close, but you didn't feel it," Jordan said softly in Swahili. "It can be much better. Touch yourself again."

"I must run. Subira will be here anytime."

Zanifa pulled on her panties. Tears formed in the corners of her eyes. She crawled off the bed.

Jordan wanted to pull her back inside and hold her tight. "I'll walk you to the door."

"No, I . . . I," Zanifa stuttered, tucking the gap shut. "I'm rushing to meet her outside the gate." She moved through the shadows.

"*Nenda salaama,*" Jordan said. Go peacefully.

"*Kwa heri,*" Zanifa said. My blessings.

Jordan lay down. The room was darker. His skin felt damp from the clouds. He wiped his hand across the bottom of his face and licked the tips of his fingers, then slipped his hand through the folds of his *kikoi.*

Jordan stood in his office, staring at the window, studying Harbor Town with a pair of binoculars.

"Stop looking at that fucking house," Vernon Taylor's voice came from the doorway.

Jordan set down the binoculars. "I just can't concentrate."

"You've been sulking around here for two weeks now. It's pitiful." Vernon shook his head with impatient sympathy.

"I don't even know where she is."

"Put her behind you. She's not the kind to come back."

"Wrong answer." Jordan slumped into his chair.

"You'll hear from her and you'll convince her to take you back," Vernon said so lacklusterly, he actually blushed. "You're a persuasive devil."

"That's . . . better."

"You'll live happily ever after," Vernon said over his shoulder. "You've got some time coming. Go off and paint or something."

Jordan picked up the binoculars and turned back to the window. His secretary's voice came over the intercom: "Miss Demange on line three."

Jordan's heart started pounding. He picked up the phone. "Anna— God, I've been crazy. Where are you?"

"Hey, Rutledge." Her voice was tired.

Jordan waited for her to say more. She didn't. He said, "I've missed you so much. Oh, baby, I'm sorry. I'm sorry I did it. I'm sorry I lied. I won't do that again. Any of it. I don't know why I would have done anything to jeopardize what we have."

Anna was silent.

"Where are you?"

"San Francisco. I get in on Northwest tomorrow at three. Can you pick me up?"

"Sure. Of course, baby."

"Bring my bike and my books and anything else of mine in your apartment. I want this over as fast as possible."

She hung up.

# Julai 12

Jordan sat on the front porch, staring at the ruined church under a gray sky. A boy ran by the gap in the hedge, rolling a barrel ring along the lane with a stick. Jordan tried to read an old *Newsweek* but kept looking up at the gate. Women in kangas, returning from the fields, walked down the road with hoes and baskets, trailed by their children. Jordan checked his watch: Zanifa was an hour late.

An hour before dawn, Jordan had woken with a clear head. He had rushed through oatmeal and tea and then jumped on his motorcycle. He had ridden across the mountains at a manic speed, determined to cut an hour off each leg of the trip so he could return in time to see Zanifa. The day had passed smoothly, with none of the typical delays. Jordan had seemed fated to make it home in time. Rajabu had been sober and waiting at a crossroads shack café an hour early. The site Rajabu had chosen near a stream was perfect for a pond, and he'd quickly grasped Jordan's instructions. It had taken only fifteen minutes to stake the perimeter. Rajabu had moved the first hundred of fifty thousand shovelfuls of earth before Jordan had finished packing his equipment on the rear rack. The road had been dry, and Jordan had arrived home a half hour before Zanifa was expected.

Now Jordan's body tingled with a distinct feeling of anticipation he remembered from the moments when he was about to see Anna in the times when they had been in love off and on through eight years.

It's only chemicals in your brain, he thought, all the ephemeral emotions of love.

Jordan threw the magazine on the bench. He imagined defending himself in front of a jury and argued that in Tanzania a sixteen-year-old girl was of marriageable age. She was therefore an adult. Their mild sexual encounter had been consensual. Further, he had acted in her best interests. . . . He walked inside to get his short-wave radio, meaning to pass the time by listening to the BBC, and returned to the porch just as a girl in a St. Mary's uniform, carrying a basket, came through the gap in the hedge. He felt a surge of excitement, then his spirits sank when he realized the girl was not Zanifa.

"*Jambo, Bwana* Joldon," the girl called halfway across the stone path to the gate.

"Hello, Subira," Jordan said.

"Zanifa was busy at school. She asked me to bring your chickens today." Subira set the basket on the porch and backed away.

Jordan looked at the basket and then at Subira. "She never misses a chance to feed Ophelia. What's she doing?"

Subira hesitated. "She had to stay late to make up the day she lost because of Mzee Sechonge's funeral."

Jordan wondered if that was the truth. He picked up the basket. "Do you want to come inside and see the eagle?"

"I have to hurry home to carry water." Subira wrung her hands.

"Okay. Let me put the chicks in the coop." Jordan took the basket around the house. Subira was clearly scared of him. When he returned with the basket to the front yard, she was waiting outside the gate.

# Julai 15

Jordan sang "I Can't Get No Satisfaction" above the whine of the Honda engine at the end of a long day delivering minnows to several new ponds scattered across the mountains. Last month he would have been thrilled that his work had not been in vain. After a year and a half, fish farming was finally catching on in his territory. But Jordan felt nothing. Zanifa had not come for three days. He worried that he had scared her off. He wanted more than anything to see her again. Jordan turned onto the lane that led to the rectory, thinking the events of his life had always seemed without order. Now, as he neared thirty, the years composed a clear line. As a boy he had marveled when his grandfather referred to the football championship of '36 or the drought of '59, baffled how the old man could so readily distinguish one year from the next. Perhaps his grandfather had delineated the chaos of his life on his solitary binges in the marsh. Now Jordan, too, could fix the date of the memories that had surfaced in the solitude.

Stopping by the fence to kick open the gate, he saw Zanifa in her uniform. Ophelia fed from her glove.

Jordan rolled to a stop by the porch, unsure of what to say.

Zanifa smiled. "You're late."

"I didn't think you would come." Jordan climbed off the bike and dropped his rucksack, wet and heavy with fish, from his back to the ground.

"I didn't know if I . . ." Zanifa looked from the bird to Jordan. "I didn't know what I wanted."

Jordan waited for her to say more. "How'd you get in the house?"

"I saw where you hide the key." Zanifa smiled impishly.

"With that smile you could get away with anything," Jordan said.

The augur lifted her wings and shifted on the glove.

"You came to feed Ophelia?"

"Yeah." Zanifa braced her gloved arm with her bare hand. "I wanted to feed her."

"You've totally tamed her. She doesn't want to go back to the wild." Jordan told himself it was wrong to push her further and moved toward the porch.

"I wanted to see you," Zanifa whispered shyly to his back.

Jordan stopped and turned around slowly.

She murmured, "Teach me again."

"You sweet, beautiful girl." He reached out and grazed his fingers along the line of her cheek. "Let me take a shower. I'm filthy."

Jordan came into the bedroom. He was bare chested and wore a green *kikoi* wrapped around his waist. His hair was plastered flat from his forehead down his neck to his back.

"You look like a white woman." Zanifa giggled. She was sitting cross-legged on the bed beneath the mosquito net.

"Even without breasts?" Jordan said, looking into his closet.

Zanifa laughed.

Jordan pulled on a sweatshirt and crawled onto the bed through a gap in the net. He stretched out and looked up at Zanifa. Her eyes looked uneasy but not scared. He whispered, "Lie down with me for a minute. I need to lie still."

Zanifa set her head on his chest. They lay quietly, Jordan running his fingers through her hair. She clasped his sides lightly, like a child. Jordan closed his eyes. His mind drifted without thought, and he felt a rare sense of serenity. After a long time he shifted her gently from his chest to the bed. He ran his hand down her neck and along her arm to her waist. Her eyes were shut, her hands clenched tight. He pushed her skirt to her waist. She was naked. Jordan planted his mouth, felt she was already wet. Lying between her legs, he lifted her thighs gently. She pulled up her knees. Her breathing quickened. She raked her fingers through his hair. Jordan lifted his head, watched her dreamy look, and went on. She sat up and cupped her hands around his neck. Her breath came in warm gusts through his hair.

"Stop." She pushed him away. "Stop. It hurts."

"What?" Jordan wiped his mouth.

Zanifa pushed her skirt down. "It hurts—I don't . . . I don't know."

"It's okay." Jordan sat up. He lay down beside her and pulled her head back to his chest. "We've got to go slowly."

Zanifa was silent. She clasped his sides lightly.

Jordan was hard and unable to lie still. "Do you want to feed Pasipo?"

"Okay," she said in English.

They climbed off the bed and brushed their skirts down to their knees. Jordan followed Zanifa through the house.

"I don't know if I can still hold her, she's so big now." Zanifa pulled on her glove in the kitchen.

"It's got to be easier than putting a five-gallon bucket of water on your head." Jordan handed her a fish from the rucksack.

"That's true." Zanifa laughed and went through the screen door.

*Quee-quee-quee!* Pasipo screamed and flew from her perch across the room, knocking over Jordan's easel. She glanced off the latticework screening one end of the porch and landed in a clump in a corner. *Quee-quee-quee!*

Zanifa held out her arm and flopped the fish back and forth in the glove.

Pasipo hopped across the porch, her talons sliding across the floor between leaps. She slid to a stop near Zanifa. She stood as tall as Zanifa's waist and looked up at her face. *Quee-quee-quee!*

*"Njoo."* Zanifa told her to come. She spoke to hawks only in Swahili.

Pasipo jumped to the glove and tore off the head of the fish. Zanifa backed up to the stone wall of the cottage. She leaned against it, bracing the elbow of her gloved arm against the nine pounds of the young eagle. Jordan had read stories of eyas raptors, severed from their genitors and raised unnaturally, suddenly turning on their surrogate parents. Pasipo looked as though she could rip your face off your head.

"What is America like?" Zanifa looked across the porch at Jordan.

"You want to go?"

"Everybody wants to go." Zanifa bent down, reaching into the rucksack for another fish.

"To the land where everyone is rich?"

"Yeah." Zanifa dangled the fish in front of Pasipo's beak.

"It's not like that." Jordan looked out over the steppe at a line of peaks growing distinct on the horizon in the late light. "It was a beautiful country once. But the *mzungu* killed the great herds of animals, cut the forests, poisoned the rivers. Now the people aren't as happy as the people in the villages here. You don't want to live there."

Zanifa set Pasipo on the perch nailed to the floor of the porch. "Then why are you going back?"

Jordan hesitated. "I don't know."

# Julai 23

Beneath the net, in the afternoon shadows, Jordan moved his tongue slowly. Zanifa cried out as if in pain. Jordan looked across her taut belly, the rise of her breasts. She was staring at the top of the net, taking long, rasping breaths. She cupped her small hands behind his ears and pulled his mouth down into her. She began to moan each time she exhaled then gasped to fill her lungs. She bunched his hair in her fists, squeezed his face with her smooth thighs and moaned louder. She screamed and pushed his head away.

Jordan rose up on his arms and whispered, "Are you okay?"

Zanifa lifted his chin with one hand. She looked in his eyes and opened her mouth to speak but said nothing. She took a few last deep breaths. "Every time before I felt good, but then it began to hurt and I got scared." Her eyes were different—softer than he had seen them before. "Today when the pain came, I didn't make you stop. Then the pain changed into something bigger." The corners of her mouth lifted in a soft smile. Her face was dreamy.

Jordan pulled himself up beside her and held her against his chest. He smiled back at her, happy that he had given her something. "It's called an orgasm."

"Orgasm," Zanifa said slowly. "Orgasm. I don't know the word in Swahili."

"There is no Swahili word for a woman's."

JORDAN SAT BY THE GATE, WAITING FOR ANNA'S PLANE. THE night she'd run off, he had made a list of his infidelities over the last three years and taped it on his refrigerator. Seven women on nine separate occasions. He'd rationalized that he would stop whenever they got married. Taylor and Stoval had urged him not to confess anything, and a therapist had told him that it was a sign of maturity to know what not to tell to one's mate in order to avoid hurting her, but he wasn't sure. Maybe if he told her everything, he would be absolved by the pain, both of theirs, and they could begin again.

He watched the travelers moving along the concourse and thought that he was by no means the most promiscuous of his friends. He remembered a drunken exchange at a wedding reception between two brokers—one the groom—about their last trip to a whorehouse across the river. His own infidelity was mild by comparison. A few junctures of lust, boredom, alcohol and weakness. In the worst moments of guilt, Jordan was afraid that he would become a chronic philanderer like his grandfather, who had abandoned his wife and sons for a rich woman in the Depression and who, after his second marriage, had an illegitimate daughter by his secretary. Jordan had seen this half-aunt only once, during college, when he had come from Nashville to Memphis to see his grandfather on his deathbed in the house of his second wife, Pauline, a sparrow-size woman in her seventies who still possessed a smooth, pretty face. Pauline had served him a Coke in the dark, musty front room of her Victorian home in the garden district. Through the window they had silently watched a pickup pull into the drive behind Pauline's white Cadillac. The back of the truck had been full of dirty kids in T-shirts and jeans. At first Jordan had thought they'd come to mow the yard. Pauline had gone out onto the porch and talked to a young woman about his age. In his memory the woman was dressed in overalls, but surely that wasn't true. Pauline had given her money and then come back in and told him the woman was Pat, his half-aunt. No one ever told him Pat's last name. Jordan's father's reaction to the desertion was to become a devout Episcopalian and devoted husband. Jordan was sure he had never cheated on his mother, though Jordan had heard from one of his father's high school friends that he had "sown his share of oats."

Outside in the brilliant light, a Northwest airliner drew up slowly to the gate. Anna was one of the last passengers to come through the door. She had a dark tan, was wearing black leggings, a white shirt and a linen blazer. She saw him and her face wavered between smiling and crying, then her eyes hardened and she bit her lip. Jordan rushed up and hugged her, and she pushed him away.

"God, it's so good to see you." Jordan took her bag.

"Did you bring all my stuff?" she asked, walking briskly.

"It's in the car."

"The only reason I asked you to pick me up is to get my things. It's over, Rutledge. I can't trust you."

Her words caught him by surprise, though they were not unexpected. "I didn't know what I was doing. It wasn't serious—the girls didn't mean anything." Jordan realized what he'd said too late, or perhaps he had meant to say it. "Most of the men in Memphis have betrayed their wives. Everyone makes mistakes."

"Girls?" Anna stopped. "I knew there were others. I just never wanted to believe it. How many?"

"Seven," Jordan said. "Now you know everything."

Anna looked as though she were going to throw up.

"I was drunk——"

"That's comforting to know." She took a deep breath and walked on.

"Anna, you don't know how sorry I am that I hurt you." Jordan was starting to cry. "You don't know what torture I've been going through. It's changed me. I'll never do it again. I swear."

"Rut—this is the deal. It's real simple: One of us tells the truth, the other's a liar. How can I believe a word you say?" Her eyebrows were raised in fury. She looked as if she would slap him, then started down the concourse.

"I'll never lie to you again." Jordan hurried alongside her. "I love you."

"Who needs love like yours?"

"Goddamn it, we've been very happy. We can be happy again."

"I was happy with someone else. Not you. You're not who I thought you were."

"I am deep down. I was just following my worst instincts," Jordan said, going down a set of stairs to the baggage claim.

"Why don't you go get the car?" Anna said, walking away from him.

"So how was San Francisco? Madeline and Melanie still out there?" Jordan asked, driving out of the airport.

"Can we not talk?" Anna glared at him, then turned to look out the window.

They rode in silence for fifteen minutes past the strip malls, the Defense Depot, the Liberty Bowl and into the tall trees and mansions of midtown, Jordan remembering the last time they'd driven from the airport after a week in Mexico. He turned onto Vinton and pulled up into the driveway of a stucco Spanish bungalow.

"Please put the bike in the garage," Anna said, sliding out of the car. She crossed the yard and went in the front door. Jordan opened the back of the Wagoneer and lifted her Stumpjumper and rolled it into the garage, squeezing past her Saab, and placed the bike against the back wall. He took a box of books and clothes out of the car and brought them inside. The house was hot and stuffy.

Anna sat on a big sofa with white cotton slipcovers, sorting through a pile of mail on a glass table. A ceiling fan whirred overhead, stirring the papers.

"Just put 'em down." Anna looked up. "Thanks, Rutledge. I really want you to leave me alone for a while. I've got to go over to my mother's now. So . . . I'll see you around."

"I love you, Anna, more than I've ever loved anyone. The mess I've made is killing me." Jordan set down the boxes and moved toward her.

There were other girls he could turn to, but he didn't want anyone else. He wanted another chance. He believed he could be faithful to her now. "Oh, God, I love you." He dropped onto the sofa beside her. "I'll go. Just let me hold you for a second."

Anna's face softened as her eyes reflected his pain. She reached her arms out and Jordan leaned against her, holding on tight. He began to cry against her shoulder. She stroked the back of his head and said resignedly, "You're such a self-absorbed bastard."

"I'm sorry," Jordan said, pulling his head back to look in her deep brown eyes. There were tears on her face. "I can start over."

"Sorry only goes so far."

Jordan put his mouth on hers, felt tears smearing on their faces. She took his tongue. He covered her face and neck with kisses, started opening her shirt, moving his lips down as each button popped loose.

Suddenly she stiffened and pushed him back by the shoulders.

"Get out of here now." Her voice rasped between sobs. Then she screamed, "Get out!"

# Agosti 21

Standing inside the screen door, Zanifa and Jordan could see Pasipo waddle across the back porch. The sky leopard's coat of feathers was fully grown. Her wings and head were black, her chest a snowy white.

"The book says she won't get her orange and black feathers for four years," Zanifa said.

"You'll be a sophomore in college by then." Jordan pushed back the collar of Zanifa's white blouse and tasted the sweat and smell of woodsmoke on her shoulder. She unbuttoned his denim shirt. The undersides of her slender fingers were inked with thin arabesques of henna. He unsnapped her blue school skirt and pushed it over her hips. She slipped off her blouse.

"God made you so perfectly."

"You don't think my bottom is too small?" Zanifa asked in Swahili.

"No. It's perfect the way it is." Looking at his reflection in her black eyes, he carried her out to the back porch. He murmured, "Why don't Africans kiss?"

Zanifa jabbed her tongue in and out of his mouth. She flopped her head back in his arms and laughed.

"You think this is a game?" Jordan knelt and laid her on a cotton futon.

Zanifa grinned and pulled him down beside her. She kissed him hard on the mouth.

"Softer. Try to kiss softer. Like this." Jordan brushed his lips against hers, touched his tongue to hers.

"A mouth must be the softest thing in the world," Zanifa said. She kissed him lightly, then guided his shoulders down her belly.

"Don't be in such a hurry." Jordan chuckled.

She pushed his shoulders down harder, for the first time eager.

When he put his mouth on her she opened her legs wider and sighed. Jordan settled comfortably on his arms. Two days ago she was uneasy, and it took an hour of cuddling her and caressing her with his fingers and mouth to make her come. For a month Jordan had kept his promise not to take her virginity. Every Monday, Wednesday, and Friday, when Zanifa delivered chickens or stopped by to take notes on Pasipo and Ophelia, Jordan woke at dawn high-spirited and the hours passed quickly on his rounds to the ponds. Time streaked along while painting cloudscapes off the cliff or drinking with Ionides in the bar of the Lawns. On the days she didn't visit, Jordan brooded and followed his routine under the gray winter sky and began to indulge in fantasies of fucking a virgin and memories of Anna that filled him with longing.

After a few minutes Zanifa began to rake his scalp. Her legs started quivering. Jordan was surprised by the speed she was approaching climax. Already he felt a premonition of melancholy—soon she would leap up and scamper over to her clothes, afraid of being late returning to the village. She moaned and pressed his face with her thighs. She was suddenly quiet and her tense body went slack. Jordan crawled up beside her. She laid her head on his chest.

"I'm happy you taught me this," she said in Swahili.

Jordan smiled and smoothed a curl of black hair out of her eyes.

"That thing scares me." Zanifa touched him through the *kikoi.* "Do you want to put it in me?"

"Yes, but I'm not going to. It's not right."

"Why not?"

"Because you should stay a virgin."

"Why?"

"Because you should save that for someone you might marry."

"For Bwana Kimweri?"

"If that's who you choose," Jordan said. The fantasy, the few pleasant minutes in the long, lonely day, vanished. Jordan felt slapped in the face by the facts. She would be a pretty decoration at his palace, a sex slave who would be young and beautiful for years. She would entertain guests with her hawks.

"Your face is sad." Zanifa rubbed her nose against his.

"I was thinking about you giving up your life for Kimweri." Jordan hugged her.

She moved her hand slowly, feeling the shape of his *mboro* through the cotton. "Sometimes it's soft. Now it's very hard."

"It's excited." Jordan felt himself blushing.

"Why?"

"From touching you. Because you're so beautiful."

"Sometimes you rub yourself like this when you are touching me." Zanifa smiled.

"That feels very nice." Jordan closed his eyes.

"On Wednesday there was a wet spot on your *kikoi* when we finished."

Jordan opened his eyes and saw Zanifa was looking down at her hand.

"Was that pee?"

"No."

"That was semen?"

"Yes."

"You had an orgasm?"

"Yes." Jordan laughed. "I feel like a biology teacher."

Zanifa looked at him solemnly, then untied his *kikoi* and pushed back the folds. She reached for his *mboro* carefully, as if picking up a nestling. "It's very ugly."

Jordan laughed. "I thought so when I was your age. It doesn't bother me now."

Zanifa started rubbing him.

"Ow! That's too hard!"

"Sorry." Zanifa laughed. "Do American girls do this?"

"Uh-huh." Jordan placed his hand on hers and moved it slowly. "American girls put their mouths on it."

Zanifa puckered her face in distaste. "Really?"

"Like I do for you."

He felt the heat gathering and watched Zanifa's face as she touched him. The tip of her tongue stuck out of the corner of her mouth. He moaned. For a moment he could be anywhere. Zanifa's jaw dropped and her eyes widened at the sight of spurts of come arcing through the air.

"That's the semen?" Zanifa whispered.

"Right." Jordan felt sad and sort of dirty. "Class dismissed."

Zanifa leapt up and looked at Pasipo on her perch, gazing out over the cliff.

"*Kwa heri, Pasipo.*" Zanifa said good-bye. Pasipo turned her head at the sound of her name. Zanifa ran in through the screen door and picked up her skirt. Jordan shook out her blouse and slipped it onto her arms. Dressed, she seemed a different person, younger, a school-girl again.

Zanifa's eyes filled with worry.

"Now you look sad." Jordan wondered if she could take any strength away from here to face her mother and Kimweri.

Zanifa stepped in close and held his sides with her small hands.

"Don't be scared." Jordan rocked her. "Be brave."

# Agosti 23

Outside at dawn, dark fog lay over the lawn, obscuring the ruin except for the steeple, which jutted up through the grayness like the mast of a ghost ship. Omali was hunkering on the front porch, warming his hands over a charcoal brazier. Jordan opened the front door, said in Swahili, "What's the news of the night, bwana?"

"Peaceful," Omali muttered morosely.

"You're always awake on payday." Jordan shivered in his *kikoi* and sweatshirt. "One night a month."

"I stay awake every night," Omali lied with an earnest face.

Jordan guffawed. "And I'm the president of Tanzania."

Omali smiled and changed the subject. "Are you going to the ponds today?"

"No. No appointments today." Jordan counted out forty dollars in shillings.

*"Asante, bwana,"* Omali said. "See you in the evening."

Jordan nodded and watched him shamble off in the long lime coat. "Try not to drink it all up at once."

"Of course, bwana," Omali called back, disappearing in the mist.

*Kow-kow-kow!* Ophelia screamed from somewhere. *Kow-kow-kow!*

Jordan looked around but couldn't see the buzzard. He went back in the dark house and found a raw chicken breast in the kitchen. Pasipo was perched on the back porch, staring into the fog, listening to the sounds of invisible swifts and ravens. A cold wind blew in from the cliffs.

"Pasipo," Jordan called from the screen door. She turned and regarded him silently. Jordan swung open the door and tossed the meat. Pasipo caught it with one claw. "Nice snag, shortstop," Jordan said as the door slammed shut. He made café au lait and a pot of oats with raisins and bananas and carried a thermos and tray to the front porch in the lee of the wind. The fog was lightening from gray to white. He stretched out in a chaise longue.

*Kow-kow-kow!* Ophelia sounded as if she were high in the albizzia.

Jordan could just make out the outlines of the tree. He set the bowl of oatmeal in his lap and brought a spoonful to his mouth.

*Kow-kow-kow!*

Jordan swallowed.

*Kow-kow-kow! Kow-kow-kow!* Ophelia watched him, wailing while he finished his porridge. *Kow-kow-kow! Kow-kow-kow! Kow-kow-kow!*

Jordan felt a pang of guilt. He'd read that novice falconers sometimes starved hawks to death by accident, usually trying to persuade them to come to the glove and eat. Now, the point was for Ophelia to hunt on her own, to feed her only if she were on the brink of death. The fog lifted foot by foot from the yard, rising like a curtain. Ophelia wouldn't shut up.

*Kow-kow-kow! Kow-kow-kow! Kow-kow-kow! Kow-kow-kow!*

"Zanifa will kill me if I feed you!" Jordan yelled in frustration. He tore off corners of a paper napkin and rolled them into earplugs. Ophelia's cries were muffled. He picked up a tattered paperback of *Lord Jim* that he'd bought on the street in Dar es Salaam. Ophelia screamed throughout the first thirty pages, then Jordan saw her fly out of the tree and glide just below the surface of the cloud across the yard toward the porch. She looked him in the eye and vanished around the corner.

Jordan read for three hours, lost in the novel, far from the present. He fell asleep in the lounge chair and dreamed of Anna and Zanifa and woke at noon. The fog had risen thousands of feet and formed a fleet of cumulus tufts below the winter dome. Jordan thought of riding into town to the post office, but he knew that he would find his box empty and ride home disappointed. She'll never write back, he repeated to himself every day, yet he still hoped. In the side yard, by the chicken coops, he worked out with barbells he had made from water pipes and various-size buckets of cement. He showered and fed Pasipo and warmed up last night's chicken and rice, then settled in the chaise on the front porch with *Lord Jim.*

"Joldon!" Zanifa called from the gate in the hedge. She jogged across the yard. A baggy burgundy St. Mary's sweatsuit hid her figure.

Jordan walked out into the yard. Dark strips of blue sky fractured the dome into thousands of jagged pieces that would re-form mysteriously in the night.

Jordan kissed her on the mouth and hugged her close.

"Someone might see us." Zanifa pulled away and glanced back at the road through the gap in the hedge. She looked at him and grinned. "Joldan."

"Call me Rutledge." Jordan walked toward the house. "Americans don't call each other by last names very often."

"Lutledge."

"Rutledge or Rut for short. My friends call me Rut."

"Lut."

"Rut, not Lut. You need to work on your r's."

"Llut." Zanifa giggled. She looked at the albizzia tree. "Where's Ophelia?"

*"Mungu anajua tu."* Jordan shrugged. God only knows.

Zanifa pointed over the escarpment. "Is that her?"

The black silhouette of a hawk hovered perfectly still several hundred feet over the cliff line, parked in the wind rising up the mountain wall.

"Maybe. Looks like she's hunting."

A thousand feet higher two raptors cruised toward the lone hawk, who didn't move her wings, scanning the ground for prey. The pair dove.

*"Haah!"* Zanifa gasped.

Tucking their wings to their sides, the two raptors slanted down like missiles. Jordan ran to the porch for the binoculars. He focused on the stooping hawks. "It's augurs. Our resident couple." He fol-

lowed the pair down through the sky and the lone hawk, still hover-
ing, came into sight. "They're attacking another augur buzzard. It's
called territorial aggression."

"Ophelia," Zanifa whispered.

The first hawk struck Ophelia with balled fists as it passed, sending her somersaulting. Ophelia righted herself, saw the second hawk
angling in, and flipped upside-down to grapple talons. The first augur,
fifty feet above Ophelia now, plunged again while her mate climbed
back into position for an attack dive.

"They'll kill her." Zanifa looked at him, terrified. Jordan thought
it possible but kept silent. He put his arm around her back, felt that
her body was taut.

Ophelia rowed away from the escarpment edge toward the rectory.
The augur pair took turns strafing her. She capsized and struck her
talons when the attackers swooped past. All three birds were screaming at once. *Kow-kow-kow. Kow-kow-kow. Kow-kow-kow.*

"They're killing her!" Zanifa yelled.

"She'll make it." Jordan squeezed her shoulder. "They're just scar-
ing her."

*Kow-kow-kow! Kow-kow-kow! Kow-kow-kow!*

Ophelia came in over the rectory and landed on a low branch of
the albizzia tree.

"I'm going to feed her." Zanifa ran for the porch.

*Kow-kow-kow!* The augur couple circled over the rectory yard twice.
Jordan threw stones at them until they flew on along the escarpment.
*Kow-kow-kow!*

Zanifa came out of the house with a fish in her glove. She looked
up at the sky.

"They're gone now. I think Ophelia's fine." Jordan followed Zanifa
to the tree. He saw that she was crying and wiped her tears away.
"She's fine."

"We should take her back to where we found her." Zanifa held the
glove toward the limb and looked up at Ophelia. "In her own telli-
toly."

"She knows where it is. Just over the ridge. I watched her fly back yesterday. She'll go back when she's ready. She's smart enough not to hunt in their territory again."

"She'll make it back?" Zanifa's eyes were red. "Are you sure?"

"Yeah, but we could walk her over one afternoon if it makes you feel better."

From the branch Ophelia watched Zanifa flapping the fish back and forth in her glove. Then she ignored Zanifa and began to smooth her feathers with her head and wings.

"Okay. Let's take Ophelia home next week." Zanifa brushed her eyes with the back of her hand and smiled. "She's not hungry."

"She must have caught something before we saw her." Jordan followed toward the house.

Due west out over the steppe a cloud drifted south across the horizon, uncovering a low sun; suddenly strong yellow light hit the porch at a right angle, like the beam of a film projector, throwing a net of lattice shadows against the back of the rectory.

"Oh, God." Jordan held himself tightly and came on the corner of her mouth.

Zanifa jerked her head back. She spat on the floor by the futon.

"It's okay. It's not dirty." Jordan wiped her face with the *kikoi*. "American girls swallow it." He laughed. "Some do, anyway. I guess some never like to."

"Sperm." Zanifa tasted a little on her tongue. "It's salty."

Jordan lifted her up from the futon and clutched her tight. Zanifa broke free and stepped into her sweatpants. Jordan pulled her top over her head.

"*Kwa heri*, Pasipo," Zanifa said.

Pasipo turned on her perch.

Zanifa waved at the eagle.

Backlit by the late sun, a thunderhead the size of a mountain range dragged a web of gold rain across the purple plains. Farther south a nimbus anvil exploded slowly into a massive mushroom cloud, dark and encircled by fire.

"That's spectacular, isn't it?"

"*Safi*," Zanifa said. Cool. She hurried through the house and stopped on the front porch to put on her sneakers.

"Are you going to tell Kimweri that you won't let him cut you?" Jordan sat beside her on the porch edge. "Stand up to him. Tell him you're a modern woman."

"I don't know if I can say that to him. My mother would beat me."

"Keep thinking about it." Jordan clasped her knee. "Think about running away."

Zanifa took a deep breath. "Let's take Ophelia to her home on Sunday afternoon."

"*Sawa*," Jordan said. Okay.

"There's Subira." Zanifa ran across the lawn, her elbows out like a distance runner.

Jordan stood and waved at Subira. He watched them walking away, holding hands, their heads bent forward, close together, two schoolgirls whispering secrets.

# Agosti 25

On Sunday morning Jordan was too restless to read. After canceling his weekly matches with a note to Kimweri, claiming his tennis elbow was acute from the pond rush, he found little else to do in Lushoto. The first year he had hunted with Ernst in the reserve at the northern foot of the mountains. Hunting with his camera was a pleasant diversion, but Ernst shot an antelope every few trips, and the wounded, writhing animals left Jordan with mounting distaste. He quit the Sunday safaris after the eyes of a dying gazelle appeared in his dreams. At the Lawns, Ionides would tell him one of a hundred stories he had heard before. For twenty-one months he had been putting off a promise to his parents to attend an Anglican service, so he rode under the gray sky to a hill where a stone church overlooked Lushoto.

The red arched doors of the colonial church were closed. Jordan parked by a bicycle stand. The congregation was singing "Amazing Grace" in Swahili to an electric bass guitar. Jordan cracked the door and slipped inside. The pews were about half-full. A few children turned and looked at him. Jordan sat in a back row. The hymn came to a close.

"We welcome a stranger, a guest!" the rector boomed from the pulpit in Swahili. He looked like a black friar, short and fat and gray haired with round wire-frame glasses. "You are very welcome."

Jordan blushed as the entire congregation turned to smile at him.

"Please, Bwana Guest, introduce yourself."

*"Jina langu ni* Rutledge Jordan." He cleared his throat. "I'm a Bwana Fish with the Peace Corps. I'm sorry my Swahili is not very good, but little by little you fill up the pot." *Haba na haba kujaza kibaba.*

The congregation broke up laughing at a *mzungu* quoting a proverb.

*"Karibu, Bwana Samaki,"* the rector welcomed him again. *"Karibu sana."*

The rector moved behind the altar and began to consecrate the eucharist. Jordan realized he'd arrived when the service was nearly over. The bass guitarist played an African hymn, and the congregation started to file toward the altar. Jordan was too preoccupied to translate the words, visited by images of Anna his last time in church. He knelt and took a wafer from the rector. "Dear God," Jordan whispered, "look after the health of Nanny and Mom and Dad and Sophie and Bob and their babies. Let Anna be happy. Help Zanifa to become a doctor. Help me to find my way." He dipped the wafer in the chalice and tasted sweet wine.

Outside, the parishioners crowded Jordan. He found himself with a smile stuck on his face, shaking hands with a long line of women in kangas and turbans and men in worn suits and barefoot children. The rector waited at the end of the line.

"Bwana Jordan, I am Safari," the rector said in English with a hardy handshake.

"Father Safari, it's good to meet you. I apologize for being late."

"This is Africa." Safari laughed. "Are you an Anglican?"

"Episcopalian."

"Of course. You are an American." Safari held his hand. "Well, we both look to the archbishop of Canterbury. There are not many of us in Tanzania."

"We seem to be dying out in the States, too," Jordan said.

"Will you come to my house for lunch?"

"I'm sorry, Father, I have an appointment I must rush to." Jordan smiled and freed his hand.

"Come again," Safari said as Jordan started the Honda. *"Karibu tena."*

"Next Sunday I'll be on time."

Zanifa was sitting on the front porch.

"You're early." Jordan climbed off the bike.

"I told my mother I had work to do at school." Zanifa smiled and touched his arm tentatively. She was wearing jeans and a St. Mary's sweater and sneakers.

"I've turned you into a liar," Jordan said.

"Everyone tells lies."

Jordan laughed sadly. "How come you're so wise?"

"My mother says that." Zanifa giggled. "Have you seen Ophelia today?"

"No, but that reminds me to feed Pasipo."

"I fed her."

"That was kind of you."

"I wonder where Ophelia is."

"Maybe she's gone home over the ridge," Jordan said, going in the door. "You hungry?"

"A little."

"I'll make pasta."

"*Nini?*"

"You know, noodles."

"You mean like spaghetti?"

"Yeah. You like it?"

Zanifa made a face. "I hate the spaghetti in the cafeteria."

"Maybe you'll like mine."

"It's strange for a man to cook," Zanifa said. "Do all American men cook?"

"No. Mostly those who live by themselves." Jordan boiled water and chopped tomatoes.

Zanifa reached for his hand. "I can't just sit and watch a man cook. It's not right."

"You're too traditional, Zanifa." Jordan held the knife away from her. "You think women aren't as good as men. You think you're supposed to serve them. For thousands of years African men have made women think they're slaves."

Zanifa sat on a stool. "It's hard for me to understand."

"That's because you were raised to think you're a slave. African girls start carrying water when they're tiny, but the boys never have to."

Zanifa nodded.

"*Mzungu* women are free. They don't go through *jando*. It's slavery. You don't have to be Kimweri's slave. You can be whoever you want to be." Jordan poured the pasta on two tin plates. "Imagine what it would be like to be free. To do what *you* want to do. Not what your mother wants you to do or your village expects of you."

They ate sitting on the futon on the back porch. Zanifa leaned her back against his side. Pasipo sat quietly on her perch, looking out over the plains. Far below, an ant-size bus moved silently along a stretch of the great north highway.

"Watching the cars makes you want to go somewhere new," Zanifa said.

Jordan grinned, for she had never before spoken of leaving. "It's the airplanes that pass over the mountains on their way to Europe that make me want to go."

"I want to ride in an airplane."

"You will one day."

Zanifa put down her plate and kissed him. Jordan thought perhaps he had gone too far. You fall in love by making love, he remembered being told by a professor in her forties he had slept with in law school.

"*Bwana Samaki,*" Omali called from the front porch. "*Hodi. Hodi.*"

"*Subiri bwana,*" Jordan yelled for him to wait.

"I don't want him to see me here today," Zanifa said.

"Okay." Jordan saw fear in her eyes. He clutched her hand for a moment, then walked through the house.

"Bwana." Omali stood outside the screen front door. "A boy is here. He has a hawk. I think it's Zanifa's."

Jordan ran across the yard toward the gate, where a boy stood outside, holding a bag. Omali shuffled along behind him. Jordan shouted, "*Unayo mwewe?*"

The boy answered by raising a burlap bag. He looked to be about seventeen.

Jordan reached over the gate for the bag. "How did you catch it?"

"They stoned it," Omali said. "It was trying to steal their chickens."

Jordan opened the bag and saw the bloody corpse of an augur buzzard. He pulled it out and recognized Ophelia by the small metal band on one leg. Jordan glared at the boy. "You killed it!"

"It was trying to steal their chickens, bwana," Omali said.

Jordan was wordless, thinking of how Zanifa would be hurt. He started for the rectory.

*"Bwana Samaki,"* the boy said.

Jordan turned his head.

"One thousand shillings." The boy had a pleading face and held out empty hands.

"You're crazy if you think I'm paying you for killing my hawk."

"It was my cousin, not me."

"Thanks for bringing it here, young bwana." Jordan tossed him the empty bag. "Omali, I'll be up late, you can wait until midnight to come."

*"Sawa, bwana."* Omali raised his stick at the boy and told him to run along. *"Nenda bwana. Nenda tu."*

Jordan thought he would hide the carcass, then decided Zanifa would hear about it from someone. He remembered crying when his dog was hit by a car when he was fifteen. He carried Ophelia inside and laid her on the big table. If Pasipo saw the body, she might think it was food and start screaming. Walking slowly to the back porch, he tried to think of what to say. *Hamna maneno,* Africans always said when someone died: There are no words.

Zanifa was standing by Pasipo, telling her she would fly next month.

"Zanifa."

She and Pasipo looked at him.

"Come here."

She crossed the porch. Jordan held her close and whispered, "Some boys killed Ophelia. She was trying to take a chicken."

*"Nini?"* She looked suddenly confused.

"Ophelia's dead. I'm sorry." Jordan stroked the back of her head. *"Poleh. Poleh sana."*

"Where is she?"

"On the big table."

Zanifa ran into the house and stopped by the edge of the table. Gently she spread out the wings. Her mouth was open slightly, her lips trembling silent words. She leaned on the table and started sobbing.

"Her spirit will live in the sky." Jordan rubbed her shoulders. He took her by the hand and led her to the futon on the back porch. They sat side by side with their backs to the stone wall. Zanifa wept, taking short breaths.

Jordan wiped tears from her face. She asked, "What will we do with Ophelia?"

"I'll burn her body tonight and cast the ashes into the wind. That way her spirit will fly over the mountains."

"I'd like to see that."

"You'll be home in bed. Maybe you'll dream about her."

"Oh, God. Oh, God," Zanifa cried out as the wave rose through her body. She must have picked that up from you, the last time, Jordan thought. She thrashed her shoulders from side to side, violent for the first time, from the sadness. She clenched his hair and screamed as the wave broke. She tugged him by the arms until he moved up to her face. She kissed him fiercely, then said, *"Weka ndhani mimi."*

*Put it inside me.*

Jordan paused, disoriented. He said slowly in English, "What?"

Zanifa leaned forward and unzipped his khakis and tried to push them over his hips. She gave up and unbuttoned his denim shirt and pulled it off. She reached again for his waist. His fantasy was coming true. She was giving herself to him. He rolled onto his back and let her pull off his canvas boots and trousers. She put her mouth on him, moved it up and down, too hard, too fast.

*"Poleh. Poleh,"* Jordan said. Easy. Easy.

She moved gently with her mouth and her hand. Jordan lay with his eyes closed, imagining himself moving slowly into her, her face changing as she felt him inside her for the first time, the pain turning slowly into pleasure. He didn't want Kimweri to have that. It was going to be his now.

She looked up at him. "Put it in me."

Jordan pulled her up alongside him and kissed her softly. "You're a beautiful girl. Are you sure you want me to fuck you?" He used the Swahili slang—*kutomba*—to scare her.

"*Unitombe.*" She moved his hand down her belly. Fuck me.

Jordan rolled her onto her back. He pulled off her sweater and unsnapped her bra. He cupped one of her breasts, kissed the other. She pushed his hand down her belly.

"Will it hurt?" Zanifa lay perfectly still, her legs open wide.

"At first. You might not like it the first time."

Jordan knelt and began to ease himself inside her, felt the hymen. "No. I can't." He fell sideways onto the futon and lay on his back. He held her hand.

"You don't want to?" Zanifa laid herself across his chest. "Something's wrong with me?"

"No. You're beautiful, perfect. It's just not right. You're . . . I was trying to teach you what you were going to lose in *jando*. Now you know. You should wait for someone you love."

"I love you," Zanifa said in English, easily, as if she had practiced.

"I love you, too." Jordan didn't want to tell her that he could never marry her until after she'd decided to run away. "But I'm too old for you."

"You're not as old as the sultani."

"Almost. But the point is *you're* too young. You need to grow up and then pick your husband."

"Don't you love me?"

"Of course I do. That's why I offered to send you to college."

Nodding, Zanifa bit her lip. Jordan kissed her softly on the lips and rubbed her nose with his. "You should go now. I'll see you tomorrow."

"You're not going to the rally?" Zanifa reached for her sweater. "Everyone at St. Mary's is going by bus."

"What rally?"

Zanifa opened the screen door.

At the other end of the porch, Pasipo leapt from her perch to the floor, flapping her wings.

"Sultani Kimweri is introducing *Chama Cha Uhuru.*" Framed by the doorway, Zanifa slid her legs into her jeans. She said in English: "The Freedom Party."

"Oh, yeah." Jordan pulled on his khakis.

"Father William is taking the whole school."

"*Sawa*, you can bring the chickens on Tuesday." Jordan tucked in his shirt and followed her to the living room.

Zanifa stood for a long time looking at the carcass. Her face contorted as if she were crying. "Good-bye, Ophelia."

They walked to the gate without speaking.

"I love you," Zanifa whispered, and touched his hand.

"You've been reading too many of those illustrated romances." Jordan smiled. "You're too young to fall in love."

"I want to kiss you, but someone might see."

"Save it for Tuesday." Jordan held the gate.

"See ya," Zanifa mimicked him.

"See ya, soon." Jordan blew her a kiss.

"That's funny." Zanifa smiled. "What's that?"

"A secret kiss."

She made a kiss, then puffed as if she were putting out a birthday cake.

Jordan watched her hurry off. It seemed unreal that he was planning to help her escape. He walked around the side of the house to get a chicken for Pasipo and was startled to see Omali near the back porch, opening the chicken coop.

"What's the news of the evening?" Omali said.

"Not good. Not with Ophelia dead."

"It's a bad thing." Omali threw a handful of feed into the coop. The chickens leaped around inside, clucking and pushing to get the grain.

"You fed them already this morning." Jordan tried to read his eyes.

"*Mimi ni pumbavu. Nimesahau.*" Omali laughed and closed the coop. I'm an idiot. I forgot.

"I told you to come at midnight. Why'd you come back?"

"I thought I had to feed the chickens."

"You just got here?"

"Yes, bwana."

Jordan knew he was lying.

JORDAN CAME INTO ST. JOHN'S DURING THE SERVICE. THE CON-
gregation was standing, singing a hymn. An usher escorted him to a
space on the rear row. Jordan squeezed into a pew, knelt, prayed for
forgiveness and the health of his family, stood and picked up a hym-
nal. The song drew to a close before he found the page and the congregation sat down.

"Let us pray," the rector's voice came from the sanctum. Everyone
kneeled. Jordan found the page in the Book of Common Prayer and
followed the service. He searched the church for the back of Anna's
head. She was close, a few rows up on the other side of the aisle with
her parents.

The congregation sat down. The ushers moved slowly from the
front, passing brass plates from pew to pew. Jordan looked at the
Georgian details, the abstract stained glass. There was a mural of
Christ on the cross behind the altar that made him look like a muscular superhero. How could they believe? Jordan didn't think that he
had ever believed. Maybe he had as a kid. He remembered the guilt
he had felt when he was twelve after a spree of shoplifting candy and
the relief that came with confession to a minister who had told him
he was forgiven, that he had only been doing it for the thrill, as if that
made it acceptable. The thrill. The same reason he had been unfaithful to Anna. The question of God had preoccupied him late in high
school and through college. The time he tried LSD in his senior year
at Vanderbilt, the idea of a meaningless universe and oblivion so terrified him that Anna had to hold him for five hours, soothing him
with ideas from her world religion class. In law school he stopped
thinking about God. He had been too busy. Jordan put a hundred-
dollar bill in the plate and passed it to a fat, balding guy in an olive
poplin suit. The man looked at the bill and smiled.

During communion, as pew after pew filed to the altar, Jordan watched a young couple leading a little boy in shorts between them, holding his hands. Jordan felt a tear sliding down his cheek and thought he cried too easily. Anna stood in line behind her parents. As she walked back, her hands were clasped in front of her waist, her gaze at her feet. Jesus would forgive me, he thought—why can't you? If the roles were reversed, he would forgive her. He would never leave her. The usher stood just behind his pew, and Jordan rose and walked up the aisle, conscious of his shoes tapping the marble. Coming alongside Anna's pew, he glanced sideways. Anna and her mother knelt in prayer. Her father saw him and frowned. Jordan walked up three steps, passed between the choir stalls, and knelt at the rail.

"The body of Christ." The rector, in a white robe, handed him a small white wafer. "The bread of heaven."

Jordan prayed that Anna and he would love each other again.

"The blood of Christ." A second minister tilted the chalice to his lips. "The cup of salvation."

Walking back to his pew, Jordan caught Anna's eyes. She looked away.

After communion the congregation sang "For All the Saints" and the acolytes led the procession down the center, trailed by the rector, who paused at the door to shout, "Go forth in the name of the Lord." The congregation responded, "Thanks be to God." Then it was quiet for a moment. Everyone stood and began to talk and file out of the church. Jordan walked out in the sunshine and waited in the crowd chatting on the steps. Anna shook hands with the rector, saw Jordan and walked over.

"You look lovely, all dressed up," Jordan said. "Remember when we were confirmed? That was the first time I saw you. God, sixteen years ago."

"When did you start coming to church?" Anna's half smile seemed to say, Look what you've sunk to now.

"It's been twenty-three long days and nights," Jordan said slowly.

She stared at him and the hardness left her face.

"People keep seeing you with different guys around town."

"So what?" Now her eyes were angry.

"It's just hard for me. Can't we spend a little time together? It might soothe our wounds."

"Anna," her mother called from behind. "Come here, darling. I want you to meet Mrs. Palmer's grandson."

"I'll come see you tonight." Anna touched his arm quickly. "Get some rest. You look awful."

Jordan walked to his car, calmed by her promise. He drove to Chickasaw Gardens, where his parents lived by a lake in an imitation Williamsburg carriage house. His mother and Anna had grown close, and Anna had been to see her after she got back from San Francisco. His mother was angry at Jordan and told him so, but she decided not to tell his father why Anna had left him. His father had enough on his mind with the housing market in the doldrums and his contracting company going broke. Only his mother's Taurus wagon was in the drive, which meant they weren't back from St. Luke's, so Jordan drove down Union to Tops Bar B Q and considered ways to kill time.

Anna stood on the landing and met his smile with an indifferent look.

"Thanks for coming." Jordan bent to kiss her, expecting to be pushed away, but she let him touch her lips for a moment. He suddenly felt at a loss. "Like a beer?"

Anna nodded and followed him to the kitchen. Jordan opened two Coronas, pushed a slice of lime into the mouth of each bottle.

"Here's to all the great years." She raised the bottle, squinting her eyes.

"God, Anna, don't tell me it's over."

"*What* do you want?" She slammed the bottle on the counter. "You want it all. I'm supposed to—what? Marry you and just stop wondering who you're fucking on the side?"

"No. There won't be anyone else. I don't want anyone else." Jordan felt the heat in his eyes, the tears coming. "Excuse me. I'm such a crybaby." He tore a paper towel from a roll. "Every night I wake up about three missing you beside me . . . the sound of your breath. I can't fall back asleep."

"You must be tired." Anna laughed. She walked into the living room and flopped down on the couch. "Would you like to fuck?"

Jordan was unsure if she was serious.

"We can't make love anymore." Anna had a playful look he'd not seen before. It frightened him a little. "We might as well fuck."

# Agosti 26

He was forced down the middle of the tarmac road by crowds of women burdened by baskets of vegetables on their heads. He passed a German sign for Jaegertail, "Hunter's Valley," and then the circular drive up a hill to the Lawns. He turned onto a dirt road by the bus stand and saw the *soko* beyond, a great teeming grid of women with wares laid out on mats.

In front of the Saddam Hussein dry goods shop, Jordan locked the Honda and entered the rows of hunkering women, a babel of Sambaa, Swahili, and English. He bought beans from a wide-eyed eight-year-old boy who counted shilling notes with the rapidity of a bank teller. He meandered through the chaos. Old women called out, "My son . . . My child . . ." The grinning crones offered oranges, mangos, papayas, avocados, holding them in gnarled fingers.

Staticky Swahili voices carried over the market from a field on the far side of a cluster of pastel cinder-block houses. The crowd began to move from the *soko*, the women in colorful kangas, the men in American cast-off clothes, many with white muslim caps. Jordan slung his backpack over his shoulder and threaded his way through the squatting traders.

By the BP station, Jordan ran into the director of the German Usambara erosion control program. Hans Schafer's manner was so cold and stiff, his Tanzanian staff called him *Jinamizi*—Nightmare.

"*Jambo*, Hans." Jordan shook his hand and went on in Swahili. "It's been a long time."

Nightmare was reluctant to respond. "*Jambo*, Rutledge."

"What's your opinion of the new Freedom Party?" Jordan put down his rucksack.

"Will it be any different?" Hans squinted at the crowd streaming by. "Perhaps the parties will start a war, or perhaps the army will decide to place itself in power. Who can say?" He smiled ominously and looked away.

"Tanzania seems too peaceful to become another Rwanda."

"Anything is possible on this continent." Hans looked gravely at Jordan.

Jordan brushed his hair out of his eyes. "You're not going to the rally?"

"No." Hans surprised Jordan by flashing a peace sign. "Back to the office."

Jordan flowed with the throng from the market to the stadium. Within a few minutes several thousand people packed the open soccer field. In the crush of strange faces, Jordan looked off to the dark mountain peaks surrounding the town and longed for the green hills of Tennessee.

The ruling party occupied the west bleachers. Over the east bleachers fluttered banners of the Freedom Party and two smaller parties. On high ground overlooking the field from the open south end of the stadium, Jordan saw uniformed St. Mary's girls standing against a green school bus, but they were too far to distinguish clearly.

"*Karibuni watu wote!*" a disembodied voice crackled through the stadium. A thin man in a baggy suit called out from the stage at the north end. "Welcome, everyone! We are here today to celebrate a great step in the development of Tanzania," the man said in Swahili. "Our beloved Teacher himself calls for peaceful, open *demokrasia*. The Teacher asks you to respect those of parties other than your own. Remember our national motto—'Unity and Progress!' "

The crowd cheered halfheartedly. The thin man introduced the incumbent MP, Bwana Cosmos Chamshama—a short fat man in a dark suit. The party members in the bleachers clapped and shouted. Old women in kangas with the black and green party colors began to dance around the platform, ululating—a high, animal sound. There was scattered applause around Jordan in the middle of the field. He worked his way toward the stage.

"Today I take great pleasure in greeting a son of the Usambara Mountains, Bwana Julian Kimweri of Vooga, the candidate of the Freedom Party."

A loud roar gathered in the standing crowd and burst into sustained applause as the sultan strode across the stage in a flowing white *kanzu*, an embroidered Arab vest and matching red fez. He held a carved staff in one hand.

Cosmos Chamshama stood behind the podium. He called for silence, and the people obeyed. His face was genial. "The Party of the Revolution guided Tanzania from the first days of independence. The party has struggled to make a country where no one is rich and no one is poor."

"Where everyone is poor," muttered an old man in front of Jordan.

"The party has worked to make a country where every man is his own master. It has tried to provide education and health care to all the people."

"There is only one government hospital in all of the Usambara Mountains," said another old man. He wore a patched wool suit coat, patched black trousers and sandals, one of the intelligentsia. Jordan knew that the farmers far from town were disturbed by the idea of new parties—how could they afford a second party on top of the first interfering with the business of their lives? *Demokrasia* was difficult to grasp in the bush.

Cosmos Chamshama stopped to wipe his brow. He blamed the dire economy on the falling price of sisal, coffee and tea on the world market.

"Why not let us sell our tea to private buyers instead of the government?" a tall man yelled not far from the stage. He had the coloring and features of the Kilindi clan—like the sultan and Zanifa.

"Get rid of the tea board!" another Kilindi yelled.

"The teachers haven't been paid for six months!" Shouts came from all corners of the crowd. "What happened to the money for the new hospital!"

Cosmos Chamshama surveyed the moody audience and changed tack. Rising on his toes, he shouted, *"Comrades,* listen. Is it a good time to turn over Parliament, the voice of the people, to men who know nothing of the day-to-day running of a government?"

The old MP paused. The stadium was quiet.

"Will you elect men who want only to make their names big in the country? Men who might plunge our nation into bloodshed like Rwanda or Somalia? The Teacher put us on a slow but peaceful course." Chamshama smiled and raised one hand. "The Party of the Revolution has brought three decades of peace to Tanzania. We will lead the country into the new era." He hurried across the stage.

Kimweri traversed the platform to the microphone. He said something in Sambaa, and the crowd broke into wild laughter. Jordan thought it dangerously tribal to address a public rally in a local language. Then Kimweri started slowly in perfect classical Swahili. *"Watu wote wanaweza"*—nearly every word rhymed or alliterated. The sultan's stage voice was resonant and soothing.

"The Honorable Bwana Chamshama called for the old party to guide our nation through this crisis of poverty." Kimweri banged his staff on the stage. "But I tell you, my brothers and sisters, it is his party, the Party of the Revolution, that made this crisis. You know it's true. You laugh and joke about it on the street every day."

Kimweri stopped and raised his staff high in the air. He said softly, "The time is coming when jokes bring change." His voice boomed: *"The time is coming when your hopes and dreams become real!"*

Kimweri spoke of the days before independence when workers could afford twenty times more bread and kerosene and clothes than they could today. Gesturing to the incumbent, Kimweri blamed the Party of the Revolution. He called for an end to government monopolies. The crowd was rapt. This was the first time these taboo ideas had been voiced publicly in the mountains in decades.

Kimweri raised both fists over his head. The flowing arms of the white *kanzu* made him look like an angel. His deep voice thundered: *"The time has come for a change to the past!"*

On the backdrop behind him, a red banner rolled down, slowly covering the green-and-black flag of the old party. The banner was spotted with symbols Jordan couldn't make out.

Kimweri turned and pointed with his staff. "This is the flag of the new party. These are the old crests of each tribe. The flag represents the unity of all tribes and a call to the prosperity of the past."

"*Turude zamani!*" Kimweri shouted. Let's return to the old days! "*Turude zamani!*"

"*Turude zamani!*" The Kilindi throughout the crowd echoed the sultan. The cry gathered strength farther and farther from the stage. "*Turude zamani!*" Within a minute the whole crowd was shouting in unison. "*Turude zamani!*"

Jordan was jarred from behind. Before he realized what was happening, he was being dragged by his arms through the crowd. He looked at his escorts: the two Kilindi warriors who had saved him from the mob on the road. They both wore dark sunglasses and white polo shirts. Jordan tried to wrench his arms loose, but their hands only squeezed his biceps harder. They glided him through the chanting Sambaa, around one grandstand, along the edge of a marsh and under a section of bleachers. Jordan yelled. One warrior clamped his hand over his mouth. The staticky voice of the thin man who had introduced the candidates thanked the people for coming. On the other side of the bleachers, the crowd streamed out of the stadium, the chanting and ululating growing fainter.

The two warriors released his arms and pushed him back into the shadows.

"*Vipi sasa?*" Jordan thought it was some kind of a joke. What's happening?

"Just wait," one of them answered. Both had kept their glasses on in the shade.

Julian Kimweri appeared in the striped light beneath the stands, flanked by bodyguards. The red fez tipped forward as he crouched to come closer. "How good of you to come to my campaign kickoff. You think it went well?"

"You bet. Your platform makes perfect sense." Jordan tried to walk toward Kimweri. One warrior pushed him back.

Coming closer, Kimweri stepped into shade. "Have you no re-spect?" His laugh was new. "I admit you were clever in your method of persuading Zanifa. But you forgot that I saved your life, no?"

Kimweri moved forward into a band of light that illuminated his black eyes. "I wonder how you'll enjoy a taste of your own medicine?" Kimweri removed his fez and handed it to an aide. His hair was short. A thin part was cut along the top of his head. "You're a guest in Tanzania, and you tamper with a traditional ritual thousands of years old." He ordered the warriors in Sambaa. One twisted Jordan's elbow behind his back while the other two spread his legs apart.

"Do not under any circumstances talk to the girl again." Kimweri leaned forward and whispered into Jordan's ear. "Then you might live to go back to America."

Jordan yelped as Kimweri slapped his crotch.

"It's true what they say about *mzungu* men." Kimweri kneaded Jordan roughly. "There's really very little between their legs." He closed his fist.

Jordan screamed.

The warriors forced Jordan onto his knees.

Kimweri cackled. "Your life hung on that thin tissue. I had a mid-wife examine her. If you'd fucked her, you'd be dead already." The sul-tan drew the front of his robe up to his waist and clutched a hard, uncircumcised penis by the base. He massaged it tenderly.

Jordan turned his head and tried to jerk away from the two war-riors.

"Seeing fear is exciting." Kimweri laughed. "This must be what motivates a rapist."

Jordan looked up at Kimweri's face. "I'm sorry, Julian. I went too far, I—"

Kimweri backhanded him across his cheek.

"I'll forgive you if you give me the pleasure you gave Zanifa." Kimweri rubbed his hand up and down the shaft of his cock.

"I can get a transfer from the mountains." Bracing himself for an-other slap, Jordan hoped Kimweri would just beat him up and not rape him. He flinched when Kimweri stroked the red mark on his cheek.

Kimweri said something in Sambaa. A warrior placed one arm around Jordan's neck and with the other clenched Jordan's hair. He forced Jordan's head forward.

"If you so much as scratch me with your teeth, he will break your neck," Kimweri said, pushing the head of his penis against Jordan's lips, which were pursed shut. "Open up."

Kimweri whispered in Sambaa. The warrior squeezed Jordan's throat until he couldn't breathe. Jordan choked and his mouth opened.

"Wider."

Kimweri pushed his penis slowly into Jordan's mouth. Jordan tried to force it out, and Kimweri shoved it in farther, making Jordan gag. "Wider." The warrior ripped a handful of Jordan's hair. Jordan screamed silently and opened his mouth wider. Kimweri breathed faster, ramming his cock against the back of Jordan's throat. Suddenly the sultan stopped and pulled back slightly, resting the head of his penis inside Jordan's cheeks. Jordan felt the penis throbbing, the warm, salty semen filling his mouth. Kimweri took it out. Jordan gagged and spat on the ground. The warrior released him.

"Lovely boy. With all that hair you could pass for a girl." Kimweri wiped his penis on Jordan's shirt and dropped the robe to his feet. "A transfer—that's a wise idea. But let's do have one last match at the Lawns before you go."

Jordan spat and rubbed his neck.

Kimweri said something in Sambaa. Laughing, without looking back, the royal entourage withdrew from the louvered light of the bleachers, leaving Jordan alone in the shadows beneath the empty stadium. He continued to spit every last bit of moisture from his mouth.

Ionides sat on two pillows, leaning forward from the front of the seat, his legs barely reaching the pedals and his chin not far above the steering wheel of his Land Rover. He drove fast down the steep road, jerking at the last moment into the corners. The tires screeched.

"You're going to kill us," Jordan said. "Why don't you let me drive?"

"I allow no man to drive my Land Rover. I've been a Landy man since 1952," Ionides rasped. "That has always been my policy."

"If it weren't for power steering, you couldn't even turn the wheel," Jordan shouted.

Ionides grunted. "You should go straight to Dar es Salaam. There will be fifty buses passing through Mombo tonight."

"The Peace Corps would never let me come back to Lushoto if I told them why I fled. And I can't leave Pasipo now. She's not ready to be released." Jordan touched the burning place on his scalp.

"If you don't keep your promise about a transfer, he'll kill you. Forget that bloody bird. Move to the other side of the country."

"I'll write Kimweri a note that I've applied for a transfer and I'm working fast to release the eagle," Jordan said. "He ought to understand. He has a Green Peace sticker on his car."

"You're mad."

The road came down off a ridgeline and pointed toward a deep gorge, presenting a vista of umbrella acacia trees studding the savanna a thousand feet below.

"How many times did I warn you not to get involved with that girl?" Ionides cawed. "Your ears must be full of wax. You think I've been here fifty years for nothing?"

"It had to be Omali. That fucking drunk. I never trusted him."

"Omali won't come around when he sees whom you've hired to replace him." Ionides downshifted to slow the car. "The Maasai started rustling Sambaa women and cattle three hundred years ago. They still rustle cattle." Ionides's laugh was high and hoarse. "The Sambaa are scared of them."

They passed the turnoff to Vooga in silence. A black bus named Death Row labored up the road, trailing a cloud of black diesel smoke.

"Bad piston rings," Ionides mumbled. "Bloody Africans."

They rounded a bend and saw Mombo, a triangular set of streets and shimmering tin roofs where the alluvial fan of the mountains met the flat plain of the Maasai steppe. On both sides of the town, orderly rows of sisal ran in perfectly rectangular hundred-hectare swaths along the north-south highway. They passed through an abandoned toll booth with missing windows and drove down a steep slope into town.

Tall palm trees swayed in a hot wind by the Caltex station. In front of the California Bar, Check Bobs, young men in shades and tight pants cut above the ankles to show off their loafers and high-tops, milled and danced. Ionides drove slowly through the town until he spotted three Maasai cowboys wearing red Roman tunics and scabbards on their hips. Their spears were stuck in the ground around a table with a Cinzano umbrella in front of the pink, cement New Paris Hotel.

Ionides parked the car and climbed out slowly, groaning as he lowered his short frame to the road. The old Greek waddled in his safari suit toward the table. Jordan followed. Ionides hailed them in Maasai. *"Entasoba!"*

*"Eba!"* They shouted back in unison.

Ionides sat at the table in an empty chair and spoke at length in Maasai. Jordan stood behind, listening, understanding only *shillingi*— shillings. Upon arriving in Tanzania, Jordan had been shocked by the way the *mzungu* employed large staffs of Africans at slave wages. He'd quickly grown accustomed and now was grateful that the Peace Corps paid for "security personnel."

The three warriors began to jabber quickly among themselves. Ionides listened, then turned to Jordan. "First they thought I was joking—fifty dollars a month is twice the salary of a government clerk. I should have offered less."

Jordan said nothing. He was considering whether Kimweri could have infected him with AIDS. He felt his mouth for cuts.

One of the warriors stood. He was about Jordan's age and size— late twenties, six feet tall, a hundred and sixty pounds. His hair was tied into long, thin braids, and he wore a little plastic film canister in a hole in his earlobe. He shook Jordan's hand limply and said in Swahili: "Call me Shabu."

"I'm Jordan."

He turned to Ionides to ask if his girlfriend could come and visit.

"Of course," Jordan answered. "And your mates are welcome, too."

"How many months?" The warrior looked at Jordan.

"Four," Jordan said. "Then I go back to my homeland." He pointed above the tall trees at the sheer gray cliffs that rose three thousand feet. "You can see my house on the edge of the mountain a few miles north. Do you see the old church on the point?"

"*Ndiyo.*" Shabu nodded.

"Right there."

"There is a cattle track that climbs those cliffs near your house." Shabu pointed to a thin zigzagging line.

"Yes. Your friends can use that path." Jordan let go of his hand. "But you start tonight."

Shabu tucked his red faux braids under a black beret and pulled his spear free.

# Agosti 27—Septemba 8

In the second moon of the dry season, the Africans lit fires across the country, wherever they intended to plant corn or graze cattle or wherever children—inspired by a collective pyromania—set the bush ablaze. Countless columns of smoke rose like white threads from the slopes of the mountains and the flat reaches of the steppe. A dead sea of air settled onto the country, and a yellow brown stratum several thousand feet thick floated over the savanna, smogging out the distant peaks and refracting the light into bloody sunsets. At night the fires were scattered across the blackness far below like coal red constellations.

No longer at ease outside the rectory grounds, Jordan sent Shabu in town to post a note to Kimweri, asking for time to arrange a transfer and release the eagle, assuring him he would avoid Zanifa. Jordan spent his mornings trying to read and his afternoons smoking *bhangi*. He picked up *For Whom the Bell Tolls*, *The Rules of Attraction*, *Dog Soldiers*, paperbacks left over from college, but couldn't get beyond the beginnings. The memory of the stadium troubled his dreams, woke him in the night to walk with Shabu around the yard, setting trip wires. Shabu wanted to run to Maasai Land for more warriors, but Jordan was too wary to stay alone even for a few days. As the days passed without a reply from Kimweri, the uncertainty slowly accumulated in his mind until he was waking at every sound in the night.

During the day, Pasipo exercised her wings, leaping from chair back

to tabletop to porch rail onto the grass of the yard between the rectory and the church and then back into the house. Shabu sat in his red
tunic, braiding beads into the ends of his ocher locks or reading a
stack of last year's *Mfanyakazi*—the *Worker*—a Swahili newspaper. He
kept an eye on the sky leopard whenever she ventured outside, having
befriended Pasipo, and more often than not used the glove to feed her
when Jordan was listless or stoned or asleep.

Late one morning Jordan woke and walked out onto the porch. Six
head of scrawny cattle were grazing in the yard of the rectory. Their
ribs showed through their slack hides, their wide horns angled up at
the tips.

"*Umeamkaje, bwana?*" Shabu, in a red tunic with a tartan cloth
wrapped around his shoulders, asked how he slept.

"*Vizuri.*" Jordan rubbed his eyes. Fine.

Behind Shabu was a warrior dressed in a red tunic and two girls
with shaved heads in matching blue tunics tied with belts of beads.
Shabu introduced his girlfriend, Kisene, who bowed with her face
averted as she shook his hand with both of hers. Shabu had told
Jordan that it was Kisene who had given him the bracelets and neck-
laces of beads that he wore every day. She had been his girlfriend for
some years, but now that she was thirteen, she would soon pass
through *jando* and be married to an older man, traded for ten cows.
The other warrior, Lesuyu, had accompanied her and his own girlfriend, Malamai, from their village eighty miles west on the flat
steppe.

"They have come to stay for two days," Shabu told Jordan. "Then
they must return my father's cows. There is little to graze in your yard,
and the Sambaa will not let us graze on their land."

"*Karibu sana,*" Jordan said, welcoming them.

Shabu shot an arrow from two feet into a big vein on a heifer's
neck. Blood spurted from the wound into a gourd one girl held.
Kisene mixed the blood in a wooden bowl she had filled with fresh
milk and whipped the liquid by rolling a stick rapidly between her
hands until there was a pink froth on top of the bowl. The girl of-

fered the Maasai milkshake to Jordan, who declined. Shabu shook his head sadly.

Late in the day Jordan decided to throw a party for his guests and gave them a goat. Shabu and Lesuyu cut its neck and drained the blood. This time when Lesuyu presented Jordan the steaming bowl, he took a mouthful. It tasted like human blood and goat meat. "Now you are a Maasai," Shabu said, leaning against him with his arm draped over his shoulder. The warriors dismembered the goat and the girls cooked the pieces on stakes set in a bonfire in the lawn. Meat was a rare delicacy for the Maasai, and they ate happily, laughing and joking, while Jordan gnawed silently on a leg, envying their simple pleasure. After dark the girls appeared with their necks encircled by disks of beads bigger than LP records. They stood opposite the warriors, bouncing the disks up and down as they danced in place, all of them chanting, "Yah, yah, yah, yah!" The warriors moved in the same rhythm and sang, "We are here with you beautiful girls." The girls sang, "You called us to play together. Jump and I will choose one of you to love." Lesuyu bounded toward the girls and leaped high off the ground. "Yah, yah, yah, yah!" Shabu leaped higher, then grabbed Jordan from where he sat by the fire and pulled him into the contest. Jordan could jump only half as high, but the Maasai all cheered him on and he danced and leapt by firelight, lighthearted for a few hours, until they suddenly called an end to the night and he went off to his bedroom alone.

The day the three guests left, Pasipo hopped into the living room, screaming, *Quee-quee-quee!*

Jordan looked up from the sofa. "Hungry, are you?"

*Quee-quee-quee!* Pasipo leapt from the floor and skidded across the tabletop. *Quee-quee-quee!* She jumped from the table, banged off the wall, and landed in an armchair. She tore a hole in the bottom cushion with her beak and tossed kapok stuffing onto the floor. *Quee-quee-quee!*

Jordan put out a joint and walked into the kitchen, then came back with a chicken breast. He was looking around for the glove when Pasipo leapt across the room and sank her talons into the chicken.

After she finished, he coaxed her onto the glove, then jessed her tightly to the perch. He decided he wouldn't feed her again that day and the next he would start her training.

Blown by wind streams, the drab dome of winter broke up slowly over a few days like an ice pack, cracking into a startling electric blue sky. Jordan studied the change during the long hours of training Pasipo. Two days were spent standing with a fish in the sun before the eagle was finally coaxed, with a long line attached to one leg jess, to cross the yard to the glove. The next day she winged over the yard twelve times at sunrise and sixteen at sunset, receiving her meals bite by bite. The following day she flew twenty times from the front porch of the rectory forty feet to the picket fence and on another fifty feet along the side of the church to where Jordan stood on a wide path. At twilight Jordan jessed her to a perch on the back porch to keep her from destroying the house. Pondering the possibility of running away with Zanifa, Jordan stared into the first starry night in months with the binoculars, tracing the flight of a blue white Venus and an amber Mars. He found himself singing the Maasai song: "Jump and I will choose one of you to love. . . ."

# Septemba 9

*B*wana, njoo sasa!" Shabu called from the yard.

Jordan set the spliff on the table and rose slowly. He looked around the living room at the walls covered with watercolors of Pasipo, trying to remember what he was going to do before he smoked—paint the eagle?

"*Njoo sasa hivi!*" Shabu shouted. Come right now! Jordan walked outside, shirtless in khakis and leather sandals.

Shabu was climbing over the tall hedge between the yard and a cornfield, his bare ass exposed beneath the tunic, his spear resting against the fence on the inside of the hedge.

"Pasipo *ametoka!*" Shabu dropped into the cornfield.

"How did she escape?" Jordan yelled, running to the hedge.

"She pulled her jess loose." Shabu leapt through dead corn stalks toward the edge of the cliff.

Jordan was about to curse Shabu, then remembered it was he who had jessed her to the porch. From the top of the hedge he could see Pasipo thirty yards from the edge of the cliff. If she launched again, she might land three thousand feet below in the woodland. She wouldn't be able to fly back up the mountain wall. Jordan yelled for Shabu to circle slowly around in front of her. He ran back to the porch for the glove and the falconry bag and dashed back outside to the hedge.

Pasipo stood in the broken clay near the edge, looking out at the smog. Between her and the edge, Shabu was on his hands and knees—less of a threatening giant from the eagle's perspective—crawling toward her. Jordan jogged through the dry corn from behind her. He knelt and held the glove before him, offering a large chick. "Pasipo."

The eagle jerked her head around a hundred and twenty degrees. *Kio-kio.*

Jordan shuffled closer on his knees, slowly, wiggling the chick in the glove to attract the raptor. Her eyes were designed to focus on small movements. "Pasipo."

The eagle spun her head back toward the edge of the escarpment. Shabu was five feet from her, crawling in slow motion.

"Pasipo." Jordan wiggled the chick.

The eagle spread her wings and leapt over Shabu.

Flapping, she arced toward the edge, cantering awkwardly on fledgling wings.

Jordan's stomach dropped, and he pushed himself up from the ground.

Pasipo wobbled over the cliff and disappeared.

Jordan and Shabu ran to the edge. There was no wind. Pasipo glided toward the savanna, already hundreds of yards away. Jordan cursed under his breath. The Maasai was silent.

Pasipo was spiraling down toward the dry thorn forest in the foothills.

"It will be impossible to track her in that bush," Shabu said. "A *fungo* will find her first."

They watched uselessly until Pasipo was too small to discern against the treetops a half mile below.

"Goddamn it," Jordan said.

Coolly in Swahili, Shabu said, "I shall take a water bottle and flashlight and run down there and look for the sky leopard. Like looking for a bead in a thorn bush." He waited for Jordan to reply.

Jordan stared out into the smog, then turned and looked at Shabu. "Maybe I should go."

The Maasai waited.

Jordan looked down at the dark umbrellas of the acacias in the foothills. Just above the treetops he could make out a raptor circling, rising in an updraft.

"It is your sky leopard," Shabu said.

"Are you sure?" Jordan squinted.

"*Utaona*," Shabu said gleefully. You shall see.

Her black wings were cantering up and down. Her body yawed fore and aft, barely under control. She circled up from the depths. Jordan watched, growing calm as she climbed closer, amazed at her instinct to navigate an invisible thermal gyre. She floated even with the cliff, a hundred feet out from the mountain wall, and spiraled higher. From below they could see the white undersides of her wings and black-and-white stripes of her broad tail.

"Pasipo!" Jordan waved the big chick in his glove.

Pasipo glanced at him, fell sideways in the turbulence of the thermal, righted herself and screamed: *Koi-koi-koi!*

Then Jordan saw the resident augur buzzards following the cliff line five hundred feet above the eyas. Jordan braced himself for the attack dives. The buzzards' flight paths undulated as they encountered the thermal turbulence. They brought their wings together and dove through the thermal, passing a hundred feet over Pasipo, who watched them open their wings as they pulled out of their dives. The buzzards kept heading south along the cliff line, oblivious of a raptor of another species. Learning from their example, Pasipo tucked her wings and dove out of the thermal.

"Pasipo!" Jordan waved the glove.

A black wedge, the eyas shot down toward the edge of the cliff. She spread her six-foot wingspan and swung her yellow hand-size claws out front.

Jordan flinched at the sight of the sky leopard coming toward him like a pterodactyl.

Pasipo hit the glove like a stone, swinging Jordan's arm behind his shoulder. Jordan fell backward as Pasipo somersaulted onto the clay. She righted herself and looked over at Jordan. He got to his feet and hesitated before offering the glove with the head of the chicken lying limp, beak to the sky, in the center of his fist. He took a deep breath. Pasipo hopped lightly onto the glove.

A PILE OF CORPSES IN BOSNIA UNDER A GRAY SKY. A BRUNETTE anchor lady. African children with big heads, swollen bellies and skeletal limbs. Images on the screen flashed by without sound. Jordan's mouth was dry. His head throbbed faintly after having drinks with Vernon Taylor. He lay on the leather couch, willing her to appear. His stomach rumbled. He hadn't eaten since breakfast. On the screen bulldozers moved deeper into the Amazon, razing trees like matchsticks.

There was the sound of a key in the lock. Then Anna. Her hair was pulled back and she was wearing the brown double-breasted suit she had worn when they took his great-grandmother to dinner last fall in Nashville. He had watched them talking about gardens and politics, laughing together. When Anna was away from the table, Nanny had leaned forward and put her wrinkled, shrunken hand on his and said, "Anna's got gumption. She knows how to take hold. Cherish her, Rutledge. You're a lucky young man."

"Hey." Anna set a leather satchel by the door.

"I must have called you ten times." Jordan rose up on an elbow as she crossed the room.

"Twelve." Anna lay down beside him.

"Why didn't you call back?"

"Why? What's to talk about?" She pulled his tie loose from his collar, started on the buttons.

"The nights you come." Jordan was tempted to say that Sunday must have been a record: had anyone else ever made her come three times in a row? There was no other way now to measure what went on between them. When she had left Sunday night, she had told him not to walk her to the street. Through the kitchen window he had seen her crying when she got in her car. He ran his little finger along her lips. "The passion that's still there."

"You're much more attentive. You're trying to hang on," Anna said, not unkindly.

"There's no sweetness left when we make love," Jordan said. "Are you punishing me or easing me out or both?"

"What do you want me to say?"

"That you come by because you hope we have a future."

"I don't know if I can say that. It's going to take time. I don't know how long it will be before I trust you again. You broke something in me. I feel used up."

"I'm sorry I hurt you." Jordan pulled her to his chest. "I never meant to damage you. I feel like such a bastard."

"Don't be too hard on yourself. Don't think that I don't know that a lot of people out there don't have half as much good in them as you." She laughed sadly. "The sex is a comfort. We've always had great sex. But I don't know how long that will last."

# Septemba 25–Oktoba 5

An arid gale howled out of the south, roaring along the mountain wall at fifty miles an hour, washing the yellow brown out of the sky, blowing the haze north over Kenya. Jordan spent the first day of the windstorm, a month to the day since he had last seen Zanifa, teaching Shabu to play backgammon in the living room. Hour after hour they played in silence. Zanifa seemed remote, like a dream, the romance a dangerous indulgence. He resolved to forget. At dusk Shabu rose from the table to light the lanterns. Jordan eyed the bookshelf, the surest escape, next to sleep. He was reading again, devouring novels between training Pasipo and a few appointments at the ponds. He sighed and closed the lid of the backgammon case.

"Bwana, this wind will blow for three or four days. No one will come while I'm gone." Shabu set a lamp on the table.

"What?" Jordan took *Folly* from the shelf.

"I'm going to see my cattle. I'll be back in a few days with some friends."

"Your girlfriend was supposed to send them," Jordan said.

"They haven't come. I'll go get them myself."

"I don't want to stay alone. Kimweri's warriors might come and kill me," Jordan said. Kimweri had yet to reply to his note, so he had ventured out only when one of his serious farmers had a problem and made the effort to send him word.

"Ah, bwana. You're too scared. The Sambaa are cowards." Shabu laughed and put his arm over Jordan's shoulder. "They won't come during a windstorm. They haven't come yet. They won't come now."

"I'm paying you to be here until I go back to America."

"I'll be back with some friends." Shabu picked up his spear and pointed it at the door. "I'll leave you with this. I must see my cattle, bwana."

"*Sawa,*" Jordan relented. He pulled the film can out of Shabu's earlobe and poured a black line of snuff on his thumb. After snorting it, he felt his nostrils burn and his mind rushing through nowhere.

Shabu watched him, grinning, then took a pinch.

The dawn sky was clear and the wind was howling. Shabu stood on the front porch, wrapped in his tartan blanket.

"Hurry back. Don't waste any time."

"Three days. Don't worry, no one will come while I'm gone."

"I just hope you don't come back and find me gone."

Shabu laughed and slapped his hand. He said good-bye in Maasai: "*Sere.*"

"*Sere.*" Jordan watched him trot off through the trees on one side of the yard. He found the binoculars on the bookshelf and went to the back porch, where he followed Shabu's zigzagging trail between boulders down a buttress that sloped toward the plain, half expecting him to be blown off the cliff. A thousand feet below, a tiny stick figure, the Maasai disappeared onto the far side of the buttress. On the back porch Pasipo hovered motionlessly two inches above her perch, held by leather thongs, balancing in the wind. The tin roof of the rectory rose with the great gusts, then heaved back into place when the howling dropped. Jordan said to Pasipo, "You're the only one left to talk to. I wonder how Zanifa's riding out the storm. You think she's in school today?"

Her beak pointing in the wind, gliding in place, Pasipo didn't look at him.

The gale carried Jordan eight years back to a typhoon off the Azores. The wind had sheared the swells into cliffs for the first few days. When it topped out at eighty knots, it drove the huge waves flat, turning the Atlantic into a sheet of glass searing with spray. Jordan recalled a shouting match with Anna in their cabin during the storm while the captain and his wife were on watch. Anna's hair was pulled back. She wore a bikini top and cut-offs. She lay down on the bunk beside him but was too angry to sleep and kept him awake through the night until it was his turn to go up. Jordan couldn't remember what they were fighting about.

He went into the house and lay on the sofa, watching the roof rise and fall like a great lung. He dug through two tall woven baskets filled with letters and old magazines until he found an envelope with photographs of Anna nude on a deserted beach. He wondered if she hadn't written back in a year because she no longer cared or if she'd stopped writing as a survival technique to kill him off in her memory. He sat at the table with thin sheets of airmail paper and a pen.

*Dear Anna,*

*"I will love you forever," you promised and then you forgot.*

He set the pen down. There was no reason to believe that she would reply when his last dozen letters had gone unanswered. He lay back on the couch with a tube of skin cream. He touched himself, looking at the photos, but his mind wandered to Zanifa. She must have been scared when the midwife who would cut her spread her legs apart to examine her for Kimweri. Where did they do that? Vooga or Lushoto? He looked down at his hand, then wiped the lotion off on his thigh and picked up a novel.

During the last fifty hours of the gale, Jordan fed Pasipo at dawn and dusk, forcing her to fly ten feet across the room to his fist over and over through the course of her meal. Jordan slipped into a dream time of napping and waking to reread a tattered paperback by lantern light through the night. He ate once or twice a day and more often jerked off to the photographs of Anna and a medley of vague images of old lovers, regretting each time that he had never photographed or sketched Zanifa nude. He watched the path up the mountain wall with the binoculars, wondering if Shabu was coming back.

Purple light glowed through the windows. Jordan sat up in bed, unsure if the sun was rising or setting. Something made him uneasy. He crawled out from the net and realized it was the silence. The wind had stopped. He fed Pasipo and painted on the back porch, taking breaks to scan the cliff side with the binoculars. In the late afternoon a party of three appeared at the bottom. An hour later, midway up the escarpment, their spears were distinct. Jordan let out a whoop of relief and pictured them spearing Kimweri's bodyguards through their polo shirts. Surely with the three of them it would be safe to stay until the end of his contract. With luck, if he trained the eyas as quickly as possible, she would be able to hunt on her own by the first of December.

*"Entasoba,"* Jordan called to them as they came into the yard. Pasipo shifted on his glove but stayed quiet.

*"Eba,"* they called.

"Shabu, Lesuyu, welcome back."

They rested, leaning on their spears with their hands clasping the shaft just below the blade. The third Maasai grinned and looked at the eagle. Loudly he asked Jordan something.

"I can't speak Maasai," Jordan said in Swahili.

"He doesn't speak Swahili," Shabu said. "His name is Parmet."

Parmet shook his hand limply.

Jordan said, "My house is your house."

"What about the money?" Lesuyu said.

"The same as Shabu's. I'll pay you by the first day of the new moon." Jordan wondered if Ernst or Ionides would lend him the money and how he would pay them back. "I haven't left the yard in days. Shabu, will you come with me?"

*"Sawa,"* Shabu said okay, smiling.

Out on the lane, Omali's daughters rushed up but stopped six feet short of the eagle. Pasipo screamed her territorial call at the children. *Koi-koi-koi!*

They turned and ran back into the house.

"You think you're a person, don't you?" Jordan asked the eyas.

Walking past Omali's house, Jordan peered in the door, wondering if he was inside.

*Koi-koi-koi!* Pasipo screeched at three women carrying water on their heads.

"Don't be afraid. I'm holding her." Jordan smiled and waved his free hand.

*Koi-koi-koi!*

The women stepped off the path, wary of the eagle and the Maasai.

"Pasipo, you've got to shut up," Jordan said. They walked past groves of spindly wattle trees and fields of corn stunted from soil sapped by years of planting and abandoned fields being reclaimed by low bristly shrubs that fertilized the soil for larger trees. Gradually Pasipo began to ignore the people on the road. In a relic patch of primeval forest, she became fixed on a clan of small vervet monkeys. Silently, she seemed to study them hopping from branch to branch.

Jordan skipped Pasipo's breakfast and told Shabu not to feed her no matter how she screamed. In the afternoon, in an abandoned field with Lesuyu watching from a distance, Jordan tied a leash onto one jess and set Pasipo on a stump. He paced off a hundred feet, winding out the leash. He waved a long sliver of beef, and the eyas winged across the field and touched down lightly on his fist. *"Safi sana,"* Lesuyu yelled. Very cool. Jordan set her on a boulder, walked a little farther away and called. Staying low over the ground, she rowed on a straight line to his fist. She flew twelve times, covering a half mile, before she was full. Two days later Pasipo was crossing a distance of two hundred yards to Jordan's fist twenty times before she refused to fly. Jordan decided she was ready to fly without a leash.

# Oktoba 13

Jordan opened his eyes. The mats curtaining the windows were edged in hot, white light. The house was quiet. He lay waiting for a phalanx of warriors to burst in through the door, a recurring nightmare he'd had the last few days. If he were in Memphis, he'd call a support group for the raped, he thought, listening to Pasipo crying on the back porch. The bird screamed on and on. He lay for a half hour, hesitant to crawl out from under the net. The eagle screamed and beat her wings against the latticework, probably at passing crows. An inspiration of how to exorcise the sultan made him smile.

He heard the three Maasai laughing on the front porch and went to the kitchen and found some porridge they'd left for him. He took a coconut onto the back porch. The visibility across the Maasai steppe was unlimited today, stretching as far as the twin peaks of Kilimanjaro, high and white and wide. While Pasipo perched on the back of a chair across the table, Jordan punched two holes on one side of the coconut with a hammer and screwdriver and another two, closer together, in the folds of hard skin on the bottom. Pasipo watched intently then started screaming. *Kiu-kiu-kiu!*

Jordan went to the front porch and greeted the Maasai. He whittled a piece of wattle into an isosceles wedge that he hammered lightly onto the coconut with a finishing nail. He cut two ovals of leather from an old safari boot and nailed one on each side of the coconut. He mixed black and purple for the lips.

*Kiu-kiu-kiu!* Pasipo screamed from the back porch. *Kiu-kiu-kiu!*

Jordan dug through his dirty clothes until he found a sweatsuit. He stuffed the top and bottom with dried banana leaves from the yard. With monofilament fishing line he sewed the pants to the shirt and closed the ends of the arms and legs. He poked four holes in the shirt around the neck and ran sisal twine through the holes. He cut the bottom out of a margarine tin, then threaded the four sisal lines through the tin and through the holes in the bottom of the coconut. Finally he pushed a red fez down over the top of the coconut head.

"What are you doing, bwana?" Shabu asked.

"You'll see," Jordan said, setting the effigy in a chair. He went out to the yard and ran fishing line through a large washer and strung the line back and forth between two trees, twisting the filaments to form one strong cord. He tied the dummy to the washer on the line and, with safety pins, clipped two lengths of sisal cord to the front and back of the stuffed shirt. He ran through the yard, pulling the cord. A noodle-necked drunk staggered jerkily from tree to tree. He cut strips of lean steak and tacked them over the eyes and mouth of the coconut head.

*Kiu-kiu-kiu!* On the back porch Pasipo stared fixedly at him from her perch on the back of a chair. Jordan pulled on the glove, and Pasipo parachuted down to his fist. She looked in his fingers for meat and screamed again.

In the yard, Pasipo focused immediately on the red fez, her sensitive eyes irritated by the unusual bright color. She raised her crown and hissed. The red-topped head resembled the wig of a red colobus monkey, awakening a genetic memory of preferred prey. Jordan jerked one of the sisal cords. The coconut man lurched toward them.

"*Piga!*" Jordan yelled. Hit! He threw the sky leopard at the oncoming dummy. Pasipo pumped her huge wings and accelerated across the yard. The thud of the impact was audible at forty feet. She perched on the coconut head, forcing the fishing line down, and tore the strips of meat from the eyes and mouth and swallowed them in quick gulps with her neck and beak raised toward the sky. The three Maasai cheered from the porch.

Jordan whispered her name, and she swam over in a few strokes and settled lightly on his glove.

Jordan jessed the sky leopard to the railing on the porch and tacked more meat to the face. He pulled the dummy to the tree near the house, then walked with Pasipo to the far side of the yard and stepped behind a bush. He jerked the dummy across the line. When it reached halfway, he jumped out from behind the bush and yelled, "*Piga!*"

Pasipo shot from his glove and thumped into the head.

Parmet yelled a war cry.

Jordan repeated the exercise from different points around the yard, sometimes starting with his back to the dummy and spinning around to release the hungry raptor. He practiced again and again, tacking only small bits of meat on the head to keep Pasipo keen. He decided to quit while she was still hungry and carried her to the house. The Maasai laughed and slapped his hand, a new respect in their eyes. Jordan put Pasipo on the back porch and waited for darkness.

"You are a shaman with that eagle," Lesuyu said, gnawing on a piece of steak.

Shabu agreed and translated for Parmet, who nodded.

"Thanks." Jordan burped loudly like a Maasai.

Pasipo screamed hungrily from the back porch.

Parmet collected the plates from the table.

"In a little while I'll show you some new magic." Jordan stood up and went to his bedroom. He removed a floorboard, where he kept the Peace Corps—issue equipment: the big first-aid box and a heavy-duty, waterproof Maglite. Jordan admired the flashlight, heavy enough to use as a weapon, its beam far more powerful than the head-light of a car. He was never sure why it had been included in the kit. He imagined volunteers across the third world blinding intruders and then clubbing them to death or crawling through twelve hours of un-expected darkness. He lifted the Maglite from the hole and went to the back porch for Pasipo.

"Come on," Jordan said, walking through the house with the eagle.

The three Maasai, wrapped in tartan cloaks, followed him out to the front yard. There was no wind to stir the darkness of the clearing. The moon was blacked out by clouds. The eagle felt heavy on his fist. With the beam on narrow focus, Jordan pointed Shabu to the sisal cord in the yard, told him to take the cord and hide behind a bush.

The dummy skimmed the ground, stopped, skimmed again.

"*Piga!*"

The eagle flew down the concentrated beam, an acrobat gliding down a spotlight. *Thwap!* She slammed into the head even though there was no meat on it.

The Maasai whooped. Jordan cut the light, betting that the diurnal raptor would stay perfectly still in the dark. He trained the light on his fist, clicked it on, heard the great billows of her wings. Out of the darkness Pasipo touched down softly.

"You're a shaman, truly," Lesuyu shouted.

Twice more the eagle streaked down the beam of the powerful light and attacked strips of steak on the coconut head before she was full. Jordan gave Shabu the glove and asked him to put her back on her perch. He told Lesuyu to light the pumpkin on the front porch and collapsed on his bed.

# Oktoba 18

In the half-light beneath the trees, Jordan and Shabu walked down an alley of shoulder-high coffee bushes. *Whoosh. Whoosh.* A sound like great bellows came from behind. Pasipo glided inches over his head and disappeared down the trail. Jordan rounded a bend in the path and saw her sitting in the shadows, camouflaged, on a branch forty feet off the ground. She swooped down and grazed his hair with her balled talons, banked a hundred and eighty degrees with sheer momentum and rowed down the trail. *Whoosh.*

Jordan emerged into the bright sunshine, blinded momentarily. He squinted and looked down at a low bush hung with furry pods. "This is a stinging bean," Zanifa had told him, pointing to the bush. "The juice of this bean can make you itch like you're covered with army ants. I've seen people brush against it and an hour later scrape their skin off with knives." She had spoken evenly, in the manner of a model student. "The lowland people believe there is no cure, that you must wait a week for the itching to stop. But my great-grandmother showed me an herb that will stop the torture."

Zanifa had pulled a leather pouch from her sisal-and-leather handbag. Her black eyes had seemed older than the rest of her face.

"I need an herb that will make me forget."

"Forget what?" Zanifa had asked seriously.

"Heartbreak."

"I know no herbs for diseases of the heart," Zanifa had said, turning away.

Jordan fondled the leather pouch hanging by his Maasai sword, considered thrusting his hand in the bush to test the powder. He tried to place the month Zanifa had showed him the bush. . . . It was June, before he had seduced her.

*Ki-ki-ki-ki! Ki-ki-ki-ki!*

A band of vervets appeared in an albizzia tree that mushroomed above the canopy. Black faces suspended on stick arms, peering out of the forest into barren land. Suddenly they all scrambled higher in the tree, then paused again and started to chatter. Jordan went down the slope beneath the tree and stared up at the thin, greenish white monkeys. One of them pulled a dried seed pod. It rattled as it fell through the air and landed by Jordan's feet. Another shat in his general direction. Vervets came out of the forest to steal corn and then escaped back to their sanctuary. Jordan had seen gangs of vervets and school kids taunting each other. Another vervet swung its ass over the branch. Jordan jumped sideways. Seed pods rained from the branches, clattering around him on the dirt. Something warm, thick and wet splattered against the back of his neck. Vervets were supposed to carry a dozen deadly diseases. Stiffening, he backed out from under the tree, looking for a stone. Shabu stood back from the tree, laughing.

Over the chattering of the monkeys, Jordan heard the sound of a projectile cutting a hole through the air and a soft explosion of leaves high on the far side of the tree. Quietly the vervets raced away from the sound into the darkness of the forest. Pasipo appeared, rising from behind the tree with slow wingbeats. A vervet was dangling in her talons. She rowed over the tree and across the ridge in the direction of the rectory.

JORDAN PARKED IN A LOT FULL OF MERCEDES, LEXUS AND CADILLACS outside the Memphis American Museum of Art, a stone building in the fashion of an Italian Renaissance villa that hunkered against a black wall of trees beneath a gloomy autumn sunset. He waved his invitation at a guard inside the glass doors. A bright hall led past dark galleries to the rotunda, where two hundred people sat on folding chairs below the high domed ceiling.

". . . Thomas Hart Benton, Edward Hopper, Georgia O'Keeffe. The permanent collection at the MAMA now rivals museums in Houston, Miami and Atlanta." Anna stood at the podium in a black suit Jordan had bought her on a trip together to New York in the spring. Her voice echoed off the marble floor and limestone walls. "You've made a lasting contribution to the city of Memphis."

There was a moment of silence, then a wave of clapping rose from the front row, swept across the room and ebbed as a string quartet began in the rear. Jordan took a glass of white wine from a waiter's tray and watched Anna smiling and shaking hands. A few feet behind her he noticed Truman Tharpe, an orthopedic surgeon who had played linebacker at Washington and Lee. You hit him and he's going to humiliate you in front of everyone, Jordan thought, finishing the wine. Anna would never talk to you again. Or maybe she would see how much you love her. He found a waiter, took another glass.

"Howdy, Rut."

Jordan turned and saw Jody Simpson from his class at Episcopal High and tried to sound cheerful. "Never took you for a patron of the arts."

"Sissy made me come." Jody shifted his shoulders inside his jacket. "You're the only one I know who'd come here willingly. I just want to get home in time for the game."

"Game?" Jordan said, glancing away.

"Ever heard of Monday night football?" Jody's eyes followed Jordan's across the room toward Anna, then he placed his hand on Jordan's shoulder.

Jordan saw the solicitous look. "Later, old buddy."

He wove through the crowd, trying to avoid familiar faces. He grabbed another wineglass off a passing tray, worked over to a wall and swallowed, tasted a splash of bile deep in his throat. He had been drinking heavily since Anna had stopped coming around, drowning a thought that haunted him: He had lost her forever for a few nights that he could barely remember. It had been a mistake to confess. It had ended right then. There was no return. Jordan gulped down the rest of the wine and set the glass in the pot of a Norfolk pine and stepped back into the crowd. Near the podium, he stood a few feet from Anna, waiting for her to finish talking to an elderly lady. His stomach felt bloated from the wine. He looked over his shoulder at Truman Tharpe.

Tharpe grinned at him.

Jordan approached Anna from the side. He smiled at the lady. "Pardon me."

Anna looked startled, then introduced them.

"Nice to meet you," Jordan said, then looked at Anna. "May I speak with you for a moment? Now?"

"Go right ahead," the woman said. "I need to find my husband. He seems to have vanished. Ninety to nothing he's sleeping in a corner."

Anna looked at Tharpe and shrugged. He smiled benevolently.

Jordan took Anna's arm and guided her up a wide flight of stairs that curved around the rotunda.

"Congratulations on the timing," Anna said halfway up the staircase. "That was a big donor. Are you drunk?"

"Sorta." Jordan put his arm around her waist, pulled her close.

"Maintain a sense of decorum," Anna said.

Jordan let go.

Reaching the balcony, Anna asked, "What do you want? I've got to get back down there."

"What do I want?" Jordan said softly. "I want you."

"That's it?" She glared at him. "You dragged me up here to say that?" Then the sarcasm left her voice: "We loved each other. We always will."

"That old cliché," Jordan said, defeated.

"I just meant that nothing will undo that depth of feeling."

Jordan took deep, slow breaths, trying to relieve the pressure in his gut.

"Are you all right?" Anna touched his shoulder.

"Something's happened to my stomach." Jordan leaned forward over the rail, vaguely amused by the thought of vomiting onto the heads below.

"Don't drink so much." Anna put her arm around his back and led him past glass cases of South American masks to a bench.

"Remember when I first asked you to marry me?" Jordan sat hunched over, concentrated on his breathing.

"I said yes then, and I meant it." She smiled sadly, as if she might cry. "You used to ask me twice a day. That's what's so tragic. The quality of love—"

"If you hadn't gone back to London for three months, we would have been married."

"Maybe you were committed before. But you weren't when I got back. Makes me wonder if you ever really were."

"I am now."

"You silly boy." She wrapped her other arm around his chest and hugged his side.

"You're fucking Tharpe now, huh?"

"Rutledge," she whispered.

Jordan groaned and slumped back against the bench. He looked up at scenes of Tennessee history on the dome of the rotunda. "Where are the Chickasaws and slaves?"

"A whitewash," Anna said, laughing a little. She wiped his eyes with a cocktail napkin. "Baby, you've got to take better care of yourself. I haven't stopped loving you. You know I'll always love you." She kissed his cheek and walked along the balcony.

"Nice ass," Jordan called.

Anna smiled over her shoulder and went down the staircase.

# Novemba 3

*M*alayka, *nakupenda malayka* . . . Angel, I love you, angel. A low voice and tinny notes of Carib-Afro steel blared from speakers hanging from a thatched roof at the corners of a concrete patio. The song, a melancholy 1950s hit still among the most popular in East Africa, pulled dancers from the tables around the patio and thinned out the crowd at the bar. The song spoke of the plight of every young man too poor to marry his true love, who would be sold off to a rich old man.

By the end of the first verse the dance floor was crowded with men bobbing up and down in pairs and trios, rarely lifting their feet but rising and falling from their knees. The disco was packed tonight because it was a *siku kuu*, a big day, this one commemorating the founding of the first African political party in the fifties. Ernst had driven out to Jordan's house and dragged him into town. Ernst towered above the Tanzanians in blue jeans and a leather jacket. Every few seconds a flash from a makeshift revolving ball revealed the Dutchman's drunken smile, his eyes focused on his partner, one of the few girls on the floor, a Kenyan with *matiti mzigo*, "tits like suitcases," a slender hourglass figure and faux braids that bounced as she swung her hips—a veteran of cosmopolitan discos in Nairobi and Mombasa.

"Come." Rose's English was stiff and sounded faintly hostile. "You dance with me, baby."

Jordan looked at Rose, the younger sister of Ernst's lover, identical except she had dyed her hair henna to match her braids. Jordan pondered the origin of the orange fibers. Rose smiled and tugged at his sleeve. Jordan smiled sheepishly, shook his head.

"*Kidege wasumbuwa loho yangu,*" the singer crooned, sorrowfully accompanied by a xylophone.

"These birds hurt my heart," Jordan translated, looking into Rose's brown eyes. She smiled, slipping her hand along his thigh. Smiling, he pulled her hand from his crotch and placed it gently on the table, thinking it funny that in both Swahili and English, men called women birds. It suddenly reminded him of Pasipo, and he stopped smiling, confused.

Rose laughed woodenly. Her long black hand, pink white on the underside, curled around a glass of plum wine. "You do not like to dance?"

"Not until I'm drunk." Jordan threw back a shot of clear Konyagi and chased it with Sprite.

A driving dual disco beat—snare drum and synthesized bass—interrupted the fading notes of "Malayka." A pulsating six-count repeated itself dramatically several times, leading into Michael Jackson's soprano. The young men on the dance floor kept bobbing up and down from their knees with the exception of one teenage boy, who spun and side-slid across the concrete, drawing his arms along his body and then pointing them into space.

"*Kijana huyu anaweza kucheza,*" Jordan told Rose. That kid can dance.

"He was seeing Michael Jackson videos." Rose refused to answer in Swahili, a Kenyan prejudice.

"How do you know?"

Rose lit a Sportsman. "He is learning where else?"

Jordan nodded, sipped Konyagi from a glass.

"Get up and dance, man," Ernst shouted, approaching the table with his arm around Rose's sister, Beatrice. "*Vipi?* I've seen a lot of depressed American volunteers in Africa, but *you* are clinical."

"To the happy Dutchman." Jordan raised the Konyagi bottle.

"You'll never know how happy," Ernst said.

Jordan brought the Konyagi to his lips and forced the burning liquid down until the glass was empty. His stomach quivered, on the edge of recoiling. Ernst slapped his back, laughing. Focused on the bitter aftertaste and a rising nausea, Jordan reached slowly for the green bottle of Sprite. The relentless beat grew louder. After all this time, after the thousands of hours building fish ponds, after saving the eagle, Jordan wondered if he had changed. He felt no sense of absolution. Anna would never forgive him. He was irrelevant to her now. Zanifa would soon be held down by four midwives while the oldest witch cut her with a razor.

"Do they ever play anything slow?" Jordan shouted, holding on to the table from his chair.

"Only 'Malayka.'" Ernst laughed. "The Sambaa are too shy to dance up close."

"I think I'm going to be sick," Jordan said, standing. He smiled and pushed off into the crowd, keeping to the edge of the dance floor. He crossed a dark lawn to a yellow light pouring out from the open door of the *choo*. A puddle covered the floor, so he retreated behind a bush and tilted his head against a wall and spat up a mouthful of Konyagi.

Walking slowly back toward the noise, Jordan stopped in the middle of the lawn to look up at a starless sky. He breathed deeply. A new song started. The notes were familiar. Jordan neared the flashing red and green lights, trying to place the strong female voice. He rolled his stride slightly with the music. Tina Turner sang "What's Love Got to Do with It." Jordan reached a vacant place on the concrete floor between bobbing young men. As she hit the refrain, Jordan sang along, his eyes closed and feet still, rocking back and forth from his waist, ripped back through time by the force of the music and the repetition of the movement until for a few seconds he was dancing with Anna somewhere in South Carolina. She was sweaty and drunk, singing loud.

The Congo Bongo Man cut off Tina Turner midverse. Jordan was jerked back into a present of another Konyagi chased with Sprite. He looked across the dance floor at Ernst and the Kenyan girls, spun on one heel and steered through the crowd, whispering aloud to Anna. Halfway along the bar, Jordan found a spot large enough to squeeze in sideways.

The bartender, a big woman in a yellow turban, waddled away, and Jordan rested his back against the bar. He stared glumly around the disco, grimacing between sips of Konyagi. A group of girls in St. Mary's sweaters and jeans were filing in through the door, led by a young teacher in a windbreaker and dress. He felt his pulse race involuntarily, the vibration of his heart in his chest.

She walked in last, talking to a second teacher, a thirtyish light-colored woman in jeans.

The first teacher led the girls along the wall toward one end of the dance floor. There was a single empty table, held by an older *mzungu* in a tweed blazer who was standing, waving. Every few seconds the flashing lights caught the headmaster, Father William. Jordan thought the cross-breed teacher must be one of the monk's daughters.

Jordan moved away from the bar and worked his way through the bobbing dancers. Bob Marley gave way to Paul Simon's African band, singing about how earth looks to distant dying constellations. Zanifa appeared to be concentrating on the lyrics, with her head cocked toward the nearest speaker. Jordan listened to the American voice he had grown up with, realizing only a handful of the people here understood the words. Zanifa mouthed the lyrics, then turned and leaned across the table toward the teacher as the song faded. A synthesized beat and German female vocalist blasted from the speakers. Jordan approached the table.

Fifteen feet across the floor, Zanifa saw him. Her face changed, but shadows obscured her expression. Jordan stepped forward. Zanifa lifted her hand off the table without raising her arm, shook her head faintly then looked back at her teacher. Jordan changed course and slipped into the crowd.

"Fuck her," he whispered, tapping the empty shot glass against the bar, listening to his voice as if it were someone else's, studying the long sandy hair, the deep tan, the pale blue eyes in the mirror above the bottles as if he were a stranger.

"Excuse me," someone shouted through the music from the side.

Jordan turned slowly and saw a girl in a blue St. Mary's pullover. It was Zanifa's friend.

Subira smiled and stared at her feet.

"Would you like a drink?"

Subira looked up, her face serious, and said in English, "No. The St. Mary's rules forbid alcohol."

"I was just joking," Jordan said. "I'm surprised Father William let you come here at all."

"One of our classmates wanted to enter the dance contest. Father William says she is showing individual initiative and that we should support her." Subira kept her two fists hanging by her side.

Jordan leaned against the bar, suddenly weary. "Father William is a wise man."

"Bwana Joldon, Zanifa asked me to say to you that there is danger here. Many Kilindi are at the disco." Subira stood on her toes to reach Jordan's ear. "If they see you and Zanifa talking, there could be much trouble."

Jordan sighed and turned toward her. "I got the message." He looked away and waved his hand at the barmaid, who ignored him, flirting with a tall man in a dark suit. Jordan slammed the shot glass against the bar and shouted in English, "Please!" The barmaid glanced at him coldly, shouted something about rude *mzungu*, then moved to the other end of the long bar.

"Please listen, bwana," Subira said.

Jordan turned toward the girl. "You're still here? Would you like a Coke?"

"*Mlevi sana.*" Subira giggled. What a drunkard. "Zanifa and I are going to see my sister. She is the telephone operator. Meet us behind the *posta* after one hour. Watch that no one follows yourself."

It took Jordan a full second to comprehend.

The darkness outside the disco was total. Streetlights, set every quarter mile, illuminated wisps of fog, and in the long stretches of blackness Jordan passed disembodied voices gaily chattering Swahili and the ominous footsteps of lone walkers. He gradually picked up his pace until he was jogging blindly toward the yellow orb of a damaged streetlight. Something rose from the road, and he fell forward onto dirt and gravel. He stood on his knees, ran his fingertips over the rips in his shirtsleeves and the skinned undersides of his forearms, then crawled back to a cold, heavy object, round—a tire rim. His shins throbbed as he walked on.

When he reached the main road, the world grew distinct. Tall street lamps painted the black tarmac hazy white and threw gray light out on hedges and rock walls, allowing glimpses of the tops of colonial houses set back from the road. It reminded Jordan of a midnight walk through Tangier with Anna, holding hands out of fear and the promise of the bed to come. His head reeled from memory and alcohol.

A group of people stood outside the bar by the BP station. Jordan turned up his collar, kept his head down and crossed to the far side of the road. A hundred yards past the station, at the corner of a little cemetery filled with German settlers, he stepped into the shadows and climbed over a low stone wall, stumbling. Sitting in the darkness with his back against a tombstone, he watched the road. After five minutes he left the cemetery from the rear and shuffled blindly through a grove of trees before finding the weak light slanting from the barred windows at the back of the post office.

Jordan checked his watch then climbed the stone foundation, clinging with his fingertips to the bricks, and peered in a window at an antique wooden switchboard with dozens of black cables looping between rows of plugs. Across the room Subira and her sister sat at a table, drinking tea, gesturing without sound.

Someone laughed behind him.

Jordan pushed off the wall and spun as he dropped to the ground. Dizzy, he leaned against the building.

Zanifa slid her arms under his and clasped his back hard, pressing her face to his chest. She said in Swahili, "I missed you."

"I think about you every day." Jordan hugged her hard and planted his face into the crook of her neck and shoulder, feeling the rhythm of her breathing. Zanifa said nothing. Jordan pulled her back by her shoulders until her face was visible in the light from the window.

"How's Pasipo?" she asked in English. She was crying.

"Healthy. Hunting monkeys." Jordan found no words to console her, or for the feeling of her warmth after so long. He hugged her again. Her tears smeared on his neck. She sobbed, and he heard his own scratchy voice coming from far away. "Don't cry."

Zanifa pulled away and wiped a tear from her eye with the knuckle of her thumb. She asked in English: "She flies on a leash?"

"She follows me on walks through the forest."

"Cool," Zanifa said, a word she'd picked up from him. Her laugh caught in her throat.

He slipped his hands down underneath her jeans and cupped her bottom. Zanifa sighed and settled against him. Jordan lifted her legs over his hips and staggered into the dark, squinting into the blackness. Crossing her legs, Zanifa scissored his waist playfully. They passed through the black gap in the hedge. Jordan shuffled forward slowly, one arm cradling her back, the other extended, groping between pine trees, brushed by invisible branches. He sank to his knees on the spongy floor and tried to lower Zanifa gently onto the matted needles, but his balance was off and she landed awkwardly.

"It's too dark," Zanifa said in English. "I want to see your face."

Jordan lowered his face blindly.

"Your breath isn't good." Zanifa slid her tongue in his mouth.

"Do you want to marry him?"

"I . . . no . . . I don't know," she whispered.

Jordan moaned, pulled out her shirttail. He skimmed his lips along her belly until he found her naked breasts. She stroked his head. He slid his hand down her pants, felt her wetness. She started to hum and unbuckled his trousers.

"Run away to school. Let's go to Kenya." Jordan pulled off her sandals and jeans. She opened her legs. Tasting her, he reached one hand up to caress her neck. He licked her clitoris and couldn't help but imagine a lump of scar tissue. Her body relaxed and she moaned softly. Jordan paused to kiss her.

"There's no time now." Zanifa pushed his shoulders up gently, saying urgently, "I would like to love you tonight. Subira is waiting."

Jordan felt the lines of her face with his fingertips. "You can't let them cut you."

"My mother tells me that she still has pleasure." Zanifa rested her head against his hand. "It will only be different."

"You're brainwashed."

"Brain what?"

Jordan thought a glimmer in the blackness was her mouth. "Brainwashed." An explanation was too difficult now. He didn't want to talk. He wanted to reclaim her. "Deceived."

"What?"

"They keep lying to you until you believe their lies."

"Subira and I must return to the disco." Zanifa sat up and pulled her blouse and sweater to her waist.

"Just wait a few minutes."

"I can't. There is no time."

One of her feet brushed his face as she turned over onto her knees. Jordan touched her hip, felt her start to stand, rose up off his knees and hooked his arm around her waist. For a moment he hesitated, fought the rush of drunken lust, then he pulled her down, breaking the fall with a forearm. Zanifa sprawled facedown against the pine needles, her legs exposed up to the hem of the sweater.

Jordan pushed his knees between her legs. His pupils fully dilated now, he could see faint gleams of her thighs and calves, the darker black of the sweater.

"Not that. He'll know. He'll punish us both."

Jordan sucked his thumb, found her sphincter, and ran his finger around the rim. Zanifa squirmed, so Jordan let his chest fall onto her back.

"Let me finish," Jordan whispered into her ear.

"Please, let me go," Zanifa whispered.

"Do this for me."

Zanifa lay still.

Jordan lathered his prick with spit and tried to push the head inside.

Zanifa gasped deeply, softly in Swahili: "You're hurting me."

Something urged Jordan to ignore her.

"It hurts," Zanifa said in English. "It hurts."

Jordan pulled back without entering and dry humped the cleavage of her ass for a few seconds, then moaned, ejaculating onto her back.

Zanifa was silent.

Jordan wiped her back off with his shirt. He heard her turn over. Her pants legs scraped against the pine needles. She breathed heavily as she raised her legs up in the air and pulled the jeans over her hips. The snap popped in place.

"I'm sorry. I'm drunk. I'm sorry. . . ." Jordan slipped her sandals on her feet. Zanifa said nothing. He wondered if she was crying. He buckled his belt and followed her through the trees.

"Zanifa," Subira called from the window, "where are you? We must go."

Forgive me, Jordan said. *"Nisa mehi."*

Zanifa hurried from the grove of pines into the building without looking back.

# Novemba 4

A gravel driveway ran through stone gates beneath a St. Mary's sign in iron scroll, wound around a steep, forested slope and ended in a lot between a grand country manor and two new buildings of a similar Tudor style. The courtyard was empty, but Jordan could see girls through the classroom windows. He parked by the house and walked through an arched door. An African nun rose behind a desk. They traded Swahili greetings, and Jordan asked to see the headmaster. The nun directed him three flights up a circular stone staircase to a smaller arched door.

"*Hodi*," Jordan called.

"*Karibu*," said a cheerful voice.

Jordan entered a round room lined with bookcases. A carved African crucifix hung on a big curved window, suspended against treetops, white clouds and blue sky. Standing behind a desk with his back to the window, Father William wore a denim shirt, blue tie and jeans.

"My fellow American . . ." Father William smiled broadly. It was the beatific smile of a man who loved his neighbor as himself.

Jordan approached his desk.

"*Habari za siku nyingi?*" Still smiling, Father William sounded like a Swahili. What's the news of many days?

"*Salaama.*" Jordan shook the monk's firm grip. He looked up several inches to Father William's face. Peaceful.

"It's been months. You must be near the end of your contract,"

Father William said with a New England accent, gesturing for Jordan to sit on an antique sofa of worn red brocade.

"I'm a free man at Christmas." Jordan noticed that he had tracked mud onto an Oriental carpet, a relic of the English heiress who had built the mansion some sixty years before.

Father William waved his hand dismissively. "Tea?"

"Please." Jordan took off his jacket and sat down. "I won't get offered tea ten times a day in Tennessee."

"You must be sad. Nobody likes to leave Tanzania." Father William poured from a thermos into Wedgwood cups on a low table in front of the sofa.

"Endings are always sad." Jordan sighed. "I miss my family, of course."

Father William sat in a wingback chair. "Didn't they come over last year on safari?"

"My father loved the Serengeti. My mother was terrified by the idea that a lion would get in her tent." Jordan mixed powdered milk in his tea.

The monk laughed. "My mother was the same. It's hard to convince them that it just doesn't happen."

Jordan sipped the tea and watched a cloud sinking toward the treetops out the window, not sure how to start. He felt a strange compulsion to confess what had happened last night with Zanifa. "We never built a fish pond for the school."

"I've been expecting you for two months. You said we would start at the end of August." Father William smiled as he talked. "After the soil had dried from the long rains."

Jordan considered telling him that he was withdrawn and depressed and too scared to leave his house but decided it was safer to lie. "I had a lot of farmers up at the north end of the range. I was commuting four hours a day on the bike, plus raising the eagle. I'm sorry. But there's still time. We can start next week."

"That would be great. Terrific for the school." A trace of the smile lingered on Father William's face. "How is the sky leopard?"

"Come see her fly. It'll blow you away." Jordan smiled back. "I'm setting her free soon."

"I've only seen them in books and in your paintings. Zanifa Hering showed me. It was good of you to help her with her project," Father William said with a look of admiration.

"She's a smart girl." Jordan reached for a biscuit.

"Very bright."

"She wants to be a doctor." Jordan glanced up at his face.

"There is a profound need for doctors here." Father William waited for Jordan to continue.

"She's going to marry Julian Kimweri soon." Jordan thought his voice sounded too urgent. "Do you think he'll let her go to medical school?"

"I don't know." Father William set his cup on the table. "I should hope so."

"He's going to turn her into a concubine," Jordan said softly.

"I certainly don't condone polygamy. And I hate to see girls married off so young." Father William settled back in the chair. "But it is part of the Muslim culture in Tanzania."

"Kimweri's going to send her through *jando*."

"*Haaah*." The monk expressed surprise like a Tanzanian. "No one told me."

"We can't just sit back—can we?" Jordan leaned forward suddenly, sloshing tea in his lap.

Father William handed him a cloth napkin. "What would you propose to do?"

"I was thinking of finding a boarding school in Kenya and promising her mother that I will send Zanifa through medical school in Africa or maybe even the States." Jordan was thankful that his voice sounded calm, even though the words spilled out of his mouth. "There must be scholarships for Africans back home. In any case, I can afford to send her to the University of Dar es Salaam."

Father William looked at Jordan. "Do you have a romantic interest in Zanifa?"

"No." Jordan laughed. "I just don't want to see her life ruined."

Father William nodded. "Why not persuade Kimweri not to put her through it?"

"I've tried." Jordan sat back on the sofa. "I'd prefer to talk to Mama

Zanifa. Do you know any Kenyan schools? I think we should secure her a place far from Lushoto before I speak with her mother."

"Are you sure Zanifa wants to go?" Father William didn't take his eyes off Jordan's face.

"I know she wants to be a doctor." Jordan strained to keep from looking away. "I haven't had the chance to ask her about boarding school. She envies the boarders here."

"Don't you think she has the right to decide for herself?"

"Of course. That's my point. But I haven't been able to speak with her." Jordan set the wet napkin on the table. "Kimweri has forbidden her to see me."

"Why is that?"

"Because I've been trying to persuade her not to go through *jando.*" Jordan crossed his legs, trying to read the monk's look.

Father William nodded quietly. "Why don't we call Zanifa in?"

He knows, Jordan thought. *"Sawa."*

Father William went to the desk and spoke into a phone. Outside the window, a hawk circled against the clouds. The monk came back and picked up a teacup. "At the very least it won't be easy to get a school to take her midterm."

"If you give me a list of good schools, I'll call them from Dar. I'm on my way."

"It would be better if I wrote them directly."

"A letter will take weeks. There's not time."

"We can't rush into this. I would hate to see the girl initiated—"

"Mutilated is the word."

"I don't want to see it happen. But we've got no legal right to interfere." Father William furrowed his forehead and shrugged.

"Then give me the names of a few schools. Nothing else."

There was a knock at the door. *"Hodi."*

*"Karibu."* Father William stood up.

Zanifa walked in. She paused at the edge of the table and clasped her hands, bunching her white blouse at the waist of her burgundy skirt. "Good morning, Father." She bowed slightly. "Good morning, Mr. Joldon."

"Hello." Jordan feared that the embarrassment of seeing her now in the daylight would show on his face.

"Sit down, Zanifa." Father William gestured toward the sofa.

Zanifa perched on the far end.

"Zanifa, I've been discussing your future with Mr. Jordan," Father William said. "He is concerned that you will not continue your education if you marry Mr. Kimweri. You are a smart and motivated girl. But it is not our place to interfere with your mother or Mr. Kimweri. How do you feel about your marriage?"

"My mother wants me to marry him," Zanifa said so softly that Jordan had to lean forward to hear.

"Then perhaps the best thing—" Father William rose from the chair.

"Zanifa, what if I can get you in a good boarding school?" Jordan's voice was thick. "You can finish high school in Kenya. I'll help you go to university. Isn't that what you want?"

"Yes . . . but . . ." Zanifa looked at the Oriental rug. "I don't know."

"I'm going to Dar for a few days. I'll call some schools to see about a place for you." Jordan's voice was normal again. "Just think about it. Maybe we can convince your mother and Bwana Kimweri."

"Okay." Zanifa's face was vacant. She glanced at the headmaster and then at the door.

"This is Mr. Jordan's idea. I'm not sure if it is best for you." Father William spoke carefully in English, looking at Jordan, then to Zanifa. "Ask your mother to come see me tomorrow."

"My mother is in Moshi buying chickens." Zanifa's voice was a little louder now. "She'll be back tomorrow night on the bus."

"Ask her to come as soon as she gets back." Father William smiled at her. "You may return to class now."

Zanifa shot Jordan a look and hurried out of the room. Was it a look of fear or an appeal?

"I think you should abandon your plan," Father William said. "She's underage. She can't make those decisions for herself. I don't know why you want to do this."

"I can't believe you'd let her go through *jando*," Jordan replied calmly, hiding his anger. "I'm scared of Kimweri, too, but we can't just sit back . . ."

"You haven't been in the country very long, Rutledge. And you're leaving soon. Do you forget that we are only guests here?"

"I'm simply going to investigate the possibility of enrolling her in boarding school. Then I'll speak to her mother."

"Rutledge, why are you doing this?"

"I told you. I don't want to watch Zanifa go through that torture. Isn't that enough?" Jordan picked up his jacket from the sofa. "Would you please give me the names of some schools?"

Father William pursed his lips.

"I guess I'll check with the International School in Dar," Jordan said. "They ought to know."

"I'll save you the trouble," Father William said. "If you promise you'll tell me what you've decided before visiting Zanifa's mother."

"Okay, Father." Jordan slipped on his jacket. "And I ask you not to mention anything to Kimweri until I'm back and we've talked."

"I'm sure I won't see him," Father William said, going to the desk. He flipped through a Rolodex, pausing to scribble on a pad. Jordan moved slowly toward the big window. The monk tore a sheet off the pad.

"Thank you, Father." Jordan glanced at the names and phone numbers.

"We'll talk when you're back from Dar." Father William smiled. "Travel safely."

"Thanks. I'll drop by straight away." Jordan shook his hand. "Take care of your girls."

The sky was a deep, burning blue. On his bike on the serpentine tarmac road, gravity canting his body in and out of the turns, Jordan's mind was emptied by wind and high speed and filled with the sensation of plunging faster into space. Five hundred feet over the savanna, the cool air stopped suddenly and simmered from warm to hot as he dropped down the last stretch of road toward the rooftops and tall palms of Mombo. He stopped at the junction of the north-south highway and looked up at the chapel ruin high above on the cliff edge and hoped the Maasai would take care of Pasipo.

Check Bobs in sunglasses and high-tops loitered around the Caltex station. Jordan topped off the tank on the Honda and turned south. Spangled buses, adorned with colored lights and garish murals, walled off the sides of the highway. The heat of the steppe trembled in pools in the distance. Jordan held the throttle steady and settled into the detached mind drift of the open road. The towering wall of the Usambara range—gray cliffs hanging with dense foliage—curved east and dwindled into low clouds over the coast.

Two hours down the road the Honda's engine was on the verge of overheating. There was no temperature gauge, but Jordan could feel the heat on his shins. He let go of the throttle, then held it at thirty miles an hour. The landscape crept by. At the first roadside village he parked in the shade of a baobab tree. From a distance the odd tree looked squat beneath its heavy crown of branches upturned like antlers. Up close the gray trunk was as fat and tall as a silo. In the still heat, Jordan sat under the narrow thatched roof of the Top Club at a table specked with damp rice and tiny puddles of tea. A girl with dead eyes took his order without speaking and returned with a dirty glass and a Sprite. After a last mouthful, though he knew it was too early, he felt the engine, nearly scorching his hand, and thought the essence of the American attitude was fatalistic impatience while the African's was fatalistic patience. He felt faint from the sun when he kicked the Honda starter and accelerated into the wind and retreating horizon.

The road rose and fell through desolate hills of dense brown and olive bush. He rode for hours without seeing any game and remembered Ionides's story about the rhinoceroses that used to charge passing cars here thirty years ago. Villages of rusty tin roofs blended with the red brown daubed walls and yards of hard clay. Occasionally a cratered section of tarmac interrupted the gravel. Jordan passed the time by compiling a mental list of buses—City Guy, Computer, Fax Machine, Air Dar es Salaam—and their slogans—*Hakuna Kama Mungu:* Nothing Like God—that roared past, drowning him in small squalls of dust. The endless bush flattened out into a wide plain, green shimmering rice paddies. The road climbed out of the plain into rolling hills checkered with cassava and beans. In a deep trough between hills, a truck, turned on its side, was blocking the road. It was the sixth accident Jordan had seen since morning. Garages, restaurants, and shops flashed by with increasing frequency. The soil by the roadside was no longer red clay but light brown sand. Seven hours since he'd set out, Jordan was on the outskirts of the capital. From the top of a hill, overlooking the narrow coastal plain, he could see the thin blue haze of the Indian Ocean and the scattered skyscrapers of Dar es Salaam, the Harbor of Peace.

Long red buses thundered through the swarming junction of University Road, Nelson Mandela Boulevard, and the Western Highway. The buses were jacked high off the road, with soot-smeared windows and men and women dangling through the doors, clinging to handrails, their shirts ballooning in the wind. Holding his breath, Jordan wrenched down on the throttle and dodged between the black clouds of burnt diesel. In an area called Soweto after the notorious South African township, the crowds were so heavy that the traffic stalled, but Jordan was able to creep along between the lanes. The traffic flowed again on a causeway across a swamp, then the road climbed a hill and dropped down into City Centre, whose edge was defined by a wall of semicircular concrete high-rises, balconied, in lime and pink pastels. The top floors were painted with huge advertisements for Duracell, Kellogg's, Pepsi, and Coke.

THE VOMITING FIRST BEGAN ABOUT TEN IN THE MORNING, WHEN Jordan was hurrying to finish a brief and the low-grade nausea that had been constant for days suddenly welled up, forcing him to rush out of his office to the toilet. After he emptied his stomach he sprawled on the tile floor, breathing easy for a few minutes until the queasiness rose into a convulsive set of dry heaves. His secretary shouldered him to a couch. Vernon drove him home, stopping to buy Mylanta and Excedrin P.M. Vernon was certain it was brought on by alcohol.

Alone in his apartment, Jordan staggered for several hours between his bed and the sofa by the TV and a bathtub of hot water, trying to find someplace where the nausea would go away. The dry heaves seemed to come every fifteen minutes. In the afternoon Vernon showed up and took him to the Baptist General ER, where two doctors both suspected food poisoning. Between the heaves they took blood, stool and urine samples and a nurse jammed in a suppository for the nausea. Vernon insisted on depositing Jordan at his parents' house.

His mother opened the front door. The strength and beauty of her fifty-two-year-old face appeared clearer than usual to Jordan. She remarked that he was the spitting image of his grandfather at the end of a binge. The suppository reduced the nausea to a tolerable level, and Jordan stopped puking altogether before his father came home. His mother told his father only what the doctor had said. His father came up to Jordan's old room, where he lay surrounded by artifacts of his youth. He was sixty now, and his hair had gone from black to snow white. He told Jordan a new lawyer joke, but Jordan didn't laugh.

The nausea woke him. Lying in the dark, Jordan felt it building and kept hoping to pass out until a fit of retching racked his body and he finally flicked on the light, saw it was 4:28, found a suppository on the nightstand. He paced the room, picking up high school yearbooks and cross-country trophies, photo albums of backpacking trips with his father in the Appalachians and the Rockies. He crawled out in the dark hall, less queasy somehow on all fours, down the hall to his sister's room, another museum of adolescence, four years older, a better-preserved reflection of high school because Sophie had spent little time in Memphis since. She'd worked college summers in places like Nantucket, graduated from Duke and followed her boyfriend to Boston, married, and had a child. Curling at the edges away from the twine-color walls were three faded posters—a young Mick Jagger, James Dean and a still from the movie *Romeo and Juliet*, the lovers kissing. About five-thirty he heard his father leave the house for his daily five-mile run, a routine that predated Jordan's birth. At daylight his mother found Jordan breathless on the upstairs bathroom floor. It took two more days of the dry heaves—Jordan was gaunt, dehydrated, plugged to an IV—before the doctors thought of X-raying his stomach, because no one imagined a twenty-eight-year-old could have a duodenal ulcer, the kind that came from stress and diet—the kind you gave to yourself.

"Oh, Rut," Anna said in the doorway. She was wearing a blazer and blue jeans. "I came as soon as I heard."

"I wondered if you'd come." Jordan hit the button that raised the back of the bed.

"You should have called me." Anna's shoes tapped across the linoleum. She was carrying a plastic gallon jug. "I heard you were here and thought you must have cracked up your car or something till I called your mother."

"You're the first person I thought of calling. Then I thought I might feel worse."

"Do you want me to leave?" Anna set the jug on a table by the bed.

"Hell, no. Make yourself at home. What's that?"

"Aloe vera juice. My acupuncturist recommended it."

"That was thoughtful. Thanks. Who told you?"

Anna frowned and sat on the edge of the bed.

"Tharpe, huh? I thought he might work here."

"Sweetheart, you have to take hold." Anna brushed the hair out of his eyes and let her hand rest on his cheek. "It's not the end of the world." She laughed. "There's a lot of women who're glad you're on the market."

"I don't want anyone else." Jordan put his hand on hers, pressed it hard against his face. "Please, let's give it another try."

Anna shook her head slowly, looking as if she were holding back tears. "There's too much hurt."

"I could make it up to you."

"It's too late now." She hugged him. "We've got to move on."

"You did this to me," Jordan whispered in her ear. "You put me in this fucking hospital."

Anna let go and sat back. She looked puzzled for a second, then angry. "No, Rut. You did this to yourself." She stood up and backed away from the bed. "You made me feel bad and I didn't drink myself to death. Now it's your turn to feel bad. You're right. I shouldn't have come."

Jordan watched her walk through the door. He called out, "Anna, come back. I'm sorry." He got out of bed and unhooked the IV bag and ran into the hall and she was gone.

# Novemba 5

Jordan woke to the noise of trucks below and the steady rattle of an old air conditioner and walked out on the balcony of Hotel Mawenzi. A river of buses roared down Maktaba Street past the dome of the Anglican cathedral and emptied crowds from the surrounding shanty towns in front of the long colonnade of the Central Post Office. Since he'd last been in Dar, the Japanese had magically transformed the streets of the city from a gauntlet of potholes into smooth asphalt. He showered and shaved and put on a clean pair of tropical-weight khakis and a light cotton safari shirt and walked into a pale green corridor, where the air was twenty degrees hotter than his room. He passed an Indian woman draped in saris, her brown belly bare, a red dot on her forehead, and hurried down a set of terrazzo stairs out of the hotel onto the street.

The heat and humidity felt like a wet wool coat. Jordan walked along Maktaba Street. Within minutes his shirt and trousers clung to his limbs with sweat. By the British Airways office, Check Bobs in dark glasses called out in English:

"Hey, man, change money? Good rate."

"Pssst!"

"Hello, brother, you like adventure safari?"

"Sail to Zanzibar?"

"*Bhangi?*" one whispered.

Pedestrians clogged the sidewalks and trickled across Samora

Machel, one of the avenues named after African dictators. A sauna in the morning rush hour, Jordan thought, imagine the afternoon. Orphans, homeless grandmothers, lepers of indeterminate sex, sat clumped in the shade beneath the long eaves of three-story buildings left over from the German and English colonial eras. Jordan handed out a few dollars in shillings and averted his eyes.

He bought a tattered copy of a recent *Economist* and the local papers at a stand outside the Salamander café. The tables under the fans outside were occupied by white travelers in sandals and shorts. The expatriates who lived here adopted the African custom of shoes and long trousers. Jordan's eyes automatically swept the veranda for white females among the long-haired Germans and Australians. Passing through the glare of the street to the dimmer light of the veranda, Jordan saw a blond woman in a red tank top and leopard-spotted leggings. She smiled and glanced away. At the buffet he picked up a piece of mango pie, a spicy potato ball, a passion juice, and an espresso.

"Two hundred shillings," said the Bantu cashier. Fifty cents.

Jordan carried his tray toward the blond woman talking to her companion through the arched window. He suddenly felt not so gregarious and chose a seat directly under a ceiling fan. He skimmed the headlines of the *Daily News* between sips of espresso: RWANDAN REFUGEES FLOOD LAKE DISTRICT . . . DONKEY EATS CHICKEN. The fan blew the damp heat from his skin. 3 GIRLS KILLED & HUNDREDS RAPED IN SCHOOL FRENZY. He read a story about a joint Catholic-government high school in Kenya where the boys laid siege to a girls' dorm, crushing three girls as they swarmed into the building and raping several hundred before police arrived. "Girls are raped individually on a regular basis," the headmistress was quoted. "It is part of the culture. But this sort of behavior is intolerable." Jordan pulled out Father William's list of boarding schools in his pocket notebook and circled the names of the private academies. He picked up the *Express*, a weekly that sprang up when the party eased its monopoly on the press. FREEDOM PARTY WINS SUPPORT ACROSS COUNTRY. The cover story quoted Julian Kimweri extensively. The Indian journalist called him "the sultan of voter swing."

Jordan looked out the arched window. The blond girl was gone. He flipped to the classifieds and read the ads for automobiles. He envisioned himself racing across the Serengeti Plains with Zanifa in a Range Rover, herds of zebra and giraffe galloping alongside. He caught himself, ashamed of his daydream. He'd woken up excited by his plan but now felt solemn seeing how he'd treated Zanifa as a product to be consumed—medication for loneliness and guilt, a human drug.

The commuters had thinned out, exposing the beggars along the walls. Jordan took a side road from the Salamander to a boulevard along the harbor. Pale pink and mint green cement facades of the Indian buildings took up the skyline. Dar es Salaam was like a dirty version of Miami Beach. Wheeling in microcurrents of hot air above tension lines strung between the rooftops was a squadron of black kites, urban raptors. One swooped down and plucked a slice of grilled cassava from an angry African. The thought of Pasipo struck Jordan like a mother waking to worries of a distant child. Indian women in flowing robes and veils of silk glided down the street, dragging thin brown children in school uniforms. Occasionally a lone maiden in the long robe of her ancestors, walking briskly, determined, her delicate features hidden by a veil, appeared, disappeared.

Jordan approached a drab modern building with a sign that said *"Uhamiaji."* The windows from the third floor to the top of the immigration headquarters were shattered, and the facade was stained black by smoke. Several months before, a fire had destroyed the upper stories, covering someone's tracks. In Jordan's first year someone burned down the central bank. Inside, minutes after opening, the lobby was chaos. Uniformed officers behind a counter along one wall were mobbed by the crowd. Jordan pushed through a group of Somali women to the front. Nobody objected because he was white. He smiled at a woman in a blue uniform and placed on the counter two nearly identical photos of Zanifa, cut to passport size from two snapshots, and a letter he had typed on Peace Corps stationery. In Swahili he explained that Zanifa had won a study tour in Kenya and needed a travel pass today.

The woman glanced at the letter. "It takes at least two weeks to process." She handed him a form.

"But the tour starts in three days."

"I'm sorry, bwana. These are the laws." She looked over his shoulder at a Somali woman wearing a yellow scarf on her head.

Jordan leaned forward and whispered, "I don't want my friend to miss the tour. I'll be glad to pay for express service. Would a hundred thousand shillings allow you to process it faster?" He offered her four months' salary, but she probably suspected nothing illegal, as most *mzungu* were millionaires.

The woman smiled, showing a gap between her front teeth. "Fill out the form and come at three."

In the hot green hallway Jordan knocked on the door of 101. He waited a minute, then knocked again. *"Hodi. Hodi."*

*"Nani upo?"* a coarse voice called out.

"Rutledge."

"It's against my principles to be disturbed in my room." The voice spoke English with a Greek accent.

"Come on, Paul, open up."

The Mediterranean voice issued faintly from the other side.

The door swung open to a blast of frigid air. In a yellow silk bathrobe, Paul Ionides, his gray hair standing on end, his long mustache drooping, looked Jordan up and down through thick rose-tinted glasses. His snarl changed to a benign smile that consisted of a few long, stained teeth.

"Since you interrupted my morning exercises, you might as well come in." The old man turned and shuffled off into the semidarkness of the cold room. Jordan could make out three forms lounging on the double bed.

"Are you trying to refrigerate all of Dar es Salaam?" Ionides yelled. "Close the door!"

The forms on the bed giggled as Jordan pushed the door shut.

"Sit down. Sit down. Coffee? Tea? I'll call room service," Ionides said expansively, reaching for the phone on the bedstand.

"No thanks."

The giggling girls looked as though they were Zanifa's age or younger.

"Well, what's wrong with my brother?" Paul Ionides dragged a chair for Jordan. "Is he drinking too much? In the hospital? Did the Africans finally string him up?"

"He's fine," Jordan said. "He's been on the wagon for two months."

"He's a bastard. A crazy old bastard. Let me make that abundantly clear." The old man sank onto the edge of the bed. One of the girls, draped in a blue *kanga*, rose off the mattress onto her knees and began oiling Ionides's hair. "How's your work going?"

"Coming along." Coming to an end, Jordan thought.

"You're doing a marvelous job. You're helping the poor." Ionides tipped his head back as the girl combed his hair. "The poor need it. The rest—fuck them."

"What's with the harem?"

"My *sungu-sungu* girls." Possibly untranslatable slang that originally meant young vigilantes. Ionides's laugh was high, like his brother's. "All the young in the city now, they are coming out for sex. They are sent by their mothers to bring money into the house for the daily bread. You see, in my day, we didn't have this tragedy." Scowling, Ionides took a box of Rothmans from his robe. "Now the younger generation has become very abusive of morals. You can advise these girls from dawn to dusk. You can plead with them to go home and stay there. You can give them money and bus fare." He lit a cigarette, exhaled smoke. "But they won't go."

Jordan looked at the half-clothed girls. They averted their eyes or watched Ionides. Jordan felt an uncomfortable confederate sense of corruption.

"They say . . ." Ionides's voice rose: " 'No, Baba, we like to stay with you. If you don't take us, someone else will. We don't like to go with Africans. They pester us. They hurt us. You are too kind, too gentle. We want to stay with you and teach you the modern sexuality.' "

The girls laughed at his imitation, not understanding a word, and Ionides joined them. Jordan smiled politely.

"The girls are getting a lot of service, a lot of food, no boozing, but they want a lot of fucking." Ionides sighed, shaking his head. "This is the problem."

"How do you cope?"

"A half a kilo of fresh onions a day. Your bloody cock never lies down. Also the onions destroy amoebas, and, the biggest secret"—Ionides leaned in, whispering—"onions neutralize most African poisons." He sat back. "What brought you from the bush? Kicks? Newcomers to Africa are funny. You would fuck under a full moon for kicks. Everything you see is extraordinary in your eyes." The old man laughed.

"Nicholas said you needed another courier."

"*Mungu ameniheri.*" Ionides smiled. God has blessed me. He fixed Jordan with his thick glasses. "Nikos told me you weren't interested."

"I changed my mind." Jordan shifted in his seat, wondering if it was too late to turn back. "He said you lost a courier."

"A Check Bob. He's in jail in Zambia. He was stupid," Ionides said. "But you have nothing to worry about."

"How long is he in for?"

"Who knows?" Ionides said through a corrugated drapery of smoke. "But you will walk right across the border. You're white. An American. A volunteer, for Christ's sake."

"Nikos said you'd gone up to five thousand sponduliks."

"The law of supply and demand," Ionides said. "You're running round-trip this time."

"I need six thousand." Jordan managed to keep a poker face. "Up front."

"You're a pirate." The old man coughed. "That's twice what you got last time."

"Last time was one-way."

"*Sawa,*" Ionides said, tapping the cigarette on the lip of a carved tray shaped like a *shetani*, a devil with a leering grin, that one of the girls held out to him. "Six thousand. *Half* up front."

"*Hapana,*" Jordan said no. "I have to transfer several thousand in Mombasa, and I want money to buy my way out if I'm busted. Six thousand up front."

"Five thousand up front. The remainder on delivery. I need some security." Ionides stubbed out the cigarette on the devil's belly. "If you hurry, you can catch the afternoon express to Mombasa. This shipment is weeks behind." Bracing himself on the bedstead, the old man rose stiffly. Paul was taller and thinner than his older brother, though less agile because Nikos lived in the mountains, running the hotel and a farm. Paul shuffled across the carpet to a wardrobe, unlocked it with a key from his robe and pulled out a blue duffel bag from the bottom shelf. Jordan knew there was a false bottom sewn above a padded package.

"If you catch the four o'clock, you'll be in Mombasa by ten." Ionides crossed the room. "Tomorrow deliver it to Hatam Patel. You remember his shop?"

"I'll never forget it." Jordan took the bag.

"He'll give you a duplicate duffel. Bring it back to me." Ionides tightened the belt around his silk robe. "You should arrive here by sunset tomorrow."

Jordan weighed the duffel with one hand. It wasn't unusually heavy. "What's in the bag?"

"Rubies, diamonds, tanzanite."

"What am I bringing back?" Jordan's damp clothes had turned cold.

"A payment." Ionides coughed. He counted out fifty-one hundred-dollar bills. "You bear the travel costs."

Jordan put the money in his rucksack and the rucksack in the duffel.

"Buy a couple of bottles of whiskey and Cuban cigars in Mombasa." Ionides followed Jordan to the door.

"What am I?" Jordan said. "Your personal delivery boy?"

"Buy something so it looks like you had a reason to go all the way to Mombasa for one night. Jack Daniel's is my brand."

"Sawa." Jordan's face was grave.

"Don't worry." Ionides slapped him on the back. "You'll stroll through customs like a diplomat."

The hall was stuffy. A few feet from the door, he bumped into a muscular African in gray slacks and a black print shirt with a pattern of oversize white dollar bills. Up one flight, in 203, he ordered a mushroom-and-cheese pizza, showered, and changed into another pair of khakis and a clean Peace Corps T-shirt. He called the front desk and asked for a Nairobi number, then sat and loaded the money into a canvas money belt. The first pizza he had seen in nine months arrived on a tray with an icy can of Heineken. Jordan had nearly finished the pizza when the phone rang.

"Hold for your call to Nairobi," the operator told him.

There was a stream of static and then a weak voice: "The Boma School."

"I'd like to enroll a student as quickly as possible. Is there someone I might speak with, please?" Jordan pressed his forehead with the cool beer can.

"You should speak with the headmistress. One moment, please."

The crackling on the line rose louder. "Pamela Calloway here. May I help you?"

"Please. I'm calling from Dar. I'm with the Peace Corps," Jordan shouted. "I'd like to enroll a sixteen-year-old Tanzanian girl who is at the top of her class at St. Mary's in Lushoto." He was relieved the static hid the anxiousness in his voice. "Father William, the headmaster, recommended I call you."

"If you send her transcript, we will reserve a place for her in January."

"Her family is in the midst of a crisis," Jordan went on, calmer now. "They'd prefer to get her away from Lushoto as soon as possible."

"The Boma School is not a haven from troubled homes, mind you." The woman laughed lightly. Her voice sounded English, middle-aged. "But we try to help. We would be happy to accommodate the girl upon receipt of a full term's tuition and room and board." Jordan smiled at how easy it was to buy Zanifa's deliverance and promised to wire the fees the next day. When she asked his connection to the student, Jordan shouted over the static that he was a family friend and Father William would contact her soon about Zanifa's arrival. The headmistress transferred him to her secretary for the exact figures and the academy's account number at Barclay's Bank in Nairobi. "You've got a chance, Miss Zanifa," Jordan said while he was on hold, forgetting his gloomy morning thoughts.

❖

Jordan carried the duffel bag downstairs, paid his bill at the reception desk, and went outside into the heat. A dozen decrepit white taxis were parked along the curb. He got in the back of an old Peugeot and told the driver, "Immigration." As the cab backed onto Maktaba Street, Jordan saw the man in the dollar bill shirt getting in a taxi.

Three minutes in the cab, he wanted to take another shower. He glanced over his shoulder but couldn't see Dollar Bill in the traffic. Near a roundabout with a weathered bronze Tanganyikan WWII soldier, Jordan leaned over the front seat and handed the driver some shillings, telling him to wait while he ran to a shop on the ground floor of one of Dar's three skyscrapers, a twenty-floor edifice stained dark brown with mold. Swinging the bag over his shoulder, Jordan rushed from the cab through the bright glare across a concrete courtyard with dead palm trees into a cool, dim pharmacy. He bought thirty Valium and a big bottle of antacid over the counter and rushed back to the taxi.

"*Twende,*" he told the driver. Let's go. Pulling back into the traffic, Jordan saw Dollar Bill in a Toyota taxi parked on the curb. Jordan twisted off the top of the antacid bottle, washed down a Valium with a mouthful of chalky liquid. Trying to be discreet, he rested his head on his palm and peered with one eye through the rear windscreen. The Toyota was two cars behind. It followed him down Maktaba onto Harbor Drive, now one car back. Jordan jumped from the taxi in front of the burned-out immigration building and ran into the crowd inside. Holding the duffel with one arm to his chest, he pushed to the counter in front of the heavyset woman in a blue uniform. She smiled and motioned him to follow her. They walked the length of the room on opposite sides of the counter. At the end she opened a gate and he followed her back into an office with a table and two plastic chairs.

"It's ready," the woman said, handing him a badly typed document stamped in three places with a photo of Zanifa pasted in the top right corner. Jordan read it quickly. It was valid for a year of travel between Tanzania and Kenya.

"*Asante sana,*" Jordan thanked her, zipping the paper into a side pocket of the duffel. He gave her two hundred-dollar bills. *"Asante, mama."*

"The travel pass costs ten thousand shillings," she said in Swahili.

*"Sawa,"* Jordan paid her the equivalent of twenty bucks.

She handed him a receipt.

"It's so crowded out front," Jordan told her. "Is there a door back here?"

*"Ndiyo, bwana. Njoo."* She walked out of the office and down the corridor to an open door in the back of the building.

*"Ninashukuru."* Jordan said he was grateful, and started across a dirt lot toward a gap in a sheet-metal fence.

*"Karibu tena,"* the immigration officer called from behind. Come again.

Jordan went through the gate onto Kibo Street, wondering who Dollar Bill was if he had in fact been following him. He checked his watch: 3:28. The boat left in a half hour. Crossing town by foot would be faster. At a near run, he kept to the small roads and alleys through the Indian quarter, passing white Hindu temples and the plate-glass windows of little dealerships that sold used cars imported from Japan. He hurried by discos and brothels frequented by Greek sailors and the tall balconied apartments of the Arab quarter. His clothes were dripping wet, his stomach burning. Twice he stopped to swig antacid.

Jordan came out of an alley in front of a white Deco building with "United Nations" painted in huge blue letters across the top floor. He could see the window of an office that last year belonged to Daniela, a lonely green-eyed Roman, the only woman with whom he'd spent a full night in Africa, sixteen months ago now. He gulped a mouthful of antacid and jogged down a shady boulevard toward the harbor, which shimmered colorlessly in the afternoon sun. He took stone steps down the harbor bank into a noisy crowd of passengers, destitute porters and flashy Check Bobs outside the office of the *Zanzibar Express.* At the end of a dock, the sleek Russian hydrofoil rested low in the water, perhaps a hundred feet from stem to stern. The ticket counter was built into the exterior of a warehouse. Behind a scuffed

Plexiglas window a burnt-orange Zanzibari woman looked at the *mzungu* and said, "First class?"

"*Ndiyo*," Jordan confirmed. "Mombasa return."

"One hundred dollars and your passport," the woman said in English.

Jordan handed her a crisp bill.

The woman held it to the light, rubbed it with her thumb and slipped it through a small electronic box. She told Jordan to wait and went through a door. Jordan sipped antacid and watched the top of the steps, wondering if Ionides had given him counterfeit money.

The woman came back with a Zanzibari man in a blue shirt and black tie. They were speaking, but Jordan couldn't hear the words through the window. The man looked at the bill, ran it through the device. He looked at Jordan and ran the bill through again. He glanced at Jordan, then picked up the blue American passport. Jordan considered running. The man handed the passport to the woman and left the room, taking the bill with him. The woman stamped a ticket, placed it in the passport and passed it through the hole in the window.

"Thank you," Jordan said.

The woman said nothing.

Jordan walked slowly around the warehouse, wondering if the man took the bill to alert customs. He could see the headline in the *Daily News:* PEACE CORPS VOLUNTEER NABBED SMUGGLING GEMS. He thought a Tanzanian jail would be worse than he could imagine.

The warehouse was half-dark, oven hot, the air stagnant. A crowd of Zanzibaris and a few hippie travelers formed a line to the immigration table manned by two officers in blue uniforms. As the line moved forward, Jordan filled out a declaration form, writing on top of a magazine. He was relieved that everyone looked sweaty and vaguely ill.

"*Shikamoo.*" Jordan offered to kiss the officer's feet, stepping up to the table.

"*Marahaba*," the officer said. Delighted. He flipped through Jordan's passport. "Are you a teacher?"

"I teach farmers to make fish ponds," Jordan said in Swahili. "In Lushoto."

*"Bwana Samaki."* The officer smiled. Mr. Fish.

Jordan nodded.

"You are a good man to come from your rich country to Tanzania," the officer said kindly. He stamped the passport, looked up. "Vaccinations?"

Jordan started to hand him his yellow card.

"That's okay. Go ahead." The immigration officer turned to the customs officer at an adjacent table. He said in Swahili, "Let him go. He's Peace Corps."

The fat, middle-aged man in a tan uniform scowled at Jordan and motioned him past with a wave of his head.

Jordan entered the V-shaped first-class compartment in the bow just as the captain was sounding the foghorn. He saw a seat by a portal beside a heavy Muslim woman in a black *shuka* and veil. He squeezed past, stowed the duffel under the seat, fell into the padded chair, put his head back and tried to meditate away the molten lead in his stomach. Leaving the calm water of the harbor, the *Zanzibar Express* accelerated into the oncoming waves. Jordan opened his eyes. A film of salt stained the portals. The sky seemed yellow, the sea almost black. Approaching forty knots, the ship rose up onto its foils, the nose coming twelve feet out of the water. The air in the cabin was cool and smelled overwhelmingly of cloves and cardamom. Jordan's temples began to ache, but he could feel the Valium relaxing him. A Zanzibari offered brown, clear and orange soda in transparent cups. The large woman in black took one of each. Jordan picked an orange cup. It was tepid. He looked around the cabin and felt a contraction in his bowels: Dollar Bill was sitting two rows up on the other side of the aisle.

Jordan watched an Indian kung fu movie on a monitor in the bow. It was dubbed in Asian-accented English but nearly inaudible over the rumble of the engines and the slapping of waves against the hull. If Dollar Bill was a cop, surely he would have stopped Jordan at the port.

Unless he wanted to know where the stones were going.

Jordan glanced quickly across the aisle. Dollar Bill was watching the movie. Maybe he'd simply stopped by immigration before his trip.

So why had he been waiting outside the pharmacy?

Forty-five minutes out, halfway to Zanzibar, a south wind out of the Mozambique channel drove up a steady stream of waves, cresting five feet, stretching thirty miles wide. The stream hit the starboard of the ship, rocking her from side to side. Jordan began to feel queasy. Every few minutes the big woman beside him burped. Inhaling slowly to defuse an impulse to vomit, Jordan stood and squeezed past the veiled woman, swaying into her soft belly twice before reaching the aisle. He sprinted out of the cabin through a bulkhead and dragged the duffel through the noisy second-class cabin, jostled by the roll of the ship, bile scorching the back of his throat, weaving around crates, chickens, passengers. He finally stumbled through a second bulkhead out to a deck on the stern.

Jordan dropped the duffel by the rail and let his stomach heave over the edge into the wake.

Several men behind him laughed. Jordan lay against the rail, resting his head on his arm. The sea was a blue that seemed to glow from below the surface. The coast of Africa was no longer visible, but leaning over the rail and looking east past the bow, he could see the island of Zanzibar jutting just at the edge of the horizon.

"The sea make you sick?" one of the men asked. The three of them wore suits and smoked. All had the egg-shaped heads and the red black skin of Zanzibaris.

"In my country, this is how we pay respect to the god of the sea." Jordan sat on a bench. He breathed deeply, felt the throbbing in his brain dissipate in the breeze.

"Are you coming from England?" one of the Zanzibaris asked, smiling.

"U.S." Jordan closed his eyes.

"United States," the man said enthusiastically. "Number one superpower."

"Many tourists coming to Zanzibar these days," another said. "You will be liking it. You will be meeting many Europeans."

"My friend here works for customs," the first man said, holding the officer's hand. "You will have no problem entering."

"Thank you, but I'm going on to Mombasa," Jordan said, and leaned over the stern again.

Jordan stayed out on the deck, too wary to go back into the cabin. Figuring that he'd puked up the last Valium, he swallowed one with the chalky antacid and watched the island grow larger. The ship slowed down, lowering its bow. The harbor was encircled by Stone Town, a maze of mosques and tall houses, the shoreline dominated by the ornate facade of the former palace of the sultan of Zanzibar, one of the richest men in the world at the turn of the century. Jordan remembered a weekend with Daniela beneath a mosquito net on a king-size Zanzibari bed. He thought of Anna and Zanifa and considered the possibility that he was some sort of romantic fool. The waves ceased as the water changed from deep blue to luminous green. Near the quay, the captain put the engines in neutral, and a few seconds later the ship bumped gently against a pier.

From the stern, Jordan watched the passengers file off two by two down a gangplank forward of the main cabin. He couldn't see Dollar Bill, but he could make out only half the people disembarking in the soft evening light. After all the passengers had disappeared down the quay, a French couple in safari gear from the first-class cabin came through the bulkhead onto the stern deck. They glanced at Jordan and began to argue loudly. Jordan lay down on a bench, resting his head on the duffel, and watched the sun sink into the sea, a watery red disk melting into two thin gold streams that ran north and south along the purple horizon. He turned his head up and watched stars appear one by one in the darkening sky.

The engines turned over twice then rumbled steadily. Jordan was alone on the deck. He sat up and looked at the lights of Stone Town. He checked his watch: 10:11. The *Express* was an hour late.

Jordan flinched as a man leapt from the roof of the ship down onto the gunnels—a silhouette whose feet landed even with his waist.

Grabbing the duffel, Jordan lunged across the deck to the rail at the stern, then turned to see if it was Dollar Bill.

The silhouette stood still, the arms hanging by his sides, something in one hand.

Fight or flight? Jordan thought. You've never fought anyone. You could go over the rail into the water or through the bulkhead into the cabin.

The man bent and pulled a line free of a halyard, then threw it onto the dock.

The *Express* backed away, a cloud of diesel smoke billowing up and drifting over the stern.

Red faced, Jordan stepped through the bulkhead into the main cabin, which was half-full and almost silent without the livestock coming from the mainland. Jordan moved unsteadily up the aisle. Set in distinct groups on the rows of benches were Arabs, Afro-Arab Swahilis, Bantus, Goans, Hindus, and several German youths, their sex difficult to discern on the rocking ship; all had long hair, psychedelic leggings, fluorescent backpacks.

In the first-class cabin, sitting behind a group of Zanzibari businessmen in suits and across the aisle from the French couple, Dollar Bill was reading a sports page. The rest of the cabin was empty. The low burning in Jordan's stomach flared into a grease fire. He chose a seat by the bulkhead, farthest from anyone, took a soda from the steward and shoved the duffel under the seat. He swallowed half of a Valium with antacid, then drained the plastic cup. The Indian kung fu movie came on. Jordan watched the back of Dollar Bill's head.

# Novemba 6

Through a portal Jordan could see lights of mainland Kenya. Moonlight glimmered on the water. The *Express* passed the opening of a channel that led to the towering cranes of a deepwater harbor and then followed the shoreline of the island of Mombasa: a dark golf course. A beach lit up by a large modern hotel topped with electric letters that spelled "Casino." A park of black baobab trees. The ship turned into the mouth of a second channel under the dark silhouette of Fort Jesus, a four-hundred-year-old Portuguese ruin. Beneath a skyline made jagged by the minarets of the old quarter, the *Express* docked at the old port, between small rusty freighters filled with scrap metal from Somalia and tea bound for Pakistan.

Ten minutes past midnight, Jordan looked from his watch to the back of Dollar Bill's head. It lay on his shoulder, as if he were sleeping. Jordan carried the duffel out of the cabin. Through a portal in the exit door he watched bare-chested dock hands cast ropes toward the ship. He heard the French couple behind him, then the voices of the Zanzibari businessmen. Outside, the dock hands heaved a ramp up to the hull and swung the door open. Jordan walked quickly along the wooden dock under the faint light from a few tall lamps. He couldn't bring himself to glance behind. The air was damp and suffocating after the air-conditioned ship. He bounded up the concrete steps into a tall, turn-of-the-century customs office.

Ceiling fans creaked thirty feet overhead. First in line at the immigration table, Jordan had his passport open to his multiple-entry Kenyan visa. The officer flipped to a blank page and stamped it. As he crossed the long warehouse to a customs booth near the exit door, the quiet empty space began to echo with the noise of the second-class passengers and the dock hands carrying oversize baggage. He heard the French couple coming behind him. A woman in a red floral dress manned the customs counter.

"*Habari za usiku, mama,*" Jordan said, smiling as he placed the duffel on the counter. What's the news of the night?

"*Salaama,*" the woman said sleepily. Peaceful. She unzipped the bag and shuffled through his clothes and books carefully without crumpling anything.

The Frenchman stopped just behind Jordan. Dollar Bill was halfway across the floor, overtaking the Zanzibaris. The woman looked at his Peace Corps T-shirt and said in Swahili: "Welcome to Mombasa."

Jordan rushed out of the building and through a gate.

"Let me take your bag." A Check Bob reached for the duffel.

Another shouted, "You need a taxi?"

The first pulled the duffel to his chest.

"Where are the taxis?" Jordan jerked his bag away from the man.

"One is there," a third answered in Swahili, pointing to headlights down the block. "The boat was late. They went for dinner."

Jordan stood by the curb and watched the light coming from the doorway of the customs house. The French couple came out and were accosted by the Check Bobs.

"Bugger off," the Frenchman told one, waving his glasses at the man. A Check Bob spat on the sidewalk at his feet. Dollar Bill came out of the doorway.

A new black London taxi drew up along the curb. Jordan dove in the back. "*Twende, bwana, haraka sana,*" he urged the driver. "Manor Hotel." The taxi drove away, and Jordan watched through the rear window. Dollar Bill stepped off the curb in front of the French couple to claim a cab. "*Haraka, bwana.*"

The streets wound around the island, walled off by the stone-and-plaster buildings of the old quarter. Crowds milled about the sidewalks in front of bars, and street hawkers manned tables outside dark shops shuttered with iron gates. The cab turned onto a four-lane road named for the president.

"Moi Avenue," Jordan said, leaning forward through the window by the driver's head. "What do you think of him?"

"He's finishing the poor." The driver turned his head around and smiled. "He has eaten the country."

The taxi pulled up to the curb outside the Manor, a three-story colonial relic rising behind a white wall screened with tall palms. Under dim lights, the veranda was noisy. British and American sailors mingled with *malaya* in tight dresses and faux braids; waiters in white uniforms served drinks. Jordan walked up the terrazzo steps into a narrow lobby with a high ceiling, dark paneling and faded murals of village and wildlife scenes. He signed the register in a small room off the lobby. Foggy from the Valium, he paid forty dollars, changed another fifty into Kenyan shillings and followed an old porter up six short flights of stairs attached to the exterior of the main wing.

"You've been working here a long time, grandfather?" Jordan asked.

"Started before your father was born." The porter turned down a hall at the top. "You come from Tanzania? There they speak clean Swahili."

"Like yours," Jordan said as the old man opened the door to a room with an ornate Zanzibari double bed draped with a mosquito net.

"In Mombasa there are true Swahilis," the porter replied. He clicked on the air conditioner and sprayed the room with pyrethrum-flower insecticide. Jordan tipped him a dollar in shillings. He bowed and shuffled out of the room.

Jordan locked the door and heard a jackhammer rattling outside. From the window he saw a construction crew breaking the pavement of a BP station across the street and knew they'd be working all night. He turned on the television. On one channel was an American soap opera, a middle-aged woman asking an older woman: "When will Donna realize that a boy she falls in love with at eighteen is not the kind of man that she'll love when she's twenty-one or twenty-five?" On the other channel an African evangelist in a suit addressed a large

Kenyan audience: "These are the Last Days and you must be full of the Holy Ghost. Bow right now with eyes closed. We are praying in the presence of Jesus. Pray this prayer from your heart. Say, 'Lord Jesus, I am a sinner. I ask forgiveness. I am born again.'" The other channels were blank.

Jordan walked downstairs. Hugging the walls, trying to stay in the shadows, he searched the four bars of the Manor for Dollar Bill. The last was called the Men's Lounge, a narrow room with a parquet floor and black paneling hung with framed caricatures of famous colonists. It was empty. Jordan bought a bottle of water and went quickly upstairs. Going down the long hall to his room, he heard footsteps behind him and glanced over his shoulder. No one was there.

Jordan locked the door and took a Valium with a swig of bottled water, then dropped out of his clothes and crawled onto the bed with the duffel by his head. The jackhammers carried from across the street over the hum of the air conditioner. He stared at the roof of the mosquito net and thought of Zanifa, naked, sitting up, her brown skin against the white net. He tried to remember something tangible about the love that had existed between him and Anna. In his long solitude only the last days of their romance were still vivid. He was unable to remember the love or how it felt. The few moments that remained seemed to diminish each time they were remembered, as if he now recalled not the experience itself, but a copy of the last memory. Or maybe the memories dimmed over time because he'd never loved her. Perhaps he had been too selfish to love anyone. Or perhaps love itself meant nothing in time. For a while he had believed that rescuing Zanifa would atone for Anna. The idea was absurd.

He wiped his hand across his mouth and laughed.

Gray light from two screened windows half filled the room. Groggy, unable to wake fully, Jordan reached for the duffel beside his pillow. He stretched and crawled out from under the net. The room was frigid. His insides felt sore. Out of the window he could see the tin roofs and high balconies of the old quarter, the tall buildings of the new city. On Moi Avenue, an old Swahili man, barefoot and wearing only a kikoi around his waist and a skullcap, pulled a donkey cart of coconuts. Jordan tried to recall a dream. He had spoken Swahili for the first time, shouting across the mountaintops to Zanifa, Anna standing beside him with a sad look on her face. He drank the last of the antacid, showered, shaved and dressed in a clean pair of khakis and a Tanzania Wildlife Fund T-shirt. The traffic noise from Moi Avenue grew louder in the full light. He packed the duffel and went downstairs.

One side of the vast dining room was large arches open to a sea breeze and palm trees. The room was empty except for an elderly *mzungu* in a white suit, a Panama hat on the table beside his coffee. Jordan chose a table obscured by the column of one arch. A waiter handed him a copy of the *Daily Nation* and took his order of two bowls of oatmeal. The lead story on the front page was MAN HACKS THREE CHILDREN TO DEATH. "A man who hacked his three children to death after a quarrel with his wife was caught by angry members of the public as he attempted to commit suicide." DRUG SMUGGLERS FOILED. "Customs officials uncovered several hundred pounds of Mandraks under a false bed of a truck registered in Zambia and driven by Somalis. The smugglers escaped on foot in the darkness after a shoot-out in which two police officers were wounded."

Jordan looked up from the paper to see Dollar Bill strolling into the airy room, wearing a green batik shirt and clashing plaid pants. He saw him clearly for the first time: tall and muscular, forty pounds heavier than himself. Dollar Bill smiled and approached the table. Jordan realized he mustn't give in to the urge to bolt.

"*Jambo, Bwana* Jordan." Dollar Bill flopped down in the chair on the far side of the table. His teeth were perfect, his skin dark black, almost blue. It was hard to guess his age.

"*Salaama, bwana.*" Jordan tried to smile.

The waiter set the bowls of porridge and a bowl of fruit in front of Jordan.

"*Kahawa.*" Dollar Bill ordered coffee. The waiter moved away.

"*Je, unataka nini, bwana?*" Jordan asked what he wanted. The heat of the day seemed to arrive at once as the sun crested the city, pouring hot light through the arches, thickening the humidity.

"You're taking me to your Mombasa connection." Dollar Bill spoke in English and reached his long arms across the table and picked up a bowl. He drank from the bowl, made an expression of disgust. "This isn't corn. What sort of *uji* is this?"

"Oats," Jordan said. "I don't know what you're talking about."

"Rubies." Dollar Bill pushed the bowl back across the white table-cloth. "What's the matter? You don't like oats, either?"

Jordan sipped ice water. The veranda was starting to fill with tourists; a babble of Italian, German, and French rose softly.

"You're a fast little rabbit. All this jumping from place to place is annoying. This morning you will take me where you are going. I have a message for this friend of Ionides. After that—who knows?" Dollar Bill stopped talking while the waiter placed a porcelain coffee set on the table. When the waiter left, he said in Swahili, "I could kill you anytime, but you are with the Peace Corps. There would be an investigation. My director says it isn't worth it. It makes me very sad. I've never killed a *mzungu*." Dollar Bill smiled. "Perhaps you'll give me the chance."

Jordan picked up a spoon, put it down, picked it up again.

"One firm controls the rubies of East Africa," Dollar Bill said smoothly in English, heaping sugar in a coffee cup and shaking his head. "Everyone knows this. Ionides is a foolish old man. You—you are a child."

Jordan started forcing down oatmeal to soak up the pool of acid collecting in his gut.

"You are a very lucky *mzungu*." Dollar Bill switched back to Swahili. "The last ruby runner, I cut off his dick and stuck it in his stomach to make it look like witch doctor's magic."

Jordan cut up a slice of papaya and chewed the pieces slowly, delaying, trying to think of a way out.

"*Twende, sungu kidogo,*" Dollar Bill said. Let's go, little rabbit. He placed some bills on the table and pulled Jordan's chair back. Jordan stood, gripping the duffel. Dollar Bill guided him by the elbow across the terrace. Dollar Bill opened the door of a battered Peugeot compact with red fringe bordering the windows and sitar music blaring on the radio.

"Get in, rabbit."

Jordan looked back at the hotel, considered sprinting up the street; but he knew Dollar Bill would run him down as if he were in a dream in which he couldn't make his legs run. Dollar Bill whipped Jordan's elbow behind his back and pushed it up painfully. Jordan got in. An Afro-Arab driver in a skullcap grinned with rotten teeth. *"Wapi?"*

Jordan said, "Barclay's Bank, then the Quarter."

The driver waited for Dollar Bill's nod, then swerved the car onto Moi Avenue, behind a minibus packed seven Africans to a seat. "Scud Warrior" was painted on its rear above a crude missile.

"A clerk at the bank will tell me exactly where to make my delivery." Jordan's voice quavered faintly with the lie.

Dollar Bill's hand claimed the duffel between them.

The car passed under the thirty-foot metal elephant tusks arching over the avenue and stopped.

"The clerk won't tell me unless I'm alone."

"Go ahead and run," Dollar Bill said, walking him to the door of the bank. "Make my day."

Waiting in line inside, Jordan pulled up his T-shirt and unzipped the money belt. The clerk was a middle-aged Indian woman. He asked her for a transfer form and gave her forty hundred-dollar bills.

Seeing Dollar Bill across the room, Jordan thought he should speak to the clerk. "I have a sister going to the Boma School. Sort of a sister. In the African sense."

The woman smiled. "A cousin?"

"Where I come from they'd call her a kissing cousin." Jordan laughed nervously.

She pushed the receipt across the counter as if he were something dirty.

Jordan gave the driver an address in the old quarter. Dollar Bill took Jordan's hand and stared ahead, listening to soccer scores on a Swahili radio station. Jordan tried to slide his hand free, but Dollar Bill clasped it hard and asked affably, "Who's your team?"

"I don't have one," Jordan said. "Who's yours?"

"I played for Simba."

"They're the best, aren't they?"

Grinning, Dollar Bill tapped Jordan softly right above his heart, seeming to imply that he would like to cut it out of his chest. "Little rabbit, you don't know a thing, do you?" The Peugeot pulled in front of a sign that said "Prestige Electronics" in blue neon. Stereos, cameras, televisions and videos were displayed in the windows. Jordan pulled his hand free. Dollar Bill wiped the sweat on Jordan's pants and grabbed the duffel bag. Pushing Jordan out of the car, he told the driver to wait.

Inside the shop the air was cool. Indian clerks stood behind glass counters along the sides of a long tile floor. Jordan spoke to a woman with a red dot on her forehead. "Hatam Patel."

"The door in the rear, please." Looking at Dollar Bill nervously, the woman picked up a phone behind the counter.

"Let me speak to him first." Jordan reached for the phone. "Hatam. It's Jordan."

Dollar Bill took the phone from Jordan and spoke rapidly in Gujarati, Patel's Indian dialect. Dollar Bill paused, then shouted in Gujarati and dropped the phone on the counter. He stuck his hand into a front pocket of his loose trousers.

Jordan thought he was going for a gun, but Dollar Bill was only scratching his balls.

"*Mpaka tutapigana tena,*" Dollar Bill said in Check Bob slang: Until we collide again.

Jordan stared back dumbly, and Dollar Bill walked out the door, the duffel hanging from the strap over his shoulder.

Through the plate glass Jordan saw him get back in the taxi. A Sikh in a white turban and warm-up suit ran out the front door and chased the taxi.

"Mr. Jordan." A slim Indian with white hair in a cream linen suit stood in the rear door. "Do come in." Hatam Patel's voice was icy.

Jordan moved slowly past the whispering clerks. He followed Patel down a hall into a carpeted office paneled with rain forest hardwood. Jordan spotted a blue duffel on the floor by a leather armchair across from a desk—a thick glass case that contained the bleached bones of a warthog, reconstructed in the pose of a flat-out run. Hanging on the orange camphor paneling were large collages of bone by the same artist.

"That was a significant loss," Patel said coolly. He spat betel juice into a brass spittoon on the floor. "You led him right here."

Jordan sank into the armchair. "Nobody told me I might be followed."

"Where did you meet this man?" Patel asked, no longer disguising his anger.

"He followed me from the Mawenzi Hotel. I first saw him right outside Ionides's room. I tried to lose him a dozen times. He found me at the Manor this morning." Jordan got the bottle of Valium from his pocket. "He spoke Gujarati like an Indian. Who is he?"

"A representative of the Koreans." Patel spat into the spittoon, shrugged. "There are plenty of other stones."

"Koreans?"

"How do you say . . ." Patel's voice trailed off. He gestured to a wall map of East Africa. "The ruby mafia."

The Sikh who had chased the taxi came in and spoke to Patel in Gujarati.

"Grewal, here, lost your man. But it doesn't matter. We don't want to start a war with the Koreans." Patel smiled grimly. Grewal listened eagerly. He was about Jordan's age. He wore his black beard rolled up in a bundle under his chin, his hair hidden by the turban.

A Swahili boy in blue coveralls brought in a tray of drinks. Jordan chose a palm-size Perrier.

"There is a rumor that they will introduce dogs at the harbor, but for the time being we are safe." Patel rolled a gold pen between the thumbs and forefingers of his manicured hands.

"Dogs?" Jordan said. "What are you talking about? What am I taking back?"

"Ionides didn't inform you?" Patel paused. "No? Well, whether a man flogs diamonds or dustpans, he is a salesman. So it is with a courier."

"What's in the duffel?"

Patel continued twirling the gold pen.

"This was never part of the deal." Jordan stood up.

"Don't be melodramatic." Patel smiled. "I'll bet you've snorted it before."

Jordan started for the door, but the Sikh blocked his path.

"At a certain point there is no turning back." Patel fired a thin stream of juice into the spittoon. "You are past that point."

Jordan looked at the Nike emblem on Grewal's track suit. Grewal smiled back as if they were on the same team.

"Grewal will go with you. He's an expert in the martial arts." Patel patted his lips with a handkerchief. "Excellent safari companion."

"You assholes." Jordan's stomach flared up. "Why can't he take it himself?"

"He'll be searched."

Jordan guzzled the Perrier against the burning in his gut. He sat back in the chair and took deep breaths.

The Indian ran a hand over his white hair, a Rolex under his cuff. "In Kenya there are ten car-jackings a day. Right in front of the Norfolk Hotel in Nairobi or at any traffic light. No place is safe anymore. The Kikuyu and the Maasai are fighting upcountry. The Muslims are trying to start a war on the coast. In five years it will be time to leave."

"So you're squeezing out as much as you can before you flee?" Jordan asked.

"You are a *mzungu.* You are safe in Africa. The Africans like you, and you can always run to your embassy and run back to your country." Patel rested his elbows on the desk and touched his fingertips as if in prayer. "But the Asian has nowhere to run. He is despised by the Africans. When the rioting starts the first thing that happens will be the rape of the Asians."

"That's no reason to import devil's dandruff, Patel," Jordan said.

"If you leave now, you can catch the eleven o'clock boat." Patel smiled paternally. "Have a good trip."

Jordan hauled himself up and picked up the duffel.

"I could use you to make a run to Switzerland next month," Patel said. "I'd triple your fee."

Jordan walked out without a word. Outside in the noise and heat, Grewal followed him to a pharmacy. Jordan bought more antacid. At some open stands along the street, he got a half dozen *kikois* of various colors and a safari shirt and stuffed them in the empty duffel. In a well-stocked liquor shop run by Arabs he found fifths of Jack Daniel's. Grewal hurried him outside and hailed a taxi. On the road toward the port the traffic stalled for ten minutes. Grewal kept checking a big diver's watch and cursing the Swahilis pulling the donkey carts that jammed the road. He jumped out of the car and cleared a path through the carts.

The taxi raced through the quarter, throwing Jordan and Grewal against each other when it rounded the corners. It screeched to a stop at the gate of the old port. Jordan glided through customs and immigration without unzipping the duffel. Behind him the customs officers made Grewal unpack his Fila handbag. Jordan walked alone down the quay. He thought of throwing the duffel in the water, but he needed the rest of the money. He boarded the *Zanzibar Princess*, a hydrofoil of the same Russian make as the *Express*. It smelled of mold and clove. He chose a seat below the air-conditioning vent, stashed the duffel beneath him and swallowed half of a Valium with a swig of antacid. A group of African men in suits filed into the cabin. For a moment Jordan thought the one at the back of the line was Dollar Bill, then realized it was someone else.

Grewal, sitting by the bulkhead, watched a kung fu movie on a screen two feet away, in which Sikhs battled Chinese. The Sikhs seemed to be winning, though there were numerous casualties on both sides. To the starboard, the sky was cloudless. Off the port, a squall line approached from the east, dark purple clouds dragging a black curtain across the sea, rolling forward through the blue sky. The *Princess*, up on her foils, cut through the waves at thirty knots parallel to the black storm front. The monsoon winds were driving the storm toward the hinterland. It would rain in the mountains within hours. The first storm of the short rains would soon bless the union. Any day now Zanifa would go through *jando* so that she would recover in time for the wedding night.

Through the portal Jordan saw the waves crest higher as the black curtain closed on the last strip of blue sky. The ship heaved from side to side. The captain slowed down, lowering the bow back into the ocean. He angled the ship into the waves. The rain began suddenly to drum on the cabin. The Princess traveled crabwise, rushing southeast into a breaker, then scurrying south in the wave's trough and turning southeast again to meet the next crest. Jordan swigged Mylanta. Around the cabin, he heard passengers retching and smelled the odor of vomit. A young Zanzibari steward hopped about, handing out bags and collecting them. Jordan grabbed one. Grewal watched him, grinning.

The drumming of the rain ceased after an hour. Through the portals the sky was clear to the south. The waves receded into a calm sea. The *Princess* rose onto her foils and hit her top speed. Jordan moved to the starboard side of the cabin and watched the shoreline. Thin trunks and spindly branches of a mangrove swamp. A rain forest of a thousand hues of green. Cattle grazing in grassland. A fishing village of hollowed-tree canoes with triangular sails and palm-thatch shacks. The Arab fort at Bagamoyo, "Bury My Heart," the last point of Africa hundreds of thousands of slaves saw before they were shipped to Zanzibar and on to Arabia. A defunct fish factory. A string of resorts, a few white people on the beach. A cement factory billowing smoke. Suburban sprawl. A yacht club. Grand mansions built by Greek sisal barons now occupied by ambassadors from the industrial world. The skyline of Dar es Salaam.

A nervousness welled up in Jordan as the *Princess* cruised by the great white State House, hidden by tall palms and walls draped with bougainvillea. The ship turned into a narrow break in the coast. He pictured the fat customs officer and took a Valium. The ship chugged slowly by the colonnaded colonial-era ministries. Pedestrians swarmed along Harbor Drive. Jordan could see black figures high on scaffolds painting the steeple of the Lutheran cathedral, then the boat turned toward the dock, swinging his view back to the mouth of the harbor.

Jordan waited for half of the cabin to file through the bulkhead.

Grewal sat in a seat next to him. He smiled and said in heavily ac-
cented English, "What's the best disco?"

"Florida 2000." Jordan gave him the name of a club frequented by
Check Bobs who hated Asians. He stood up and steadied himself on
the seat back, his legs shaky from the Valium, then started for the
bulkhead. Grewal followed him a step behind. Outside, he felt faint
in the sudden heat and humidity. The passengers herded down a short
gangway and hurried along a dock, some scurrying to the front of the
throng. The two sliding doors of the warehouse were opened wide
like a hangar. In the musty air inside Jordan recognized the same immigration officer at a folding table. He smiled at Jordan and said in
Swahili: "What's the news of your safari, Bwana Fish?"

"Peaceful." Jordan handed him his passport. "Do you think the
short rains have arrived?"

"God willing." The officer looked up, smiled.

"The farmers will be happy," Jordan said. "In the mountains they
feared another drought. Last year the short rains failed."

"Everyone will be glad if the rains come." The officer stamped the
passport. "Have a safe safari home."

There were two agents at the customs counter, a thin man and a
heavy woman in tan uniforms. The line to the man was shorter.
Jordan stepped to the end of it and watched him dump a woman's
suitcase onto a table. He asked her why she had twenty new pair of
underwear and declared she must pay fifty percent duty since she
planned on selling them. The woman shouted back too fast for Jordan
to understand.

"Bwana Amerikani," a voice called gruffly. It was the same fat officer
from the day before with the same scowl. "Njoo."

Jordan stepped tentatively out of his line.

"Njoo," the officer barked, waving him to the far end of the counter.

Jordan moved unsteadily. He offered to kiss the elder's feet.
"Shikamoo, mzee."

The officer gestured for him to set down the duffel and grunted in
English, "Anything to declare?"

Jordan's arms seemed to be moving in slow motion. "No, mzee, I bought two bottles of whiskey in Mombasa, but I know the law allows that."

"Open the bag."

Jordan unzipped the duffel with sweaty fingers. The officer lifted the two fifths from the bag, set them on the table, then plunged his hands into the *kikois*. Jordan tried to appear relaxed. He glanced back and saw Grewal in the line behind him.

"Give me a bottle, you don't need two," the officer said in Swahili.

Jordan hesitated. The officer placed his hand on one fifth.

"I'm sorry. I need it." Jordan took the bottle from his fat hand and placed it in the duffel. He started to walk away from the table toward the light coming through an open door in the rear. Outside in the glare, steam rose from wet pavement.

"*Bwana Amerikani*," the officer called. "Come back."

Jordan turned.

Grewal was standing across the table from the fat customs officer.

"*Nini?*" Jordan asked. What?

"*Njoo!*"

Jordan looked over his shoulder. A soldier with a small machine gun sat on a stool to one side of the door, obscured by the bright light from outside. The soldier seemed to be watching him.

"*Njoo sasa*," the customs officer said. Come now.

Jordan moved slowly back toward the counter. Grewal spoke to the officer. Jordan felt light-headed with the flash that he had been set up. The fat officer scowled at Jordan. Grewal looked away from his eyes. The immigration officer was watching on the other side of the warehouse.

"*Nini?*" Jordan asked. His mind raced, thinking of how he could buy his way out.

The fat officer turned and spoke to the woman officer.

Jordan set the duffel on the table, said in English: "What is it?"

"You forgot your newspaper." The officer handed him a rolled copy of the *Nation* and laughed. "Please, bwana, may I have one bottle? They pay us so little."

"You can have the paper." Jordan laughed nervously.

He slumped against the plank wall of a kiosk at the top of the bank. Grewal strode around the corner of the customs house. He smiled at Jordan and bounded up the concrete steps.

"High five!" Grewal held his arms over his head and waited.

Jordan stared at him, then pointed to a waiting taxi. He heaved himself up and followed Grewal into the back of a jacked-up Peugeot 504. A stream of brown water gushed down Harbor Drive, fed by tributaries from every side street, overwhelming the new Japanese drains, brimming over the curbs. The cab cut a wake along the avenue.

Jordan knocked just below the painted numbers 101. "Open up, Paulos."

The door swung back, revealing Ionides in a pressed tan suit. He smiled. "How was the voyage, fair or foul?"

Jordan shoved the duffel in his chest. "You prick."

Ionides stumbled backward, holding onto the duffel, regained his balance, coughed.

Grewal grabbed Jordan's arm from behind. Jordan shook him off.

"Shut the door," Ionides rasped, dropping the duffel to the floor.

Grewal closed the door gently. Jordan was suddenly worried that they wouldn't let him leave.

"What's the matter?" Ionides lowered himself slowly to the edge of the bed. He motioned with one arm to the two chairs in the room.

Jordan remained standing.

"I know," Ionides said. "I spoke to Patel this morning. But it worked out. You're here."

"You never mentioned coke."

"What's the difference?" Ionides lit a cigarette.

"Just give me my money. I've got a long ride."

"We lost a lot of money today." Ionides exhaled a stream of smoke. "You've already been paid more than you deserve."

"What?"

"You'll have to make another run." Ionides tapped the cigarette into the devil ashtray.

"You're insane." Jordan moved toward Ionides.

Grewal stepped in front of him, grinning slightly. His eyes dared him to go further.

"Give me my fucking money," Jordan was shouting.

"Or what?" Ionides laughed. "Grewal, show him out."

"Let's go, bwana." Grewal took his elbow.

"Rutledge, come back when you're ready for another run," Ionides said.

"Wait a second. Let me get my stuff." Jordan bent toward the duffel. He unzipped the bag, reached inside for the *kikois* and whiskey. "Here," he said, standing and tossing one bottle to Grewal.

Grewal raised both hands to catch the bottle.

Jordan swung the other fifth against the side of Grewal's temple with a two-fisted backhand.

The bottle shattered, spraying bourbon. Grewal fell to the carpet.

Jordan picked up the other bottle, ready to hit him again if he moved. A red stain bloomed on the turban over his ear. His chest rose and fell beneath the warm-up jacket.

Ionides stood up from the bed.

"I told you I needed the money." Jordan breathed heavily.

"That was a mistake." Ionides moved toward the dresser.

Jordan shoved him down on the bed. "Give me the key to the wardrobe," he said, nudging Ionides's shoulder with the jagged bottle.

Ionides reached in his jacket, handed him the key. Grewal moaned softly. Jordan pulled a dresser over on its side, pinning Grewal's legs below his waist.

"You're a dead man," Ionides said as Jordan opened the wardrobe.

"You should have paid me." Jordan's hands trembled, stuffing a thick sheath of bills in the belt under his T-shirt.

"That hardly matters to a Sikh." Ionides coughed and lit another cigarette.

"You can keep the cocaine." Jordan kicked the duffel toward the bed. "Call it even."

Grewal groaned. His black eyes flickered open in his brown face.

"Revenge is their religion." Ionides looked at Grewal and shook his head.

Jordan opened the door and stepped into the hall, expecting to see Dollar Bill. Time was moving so fast, nothing would surprise him.

"If you leave the money, I can smooth it over with Patel," Ionides said, rising from the bed. Grewal groaned and touched his head.

Jordan shut the door and locked the deadbolt. He dashed down a flight of stairs and through a glass door to the reception desk. He asked the clerk for his helmet and slicker. As she got them from a closet, he watched the stairs through the glass.

"These are the old man's keys." He dropped them on the counter.

The woman laughed. "He just called for a set. Said he'd locked himself in and there was a man bleeding to death on his floor. I thought he was drunk."

"His room reeks of whiskey. You better send someone up."

JORDAN DROVE ACROSS THE RIVER FORTY MILES INTO ARKANSAS to a hunting camp his mother's grandfather had built in the twenties. From the porch of the main cabin on a wooded hill overlooking the edge of a wide marsh, Jordan tried to paint the first traces of autumn but kept on thinking about the chemical plants on the Mississippi and the half-built federal toxic waste incinerator and the new industrial catfish farms that he had seen on the drive out. He recalled a phrase of his grandfather's: "the juggernaut of human progress." His first time in a duck blind, when he was nine, alone with his grandfather, shotguns had thundered like war and ducks had fallen from the sky and he had wept at the slaughter. His grandfather had never told anyone. The next Saturday, before dawn, when his father and uncles and cousins were about to head to the blinds, his grandfather had given him a set of watercolors and a book of Audubon prints and instructed him to stay in camp and paint the sunrise, telling the others that someone in their clan should aspire to something higher than killing game and that his namesake Rutledge possessed the temperament.

The hundred ways we fill our days distract us from the fact that we are simply one species living on a planet that will be incinerated by the sun in a billion years. Jordan imagined the reflections of Henry Malone Rutledge and pictured the old man listening to the repetitive creaking of the rocker, gazing out over the marsh, steadily sipping corn mash from a pewter cup, the open bottle beside him on the floor. Our labors and pastimes keep us from dwelling too long on death and the pointlessness of life. For days he would rock and ruminate and drink, turning into a mean, raving shadow-self. After six or seven quarts his gut would finally rebel, double him up with pain, and the Negro caretaker would deposit him at a clinic outside Little Rock.

Jordan had never seen his granddad drunk. He had ridden with him to deliver sacks of groceries to families who were having a rough time. His mother had told him how he quit law in the Depression after defending a black man who, trying to feed his family, had stolen three boxwood trees off the plantation where he worked and ended up in prison. The gentle soul Jordan remembered didn't fit the stories of his binges, which came every few years, when he had hit his wife and terrorized his children. Jordan had once asked him why he would go back to the bottle. "The world is too painful," Granddad Rutledge had said. Rocking in the dead man's chair, Jordan searched the sky for birds with binoculars. He recalled flirting with a dozen women in a dozen bars, and his stomach shuddered at the pattern that had become the man. Somewhere beyond the horizon was Memphis, which seemed about as appealing as the Brushy Mountain State Penitentiary. Jordan didn't want to go back to his old life and he didn't want to start a new one just like it in Atlanta or New Orleans.

# Novemba 7

Under the stormclouds, the night was faultless black. The weak headlight of the Honda barely illuminated a narrow lane of slick tarmac between the mountainside and an abyss below. A few dots of light marked mountain villages miles away on the far side of the gorge. Ten minutes up the steep road from the savanna, the air turned suddenly cold. Fog swallowed the headlights. Shivering, Jordan zipped his slicker to his throat and prayed it wouldn't rain again.

Turning between tall pines onto a drive, Jordan was relieved to see the lights on after midnight in a log-and-stucco house. A BMW motorcycle and a Nissan pickup were parked under a carport. Jordan cut the engine and coasted to a stop by the front porch. Groaning, he lifted his leg over the bike, then bent over and tried to touch his toes.

"*Habari, bwana,*" a watchman called out, squatting in the shadows under a thatch lean-to, warming his hands over a charcoal brazier.

"*Salaama.*" Jordan stepped into the light of the porch.

Ernst opened the door before he knocked, feigned surprise and almost shouted, "Rut!"

"Hey, Ernst." Jordan yawned and moved toward the door.

"You look knackered, bwana. Where've you been?"

"Mombasa." Jordan felt his back ache.

"On that *pikipiki?*"

"The fast boat from Dar." Jordan followed him into a long room with a parquet floor and beamed ceiling.

"You disappeared from the disco," Ernst said. "Rose was disappointed. She left today. You probably passed her on the road."

" 'Love is a rose,' " Jordan said, recalling a folk song from childhood. " 'But you better not pick it. It only grows when it's on the vine.' "

"What?" Ernst laughed, getting two Tuskers from a round wooden cooler at the end of a leather couch. A video of *Until the End of the World* played by a fire in a stone hearth. Jordan took off his slicker and fell onto the couch. He felt like sleeping here, but he wanted to ride on home to check on Pasipo and the Maasai.

"The short rains have arrived." Ernst settled into an easy chair. "Bad news for Zanifa."

Jordan drank and stared into the fire.

"You're still worrying about her?"

Jordan turned toward him. "Can I take your bike to Nairobi?"

"No." Ernst took a sip of Tusker.

"Five hundred bucks." Jordan stretched his arms and yawned. "Easy money."

Ernst looked at Jordan as if he couldn't be serious. "When did you get rich?"

"I did another run for Ionides," Jordan said.

"What's so important about a trip to Nairobi?"

"I'm taking Zanifa to school." Jordan swallowed the Tusker.

"You fucking Americans." With an amused look, Ernst considered Jordan, then laughed. "You're saving her because you don't want someone else to fuck her."

"I'm saving her 'cause *I* don't want to want to fuck her," Jordan whispered too low for Ernst to hear.

"What?" Ernst said, still smiling.

"I'll leave the bike at your wife's house."

"Yeah." Ernst lost his amused expression. "You better not come back."

The halogen headlights of the BMW Paris-Dakar racer lit up the road like a movie set. The town was dark and empty. A few street lamps cast pools of yellow light on the antique BP pumps and the front of the police post. No one was outside. Jordan parked in front of the gingerbread post office, aimed the halogens at the porch, and leaned the bike on its stand with the engine running.

He opened his box. On the back of a postcard, opposite a photograph of an alligator pulling down a buxom woman's bikini bottom, Garret Stoval had written, "Your letters get weirder. Are you stir crazy or falling prey to pedophilia? That girl in the photo was okay but hardly Miss Tanzania. You look thin as a whip. Did you get the vitamins? How's your gut? Get your ass home in one piece." Jordan recognized his mother's handwriting on the other envelope. He tore it open and read, the low rumble of the German engine drowning out the sounds of the night. "Nanny died tonight after a week in the hospital. Grandmother, your sister, and your cousins were all there. Nanny asked about you, asked us to pray that you are safe. She was so noble and brave. She said that she was ready to leave . . . the funeral will be in a week, on the 7th . . . We will all miss you." Jordan leaned against the wall, panting. A hundred years old. The funeral was today, he thought with a rush of guilt.

In the headlights, a Maasai stood on the porch with his spear and his *shuka* like a shawl around his shoulders. The windows of the house were shattered.

"Shabu, what happened?"

"I went for a walk with Pasipo at dawn and returned at sunset. I didn't see anyone."

"Where's Parmet and Lesuyu?" Jordan took the Maglite from his hand.

"A brother died. They went home."

"Ah, shit," Jordan said in English, then in Swahili: "I paid them to stay here."

"A brother died. They'll be back in a few days."

"A brother or a third cousin?"

Shabu smiled and mumbled something about Parmet's sister's husband's brother.

Jordan stepped into a stench that filled the rectory. The buzzing of flies formed a background hum to the drizzle of rain on the tin roof. Jordan moved the beam of the Maglite around the dark room. All the furniture was overturned. Piles of human shit sat on the floor, on the sofa, on the tables, an old insult of African war parties. Green flies swarmed. The watercolors of Pasipo had been ripped from the walls and shredded into confetti sprinkled across the room.

"Sultani Kimweri," Jordan said.

They followed the beam into the bedroom. The mosquito net hung in rips from the ceiling, the mattress stuffing scattered. Cupping his hand over his nose, Jordan led the way back through the living room into the kitchen, where the floor was covered with broken plates. A perfect coiled rope of shit lay on the center of the table.

On the back porch Pasipo was sleeping on her perch. Shabu dragged the broken furniture to one end. Jordan told him to bring his bed roll, but the Maasai insisted on sleeping out front in case the warriors returned. He went into the house and came back carrying a charcoal brazier full of burning coals, his hands numb to the hot metal. He set down the stove and pulled an envelope from under his thin leather belt. "A girl brought this today at sunset."

Jordan read the Swahili by flashlight. The handwriting was large and girlish. Shabu left him translating the letter into English aloud:

*Peace, Bwana Jordan,*

*This morning, after the assembly, Bwana Kimweri came to St. Mary's. He took Zanifa. She was crying. She didn't want to go. Last night Father William came to our village and talked to Mama Zanifa. On the way to school, Zanifa told me that Father William told her mother she must be married. She wanted to come to your house after school to ask you to take her away.*

*Yours,*
*Subira*

Jordan was tired but too anxious to sleep. He found some clothes hanging on a line by the side of the rectory and told Shabu to slaughter the goat and pack the meat for a long ride in the morning. He

walked through the house with the flashlight but couldn't find anything that he wanted to take with him. At about four in the morning
the rain started to pelt the tin roof. He lay on the futon in the darkness, listening to the wind roar along the cliffs, and caught himself
drumming his fingers on the canvas, silently singing a song from college, "Should I Stay or Should I Go." He remembered singing the
song to Anna on their first date, drunk at the end of the evening. He
had stayed. If he told the Peace Corps that Kimweri's men destroyed
his house, they would let him out of the last six weeks of his contract, give him his full five-thousand-dollar payment and fly him
home. He whispered, " 'Like me who has no love which this wild rain
has not dissolved.' "

In the morning fog they rode the BMW: Jordan driving in his green
slicker and black helmet, Shabu wrapped against the wind in a bright
red Maasai tartan blanket, long braids flapping, a spear in one hand,
bangles jangling on his wrist, and Pasipo, jessed to the rack, a leather
hood over her head, her six-foot wings outstretched. Jordan chose
back roads, avoiding the main highway. Rushing through the mist, an-
ticipating cattle and children, his hands on the throttle and brake,
Jordan fixed his mind on driving. Shabu was silent. Pasipo screamed
whenever the bike leaned into a turn.

Jordan worried about the direction. Every few minutes he looked
down at the compass duct taped to the petrol tank. The needle stub-
bornly drifted east. He slowed the bike and drove on tentatively, looking for someone to ask. The fog cleared, though another bank then
drifted slowly toward them from a ridge above. Shabu pointed to
women working in a maize patch. Jordan accelerated down the muddy
road, then coasted to a stop by the field. The women turned toward
them. Jordan lifted the helmet visor and started to ask directions. The
women dropped their hoes. Shrieking, they ran up the mountainside.

From the top of a mountain Jordan studied Vooga through binoculars. A few miles off, the village was set on a lower peak—an island
rising out of the white ocean of a solid cloud bank that lapped the

mountains and stretched to the far horizon of the Maasai steppe. Houses surrounded three sides of the palace, but the back faced only banana trees. He handed Shabu the binoculars. The Maasai gazed down at Vooga for several minutes. He said, "We go up through the bananas and the wall of thorns." He drank from a gourd, then offered it to Jordan.

"What is it?"

"War medicine. It makes you so angry your arms shake." Shabu's eyes had a crazed gleam. "You don't care about anything. You aren't afraid to die."

"I could use some of that." Jordan swallowed the metallic-tasting tea.

At the edge of the banana gardens, they struggled to push the two-hundred-pound bike through soft mud into a thick clump of trees. Jordan wrapped his slicker to the BMW rack and took Pasipo on the glove. Pasipo cried, and Jordan fed her a slice of goat meat from the falconry bag to shut her up, then hooded her. They walked through the half-light under the trees. The fog thinned out toward the top of the hill. Jordan's heart started pounding like some thing trapped in his chest when he reached the hedgerow. He had come to the end of his plan. Shabu ran along the wall and disappeared.

Shabu's face was eager, his eyes more manic when he returned. "I've found a way in," he whispered. He trotted back along the thorn wall in a crouch. Jordan watched him grow smaller and followed just as he was out of sight. He reached Shabu on his hands and knees in a hole in the hedge. The Maasai hung his head and looked upside-down through his legs at Jordan.

"No one is outside. I go first." Shabu crawled into the bush.

Panting, Jordan cradled the hooded eagle, crawled into the bush.

The sun was shining. White lines of lime were drawn in squares across the courtyard. Jordan saw a low net. This was where Kimweri practiced his serve. Four adobe huts blocked the view of the compound. Only the peaks of the palace roof were visible. The windows of the huts were small, shuttered: the servants' quarters. Across the yard was the ruin of Kimweri's father's courthouse. White-necked ravens swooped into a hole in the roof.

"Which way?" Shabu whispered.

Jordan said nothing.

"We must move, they'll see us."

Jordan started panting again.

"Never think of the lion before you are upon it," Shabu said.

A dog barked in one of the servants' huts. Shabu ran away from the noise toward the ruin.

"No," Jordan whispered. "This way."

Several dogs barked in unison as Shabu and Jordan circled around the servant quarters. Naked children stood outside the huts. Thirty yards across a shady lawn, set near one corner of two walls of the hedgerow, was a ring of round adobe rooms, each with an open-shuttered window and a thatched conical roof. Jordan couldn't see the front of the palace where cars parked by the covered walkway. Sprinting, he led Shabu the other way into a dark alley formed by the back of the palace and the tall hedge. They ran crouching beneath the windows until they reached a doorway.

"What is the plan?" Shabu asked. "Where's the girl?"

Fear had scrambled Jordan's ability to translate Swahili. He wished he had drunk more of the tea.

"Inside here?" Shabu set his hand on the door latch.

"Okay," Jordan whispered. "Inside."

The door led into a narrow adobe passage to the atrium, where flame and jacaranda trees grew out of the flagstones. Through the branches of a flame, Jordan spotted Kimweri on the far end of the garden in an open area near a fountain. In a business suit and red fez, he was sitting talking with another man in a suit. Behind them, under the covered walk, a warrior in a white shirt and dark pants stood with his back turned, looking out at the barking dogs. Jordan and Shabu crept closer and paused at the edge of the trees and potted plants. Thirty feet away Jordan saw a woman's face appear behind a window screen.

She stared at Jordan.

Pasipo shifted on the glove.

The woman screamed. The Kilindi warrior ran from the covered walk into the garden. Outside, dogs barked madly across the compound.

"*Aaheeeee!*" Holding his spear with both hands from his waist, Shabu charged out of the trees and stopped a few feet from the Kilindi warrior.

Kimweri and his companion stood up quickly. The sultan's face was confused until he saw Jordan behind a jacaranda, and then he grinned. Jordan glanced behind his back, then walked forward. Kimweri laughed.

"What an unexpected pleasure." Kimweri reached into his jacket.

"Where's Zanifa?"

"Recuperating." Kimweri giggled and drew a small silver pistol from his jacket. "You're too late."

"Zanifa!" Jordan screamed, dodging behind the fountain. "Zanifa!"

"*Atcha mkuki!*" Kimweri pointed the pistol at Shabu. Drop the spear. He said something in Sambaa, and the Kilindi backed away from Shabu. Kimweri aimed the gun with both hands.

Shabu dashed for the trees.

Kimweri swung his arms in a smooth line.

Jordan jerked the hood from Pasipo; the eagle's eyes fixed on the red fez.

A shot echoed in the courtyard and Jordan yelled: "*Piga!*"

Shabu rolled across the stones.

Streaking across the atrium, the sky leopard hit the fez with a loud thump. She rode Kimweri's head down to the patio.

On his feet, Shabu shouted and pointed his spear at the Kilindi, who was staring down at Kimweri.

Pasipo tore at Kimweri's face with her beak.

"*Njoo,*" Jordan called the eagle, moving across the patio. He bent and picked up the pistol. Come. "*Pasipo, njoo.*"

The Kilindi warrior and the stranger in the suit didn't move. Three women in bright kangas rushed into the courtyard and stopped a few feet from the body.

Pasipo held one of Kimweri's eyes in her beak. She tilted her head and swallowed. The eye bulged in her crop.

The women screamed and started to wail.

Pasipo raised her white-tipped crown and mantled her wings, a territorial gesture, as Jordan crouched next to Kimweri's body. She looked at the meat in the glove, then turned her head and pecked the bloody eye socket. Jordan held his gloved fist trembling against her legs, blocking her view of Kimweri's face, until she stepped onto the glove. He stood with the eagle on his fist.

"Joldon . . ." From under the covered walkway at the front of the palace, Zanifa appeared, running toward him. Her eyes were wide, her mouth twisted with fear. She was carrying a sisal traveling bag at her waist, wearing jeans and a St. Mary's sweater.

One of the women ran screaming toward the compound gate, where a crowd had gathered.

"Run!" Zanifa stopped a few feet from him. "That witch will tell the people to kill you."

"Are you okay?"

"Yes. Come on."

"You haven't . . . they haven't . . . ," Jordan stammered in English.

"What?" Zanifa looked fearfully past him. "Please! We must run."

"Bwana." Shabu pulled Jordan by the shoulder. "Let's go."

The Kilindi warrior was still standing by the man in the suit. They stared in shock at Kimweri's face.

"Don't just sit there!" Jordan shouted. *"Kuma mayo!"* Your mother's cunt. He waved the gun. "Get him to the hospital!" The two men hurried over to the sultan.

A crowd began to pour through the gate, a few boys jogging ahead of the mass. Jordan ran after Zanifa and Shabu, across the patio and back through the narrow passage, out into the alley and along the hedgerow to the hole. They crawled through the thorns into the banana gardens and leapt down the mountainside, falling and sliding through the fog. Jordan lashed Pasipo to the rear rack. The cries of the crowd grew closer.

"I'm safest by foot from here." Shabu smiled. "They'll follow the motorcycle into the mountains while I go home down the gorge on the other side."

Jordan peeled off fifteen hundred dollars from the eleven thousand he had taken from Paul Ionides twenty-three hours ago. "You can buy ten cows now. Enough to get married."

"I'll name my first son Jordan." Shabu slapped his hand and laughed.

Jordan looked downhill into the fog and considered the fact that police could be waiting at the bottom of the road to Mombo with the gate closed. He checked Zanifa behind him. Her eyes were invisible through the visor of the black helmet sitting lopsided on her small head. Pasipo beat her wings and jerked at her jesses, trying to fly. Jordan wiped the mist from his face and turned uphill onto the tarmac.

They rode up, climbing, passing Sambaa women carrying loads of vegetables and charcoal on their heads, until Jordan saw a turn hidden by tall grass. A dirt road ran along a barren ridge top to the edge of a pass that zigzagged down the cliffs of the escarpment. It was built a hundred years before by the Germans, who had a thousand Africans drag a three-ton coal-burning saw up into the rain forest. The road dropped three thousand vertical feet in a mile and half. They rolled down slowly in first gear. Zanifa gasped when the bike slid through the gravel near the edge of an opaque abyss. Halfway to the bottom they came out of the fog. To the south the summits of the mountains scattered across the Maasai steppe were sheered off by the cloud bank, but north of the Usambara range the sky was open and clear. The air grew hotter as they descended. The vast steppe was gloomy in the gray light.

At the foot of the mountains they took a sand road between the tall plants of a sisal plantation. On the highway they turned south toward Mombo, then a mile before town veered west by the grass runway and terminal cottage of the extinct East African Airways. Jordan hit seventy miles an hour on the long flat road toward Mafi Mountain, whose dark form rose before them like a volcano.

A late light colored the cloud ceiling soft pink and brought out the myriad green hues of the canopy of the mountain forest. Jordan let off on the throttle and coasted through a turn onto a road that climbed gradually in a straight line several miles up an alluvial fan to-

ward the base of the lone mountain. The road showed no signs of recent traffic. Clumps of spiky sensivera dotted the shallow slope. At
the top of the alluvial fan the road crossed a wooden bridge and
began a steep ascent. Boulders blocked the road, and the switchbacks
were washed out, too narrow for a car. At the top of the pass they left
the twilight and entered a dark, cold forest. Jordan flicked the twin
halogen lamps onto tree stumps as big as redwoods and bark-covered
vines as wide as water pipes twisting hundreds of feet up into the
darkness.

They stopped and climbed off the bike.

"Are you okay?" Jordan asked in English.

Zanifa started to sob, harder and harder, until she was almost
choking.

"You'll be fine," he said lamely, grasping her tightly against him.

She backed away from him and vanished into the darkness. Jordan
unlashed the bags in the dim red and yellow light at the back of the
bike. Unable to see her, he asked, "Would you like something to eat?"

"No."

In the headlights Jordan climbed a smooth trunk, clutching it between his arms and legs, to a limb twenty feet off the ground. He
unwrapped large pieces of ripe goat from a plastic bag and tied them
to the limb with strips of cut inner tube, then slid to the ground and
wiped his hands on the silvery trunk. Shadowing his eyes with one
hand, he walked through the blinding light back to the motorcycle
and found Zanifa sitting on the seat, nibbling an apple. She pointed
to the crown of a fallen tree in the headlights. "That plant with red
stems that grows at the top of trees will keep you awake."

"*Khat.*" Jordan was relieved that she had spoken.

Zanifa said nothing more, dropped to the ground and walked away
from him into the white light. Jordan drank half a bottle of antacid,
then sliced a mango and watched her collect stems from the fallen
tree. She moved gracefully among tangled underbrush, then came
back to the road. Jordan put his hand on her shoulder. She pulled
away and went to the other side of the bike.

Jordan switched off the headlights and aimed the Maglite at
Pasipo. She turned her gray eyes away from the light and raised her

feathered crown, fully grown now, the white feathers three inches long, tipped with black triangles. Jordan bent and cut the leather jesses off Pasipo's legs with his pocket knife. He breathed deeply, heat gathering in the corners of his eyes, and trained the light on the meat lashed to the limb. *"Piga!"*

Pasipo swam up the beam of light to the branch. Jordan handed Zanifa the light and asked her to hold the beam on the bird. He strapped the bags back on the rack. They watched Pasipo tear into a goat thigh.

*"Kwa heri,* Pasipo," Zanifa said. Good-bye.

"Turn off the torch," Jordan whispered.

They were surrounded by blackness that seemed solid.

Surefooted in the darkness, Zanifa walked ahead while Jordan pushed the bike slowly down the road. After twenty minutes they came out of the forest. From the top of the pass they could see a few fires dotted across the steppe. Jordan swung his leg over the wide seat and switched on the halogens.

Zanifa climbed onto the bike. She was sobbing quietly.

"Pasipo will like it here. It's perfect for a sky leopard. Plenty of game." Jordan felt her press against his back as she looped her arms around his waist. She said nothing.

In the far reaches of the headlights a huge raptor stood immobile. It had a crown.

"Is it Pasipo?" Zanifa whispered.

Irrationally Jordan hoped that it was, braking the bike on a steep grade.

The raptor held still as the tires crunched the gravel. Two ear tufts poked straight up on the sides of its round head.

"Usambara eagle owl," Jordan whispered to Zanifa. The eagle owl looked big enough to catch a sleeping colobus monkey.

*Ooop-oop.* The eagle-owl spread her gray wings and flew into the dark. *Ooop-oop.*

Zanifa laid her head against his back. "What if she finds Pasipo?"

They rode out from under the clouds at the Mkomazi Gap, the scrubland separating the Usambara Mountains from the Pareh range, a point on the old slave route from the great lakes to the coast. The BMW sped over smooth highway at 110 mph. Jordan wore sunglasses to protect his eyes but his face was stung by insects. At the end of the halogen beam an eighteen-wheel truck seemed to be turned on its side. Jordan took his hand off the throttle. The engine whined as it wound down. It wasn't a truck, but a herd of red elephants crossing the highway.

"*Tembo,*" Zanifa said. "*Haah.* I've never seen one."

"They're stained by red clay."

They rode on when the elephants were gone. Nightjars froze in the bright light, fluttering out of the way just as the bike was upon them. Jordan chewed *khat* and drove slowly. A family of warthogs ran along the shoulder with funny stiff gaits, their tails thrust vertically. The moonlight illuminated the long necks of giraffe rising above the domes of distant trees like a school of surfacing Loch Ness monsters.

The game disappeared at the other side of the Mkomazi Gap, and Jordan accelerated to 80 mph, keeping to the center of the empty highway, aiming directly at Mount Kilimanjaro a hundred miles north. The moonlight burnished the twenty-thousand-foot summit of the dead volcano, whose cap of white icing dripped down the sides of the cone. They rode alongside the Pareh range, a jagged black form against the starry sky. By morning, Jordan reckoned, the police would have radioed every border post.

# Novemba 8

Jordan felt Zanifa's body shift across his back. In the rearview mirrors against the darkness he could just distinguish the black helmet wobbling on her neck from shoulder to shoulder. He slapped her thigh, spat out a bundle of ground *khat* stems from the back of his mouth and let off on the throttle. She jerked awake when he hit the brakes. Her voice was a hoarse whisper. "Where are we?"

"About four hours from the border." Jordan climbed off the bike, steadying himself on her shoulder. The *khat* had made him edgy. He wanted to run a mile down the highway or guzzle a half-liter bottle of Safari. He circled the bike, kicked the tires, felt the heat coming off the big cylinder heads. Zanifa pulled off the helmet and shook her hair in the breeze. She lay back on the long seat with her legs dangling on either side of the gas tank. "You will never leave me?"

"Sweet girl, I'll be a rock you can stand on." Jordan rushed over to look down in her face. *"Nitakuwa kaka kwako."*

"You will be my brother," she translated flatly, her face a black form in the night.

With a sizzling sound, bats swooped low and caught insects drawn to the headlights. Zanifa placed her hands on Jordan's neck and pulled his head toward her. She closed her eyes and parted her mouth.

Jordan held his face a few inches away and waited for her eyes to open. Then he said gently, "No. Not anymore."

She left her hands draped around his neck. "Where will we live?"

"You'll like the Boma School. It sounds great. You always wanted to board at St. Mary's." If we make it into Kenya, Jordan thought. He stood up. "Here, put my sweater on."

"It's too big."

"I know." Jordan tapped his fingers against the big fuel tank. "I'm going to wrap the sleeves around my waist—tie you to me so you don't fall."

Zanifa hopped off the bike and moved into the headlights. "It'll be too hot with two jumpers." She pulled her sweater over her head and her T-shirt off with it. Jordan saw her breasts in a bra and looked up at the sky.

"You're going to leave me," she said, wiggling into his sweater.

"Not forever," Jordan said softly, reaching for her shoulder.

Zanifa smiled. There was something new about her face, perhaps the first traces of guile, as if she were now aware of the power her body held over men.

"Kimweri and the police will be looking for me soon." Jordan paced around the bike, excited that he had gone this far, pushed the stakes so high. "I've got to take the first plane out of Nairobi for Europe and go on back to the States."

"Why did you throw Kimweri's gun away?"

"Maybe that *was* stupid," he mumbled, the elation suddenly gone. He opened his rucksack on the rear rack and felt around for an envelope.

"Will you take me to America?"

"One day. Of course. We have to get you a passport," he said cheerfully, afraid he would infect her with his fear. He counted out seven thousand dollars and put it in the envelope. "Here's enough for next year. It'll see you through high school. There's an extra thousand dollars for clothes or emergencies. Take it now. We'll deposit it with the headmistress at the academy. But it's yours. If you decide to go back to Lushoto, it's still yours."

"*Mimi siwezi kurudi,*" Zanifa said softly. I can't return. She hesitated a moment before taking the envelope. "I won't go back for a long time. I'll send some of this money to my mother so she can come visit me." She brushed a tear from her cheek and hugged Jordan.

She fell asleep with the helmet against the back of his neck. He stuck his chin into the high collar of his slicker against the careening bugs and chewed *khat* and kept a watch on Orion as if in a trance until the hunter passed over his head and sank over the horizon to the south in the rearview mirror. He saw Pasipo riding Kimweri's head to the ground. Ripping the eyeball from the socket. Jordan felt something cold and soulless enter him, like another being. It seemed to smile at him as if saying that it was here to stay. He thought of Pasipo flying up the light beam and wondered if the eagle would survive on her own or how long it would take for her to starve to death. The scar on his forearm throbbed, and his arms ached from holding the wide handlebars steady. He imagined meeting Kimweri at the border, the sultan in his fez wearing an eye patch. He prayed to God that he would deliver Zanifa.

The road ran straight and flat. There was no traffic. Jordan watched Polaris climb out of the north. He fixed on the north star, glancing up every few minutes from the centerline, until the star disappeared as the black edge of the eastern horizon turned a fiery liquid purple. Jordan figured it was about a half hour to sunrise.

A silver obelisk glinted in the last light of the moon. Beneath the massive granite peak were the lights of Namanga.

"Wake up, sweetpea," Jordan shouted over the wind, patting her thigh.

"*Sisi wapi sasa?*" Zanifa asked sleepily.

"The border."

"Untie me, please," Zanifa said in Swahili. "My arms are stiff as branches and my stomach is growling like a leopard."

"We'll eat breakfast in Kenya." Jordan managed to undo the sweater with one hand. Zanifa stretched and yawned. Coming into town, she nestled against his back and watched one side of the road, passing a row of dark stalls, tin-roofed bar hotels, a BP station. Jordan parked in the middle of an empty lot half lit by tall lamps in front of the yellow cement office of customs and immigration. Zanifa leapt off the backseat. Jordan leaned the bike on its stand and unlashed Zanifa's bag and his rucksack.

"That's Kenya?" Zanifa pointed at the misty country beyond a chain-link fence.

"That's right." Jordan brushed smooth his sweat-stained Peace Corps T-shirt. "Another country."

"It looks the same as Tanzania."

"God made the world, and men drew lines across it." Jordan yawned.

"I thought it would be different." Zanifa sounded disappointed.

"It will be." Jordan took her hand. "When we go in there, just do what I do, okay?"

"Monkey see, monkey do." Zanifa giggled.

"*Kinehora,*" he whispered for luck as they entered the fluorescent white light of the government post. A young immigration officer in blue stood at a counter at one end of the room. An older officer in a tan uniform slept in a chair behind a counter on the opposite side.

"*Jambo, mzee.*" Jordan called the young officer "revered elder." "What's the news of the night?"

"Clean," the officer said sleepily. "What's the news of your safari?"

"Peaceful." Jordan wished the officer would return his smile.

"*Shikamoo,*" Zanifa said. I kiss your feet.

"Delighted," the officer grunted. "Where are you coming from?"

"Lushoto. It's been a long safari." Jordan placed their passports on the counter. "She just won a scholarship to school in Kenya."

The officer passed them yellow departure forms.

"May I use your pen, please?" Zanifa asked in Swahili.

The officer pulled the pen from his mouth and offered it wet end first across the counter.

"*Habarizenu!*" A truck driver walked in smiling, employing the same obsequious strategy as Jordan. What's the news of everyone?

"Clean," the officer muttered. He unfolded Zanifa's travel papers and checked the information against the card, said in Swahili: "This girl, Zanifa Hering, is underage. She cannot travel without a parent."

"I have a letter from the Peace Corps explaining everything." Jordan found the letter in his rucksack.

The officer glanced at the letter. "Why didn't her father sign a release? A release is mandatory." The switch to bureaucratic English was a bad sign.

"My father is dead," Zanifa said clearly in Swahili, meeting the man's eyes. "My mother is traveling on business."

"You will have to go back and get a release from a family member, stamped by your village secretary," the officer said.

"It takes a day to travel to Lushoto," Jordan said.

"It is the law," the officer said drowsily.

The truck driver filled out a yellow card at one end of the counter. Jordan leaned forward and whispered, "I'll pay you a hundred dollars overtime."

The officer said nothing. His eyes were flat.

Jordan's stomach started to burn.

"Two hundred," the officer said.

"Should we go outside?" Jordan peeked at the truck driver.

"No. Here."

Jordan slid the two bills across the counter and watched him stamp Zanifa's travel pass and his passport. They walked toward the sleeping officer behind the customs counter.

"*Namanga. Sisi ni Arusha, unasema,* over?" A voice from a radio carried through a door in the center of the wall between the two counters.

The older officer in tan woke up, glared at Jordan and called across the room in English: "Where is Lieutenant Mbele?"

"Sleeping in back," the immigration officer answered in Swahili. "He got drunk with his whore on the Kenya side and stumbled in about an hour ago."

"*Namanga, Namanga,* do you read, over?"

Jordan felt a sudden pressure in the top of his chest. His palms started to sweat.

"He is crazy—that policeman." The immigration officer whistled. "He says he does not use a condom with his whore because she is like a wife. He sleeps only with her."

"*Namanga, Namanga,* come in, over."

The customs officer gestured for Zanifa to set her bag on the counter and yawned noisily, stretching his arms.

Zanifa hesitated, looked at Jordan.

"Put it on the counter," Jordan whispered in English. "Tell him that you have nothing to declare."

Zanifa looked at the officer and said, "I have nothing to declare."

"*Namanga, Namanga,* come in, over."

"Does she sleep with other men?" The gray-bearded officer stared over Zanifa's head across the room.

"What does a whore do at night?" the immigration officer answered, stamping the trucker's travel papers. "She says she always uses socks with other men."

"Don't believe it. Most men refuse to use socks with whores," the graybeard said. "They feel like they are getting cheated. Men are fools. Has Mbele had a test?"

"None of us have had tests," the younger man said. "Who wants to know?"

"*Namanga, Namanga.* Do you read? Over."

Jordan braced himself not to flinch, certain he would give himself away. He fingered a stalk of *khat* in his pocket, remembered it was illegal.

"*Namanga, Namanga.* This is Arusha. Do you read? Over."

"They sound angry. We should wake him," the graybeard said.

The younger man thought for a moment.

"Please, we are in a hurry, *mzee,*" Jordan said. He laid the BMW papers on the counter.

"Just one minute," the officer replied. He looked back across the room. "Go wake him. He's your friend."

Jordan's head hurt behind his eyes, and he looked at Zanifa and realized that she also had taken on his nervousness.

"*Namanga, Namanga,* come in. Over."

"Mbele will chew *me* out because they'll chew *him* out for not being at his post by the radio for the morning check," the younger man answered rapidly in Swahili. "He'll call in at noon and tell them the interference was bad."

"There is no pride left in the civil service," the graybeard said softly in English. "It was different when I worked for the British." He looked at Zanifa's sisal bag and told her, "Go ahead."

Zanifa grabbed the bag from the counter and hurried out the door. The graybeard picked up the BMW logbook.

*"Namanga, Namanga . . ."*

Jordan watched, afraid the man could smell his sweat across the counter.

*"Mzungu!"* the immigration officer called across the room.

Jordan tried to smile.

"Your friend is fresh. You don't have to worry about *ukimwi* with her." He winked. "Don't deliver her to school with a big belly! They'll throw her out."

". . . come in. Over."

The graybeard stamped the logbook.

Jordan thanked him and turned to face the immigration officer, smiling, on the edge of hysterical laughter. "Don't worry about that one. She'll come back and start a women's party! Women across the country will refuse to carry water!"

The officers laughed and slapped the counter. "That's the best one I've heard since all this talk of democracy," the graybeard said in Swahili. "Crazy."

*"Namanga, Namanga,* do you read, over?"

Jordan walked out into a clear dawn. Zanifa sat on the bike, folding cuffs on the bottom of her jeans. The sky was deep sea blue against the granite peak and the infinite flats of the green thorn scrub. He kissed her on the cheek and held her close, wanting to tell her he loved her, afraid she would misunderstand. He swung his leg over the seat and hit the starter button. They rode across the parking lot to a gate, a single length of metal pipe. A tired soldier in faded fatigues swung it open and they crossed into Kenya.

# Novemba 9

A sound startled Jordan from deep sleep. The heavy drapes and carpet looked unfamiliar. Horse racing scenes on the wallpaper recalled a hotel room in Louisville where after a long night on a Derby weekend he had listened to Anna talking in her sleep. He sat up in the dim light and groaned softly, his back stiff and shoulders sore. There were three soft knocks, and then Zanifa's voice from the hallway: *"Hodi. Hodi."*

*"Karibu."* Jordan tightened a *kikoi* around his waist and opened the door.

She was wearing pressed jeans and her St. Mary's sweater. "Are you sick? You've been sleeping for twelve hours. I was worrying you were sick."

"No. Just worn out."

Zanifa brushed past him and dove onto the bed. "These are the best mattresses."

"We need to buy some clothes this morning." Jordan picked up a pair of filthy khakis and slipped them on beneath the *kikoi*.

"I found a *duka* in the central market where they sell American clothes." Zanifa rolled on her back and dangled her legs over the edge. "All the Asian girls and European girls will be having nice clothes on weekends."

"You went out this morning?"

"No, last night." Zanifa smiled impishly.

"To the central market. By yourself. You could've been robbed or raped. I told you to stay at the hotel."

"You were asleep," Zanifa said earnestly in Swahili. "There were many people out in the streets. It's not dangerous. Besides, I went with a maid from the hotel. She's a Chagga from Kilimanjaro."

"You already made a friend." He laughed at his anger.

Jordan followed Zanifa through the buffet, humming while they loaded their plates with fruit, eggs and pastries. The big dining room was occupied by an army of tourists in safari gear who stared at the long-haired white man in dirty clothes leading the African girl past their tables.

"Why are the whites wearing uniforms?" Zanifa whispered in Swahili.

"That's the fashion for visiting game parks."

"They *want* to dress alike? When I finish school I'll never wear a uniform again."

"What about jeans and jumpers? That's a uniform." Jordan found a table by a glass wall overlooking a courtyard.

"I never thought of it that way." She looked outside at a large bird-cage. "You think Pasipo is okay?"

"Of course." He smiled and started shoveling eggs into his mouth, then caught himself. He was setting a bad example. A waiter brought tea. Jordan cleared his plate slowly, one hand in his lap, watching the tourists come and go.

"You're happy this morning." Zanifa sat straight in her chair. "You've been singing since we left your room."

"Was I? It was a hymn from chapel when I was your age. I can't remember the words."

"I know it." Zanifa hummed.

"You're a Muslim."

"Everyone has to go to chapel." In a clear soprano Zanifa sang softly across the table:

*Joy-ful, joy-ful, we a-dore thee, God of glo-ry, Lord of love;*
*hearts un-fold like flowers be-fore thee, prais-ing thee, their sun above.*

*Melt the clouds of sin and sad-ness; drive the dark of doubt a-way;*
*giv-er of im-mor-tal glad-ness, fill us with the light of day.*

"I'm very proud of you." Jordan smiled. "You'll do great things one day. I just know it."

"That was beautiful," a woman said from a table nearby. "Hi, I'm Flo. I think it's wonderful there are so many Christians in Africa."

"Oh, yes, ma'am," Jordan said. "More here than anywhere else in the world."

"You sound southern. Where're you from? We're from Dallas."

"Memphis."

"You look like you live here," said a man at the table. "Do you know anything about changing money on the black market?"

"No, sir." Jordan signed the check and stood up. "I'd use a bank."

"What are you doing over here?"

"I'm a missionary. Y'all have a good day." Jordan took Zanifa's hand and walked away humming Beethoven's *Hymn to Joy.*

Outside the Norfolk the air was cool and vibrating with traffic noise. Zanifa walked the streets of Nairobi with her head tipped back at the skyscrapers and her mouth open. The multitude of coats and ties was an unusual sight to Jordan. Zanifa bumped into one of the men streaming past.

*"Wewe mshamba."* The man called her a hillbilly.

"I beg your pardon, sir," Zanifa said in English.

At the Oxford Clothiers, Jordan bought a tweed blazer, button-downs, khakis and for Zanifa a V-neck sweater and loafers. At a Bata shop he bought them both suede desert boots. In the stalls of the central market he watched while Zanifa picked out a pirated Nike warm-up jacket and two pair of secondhand Levi's jeans. They walked back to the small hair salon at the Norfolk. Zanifa looked apprehensively around the room at the mirrors and rows of bottles.

"Two haircuts." Jordan guided her gently toward an Asian woman standing beside a barber chair. "Ladies first."

"How would you like your hair cut today?"

"My mother always cuts it the same way." Zanifa pointed at a poster of a mulatto girl with a wave of bangs curling around her cheeks. "Can I get that one?"

"That's a permanent."

"What?"

"We would have to straighten your hair and set it."

"Your hair is beautiful the way it is," Jordan said. "Just ask her to trim the ends so it's all even."

"Please, just trim it nicely," Zanifa said, disappointed. She gasped when the chair back lowered suddenly toward the sink. The stylist smirked and began to wash her hair. "You're not from Nairobi."

"I come here for going to school," Zanifa replied. "From Tanzania."

"You'll like Kenya. It's much better here. Tanzania." The stylist shook her head. "A backward country. Who is your friend?"

"He is my brother."

Jordan smiled, flipping through a British *Vogue*. He planned the rest of the day. From his room he would call all the airlines and the Peace Corps office in Dar es Salaam. He would call the headmistress and tell her they would arrive in the afternoon. It would be better to hire a car than show up on the motorcycle.

Asking her questions about the Usambara Mountains, the woman parted Zanifa's hair in the middle and evened the ends of the ringlets along her cheeks and in a line across her slender neck. He heard Zanifa tell her: "I miss my mama. I've never slept away from home."

"You're not so far away. My mother is in India."

"She'll come visit you soon, Zanifa." Jordan crossed the room to the chair where the stylist was brushing off Zanifa's shoulders. "Look at you! *Ah!* You'll be prettier than all the other girls." Jordan picked up a lock of her hair off the floor and wrapped it in a tissue. "A keepsake."

"Not for magic?" Zanifa laughed, but her eyes were uneasy. She leapt down and looked at herself in the mirror.

"Just to remember you." Jordan reclined in the big chair.

"The last one to cut your hair was blind?" The stylist's comb caught in a knot on the back of Jordan's head.

"Last trim I got was from a Maasai." Jordan laughed. "Cut it all off. Make me look like a merchant banker."

Zanifa tied a length of his hair with a piece of string from a tag on her new sweater. She showed it to Jordan. "A *kumbukumbu.*"

From a hill above the city, dwindling through the rear window of a London cab, the Nairobi skyline looked like a stage prop against the vast plain. When the view was blocked by trees, Zanifa turned around and sat with her feet on the edge of the seat and her chin on her knees, hugging herself as if she were cold. She stared out the window at the roofs of houses peaking above walls topped with razor wire and shopping malls rising out of islands of asphalt. Jordan took her hand. "What's the matter?"

"You're leaving me alone," Zanifa said in Swahili.

"The Kenya police might try to stop me if I wait around," Jordan said softly. "I didn't want to frighten you. The police in Dar have told the Peace Corps office that I should report for questioning."

"How do you know?"

"I talked to my boss while you were finishing lunch. You're safe. You didn't do anything wrong. I know you miss your mama and you're going to be in a new place. But you made the right choice."

"*Labda mchowi ya Sultani ataweka dawa kwenye mimi.*"

"That's what's worrying you?" Jordan laughed. "Don't be silly. Kimweri can't put a curse on you. Witch doctor magic is bullshit. You know better than that."

She looked out the window at woodland on the edge of a game park. He was bound to her now as surely as if she were his own child. He tried to picture her walking across the Memphis State campus. The obligation liberated him from his aimlessness. Then he felt somber as he realized that if he'd had the same sense of commitment three years before, he would have married Anna.

"Will you take a wife in America?" Zanifa said as if reading his thoughts. "You are too old not to have a wife."

"One day." Jordan smiled. "You won't be jealous, will you?"

"Who is she?" Zanifa threw herself on him across the backseat.

"There's no one." Jordan laughed, holding her arms away from his face.

"There will be." Zanifa stopped struggling. "You like making love too much. That's why you helped me."

"Smart ass." Jordan touched her scratch on his chin lightly in the rearview mirror, struck by the strangeness of his short hair and blazer. "Will you keep our secret?"

"I won't tell anyone," she said slowly in English. "You were teaching me. My best teacher."

A large green sign for the Boma School marked a long driveway between playing fields. Girls with hockey sticks darted back and forth across the farthest field like a flock of birds. The rains had not reached this far north and the grass was brown under the hot afternoon sun. Hidden by hedge and creepers, a fence surrounded a stand of tall trees. A uniformed African snapped to attention as the taxi passed through a gate. Two boys wearing white shirts and blue shorts, a slim turbaned Sikh and a beefy African, kicked a soccer ball near several girls, white, black and brown, sitting on the lawn. Under the trees, the buildings were settler style with the tin roofs and cedar walls. Jordan told the driver to wait and picked up Zanifa's bag. "This looks like a great place. I bet they've got computers."

Zanifa said nothing. She kept her eyes on the sidewalk crossing the lawn.

"Good afternoon," said an African girl walking with an Indian girl, wearing white blouses and plaid skirts.

"Hel-lo," Zanifa stuttered.

"She was friendly," Jordan said.

"You never can tell," Zanifa said.

"After you." Jordan held open a door. "Do you want to tell them who you are or do you want me to?"

"I will." Zanifa laughed. "I know who I am."

"I wish we could help more of these girls," Ms. Calloway said. Her grip was as firm as any man's. Jordan decided she was about forty, younger than her voice had sounded on the phone, younger than her tan face suggested after years of the tropical sun and gin and tonic evenings. She wore her sun-bleached hair short and a batik dress over a large, athletic body. She might have begun her career as a coach. She looked at Jordan admiringly. "Zanifa, you're very lucky to have such a patron."

"Yes, ma'am." Zanifa's smile was innocent. "I know."

"Rutledge, I'll see you at seven at the Norfolk?"

"*Sawa.*" Jordan thought he would make the drink a short one. A lonely white woman in Africa out for a little adventure. Leaving the headmistress's office, Zanifa looked at him with narrowed eyes. Outside, she whispered, "That mama likes you."

"Don't be ridiculous." Jordan smiled. "Ms. Calloway thinks I'm a good man because I paid your fees for the next two years. She cares about children."

"Her eyes said she wants to pick cabbages."

"Zanifa." Jordan laughed. "She just wants to question me about your history. She probably wants to know if you and I picked any."

"Will you tell her what we did?"

"Do you want me to?"

"No." Zanifa paused with her mouth still forming an *o.* "I wish I could go with you."

"I do, too." Jordan draped his arm over her shoulder. "I'll call you on Thursday when I'm in Memphis. We can talk every day." He squeezed her arm.

"I don't want these kids to see me cry."

"Don't be sad. I'll be with you." Jordan's voice caught. "I'll be thinking about you."

Zanifa's face brightened when she saw a tear in his eye. "I'll be with you, too."

The driver started the engine as they neared the taxi. Jordan hugged Zanifa, lifting her feet from the ground. Her face pressed into his neck, she let out a muted, animal wail. He set her down, expecting her to be sobbing, but her eyes were clear. She smiled weakly and said, "I love you."

"I love you, little one." Ducking his head, he stepped up into the taxi. "You're going to be fine."

"*Kwa heri, kaka,*" Zanifa said fiercely, closing the door. Go with blessings, brother. *"Mungu atakupelekie."* God will deliver you. She followed the cab to the gate, waving both arms over her head. Jordan watched her through the rear window as the car drove between the playing fields, which had filled with rugby and cricket teams. She turned and ran across the lot, looked over her shoulder and blew him a kiss, still running, then disappeared.

"I haven't used this in two years, I hope it clears." Jordan slid a card across the desk.

The Kenyan woman in a blue dress typed on a keyboard. "Better you change this one-way to a return. After a *mzungu* lives in Africa, he will never feel at home where he came from." She made an imprint of his card. "Two years. Your whole family will be coming to the airport to greet you?"

"At least my mama and *baba.*" Jordan signed the slip. He saw them in the terminal in winter coats, his mother's head not reaching his father's shoulder, both smiling, his mother ready to jump like a cheerleader. In another time Anna would have been there. He was aware now that he no longer ached with remorse. It had shrunken into a cold stone in his heart. "Do you believe you can start your life over?"

"You mean born again? Many friends of mine, they were born again, but they never changed." Behind her, a printer suddenly began to process a ticket, beeping at the end of each line. "Your card is still good. You should take me to dinner to celebrate your departure." She reached out and slapped Jordan's palm.

"I'd love to." Jordan smiled. "But I have plans."

She pretended to pout and handed him his ticket.

"You'll fly halfway around the world and Africa will be a dream." Stepping outside, Jordan found himself thinking out loud. "Maybe you'll stop talking to yourself so much." He walked down Haile Selassie Avenue to the Extelcom House, where he placed a collect call to Memphis, but there was no answer. The Norfolk was on the other side of the city center. The afternoon was turning chilly, and Jordan decided to go by foot through the rush-hour crowds. " 'The volunteer returns from deepest Africa a babbling idiot,' " he said in Vernon

Taylor's deep drawl. " 'Did you allay the guilt of your ancestors and bury the demons that drove you away?' " He imitated Vernon's cynical laugh.

"You, *mzungu!*" A minibus swerved around a corner with a young man hanging out of its open door.

Jordan stepped back onto the sidewalk as it roared past.

The barker leaned toward him and shook his finger furiously. "Watch where you go!" Painted on the rear was the motto "Too Many Tears." Jordan crossed the intersection to the mouth of Harry Thuku Road and walked alongside the shady campus of Nairobi University, wondering if Zanifa might prefer to go to college here. Looking at the Land Rovers and Land Cruisers parked in front of the Norfolk, he thought maybe he could come back when she graduated from the Boma School and take her on safari.

"You have visitors." The concierge looked at him oddly and nodded at an alcove across from the desk. A tall policeman in black trousers, a navy sweater and a peaked cap stood beside a brawny man wearing a gray suit too small for him, a white shirt and a thin black tie. There was something schoolboyish about his dress that made him more sinister.

"Oh, shit," Jordan whispered to himself. "May I use a phone?"

"Next to the toilets." The concierge gestured toward the hallway behind the approaching policemen.

"Mr. Jordan?" The man in the suit smiled.

"Yes."

"Detective Waweru." The man flapped open a wallet with a badge. "I have orders to bring you with me to answer some questions."

"Why?"

"I haven't been informed. Detective Njoroge is waiting for you."

"I'd like to call my embassy." Jordan walked past him. His fingers trembled as he turned the pages of the phone book. He gave the number to the hotel operator.

The detective stood a few feet away, his face placid. He checked the time on his watch, then caressed the big gold band with one finger.

Jordan heard a recording, a flat midwestern woman's voice: "You've

reached the embassy of the United States. Our office hours are . . ."
He hung up and took a deep breath.

"You look scared, my friend. *Hakuna matata*." Waweru took Jordan
gently by the elbow and laughed. No problem. "You'll be back at the
bar in time for a sundowner."

Jordan pulled his arm away and walked briskly toward the veranda.
Waweru passed him on the steps down to the sidewalk. The uniformed officer pulled up to the curb in a white, dovetailed Peugeot
with a license plate that ended in W, which everyone knew belonged
to the Criminal Investigation Division.

"I hardly recognized you." The Texan woman from breakfast appeared beside him. "You look much better with that haircut. Doesn't
he, Sam?"

"A real gentleman." With a wide grin, the man glanced Jordan up
and down. "Would you care to join us for dinner? We'd like to hear
about the real Africa."

"*Bwana* Jordan," the detective called from the curb, holding open
the rear door.

"Very generous of you, but I can't make it." Jordan tried to smile.
He turned and walked across the sidewalk and got in the car. Waweru
closed the door. The eight Texans watched silently as if he were an animal in a game park. Waweru circled the car and slid in beside him.
The car pulled away. The Tanzanian police had probably contacted
the Kenyans with a request to detain him, and the Kenyans were going
to shake him down before they let him fly out. The driver turned right
onto University Way.

"The police station is back there," Jordan said uneasily.

"We are going to CID." Waweru's tie knot was loose, his top button
undone, as if he had gotten the image of himself from a comic book.

"Where's that?"

"You'll see soon enough." Waweru's smile seemed deliberately
tough and cynical.

Jordan watched black kites spiraling over Uhuru Highway, dozens
of them circling in the same current like vultures in the twilight. He
whispered, "Pasipo."

The sky flashed into a sheet of blinding light.

Stars glimmered and blurred in the night. It took too much effort to hold up his eyelids against the throbbing that felt as if a spike had been driven into the base of his skull. He let them fall. He ascertained he was lying flat on his back in tall grass. Across the playing fields he saw Zanifa waving by the gate. He forced his eyes open and tried to sit up and the stars streaked across the sky. He moaned from sudden dizziness and his head fell forward between his legs.

"*Karibu kurudi,*" someone said. Welcome back.

The voice was familiar. Jordan opened his eyes and found himself in a pool of light. He saw the black slip-on shoes and gray trousers and fear welled in his chest. Waweru wasn't on duty. He must be moonlighting for Patel and Ionides. Surely they wouldn't kill him for stealing their money. He couldn't pay them back if he was dead. They just wanted to frighten him.

"You'll vomit soon. When your brain slams up against the inside of your head," Waweru explained casually in Swahili like a doctor while the other officer lifted Jordan up by the shoulders, "you get nausea after you wake."

Jordan stood unsteadily. The car headlights were shining down a dirt road that ran through a stand of acacia trees and disappeared in the darkness.

"Don't vomit on my shoes." Waweru chuckled, leaning him against a tree. Before he realized what was happening, the uniformed officer had handcuffed his arms on the far side of the trunk.

"Cousin Kimweri sends his peace," Waweru said in Swahili, placing his big hands on Jordan's shoulders. He shoved him down on his knees, and the other officer cuffed his ankles together behind the tree. "He called this morning from the Agha Khan Hospital in Dar es Salaam. They gave him a glass eye."

"I'm glad he's all right." Jordan managed to keep his voice steady. "I didn't want him to be hurt."

"He'll live." Waweru slapped his flashlight in his palm like a billy club. "With one eye."

"Where's Zanifa?"

"The girl? The girl goes her own way. Only you are to pay."

Jordan heard himself laugh. Kimweri had arranged the ultimate sacrifice. He was to die so Zanifa could live. His laugh didn't sound like his own. It seemed to mock him. He realized he had nearly been at peace with himself for the first time, and now he was going to die. He had come all this way for one day. His laugh had become a howl. He bent his neck, trying to wipe the tears off his face, but he couldn't reach his shoulder.

"*Maina, njoo.*" Waweru called the man in the uniform. "Hold the light on his face."

Blinded by the beam, Jordan remembered every word of the Lord's Prayer, then mumbled, "Let them all know I love them."

Waweru seemed to move toward him in slow motion, a shadow with a knife silhouetted in one hand. A faceless head, haloed by the backlight. "You white monkey. You come to Africa and think you are a big man. Look at you now, crying like a girl." He clasped Jordan's chin as if to kiss him.

"I—" Jordan started to speak. Waweru slashed his cheek with the knife. Jordan cried out, and the man cut his other cheek. Jordan clamped his mouth shut, swallowing his screams.

Maina was laughing. "Mark him like a Kamba warrior."

Laughing from his belly, Waweru turned and slapped Maina's palm. Then he crushed his large hand over Jordan's face and nose, pinning his head to the tree. He eased the point of blade gently across his forehead. The first slice stung, but as Waweru drew a third line over his eyebrows, Jordan felt only the blood trickling down his nose. His body went slack against the metal cuffs.

"Now you are an African." Waweru dropped his head. "One of us."

Maina doubled over laughing so that the flashlight shone on blood dripping to the ground. "Cut off his ears. Then he'll look like a snake."

"Keep the light on his face," Waweru snapped. He raised Jordan's chin and whispered, "Look at me, *mzungu.*"

Jordan kept his eyes shut and tried to will himself to faint.

"Look at me or I'll cut off your ears to make that fool happy."

Maina giggled. "Cut them off anyway."

Jordan blinked at the light through a film of blood and tears.

Waweru held his chin tighter and moved the knife slowly toward his forehead. Jordan felt the point slide between his nose and eye. He twisted away as the blade pried his eyeball. Overwhelming pain exploded through his head. Screaming, he tugged at the cuffs and thrashed against the tree, oblivious of the metal gouging his wrists, the bark scraping his back raw. Waweru stepped away. Cackling like a hyena, Maina leaned forward, aiming the light at Jordan's knees. For a moment Jordan focused clearly through the pain at his eyeball in the dirt. It was flattened into an egg shape. Tiny strips of pink muscle. The white stump of the optic nerve like an apple stem.

"Dump him at the highway," Waweru said.

"When do I get my money? This was dangerous work. You never told me he was white. I wouldn't have come if I knew he was white. I thought he was Tanzanian. Two hundred dollars isn't enough. We're talking about a white man."

"Shut your mouth and drive." Waweru sounded annoyed.

"An American is worth more than a Tanzanian."

"Shut up."

"There could be trouble—"

"We'll be protected. We never saw him."

Jordan followed their Swahili, lying flat on the backseat, motionless as if he were still unconscious, his head throbbing like a gong. The car stopped. Maina dragged him out by his feet. Jordan bit his lip when his head hit the ground but kept silent, his eyes closed. He felt a hand slide into his jacket, then slap his face lightly. Maina's voice whispered, "*Mzungu*, where do you keep your money?"

"Get in the car!" Waweru yelled, and started the engine. Maina raised Jordan on his side and patted his back pockets. The car honked. Jordan felt himself roll onto his back and Maina's spit splatter on his chin. He heard Maina crunch across the gravel and close the door. The car spun its wheels and was gone.

Jordan lay for a long time until the pain ebbed enough to form complete thoughts. Dear God, Allah, *Yesu Kristo.* He laughed and rose slowly to his feet. Gingerly he touched the torn lid hanging over the empty, burning socket. He opened his other eye. A big copper moon hung low over the savannah like a setting sun.

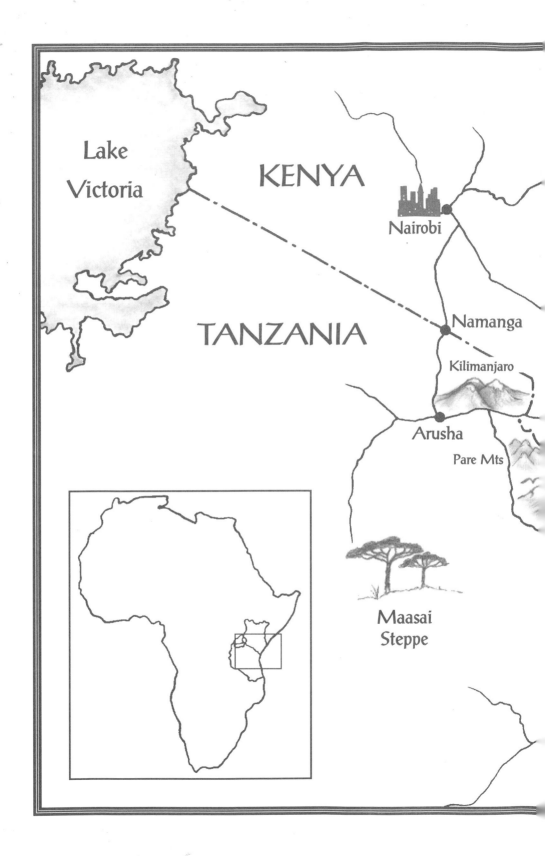